Join the army of fans who LOVE [the Ben]
Hope series . . .

'Deadly conspiracies, bone-crunching action and a tormented hero with a heart . . . Scott Mariani packs a real punch'
Andy McDermott, bestselling author of *The Revelation Code*

'Slick, serpentine, sharp, and very very entertaining. If you've got a pulse, you'll love Scott Mariani; if you haven't, then maybe you crossed Ben Hope'
Simon Toyne, bestselling author of the *Sanctus* series

'Scott Mariani's latest page-turning rollercoaster of a thriller takes the sort of conspiracy theory that made Dan Brown's *The Da Vinci Code* an international hit, and gives it an injection of steroids . . . [Mariani] is a master of edge-of-the-seat suspense. A genuinely gripping thriller that holds the attention of its readers from the first page to the last'
Shots Magazine

'You know you are rooting for the guy when he does something so cool you do a mental fist punch in the air and have to bite the inside of your mouth not to shout out "YES!" in case you get arrested on the train. Awesome thrilling stuff'
My Favourite Books

'If you like Dan Brown you will like all of Scott Mariani's work – but you will like it better. This guy knows exactly how to bait his hook, cast his line and reel you in, nice and slow. The heart-stopping pace and clever, cunning, joyfully serpentine tale will have you frantic to reach the end, but reluctant to finish such a blindingly good read'
The Bookbag

THE MOSCOW CIPHER

Scott Mariani is the author of the worldwide-acclaimed action-adventure thriller series featuring ex-SAS hero Ben Hope, which has sold millions of copies in Scott's native UK alone and is also translated into over 20 languages. His books have been described as 'James Bond meets Jason Bourne, with a historical twist'. The first Ben Hope book, *The Alchemist's Secret*, spent six straight weeks at #1 on Amazon's Kindle chart, and all the others have been *Sunday Times* bestsellers.

Scott was born in Scotland, studied in Oxford and now lives and writes in a remote setting in rural west Wales. When not writing, he can be found bouncing about the country lanes in an ancient Land Rover, wild camping in the Brecon Beacons or engrossed in his hobbies of astronomy, photography and target shooting (no dead animals involved!).

You can find out more about Scott and his work, and sign up to his exclusive newsletter, on his official website:

www.scottmariani.com

By the same author:

Ben Hope series
The Alchemist's Secret
The Mozart Conspiracy
The Doomsday Prophecy
The Heretic's Treasure
The Shadow Project
The Lost Relic
The Sacred Sword
The Armada Legacy
The Nemesis Program
The Forgotten Holocaust
The Martyr's Curse
The Cassandra Sanction
Star of Africa
The Devil's Kingdom
The Babylon Idol
The Bach Manuscript

To find out more visit **www.scottmariani.com**

SCOTT MARIANI

The Moscow Cipher

avon.

Published by AVON
A Division of HarperCollins*Publishers* Ltd
1 London Bridge Street
London SE1 9GF

www.harpercollins.co.uk

A Paperback Original 2018

2

First published in Great Britain by HarperCollins*Publishers* 2018

A catalogue record for this book is
available from the British Library

ISBN 978-0-00-748625-0

This novel is entirely a work of fiction.
The names, characters and incidents portrayed in it are
the work of the author's imagination. Any resemblance to
actual persons, living or dead, events or localities is
entirely coincidental.

Set in Minion by Palimpsest Book Production Ltd, Falkirk, Stirlingshire

Printed and bound in Great Britain by
CPI Group (UK) Ltd, Croydon CR0 4YY

MIX
Paper from
responsible sources

FSC
www.fsc.org

FSC™ C007454

This book is produced from independently certified FSC™ paper
to ensure responsible forest management.

For more information visit: www.harpercollins.co.uk/green

THE MOSCOW CIPHER

'I want a new invincible human being, insensitive to pain, resistant and indifferent about the quality of food they eat.'

Joseph Stalin, 1925

'One may imagine that a man can create a man, not only theoretically but practically . . . a man who can fight without fear, compassion or pain. What I have just described might be worse than a nuclear bomb.'

Vladimir Putin, 92 years later

'A man does not have the right to develop his own mind. We must electrically control the brain. Some day armies and generals will be controlled by electric stimulation of the brain.'

José Delgado, neuroscientist and pioneer of Intracranial Radio Stimulation, paper presented to US Congressional hearings on the Central Intelligence Agency's MK-ULTRA mind control program, 1975

PROLOGUE

The city was Moscow and the date was February 10th 1957. It was to be the last night in Leo Ingram's life, although he didn't yet know it.

The bitter cold day was turning to a frigid evening as the deserted streets darkened, urging Ingram to turn up the collar of his heavy greatcoat and walk faster along the slippery pavement. His shoes were sodden from trudging through the dirty slush. The whistling wind carried flurries of snow that threatened to re-cover everything in white.

Ingram detested the unrelenting cold, as he detested the palpable fear and oppression that gripped this city. He could see it in the eyes of the people everywhere he went; could almost feel it oozing from the grey, dirty, ice-rimed streets themselves; and the same fear was pulsing deep inside his own heart that night as he carried out his mission.

Leo Ingram was his real name, as opposed to the identity shown on the forged papers he was carrying. His spoken and written Russian were easily good enough to pass for a native, as long as he didn't get into protracted conversation with any of the locals, something he had studiously avoided since being smuggled into the USSR five weeks earlier. His cover had been carefully set up. For the last five weeks, as far as anyone was concerned, he had been Pyotr Kozlov, self-employed piano tuner. Had he been required to actually tune a piano as proof of his false identity, he could have done so, as that had been his profession before the war.

Quite how a mild-mannered, cultivated and peace-loving gentleman like Leonard Ingram could be transformed into a highly decorated British Army captain and then, post-1945, into a special agent of the Secret Intelligence Service: that was a testament to the deep, dark impact that terrible war had had on the lives of everyone it had touched.

Ingram's mission in Moscow was nearly complete. He had been planted here to play a relatively brief role, but one that was key to the success of the operation. If all went well tonight, the five weeks of perpetual nail-biting tension, of constantly looking over his shoulder, half-expecting to see the KGB thugs coming for him at any moment, would be over and he would begin the journey home. Not that getting out of the Soviet Union would be an easy matter.

If all didn't go well . . . Ingram closed his mind to that dreadful possibility.

The package thrust deep inside one pocket of his greatcoat was the first thing his plan required him to offload that night, before moving to the second phase. The package was innocuous enough at first glance, just an ordinary tobacco tin imprinted with Cyrillic lettering, identical to millions of others carried by millions of men across the USSR. But what that little round tin contained could not have been more explosive if it had been packed full of super-concentrated TNT. If they caught him with it, all was lost. Not just his own life, but all the efforts and risks taken by others in order to obtain the extremely precious and hard-won information inside.

As Ingram rounded an icy corner of the dark, empty street and a fresh blast of bone-chilling wind slapped him in the face and made his eyes water, the warehouses came into view. A mile's walk from his rented digs, this industrialised zone of the city was even more dismal and rundown than the rest of Moscow. Most of the ancient pre-revolutionary buildings were semi-derelict and abandoned behind rickety fences nobody guarded. All the same, he was cautious. The failing bulb of a street light flickered on, off, on, off, throwing long shadows that he watched carefully in case they might conceal enemies with guns.

Satisfied he was alone, Ingram approached the fence and made his way along the snow-rimed wire mesh to the hole, large enough for a man of his slender build to slip through easily, he'd cut three nights earlier.

The warehouse was an old meat packing plant that hadn't been used for many years, its doors rotted off their hinges. Ingram stepped over the half-eaten body of a frozen rat and moved into the darkness of the building. The hiding place was very specific. The package would remain there only a day or so before, if all went according to plan, his contact would collect it. It had been decided back at the start of the mission that a dead drop of this sort was a safer, more prudent way for the package to change hands. Ingram would have preferred to deliver it straight to his contact, but these were not his decisions to make.

The package carefully hidden, Ingram slipped unseen from the warehouse and continued on his way through the cold darkness. Phase two of the plan was the rendezvous with his colleague, a man he had never met and would never meet again after tonight. A small waterproof envelope in Ingram's pocket contained a slip of paper on which were written four lines of code: an enciphered message that, among other information, gave precise directions to the location of the hidden package. Once the envelope was passed on, Ingram would walk away relieved of a tremendous burden. His part in the mission would effectively be complete as his contact decoded the directions using a special key known only to a select few, then retrieved the package and whisked it away to East Berlin, where others in their organisation would be anxiously waiting to take possession.

When the package finally reached the safety of London and its contents were analysed, it would cause a sensation. Careers would be made out of this, though the men and women who'd risked their lives to obtain the information would likely get little credit.

Ingram walked on through the half-deserted streets, checking his wristwatch and his bearings and glancing behind him now and then to ensure he wasn't being followed. A police car hissed by, tyres churning brown slush on the road, and made his heart race for a moment before it passed on into the night without so much as slowing down to check him out.

His anxiety was peaking as he walked on. His meeting with his contact, however brief, would be the moment of maximum danger for both of them; when they would be at their most vulnerable if either of them had fallen under suspicion. To be caught together was their worst nightmare. 'It's almost over,' he kept telling himself. 'You'll soon be home free.'

As Ingram crossed a sidestreet, a large figure of a man in a long coat and a brimmed hat appeared from nowhere and stepped towards him. 'Good evening,' the man said in accented English. He was smiling. His right hand was in his pocket, clutching a hidden weapon. And he was most certainly not the man Ingram was supposed to meet.

KGB. The acronym stood for *Komitet Gosudarstvennoy Bezopasnosti*, the Committee for State Security. A name that

4

struck terror into the hearts of those who opposed the Soviet regime, as well as the Russian citizens it oppressed as virtual captives in their own homeland. The KGB had been created only three years earlier and already forged a fearsome reputation as a direct descendant of the dreaded *Cheka* secret police of the olden days. Its agents were as ruthless as they were efficient.

Ingram's stomach twisted as he realised they were onto him. He bolted diagonally away across the icy street, then skidded and almost fell as a second figure appeared around the corner up ahead, cutting off his escape. The second agent wasn't smiling and he had drawn his service automatic.

Had someone betrayed him? Had the KGB already caught his contact and made him talk? Had a mole inside his own agency given him away? Ingram didn't have time to ask those questions as he sprinted off in the opposite direction with the two agents in pursuit.

A shot cracked out. Splinters of brickwork stung Ingram's leg as he darted around a corner. He knew that the KGB would shoot to wound, not to kill. He also knew what kind of horrific tortures they would use to force information from him. He would give them nothing. He and his fellow agents had all been sternly lectured on the risks associated with getting caught. Like his colleagues, Ingram carried hidden in the heel of one shoe a small glass vial containing a cyanide pill, to be swallowed in the event of imminent capture. The death it offered was by no means a pleasant one – but it was, he had been assured, far quicker and kinder than the treatment a spy would receive at the hands of his or her captors.

He sprinted along a cobbled alleyway, vaulted a railing and almost broke his neck hurtling down a long flight of icy steps. A sharp right turn, then a left, then another right;

and now Ingram was quite lost in the maze of dark narrow streets, but all that mattered was getting away from his pursuers. Escape was his only hope. Ingram had killed over a dozen enemy soldiers in the war and was quite proficient at armed combat, but the Secret Intelligence Service didn't issue weapons to undercover agents posing as innocent piano tuners. The couple of tuning forks he carried about with him wouldn't be much use.

He paused, heart pounding in his throat, breath rasping. Listened, hard, but could hear nothing. Had he lost them? Maybe, but he could afford to make no assumptions.

The cipher in his pocket. It must not be found. He snatched out the envelope and looked desperately around him for a hiding place to which, if he made it out of this, he could always return later. The buildings either side of the narrow street were old grey stone, slowly crumbling with decay and neglect. He ran his fingers along the rough, cold masonry, found a crack big enough, and stuffed the envelope inside it and poked it in deep with his fingers. Then he ran on, careering over the slippery pavement.

For a few elated moments longer he thought he'd given them the slip. That was when he heard the rapid thud of footsteps closing in behind him and in front, and realised they had him cornered.

He was done. Ingram felt the strange calmness that can sometimes come over a man when he knows, and accepts, that the end is here. He reached down and slid the false heel off his left shoe, trying to get to the cyanide pill inside before the enemy grabbed him; but his hands were numb with cold and he fumbled with the vial and accidentally let it slip from his fingers. He dropped to his knees, groping about in the shadows for it, but it was too late. Powerful hands seized his arms and yanked him roughly to his feet.

A pistol pressed against his head. If he could have struggled fiercely enough to make them blow his brains out, he would have, but then a cosh struck him hard over the back of his skull and knocked him half senseless. The KGB men dragged Ingram down the street to a waiting car where a third agent sat impassively at the wheel, smoking a cigarette. Ingram was bundled roughly inside. The two who had caught him sat to his left and right, boxing him into the middle of the back seat. The car sped off.

Its destination was the infamous Lubyanka prison and KGB headquarters in the heart of Moscow, where men highly expert in extracting the truth from their victims awaited their new arrival.

The last night of Leo Ingram's life would be a very long and agonising one.

Chapter 1

Inside the confessional, filled with the serenity of the magnificent cathedral that was one of only two Catholic churches in his home city of Moscow, Yuri Petrov knelt humbly on the step and prepared to bare his soul to God.

On the other side of the grid, the priest's face was half veiled in shadow. Yuri made the sign of the cross and, speaking low, began the sacrament as he'd been doing all his life.

'Forgive me, Father, for I have sinned. My last confession was over two weeks ago and these are my sins.'

Yuri ran through the list of various lesser, venial sins, such as drinking and occasionally skipping his nightly prayers. But it was something else that was weighing so heavily on him and was the real reason he'd come seeking guidance. 'I'm struggling with a great burden, Father,' he explained nervously. 'A terrible secret has been revealed to me and I don't know what to do. I'm frightened.'

The priest listened sagely. 'Would the right course of action be to share your secret, my son?'

'Yes, Father. But in so doing, I could be in serious danger.'

'The only danger is in doing wrong, my son.'

9

'I know it's wrong to lie, or hide the truth. I've done that too many times, Father. I've been used to keeping secrets, in my past career. But nothing like this. If I tell, I'm a dead man. I need God's guidance on what to do.'

The priest reflected on this in silence for some time. 'Pray to Him, my son. Open your heart to His wisdom, and the guidance you seek will be heard.' Having given his counsel, the priest gave Yuri the penance of two Hail Marys, invited him to make an act of contrition, and ended the sacrament with the usual 'Through the ministry of the Church, may God give you pardon and peace. I absolve you of your sins, in the name of the Father, and of the Son, and of the Holy Spirit.'

'Amen.'

'Go in peace. Do the right thing, my son.'

Yuri left the Cathedral of the Immaculate Conception and trudged down the steps to Malaya Gruzinskaya Street feeling scarcely any more reassured than before. Moscow was enjoying a warm June; the sky was blue and the sunshine was pleasant, but Yuri was too taken up with confusion and dread to notice. How had it come to this, he kept asking himself. As he walked away from the grand Gothic church, he cast his troubled mind back over the events of the last few days and the path his life had taken to lead him to this awful situation.

Yuri Petrov was thirty-nine years old, divorced, single, currently unemployed and going nowhere fast. The reason he'd been so used to keeping secrets in the past was that, for over fifteen years, he had been a spy for Russian intelligence, albeit a minor and lowly one. Not that any of his former neighbours or acquaintances in Amsterdam, where he had lived for ten of those years, would have known it. As far as anyone was concerned, even (especially) Yuri's ex-wife Eloise and their daughter Valentina, he led the steady, plodding and unexciting existence of a senior technical support analyst working for an international software company based in the Netherlands. The ability to speak Russian being a key part of his phony job, the story fitted well and he'd carried it off for years without drawing suspicion. Each morning at eight he'd kissed his wife and cycled off to a fake office with a fake secretary, and got on with the real job of being an intelligence spook. Whatever that was, exactly.

While the Russian secret service had been stepping up its spying activities across Europe for some time and deploying their spooks on all kinds of cool missions such as nabbing state secrets, orchestrating cyber-attacks, infiltrating protest groups and generally helping to subvert the stability of nations, to Yuri's chagrin he felt his own talents to have been woefully underused. He was not, never had been, Russia's answer to James Bond. He had never carried, nor even handled, a gun, or been asked to do anything remotely risky. His role in Amsterdam was ostensibly to keep tabs on the intelligence agents of rival nations, but it seemed that his counterparts there had as little to do as he did – which all amounted to a life not much less drab and uninspiring than his fictitious cover, in which he had little to do except trawl the internet, drink too much coffee, eat too much stroopwafel, and become increasingly dissatisfied and frustrated with his career.

It hadn't always been this way. Once upon a time, in the bygone days before he'd been sent into exile in Amsterdam, his Intelligence bosses had seemed to appreciate Yuri's abilities. For Yuri might not have been endowed with many talents in his life, but for some reason and with very little effort on his part he just so happened to be a highly gifted code-cracker. Back in the day, Yuri's capacity for deciphering signals intelligence – or 'SIGINT' as the Americans termed it – encryptions intercepted from rival agencies such as the Brits, the Yanks or those pesky Israelis had been second to none and earned him quite a reputation in Moscow. On several occasions, when Russian Intel operatives way above his pay grade had been unable to penetrate the firewalls protecting the secret files of MI6, CIA, Mossad and others, Yuri had been called in to assist. He'd cracked security pass-codes that had been thought uncrackable, even complex fifteen-digit monsters that presented over 700 million billion billion permutations.

But that was long ago, before the relentless march of technology had taken all the intellectual challenge out of codebreaking and pretty much rendered talents like his obsolete. Nowadays it was all just a war between computers: one to weave the incredibly complex code, another to attack its defences, and the winner was simply whoever had the most powerful machine. With alarming rapidity, the human factor was being almost completely removed from the equation. After just a few years in the job, Yuri's special skills had become increasingly redundant. Then came the Amsterdam posting, and the long, slow decline. Frustration grew to bitterness; bitterness to hatred: against his employers back home, and the whole damn government.

During this unhappy period he hooked back up with an old friend from school and began regular contact with him on social media. Yuri Petrov and Grisha Solokov had known each other since the age of seven, and had the usual on-off friendship until their teens, when they'd become best buddies for a while until Yuri drifted off to university in St Petersburg to study IT and Grisha went to work for his father, who owned a radio repair shop.

During the years the two friends had been out of touch, Grisha had discovered the wonderful world of conspiracy theories and become deeply immersed. The repair shop long gone, he now operated his own internet radio station from a hidden trailer at a remote farm many miles from Moscow. He lived alone with only a dog, an assortment of feral cats and a few goats and chickens for company, and spent most of every night in the trailer streaming his rants about everything from illegal government surveillance operations to chemtrails to the Illuminati plot to enslave the human race to the covert deportation camps that really existed, according to him, on Mars.

Needless to say, in their Facebook chats Yuri had never divulged to his friend what he did for a living, for that would have instantly branded him as the enemy. Grisha had his own secrets, too. Because his show frequently attacked what he considered to be the corrupt dark underbelly of the Russian state and its president in particular, he kept his location extremely hush-hush so as to elude the government assassins who he believed were intent on silencing him.

In short, Grisha was slightly nuts.

Looking back, Yuri couldn't pinpoint the moment he'd started getting drawn into Grisha's ideology. To begin with, he'd been dismissively sceptical of the whole thing, and almost stopped with the social media contact. The stuff his friend came out with was often more than Yuri could stomach, like his conviction that lizard-like alien beings capable of taking on human form really do run the planet, and that various celebrities as well as members of the British royal family were among these evil creatures hellbent on the total domination of humanity. But the more he'd listened to Grisha's show, the more compelling Yuri started finding its less wacky theories of conspiracy and corruption at the heart of the global establishment. After all, Yuri was privy to facts and secrets that were kept from ordinary folks, and so it wasn't hard for him to imagine that all kinds of levels of secrecy existed above him. Gradually, tiny doubts about his own government, and the state of the world generally, percolated through his head and wouldn't go away, feeding his increasing sense of restlessness that he was a pawn working for dark powers.

Maybe it was just an expression of his dissatisfaction with his own job, he told himself. Yet the same creeping paranoia that fuelled Grisha's radio show started haunting Yuri as he cycled the streets of Amsterdam. He became certain he was being watched and followed, his phone tapped, perhaps even his thoughts somehow monitored. A reasonably devout Catholic since his teens, he turned to God for moral support. When an answer to his fervent prayers failed to materialise, Yuri found solace in the sins of drink and marijuana, having developed a taste for both.

What made it so much worse was that he could never tell Eloise a word about his secret life, let alone the anxieties that plagued him. As a result he ended up barely speaking to her at all, with the inevitable consequence that she felt very neglected by him. When the marriage eventually fell apart, Yuri blamed the Russian intelligence services even more bitterly for his woes and took it as proof of their pernicious influence over society. Shortly after Eloise left him and took Valentina away to live in France, Yuri returned to Moscow, handed in his resignation and found alternative employment fixing computer bugs for private cash-paying customers. He managed to persuade Eloise to let Valentina, now ten, travel to Russia for visits. Eloise was difficult about it and barely spoke to him on the phone.

Yuri's preoccupation with all things conspiracy-related

had by then grown even more pervasive. Even if he wasn't yet prepared to believe that shape-shifting alien lizards govern the planet, as a parent he was angry that his child would grow up as a drone of the globalist Deep State. He felt he needed to *do* something to make people wake up to the realisation that everything they thought they knew about the world was a lie. The media they trusted was simply an instrument for propaganda; the leaders they voted for in fact controlled nothing; the real rulers were hidden in the shadows and the whole concept of democracy was a carefully concocted myth.

He and Grisha now communicated daily on prepaid phones bought for cash and theoretically untraceable to them. On Grisha's advice, as an extra precaution Yuri followed his friend's practice of replacing his 'burner' every couple of weeks. As a means of living as much off the grid as possible in an urban environment, he also moved to a dingy hole of an apartment that he paid for in cash, utility bills all in the name of a former tenant.

He and Grisha started meeting in person. The first reunion took place at a bar in a small town eighty kilometres from Moscow. Later, as a sign of his growing trust, Grisha let Yuri in on the secret of his farm's location, way out in the remote countryside. Never had Yuri mentioned his past as a spook for Russian intelligence. That was history now, anyway.

Over the next couple of years, Yuri visited the farm often. The two friends would spend days and nights in Grisha's chaotic home drinking vodka and talking conspiracies. It was more than a hobby or belief system for Grisha, it was a total lifestyle. Yuri felt the infectious lure of that world. He was becoming seriously addicted.

'It's all building to a head, don't you see?' Grisha had

kept insisting during their most recent late-night session. 'It's coming. Just you wait. Something's going to happen that'll prove everything we've been saying. Something that'll show the world what these bastards have really been up to all along. Nobody will be laughing at us then.'

'"Something"?'

'Something huge, my man.'

Yuri believed it too, even if neither of them knew what that 'something' could be.

Then, one sunny day in June two years after he'd left Amsterdam, Grisha's prediction came terrifyingly true, in a way neither of them could have imagined.

Chapter 2

For a dedicated conspiracy buff tainted by more than a whiff of paranoia, nothing could be more alarming than happening to be walking down the street minding your own business when a mysterious black car full of mysterious men suddenly appears from nowhere and pulls up beside you.

That was exactly what happened to Yuri Petrov one day that summer as he strolled aimlessly about the streets of Moscow. He instantly knew the black Mercedes was an Intelligence Services car. Gripped by panic, he was ready to bolt as the back doors opened and two men, very obviously government agents, climbed out and walked calmly towards him.

He'd never seen either of them before. But they seemed to recognise him, even with the hair and the beard. Yuri hadn't been paying so much attention to personal neatness of late.

'Hello, Yuri,' one of them said.

The other motioned towards the car's open door. 'Let's go for a drive, shall we?'

Powerless to refuse, Yuri climbed into the back seat. The two men sat flanking him as the Mercedes sped off. 'What's this about?' he kept repeating. 'Who are you people? What do you want with me?'

'You'll find out soon enough. Shut up and enjoy the ride.'

Twenty minutes later, the Mercedes arrived at a lugubrious government building Yuri had never visited before. They passed through two armed security checkpoints, then whooshed down a ramp into a subterranean car park from where Yuri's escorts ushered him up several floors in a lift. They stepped out into a corridor that was devoid of any windows or furniture and painted institutional grey. Yuri was so nervous he could hardly control the shaking in his knees as they led him up the corridor. After two years of the Grisha Solokov academy, it seemed to Yuri like the dystopian nightmare coming true.

Yuri had no idea of what he was about to step into.

The agents stopped outside an unmarked door. 'Go in,' one said to Yuri.

Yuri did as he was told. He found himself in an office, not a cosy one. The walls and steel filing cabinets and ancient iron radiators and exposed pipes were all painted the same grey as the corridor. There was no carpet and only one window, through whose dusty glass little sunlight was able to penetrate. In front of the window was a large, plain desk, which was completely bare except for a telephone and a slim cardboard folder that lay closed on the desktop.

Behind the desk sat a man whom Yuri, unlike the men who had brought him here, did in fact recognise. It was his former chief, the man who had first interviewed and employed him in the service, Antonin Bezukhov.

The chief was a large, heavyset figure in a dark suit. His white hair was buzzed military-short and his face appeared to have been chiselled from a lump of granite. He had to be in his mid-seventies, but if anything he looked more severe and intimidating than Yuri remembered, which was saying something. This was a man rumoured to have personally

18

executed several CIA operatives, back in the glory days of the Cold War. As far as Bezukhov was concerned, the old regime had never ended.

Bezukhov invited him to sit, and offered him a ghost of a smile. 'You're a hard man to find, Yuri. We obviously trained you too well. Where've you been hiding yourself these days?'

Yuri swallowed. 'Why am I here? What do you want from me?'

'We need you to come back and work for us, one more time,' said Bezukhov.

'But I'm retired,' Yuri protested. 'Out, gone, done with the whole thing. I don't want anything more to do with any of it.'

'Consider this your heroic comeback,' the chief said, faintly amused. 'Come on, Yuri, don't you know that once you're in the club, we'd never really let you go? That's how the game is played, my friend. And now we have another job for you.'

Yuri could find nothing to say. Bezukhov reached a thick arm across the desk, and a brawny paw of a hand slid the solitary card folder over its surface towards Yuri. 'Open it.'

Again, Yuri did as he was told. Inside the card folder was a transparent plastic sleeve, and inside that a single oblong slip of paper. It was heavily aged, as if it had spent many years exposed to the elements. And creased, as though it had been folded up very small throughout that time. Long ago, someone had written four lines of text on the paper, using black ink that had faded somewhat but was still clearly legible. The writing wasn't in Russian. It used the letters of the English alphabet, though the language wasn't English either.

'It's a cipher,' Yuri said. An old one, too, dating back a

good few decades. Seeing it, he couldn't pretend not to feel a slight stirring of curiosity.

'Good to see you haven't lost your powers of observation, Agent Petrov.'

'Please don't call me that.'

'This cipher is the reason I called you in,' the chief said. 'You're going to decode it for us. Just like old times.'

Yuri studied the cipher more closely. Right away, he could tell it was like no other code he'd come across before. Even back in the pre-cybertechnology dark ages, cryptology had reached a level that was far from crude. 'It's not going to be easy.'

'Why do you think we selected you for the task?' the chief said. 'Some people haven't forgotten you used to have a way with these things, back in the old days before these fucking computers took over.' He spat out the expletive with surprising bitterness.

As Yuri went on peering at the encrypted text, the chief recomposed himself and explained, 'The cipher was discovered two weeks ago by a crew of workmen who were demolishing a block of old post-war houses in Novogireyevo District. Coming across an envelope that had been crammed into a crack in a wall, they opened it, saw it was something peculiar and handed it in to the police. Thank God for patriotism, heh?'

Yuri asked, 'What was it doing there?'

Bezukhov smiled, aware that Yuri was being drawn in despite himself. 'We believe that it was concealed there in February 1957 by a British spy working as part of a network. His cover ID was Pyotr Kozlov, real name Leonard Ingram, a British Army captain recruited to SIS after the war. He and a couple of others were inserted into the Soviet Union that January, as part of a special operation you don't need to know about. Let's just say they were stealing secrets. That was before the Anti-Fascist Protection Rampart was put up, and these shits could creep in and out almost as they pleased.' This was all long, long before Yuri's time, but he knew the chief was talking about the Berlin Wall.

Bezukhov levered himself from his chair and went to gaze out of the dusty window. With his back to Yuri he went on, 'Of course, our boys were onto them the moment they stepped on Russian soil. And we had our suspicions about what they were up to. The cipher is obviously a set of instructions of some kind, which would indicate the nature of the secrets they stole, and their whereabouts. Ingram was on his way to pass those instructions to one of his fellow spies when the KGB jumped the gun and nabbed him too soon. If they'd allowed the meeting to take place, they could have captured both of them together as well as the information they were sharing.' Bezukhov turned away from the window with a sigh. 'Mistakes happen. Anyway, when he knew they were closing in on him, Ingram managed to hide what he was carrying, presumably intending to return there if by some miracle he escaped.'

'But he didn't.'

Bezukhov shook his head. 'Before he knew it, he was carted off to Lubyanka for interrogation. Sadly for us, however, the clumsy fools who worked him over were a little overenthusiastic with their use of force. He expired before they were able to get much out of him.'

Yuri felt sick. He tried not to visualise the scene too vividly, but couldn't shut off his imagination.

'Before he died,' the chief went on, 'he revealed knowledge of some highly sensitive information. And I do mean *highly*,' he repeated for emphasis. 'We want to recover that information, and we believe the cipher is key to understanding how much he knew, who else might have been passed that information and how much damage might have been done to our security.'

'So long ago,' Yuri said, frowning. 'How could it still be important?'

'The biggest secrets are like plutonium,' Bezukhov replied. 'Their potency doesn't fade over time.'

The chief let those words hang in the air for a moment, then yanked open a drawer of his desk. 'As you probably know, the old KGB archives on dissidents and enemy spies detained during the Cold War were never destroyed after the fall of the Soviet regime. They were simply hustled away to a new location and now reside inside a high-security underground vault, one to which I happen to have access. I've examined the contents of Ingram's file and found something that may be of value to us. Ingram was carrying these items the night he was captured.'

Bezukhov took a packet from the drawer and slid it across the desk towards Yuri. Yuri hesitated, looked inside, then glanced quizzically up at the chief.

'Tuning forks,' Bezukhov said. 'Part of his cover. Never mind those. It's the book I'm interested in.'

The paperback was an old mid-fifties edition of *Lucky Jim* by the English novelist Kingsley Amis, yellowed by decades spent in secret government storage.

'Certain pages of the book appear to have been very well thumbed,' Bezukhov said. 'You know what that means.'

Yuri did indeed. Old-fashioned ciphers often made use of random phrases and passages from books, likewise chosen at random and known only to the codemaker and the codebreaker. Without the book, it could be literally impossible to decipher the encrypted message. Yuri shook his head. What a fool the British spy had been, to be caught with it.

A basic error of tradecraft, one that had cost him dear. Needless to say, Russian agents didn't make such mistakes.

'Get to work,' Bezukhov said. 'I expect results, Agent Petrov, and I expect them soon. And for pity's sake, get a shave and a haircut. You look like one of the beatniks we used to send to the Gulag.'

Chapter 3

Yuri returned to his dingy apartment, his nerves rattled by the idea that the intelligence services could just scoop him up and put him back to work like he was one of their mindless, unquestioning drones. But what choice had he, other than to do their bidding?

And if he was perfectly honest with himself, a tiny part of him was thrilled to be working on the cipher. For so long, he had lacked any sense of purpose. This was the stuff he did best, and he was determined to crack it. Not just to please Bezukhov, but to prove to himself that he still had what it took.

First impressions had been right: the cipher was indeed like nothing else he'd encountered before. It was like a modern-day locksmith suddenly faced with picking some antiquated and fiendishly complex device from ancient China or Egypt. Yuri carried it over to the cluttered work table in the corner of his tiny living room. With a cup of coffee at his right elbow, Ingram's copy of *Lucky Jim* at his left and the cipher, notepad, pen and his trusty laptop in front of him, he got down to his task with an energy he'd forgotten he had. The laptop was loaded with a decryption program he'd designed himself, called CAESAR. But, just like in the good old days, technology would be no substitute for sheer brainwork. Man, not machine, would be doing most of the heavy lifting.

The thing was a modified Polybius square with straddling bipartite monoalphabetic substitution, superenciphered by double transposition. In short, it was a tough little bastard to crack. Without the yellowed, dog-eared old book, he'd have been lost. Somewhere within its pages was the key to whatever message the British spy had been trying to pass to his colleagues. He was damned if he couldn't find it.

Yuri worked all night. And all of the next day. And all of the following night as well. He worked until he was exhausted, skipping meals, snoozing for short periods at the desk, reluctant to leave his chair even for toilet breaks. He worked until the whole room was littered with screwed-up sheets of paper covered in gobbledegook.

But he got it. Finally, as the first streaks of dawn were breaking on the third day, with just a little help from CAESAR, he got it.

When the computer finally spat out the finished decryption, Yuri fell back in his chair and stared at the screen for a long time. The decoded message was short. The bottom lines were a set of geo coordinates. The top line consisted of just five words, in English. OPERATION PUPPET MASTER IS REAL.

Those five words couldn't have hit Yuri harder if they had been bullets fired from a high-powered rifle.

'Operation Puppet Master' was the translation of the Russian 'Операция кукольный мастер', and one of the great mythical beasts in the pantheon of conspiracy theory dating back to Cold War times. On internet forums and all across the blogosphere, debate still raged among paranoid nutjobs and serious investigators alike over whether the highly classified Soviet project had ever been more than a wild fantasy.

He and Grisha had talked about it often. While Grisha was an avid believer, of course, Yuri had been privately sceptical: file under 'Giant Alien Lizards'.

Suddenly that scepticism had been blown to smithereens. 'You've got to be fucking kidding me,' he breathed.

The bastards had actually been developing this stuff all along? It was *real*?

Not only real, but worrying enough, apparently, to have drawn the attention of SIS, the British Intelligence Service, precursor to MI6, so long ago. Enough of a threat for the likes of Captain Leonard Ingram to risk and lose his life over. Things didn't get more real than that.

Yuri fed the geo coordinates into Google and discovered that they pointed to a location right here, in Moscow. It was obvious what he had to do next.

Yuri's car was an ancient Volkswagen that wheezed and rattled and grew lighter each year as more parts dropped off. Traffic was mercifully sparse at that time of morning, and the banger was able to reach its destination without expiring. The area was in the east of the city, part of the Novogireyevo district where the KGB had apprehended the British spy back in '57. The coordinates led Yuri to a fenced-off row of old Soviet-era warehouses that must have been disused even then, now decades overdue for demolition.

Ingram's decoded directions were amazingly precise. Behind a stack of rusty, jagged metal and empty crates, Yuri came across the tobacco tin exactly where the spy had left it all those years ago. He hustled back to his car to open it. The round pocket-sized tin was red with rust on the outside, but when he used a coin to pop the lid he found the airtight seal still intact, opening with a little hiss of stale air trapped in there since 1957.

Inside the tin was a roll of microfilm, then the summit of technology, nowadays easily scanned and read on a home computer. The other item left Yuri breathless. He peeled away the square of oiled cloth in which it had been wrapped, and let the thing roll into the cupped palm of his hand, careful not to drop it. It was only a few millimetres in length, oblong-shaped and rounded at both ends like a medicine capsule, but made of shiny metal that was smooth and cold to the touch. If it was what Yuri thought it was, it was beyond sensational. Its discovery could change everything. Never mind myths and speculation: here, for the first time, was the hard physical evidence that could blow the lid right off the whole conspiracy.

No wonder Bezukhov and his people didn't want this coming out. *Like plutonium*, the chief had said. The secret was as explosive now as it had been sixty years ago. Maybe even more so. What were these bastards still up to? How much more advanced must the technology be today? It was a terrifying thought.

He had to tell Grisha about this. Grisha would know what to do.

Yuri fished out his mobile, then swore as he realised that in his hurry to leave the apartment he'd snatched his regular phone instead of the burner he used to communicate with Grisha. He'd been so busy he hadn't checked his emails the last two days – and now there was one waiting there from Eloise, his ex-wife.

'Bitch!' he yelled out loud when he read it.

In her latest scheme against him, Eloise was now threatening to prevent future visits from their daughter and ending his custody rights, on grounds of poor parenting. Specifically, because for three out of five of Valentina's last trips to Moscow, he'd failed to turn up to collect her.

Yuri knew he was guilty as charged. But Eloise's vindictiveness had reached new heights. She couldn't do this! Then again, Yuri thought angrily, maybe she could. Eloise's uncle, whom Yuri had always despised, had all the money and power in the world. He was probably a lizard person, too.

The email reminded Yuri that he was due to pick Valentina up at the airport later that day. He'd been so focused on the cipher, he'd nearly forgotten that she was visiting for the next five days. He couldn't afford another no-show, in case that harpy of a mother of hers made good on her legal threat. The idea of not seeing his beloved kid again for a long time upset him enormously.

As if Yuri's mind wasn't already overloaded with stress right now. What was he going to do about his discovery? Forcing himself to think logically, he realised his options were few. If he delivered the decryption and the contents of the tin back to Bezukhov, he'd be signing his own death warrant. People who knew too much were made to disappear just as efficiently as in the days of the KGB. Maybe even more so. But if Yuri chose to deny Bezukhov his prize, he was a marked man. They'd hunt him to the ends of the earth until they found him and put a bullet in his skull.

With shaking hands, Yuri replaced the precious items in the tin, screwed it tightly shut and was about to start the car when his phone rang.

'Well?' Bezukhov's voice rumbled in his ear. 'Any progress? It's been days.'

'It's you, chief,' Yuri said, thinking furiously. It was decision time. 'Well, I, uh, you see—'

'I told you I expected results.'

'And you'll get them. I just need more time, that's all.'

'What's taking so damn long?'

'It's been tougher to decipher than I expected. I'll get there, trust me.'

Bezukhov growled a series of dire warnings about what would happen if he didn't, and soon, and then hung up.

Yuri started his engine with a rattle and a puff of blue smoke, and sped off. The thought of telling his secret to Grisha terrified him almost as much as letting Bezukhov have it. Grisha would waste no time plastering it all over the internet, and you didn't need to be a genius to figure out what would happen next.

Yuri couldn't wait to see what was on the microfilm, the final confirmation as if any were needed. Rushing back to his dingy apartment as fast as his jalopy would carry him, he dived into his desk chair and fired up his PC and scanner. The process of scanning the microfilm was a simple but time-consuming one, for such a small quantity of information. What in the fifties would take up a whole roll of microfilm now used only the tiniest amount of digital storage. But the data itself was even more astonishing than Yuri had anticipated. Everything was in Russian, officially marked with the stamp of a Soviet-era intelligence unit he'd never even heard of. It comprised a mind-boggling collection of detailed instructions and plans, blueprints, case studies and more. Yuri didn't know whether to laugh out loud, or whimper in dread. He ended up doing both.

Yuri carefully encrypted the file, stored it on a flash drive that he would keep on his person at all times, and erased all trace of it from his computer. Even just walking around the apartment, he felt as though he was carrying a megaton warhead in his pocket.

At times like these, you need the counsel of an especially wise friend to guide you. Yuri swallowed down some coffee and a stale bagel, then ran back to his car and headed to the

Cathedral of the Immaculate Conception on Malaya Gruzinskaya Street to seek the advice of the wisest friend anyone could wish for, even if He wasn't always forthcoming with His reply. A while later, Yuri emerged from the church feeling somewhat let down; but there was little time to agonise over it, as he then had to scoot over to the airport in time to pick up Valentina.

Yuri's twelve-year-old daughter was his pride and joy. So full of light and sharp intelligence, she almost made him forget his predicament as they spent the first day of her visit together. He'd promised her a super-fun time, and it was, exploring the parks, visiting the zoo, cooking lunch together, laughing at Valentina's hilarious impressions of her teachers, telling jokes, watching a goofy DVD. By evening, Yuri had managed to relax somewhat, and decided what to do. He called Grisha on his burner, but his friend didn't pick up. Drunk again, no doubt, or working double shifts warning the world of the evil plots being hatched against them.

The following day – still no reply from Grisha and mercifully no more calls from Bezukhov, though that was just a question of time – Yuri took Valentina out for lunch. Nothing expensive, because he had no money. Over a McChicken sandwich meal, conversing in Dutch as they generally did together out of habit from their Amsterdam days, he discreetly raised the subject of her mother's lawyer. Valentina appeared not to know anything about Eloise's dirty little schemes, which was just as well. Yuri tried to console himself that it was just an idle threat. Eloise was well known for her manipulative ways, and this kind of emotional blackmail was not beneath her.

It was as they were walking home after lunch that Yuri passed a newsstand, did a double-take at something he'd glimpsed on the front page of the latest edition of *Metro Moscow*, and went rushing over to buy a copy.

He had to blink several times before he was sure he wasn't dreaming.

The priest he'd spoken to the day before had been found hanging from a bridge. Suicide.

Yuri stopped breathing. Dirty bastards. If they'd pressed the poor old man for information before they murdered him . . . if they knew what Yuri had confided in him . . .

He threw down the paper and instantly glanced around him at the passers-by on the busy street. It all looked innocent enough, but Yuri was thrown into a panic. Remembering to his horror that he'd left the flash drive and tobacco tin containing all the incriminating evidence right there on his desk, he was suddenly terrified. Could *they* be watching the apartment? Did they know where he lived? Maybe, but it was a chance he had to take. He seized Valentina's hand. 'Quickly. We're going home. No time to lose, Sweet Pea.' It was a pet name she'd always loved.

'Why? What's happening?' the girl asked, alarmed at the look on his face.

'To pick up some things, then we're leaving.'

'On a trip, like the other time? To see Uncle Grisha?'

'That's right, Sweet Pea. You liked that, didn't you? But don't say his name, okay? Not until we get there.'

'Why?'

'Just because.'

Armed thugs didn't pounce on them at the apartment, and to Yuri's immense relief the evidence was still right where he'd left it. He snatched the tin and the flash drive and stuffed them into his pocket. 'Okay, that's enough. Let's go, Valentina.'

'But my things—' the girl said, crestfallen.

They could be here any minute. 'No time, baby. We can pick up anything we need on the way. Come on!'

'Wait, my phone!' It was by the bedside in the spare room. Pink, like most everything else Valentina owned.

Yuri was very aware of all the fancy geo-location toys the intelligence services could use to hack and track anyone's smartphone. For the same reason, he was frightened to bring his laptop with him. 'No. You have to leave it behind.'

'But it's mine.'

'I'm sorry, baby. I can't explain why, but you can't bring it with you. Too dangerous.'

'Don't be silly, Papa. How can a phone be dangerous?'

'It just is. Come *on*, Valentina!' Yuri could see she wouldn't listen. In his panicky frustration, he could think of only one way to end the dispute. He barged past his daughter into the spare bedroom, grabbed her phone, dropped it on the floor and crunched it several times with his heel until it was in bits. Valentina stared at the broken pink pieces, and in disbelief at her normally so placid father for what he'd just done, then burst into tears.

'There,' he said, feeling awful. 'Now you don't need to worry about your phone any more. Let's go.'

Yuri Petrov hurried his daughter away from the apartment, knowing he would never return to this place. All that mattered to him now was getting away from here.

Minutes later, the first attempt would be made to snatch them.

Chapter 4

Normandy, France
Several days later

The light summer rain filtered through the oak woodland canopy to fall as drips and splashes to the ground that was soft and spongy with decayed moss and leaves layered season on season for thousands of years. The trees grew thick and wild, blocking out the sunlight; here and there a fallen trunk overgrown with creeping ivy and barbed-wire brambles.

Once upon a time the Neolithic forest had spread far and wide, later to form a battleground for invading Roman legions and the Celtic Gaulish defenders of the land, whose swords and arrowheads still remained buried deep under layers of soil. The areas of woodland that had survived to modern times probably looked no different from when Druids had practised their strange magic and rituals here, and wild boar and red deer and roebuck roamed free, preyed on by wolves, bears and tribal humans.

Today, the prey and predators were of a different kind.

From the green shadows stepped a man. His hair and clothing were wet from the rain, his face streaked with dirt. Alone, unarmed and hunted, he had been evading his pursuers for close to two hours. At times they'd been so close to him that he could hear the rasp of their breath, smell the tang of their sweat. They were all around him, spread out through the acres of forest like a net, and they wouldn't give up until the fugitive was caught.

He paused, as still as the trees, scenting the air, his acute hearing filtering out the background hum of insects and the chirping of birds for the tiniest sound of his enemies closing in. There; three o'clock from his position, no more than twenty metres away through the foliage: the crack of a twig underfoot, followed by a wary silence. Someone approaching.

The fugitive fixed his enemy's position and moved on, padding over the rough ground as silently as a hunted animal when danger is near. His pursuers were a dedicated professional four-man team equipped with automatic rifles and sidearms. He was alone and had no weapons other than his wits and experience. Which gave him an edge over his hunters. And as he knew very well, having an edge was everything in war.

He would not be caught. He refused to fail.

The fugitive stalked his way through the trees, pausing frequently to listen and observe. Then he stopped. The man whose careless footstep had given away his position was right there up ahead, just five metres away with his back turned, quite unaware that his quarry was creeping up close behind. His rifle was slanted across his chest, gripped tightly in his gloved hands. Like the fugitive, he was dressed in military disruptive pattern material camo, except the utility belt around his waist held a holstered pistol and a commando knife. He was glancing left and right as he paced slowly between the trees. The stress of the long, gruelling hunt was telling on the man's tense body language and the rapid rate of his breathing.

The fugitive smiled. Those were good signs. The enemy

is at his most vulnerable when he's nervous. Get him spooked enough, grind down his morale, and he's ripe for defeat.

All at once, prey became predator as the fugitive suddenly struck out of the shadows. It was all over in an instant: the pursuer down on the ground, face pressed into the moss and leaves, unable to make a sound for the strong hand clamped over his mouth. The fugitive unsnapped the commando knife from the man's sheath and touched the flat of its blade against the soft flesh of his neck. The words the fugitive whispered into the man's ear chilled his blood and froze him in mid-struggle.

'You're dead.'

The man relented, and the tension went out of his muscles as he realised it was over for him. The fugitive kept the pressure of the blade on his neck as he trussed the man's wrists one-handed with a thick plastic cable tie. He did the same for the man's ankles. Then he thrust the knife into his belt and picked up the fallen rifle. He moved on, still listening hard for the crackles and snaps of the remaining hunters moving through the forest.

He could sense them not far away. The map of their ever-shifting positions was like a three-dimensional model inside his mind, marked by the points of an imaginary compass. The nearest one was roughly southwest, less than forty metres off. The fugitive's nostrils flared and twitched at the scent of him. Lesson number one: don't wear aftershave when you embark on a manhunt after a seasoned operator.

In less than a minute, the fugitive was right behind his enemy. He touched the barrel of the captured rifle to the man's back and whispered, 'Bang.' The man turned, put up his hands, immediately accepting defeat. Moments later he was trussed, gagged and helpless in the bushes, like his comrade before him. Without a sound, the fugitive dragged his captive over the ground to where he'd left the first one. The two lay helplessly side by side in the leaves, wriggling like caught fish and muttering stifled curses behind their gags. The fugitive left them to resume his stalk. The pursuit had gone on long enough. It was time to end it.

The last two were paired up together, slipping furtively through the trees when a section of shadow to their left seemed to come alive and detached itself towards them. By the time they saw the movement and the gun aiming at them, it was too late to react.

'Lose your weapons. On the ground. Flat on your faces, arms out to the sides.'

The fugitive secured their wrists behind their backs and relieved them of their sidearms. He left their ankles unbound so that he could march them back at gunpoint to reunite them with their companions. Once all four were lined up sitting on the wet ground he slashed their plastic bonds and they rose warily to their feet, rubbing their wrists and looking up at him with just a little resentment in their eyes. They were unhurt, but thoroughly humiliated and dismayed. They had travelled to this location as a team, in the hopes of demonstrating their skills. This outcome was far from the one they'd anticipated.

The fugitive's name was Ben Hope. He leaned against a tree trunk, reached into the pocket of his camouflage combat vest for one of the blue cigarette packs he always carried and went through in large quantities, and lit up with a battered steel lighter. As he contentedly puffed the Gauloise, he studied the expressions on the faces of his students and smiled.

'Don't feel so bad, boys. Education's all about making mistakes and learning how to avoid making them again. That's what you're here for.'

The location of the training exercise was a place called Le Val, in rural northern France. In some circles it had become a key facility, just about the only place in the world where certain specialist skills could be acquired by those prepared to pay the fee and take the strain. Le Val was jointly owned and operated by Ben and his business partner and longtime friend, Jeff Dekker. It had been steadily growing for some years now, the latest development being the purchase of an additional forty-acre parcel of forest to add to the existing spread of the estate. It had been a huge undertaking to fence off so much extra land to keep it secure from intruders, unwitting or otherwise – but the investment meant Le Val could now offer courses in pursuit and tracking skills on top of all the other educational services they provided to the police, military and private security trainees who came to them from all over the world.

Today's group were part of a specialist fugitive manhunt agency based in Belgium and affiliated to INTERPOL, seeking a five-day CPD training in the art and science of capturing a fleeing subject in a rural or wilderness environment. The first job of the Le Val Tactical Training Centre was to expose, break down and analyse their weaknesses as a team. That first morning's session had revealed some issues. Now it was time to start examining what had gone awry.

The post-operation debrief took place in a prefabricated hut in a pretty wildflower meadow close to the edge of the woods, outside which were parked the two long-wheelbase Land Rover Defenders that would later shuttle everyone back to Le Val's farmhouse HQ. Ben was joined by Jeff Dekker and their business associate Tuesday Fletcher to run through the results of the morning class. The various weaponry – consisting of trainer rifles, pistols and knives that felt and weighed exactly like the real thing but were made of bright blue plastic – were stacked on a table beside them, next to the obligatory canteen of hot coffee brewed up on the military Jetboil stove.

The Belgians were visibly demoralised and exhausted, and so Jeff spared them the scathing criticisms that were half-hanging off his tongue and contented himself with standing against the wall with his arms folded and a sneer of contempt on his face. After half an hour's lecture detailing the many missteps that had allowed the team's target to not only evade capture but turn the tables on them, Ben decided they had suffered enough.

'Okay, folks, let's break for the day and get some rest. You'll need it, because tomorrow we're going to repeat the exercise all over again and see if we can improve on today's performance. Any questions?'

There was a chorus of groans. One of the trainees complained, 'If it'd been for real, we'd have had dogs.'

'It's a fair point,' Ben said. 'But relying on a K9 unit is a luxury you might not always get to enjoy. Imagine the dogs have copped it. Put out of action by pepper spray, wire traps or a bullet. Now you're on your own. Depending on your own skills. That's what's being tested here.'

'Yeah, but you were an SAS major,' moaned another. 'Not even in the same ballpark as most of the crooks we go after. How many guys like you are we ever going to have to catch, in real life?'

Jeff just glared at them and shook his head. Tuesday was having a hard time not laughing – but then, the young Jamaican ex-soldier had a habit of always seeing the funny side, even when he was being shot at.

Ben shrugged and replied, 'The Roman army used to train their legionaries with lead swords, three times heavier than their regular sidearms. Why? So that when it came to the thick of battle where the metal meets the meat and a man's nerve is tested like never before, they felt invincible because their issue weapons were like a feather in their hand. If you don't believe in your abilities, you're already the loser. Belief is confidence. I want your team to leave here confident that you can catch not just some ordinary Joe, but *anyone*. Because you never know who you might be sent to take down.'

'And nobody likes making a total bollocking fool of themselves, now do they, fellas?' Jeff added, apparently unable to resist getting in some slight dig.

Ben was about to say something a little more reassuring when the thud of a fast-approaching helicopter suddenly rattled the hut's windows. The chopper wasn't passing over, it was coming in to land – and that definitely wasn't part of the day's schedule.

'Hello, what's this all about?' Jeff muttered.

They stepped outside to find out.

Chapter 5

The afternoon sunlight made little starbursts on the chopper's shiny red fuselage as it settled down to land in the meadow a little distance from the hut. Ben and Jeff walked out to meet it, both wondering who their unexpected visitor might be. The blast from the spinning rotor blades ruffled their hair and flattened a circle of grass and wildflowers around the landed aircraft. They could see the pilot through the Perspex window, shutting everything down. As the pitch of the turbine began to dwindle and the rotors slowed, a rear hatch swung open and the chopper's two passengers stepped out.

The first to emerge was an elderly man named Auguste Kaprisky whom Ben and Jeff both knew well, due to the fact that he'd been a client of theirs in the not-so-distant past. Born August Kaprisky in Rottweil, Germany, eighty-two years earlier, he had become a devoted Francophile in his middle age, moved his home and business to Le Mans and suffixed the 'e' to his first name to make it sound more Gallic.

Kaprisky might be old, but he was still fit as a fiddle and as mentally sharp as the day he'd wangled his first million, sixty years ago. He was currently ranked fourth on the Forbes list of Europe's richest billionaires, although aside from his surname and flashy corporate logo painted on the side of the helicopter nothing about his appearance hinted remotely at vast wealth. Tall and stringy in the same tatty old green chequered suit Ben remembered from every time they'd met, he looked more like a hobo clinging on to dignity than one of the continent's most powerful and influential tycoons.

His co-passenger, awkwardly climbing out of the chopper after him, was a woman a fraction of his age. She appeared expensively groomed and polished, with a mass of long fair hair tied up in an elaborate braid that must have taken a team of top-class beauticians eight hours to perfect. Ben had never seen her before; he wondered fleetingly whether Kaprisky, a widower for many years, might have finally succumbed to the same temptation as so many other fabu- lously rich old men and got himself a trophy wife.

Whoever she was, Ben noticed as he and Jeff got closer, she looked teary and distraught. The expression on the old man's face told Ben he wasn't very happy either. Auguste Kaprisky was known as 'the man who never laughs'. Come to think of it, Ben had seldom seen even the faintest ghost of a smile bend his lips. Today he looked grimmer than ever. Clearly, this unannounced visit was no social call.

Ben reached him and put out a hand to shake. 'Auguste, what a surprise,' he shouted over the diminishing yowl of the turbine. He and his client were in the habit of speaking French to one another, which Ben did fluently. Jeff was still struggling with the language, despite the best efforts of his new fiancée, a local teacher called Chantal.

'Your staff told me I would find you here,' Kaprisky shouted back, croaky and throaty. The woman was clutching at her braid to save it from being blasted to pieces by the hurricane. Kaprisky didn't have much hair left to protect, and probably wouldn't have cared anyway.

As the four of them moved out of the wind and noise of the helicopter, Kaprisky apologised for turning up so unexpectedly. 'I hope it's not inconvenient. I would have called, but—'

'Not at all,' Ben replied. 'To what do we owe the pleasure?'

Kaprisky's lined face was as hard as concrete. 'I need your help.'

Didn't they all.

'This isn't a good place to talk,' Ben said. 'Let's go back to the house.'

They climbed into the Land Rovers – Jeff, Tuesday and the four Belgians riding in the lead vehicle and Ben and the visitors following behind as they went bouncing and roaring over the meadows towards the main compound. Ben's passengers were silent as he drove. He could feel their tension and wondered what this was about, but said nothing.

The old stone farmhouse, big and blocky and more than two hundred and fifty years old, was the central hub of Le Val, and the farmhouse kitchen was the central hub of the house. While Tuesday escorted the Belgians to the separate building used to accommodate trainees, Ben and Jeff led Auguste Kaprisky and his female companion inside. The kitchen was floored with original time-smoothed flagstones and lined with antique pine cupboards. The wine rack was always full, and there was always something delicious-smelling bubbling on the range courtesy of Marie-Claire, who lived in the nearby village and came in to cook for them. In the middle of the room was the pitted old pine table at which Ben, Jeff, Tuesday and a hundred Le Val trainees had spent countless hours talking, drinking, playing cards, planning strategies and (to Marie-Claire's vociferous outrage) stripping and cleaning automatic weapons. It was all a far cry from the plush boardrooms out of which Kaprisky ran his multi-billion-euro empire, but the old man seemed too preoccupied to pay any notice to his surroundings.

They all sat around the table. Ben offered coffee, which was politely declined.

'Now,' Ben said, getting down to business. 'What is it that brings you here, Auguste?'

The fair-haired woman still hadn't been introduced, nor spoken a word. Kaprisky touched her hand. 'This is my niece, Eloise. She speaks English, German and Dutch but very little French, having moved here relatively recently. I would like her to participate in this discussion, so may we switch to English for the remainder of the conversation?'

'Of course,' Ben said in English. Jeff looked much relieved.

Kaprisky made the usual introductions, in his rather stiff and formal way. Eloise offered a small smile and a limp handshake, and said very little.

'Again, I must apologise for this intrusion,' Kaprisky said. 'My reason for being here is, as I said, that I – we – desperately need expert assistance with a matter of extreme urgency. I would have made contact to warn you in advance of our arrival, but what I'm about to reveal to you is, well, most delicate.'

Ben wasn't surprised by the lack of communication. Kaprisky was an inveterate paranoid who worried neurotically about phone taps and email hacking. Ever since the attempt on his life, when a disgruntled business rival had lost his mind and assaulted Kaprisky's home with an Uzi submachine gun, he'd spent untold fortunes turning his estate near Le Mans into a fortress within whose impenetrable walls the old man lived like a virtual recluse. When Jeff sometimes commented that Kaprisky was turning into Howard Hughes, he wasn't joking. Only a serious emergency could have prompted the billionaire to leave his stronghold.

Kaprisky paused, spread his hands out on the table, seemed about to speak, then threw a covert sideways glance at Jeff.

'Am I a third wheel here?' Jeff said, catching his look. 'No problem, I can make myself scarce.'

'Whatever you're about to tell me,' Ben said to Kaprisky, 'understand that I have no secrets from my business partner and you need have none either. I trust this man with my life.'

Kaprisky seemed satisfied with that. Eloise sat very still beside him, gazing at the table with a set frown wrinkling her brow.

'I'm guessing this matter has to do with Eloise?' Ben prompted.

Kaprisky nodded. 'She is the only child of my late brother, Gustav. She is as dear to me as if she were my own daughter.'

Ben said, 'Naturally.' Then waited to hear what on earth this was about.

Talking as though his niece weren't present in the room with them, Kaprisky went on, 'Her full name is Eloise Petrova. Personally, I thought Eloise Kaprisky sounded far better, but in fact anything would have. The reason for this unfortunate change is that she married a *Russian*.' Kaprisky spat that last word out as though his niece had married an alien slime creature. 'Fortunately, she had the sense to split from him after a mere ten years. The divorce was an extremely acrimonious one. I will spare you the painful details.'

'I'm sorry to hear of your family trouble,' Ben said. Still wondering.

Kaprisky shook his head. 'Not I. I have never tried to conceal my conviction that the marriage was a disaster from the start. Yuri Petrov is, has always been, and as far as I am concerned will always be, with no possibility of redemption

44

whatsoever should he live for all eternity, the worst kind of pathetic excuse for a human being.'

'So you don't think much of the guy,' Jeff interjected.

'There is no man alive more unsuited to be a husband to my precious Eloise, or the father of her child. He is the most indolent, self-seeking, worthless piece of—'

'We get the general idea,' Ben said.

'Forgive me,' Kaprisky said, collecting himself and wiping flecks of spittle from his lips. 'I get very worked up. It's just that this haunts our lives, even two years after the marriage ended. Things were bad enough when this moron whisked Eloise off to live for a decade in Amsterdam, where he *apparently* had some kind of employment, the nature of which has never been clear to me—'

If that was a cue for Eloise to step in and say something, she didn't respond to it. Her uncle carried on, 'She then had to tie herself forever to him by having a child with him, despite all my warnings that she would come to bitterly regret it.' Kaprisky halted mid-stream and grimaced. 'I don't mean the child herself. She brings nothing but joy and we love her dearly.'

'I know what you mean,' Ben said.

'How I pleaded for her to see sense, but did she listen? No, no. Now she must deal with the fool every time they exchange custody of their daughter. To make matters even worse, the idiot has since returned to live in *Russia*.' Land of the slime creatures, apparently.

'What's the girl's name?' Ben asked Kaprisky. There seemed little point in asking the mother, who still hadn't offered a word to the conversation.

'Valentina. She's twelve.' Kaprisky sighed. 'As much as I despise her worthless father, I dote on that child. If anything should happen to her, I . . .'

Ben sensed the tone of desperation in his voice. Now, maybe, they were coming to the crux of the matter. 'This is about Valentina, isn't it? Is something wrong?'

Eloise Petrova went on staring vacantly at the tabletop. Kaprisky slowly nodded, his eyes filling up like dark pools of despair.

'Yes, this is about Valentina. It appears that she and her father have disappeared. And we know why. The brute has kidnapped her.'

Chapter 6

Now Ben understood why Kaprisky had brought this to him.

For several years after he'd quit the military, Ben had operated as a freelance 'crisis response consultant' specialising in the area of what was known as 'K&R'. The acronym stood for 'Kidnap and Ransom'. The fast-growing industry of misery, terror and death perpetrated by cruel men against the innocent and the vulnerable. It was the most innocent and vulnerable victims of them all – kidnapped kids – whom Ben had most tried to help. The taking of a child, whether to extort money from the frantic family or for myriad other reasons, was the thing he despised the most. He'd have despised it, and its perpetrators, even if he hadn't gone through the anguish and horror of losing his nine-year-old sister to human traffickers when he was a teenager, and the catastrophic family breakdown that had followed.

Nothing he'd done in his entire Special Forces career had driven him the way he'd been driven to find those lost children, bring them home safe and punish the men who'd snatched them from their families. To this day he could remember the names and faces of every single kid he'd rescued. He often thought about them, what they were doing now that they were older, what life was like for them, whether they ever still had nightmares about being taken and held prisoner. For him, the memories of children locked in damp, filthy basements, imprisoned in cages, chained to beds, blindfolded in the dark, often drugged, too often abused in other ways, would never fade. Thinking about it now, he felt his fists clench tight.

'I haven't been involved in that for a long time,' he said to Kaprisky. 'I'm not even going to ask who you've been talking to. It's not exactly public knowledge what I used to do.'

'I have many connections, my young friend. And there are many people in this world, whose names you and I both know, who still regard you as their saviour. Rest assured they are extremely discreet to whom they divulge such information, but they will never forget what you did to reunite families torn apart by monsters.'

Ben looked at Eloise, who still hadn't said a word since they were introduced, then back at her uncle. 'And that's what you believe Valentina's father is, a monster?'

Kaprisky said, 'Parents have been known to kidnap their own children, have they not?'

Ben had indeed known several cases of that happening. It was usually done to harm the other partner in some way, the ultimate expression of a catastrophically fragmented relationship. That variety of kidnapper seldom chained their own kids up in basements or deliberately harmed them – although it wasn't unknown to happen; but there was nonetheless a serious risk of harm coming to the kids as the ring closed around the offending parent and they became increasingly desperate to get away. More than one had ended up endangering their child's life in a high-speed car chase or a volatile armed standoff with bullets flying in all directions.

That was why, in Ben's experience, the often heavy-handed tactics of official law enforcement frequently did as much damage as good. Many of the stricken families who had come to him for help in the past had heard the horror stories and decided to forgo police involvement in favour of more unorthodox, yet far more effective, methods. Ben had no problem with bullets flying, but he liked them to be properly aimed where they were meant to go: into the kidnappers themselves, and preferably not into their hostages.

'Have you reported this to the authorities?' In his K&R rescue days it was always the first question he'd asked prospective clients, bracing himself for the reply.

Kaprisky shook his head. 'Informing the police would, I agree, be the first and most obvious recourse. However, as you know, I value my privacy, and also that of what little family I have left. For that reason I would prefer not to have my niece's private affairs disclosed to strangers.' He paused. 'I am also a highly cautious man, who has learned never to step on ground without having first made certain it was safe to walk on. It takes only the minimum of research to reveal that, if the many tragic reports of ineptly mishandled cases are true, involving the forces of conventional law and order in such instances is all too often the worst error one could possibly make.'

'That's your choice,' Ben said.

'And so, that option must remain the very last resort, not the first. I would do anything to keep this in the family, so to speak, if at all possible. I consider that I owe you my life, Major Hope. That is as good as a blood connection for me. And that, as you have surmised, is why I am here.'

Ben hated being called by his military rank, but the old man got some kick out of authority titles and nothing would dissuade him of the habit of addressing Ben that way. 'I'm honoured, Auguste. But I'll only tell you what the police would have told you. Genuine kidnap cases are mercifully rare. There could be other possible reasons to eliminate before we start jumping to radical conclusions. Why don't you run through exactly what happened? From the beginning.'

Kaprisky knitted his long, bony fingers in front of him on the table. He licked his lips, as though they'd gone dry. 'May I trouble you for a glass of wine? My nerves are shattered.'

'Of course.' Ben stood, grabbed four glasses from the cupboard and a bottle of Chante Clair, Le Val's current house red, from the rack. He pulled the cork, poured out the glasses and sat down. 'You won't mind if I smoke?'

Kaprisky took a long drink of wine. Eloise didn't touch hers. Jeff knocked his down at a gulp and refilled it. Ben lit a Gauloise and leaned back in his chair.

'As I said,' Kaprisky went on, 'Valentina's father now resides in Russia. Moscow, to be precise. Since the divorce Eloise and Valentina have come to live on the estate at Le Mans, where they are very happy and Valentina is home-schooled by the finest private tutors money can buy. The unsavoury custody terms of the divorce settlement are that she spend a week with her worthless father every two months, which we have been honouring except in winter when it was too cold. As you know, I have my own personal jet on permanent standby not far from home.'

'Indeed I do,' Ben said. The previous year, Ben's grown-up son Jude had got into serious trouble off the east coast of Africa that had required a very rapid intervention by Ben, Jeff and Tuesday. Kaprisky had provided the Gulfstream G650 as emergency transport, without which Jude would be dead now.

'So, whenever it has been his time to have her,' Kaprisky continued, 'we put Valentina on the Gulfstream and fly her over, where he is supposed to meet her at the private terminal at the airport, to drive her to the dive of an apartment he keeps in some squalid part of the city. She normally stays for five days. At the end of each interminable visit, the process reverses and she flies home to us. In this way, the poor girl has been passed back and forth like the ball in a game of long-distance tennis. Scarcely the most satisfactory arrangement, but we have endured – until now.

'Four days ago, at what should have been the end of her most recent trip to Moscow, Valentina failed to come home. The pilot called us to say that neither she nor her father showed up at the airport. I eventually had him fly the empty plane back to Le Mans. We have been frantically trying to contact them ever since, without success.'

Jeff knocked down another gulp of wine and made a frown that rippled his brow into corrugated creases. 'So, Yuri just decided a week with his kid wasn't long enough, or what?'

Kaprisky snorted derisively. 'I suspect a far less wholesome motivation than fatherly attachment is at work here.'

'Four days,' Ben said, more to himself than Kaprisky. His mind was spinning through a hundred possibilities. On the one hand, a four-day absence wasn't that long. On the other, a lot of very bad things could happen in less time.

'But I have not been sitting idly waiting,' Kaprisky replied. 'No sooner had the aircraft returned without Valentina than we were ready to refuel and fly straight back there, with a team of my best men aboard. One of them, Andriy Vasilchuk, grew up in the Ukraine and speaks some Russian. I additionally employed a Moscow private investigation firm to assist the team in their enquiries. Their instructions were to go immediately to Petrov's apartment and commence the search for him and Valentina.'

'And they didn't find them there, obviously.'

'Not only that, but on questioning neighbours in his apartment block, it transpires that nobody there had glimpsed any sign of Petrov, nor of the child, for days before he should have delivered her to the airport.'

Kaprisky let out a long breath through his nose, leaned forward and fixed Ben intently with his piercing eyes. 'I am no expert and would always defer to your superior judgement in these matters. But, to me, this situation bears all the suspicious hallmarks of an abduction. Please tell me if you can think of any other possible explanation.'

Ben was thinking hard. He said nothing as Kaprisky went on staring at him with such intensity that the old man was almost trembling.

Just then, Eloise spoke up for the first time since she'd sat down. Despite a marked German accent, her English was perfect. 'There's more you need to know. My uncle hasn't mentioned the fact that, before this happened, I had been investigating my legal options to restrict Yuri's right of parental access.'

Ben narrowed his eyes at her. 'Why? Are you suggesting—?'

She flinched visibly at the notion. 'Abuse? No, nothing of that sort.'

Kaprisky gave another snort, as if to say, 'Who knows what that creep might be capable of?' His niece shot him a look and went on: 'What it is, Monsieur Hope, is that on several occasions when Valentina was sent to visit her father, he failed to show up at the other end to collect her, and she had to be flown back home without having even seen him. No apologies from my ex-husband, no attempt to explain, not even a call. Finally, after two missed visits in a row, I lost my temper and sent him a message.'

Ben could see where this was leading. 'You threatened him.'

'I had consulted my lawyers earlier that day, who were confident we could make a case against Yuri on grounds of neglect. I told him straight out that I had had enough of his behaviour, that I would be putting things in motion and that Valentina's next visit to him would be her last.' Eloise shook her head. Her eyes clouded and she dabbed at one of them with a knuckle, smearing her mascara. 'I was so angry with him. I didn't realise what I'd done. This is all my fault.'

'Absolute rubbish,' Kaprisky said. 'The blame lies entirely with that reckless imbecile. You did the right thing, my dear. How many times have you complained to me of that man's unreliability, his complete lack of responsibility, the way he pours so much vodka down his throat that he reeks of the stuff from morning until night . . . Need one say more?'

Eloise gave a tiny nod, her eyes still misted up with tears. 'It's true, he does drink far too much. I've tried quizzing Valentina about it, but she doesn't say anything, and I think it's to protect him. The fact is that he was never emotionally stable, and I think he's got worse and worse since the divorce.'

'As well as being a pathological liar,' Kaprisky added angrily. 'All those years in Amsterdam, when he was supposedly employed in some aspect of the computer business, I always thought the whole thing suspiciously vague. I was long convinced that he was leading a double life of some kind. God only knows what that man was up to, and no doubt still is. In a debauched, morally bankrupt drug addicts' haven like Amsterdam, of all places?'

'I'm past caring what he does,' Eloise said bitterly. 'Let him live how he pleases. He can destroy himself for all I care. But not with my Valentina.' She turned to Ben, eyes brimming. 'Do you not see? If I hadn't threatened him he wouldn't have taken her. *I* made him panic. *I* made this happen. And now there's no telling what could happen next. I might never see my little girl again. Am I not right?'

Ben was beginning to think she was. Which meant the worst fears of uncle and niece might very well be justified. All the indicators were pointing unpleasantly towards this being a classic parental kidnapping.

It seemed unlikely that Yuri Petrov would intentionally harm his daughter. But he would be fully intent on not being found. That was the tricky part.

'Please,' Kaprisky said. 'Will you help us?'

Ben said nothing for a long time. He stubbed out the butt of his Gauloise. He could feel the three pairs of eyes on him: Jeff's as well as Kaprisky and Eloise. Finally Ben asked, 'Do you still have men watching the apartment?'

Kaprisky nodded. 'If Petrov had returned there at any time since his disappearance, I would know about it. I also have some connections at government level, who would have notified me if Petrov had attempted to leave the country. As far as we know, he is still in Russia.'

'Russia's a fairly large place,' Ben said. 'Any way to narrow that down a little?'

'I am afraid not, no. We have no idea where he could have taken her. They could be travelling even as we speak.'

'Then you have a problem,' Ben said. 'A bigger one than you perhaps realise. This isn't about scouring a few known haunts, talking to his drinking cronies and sniffing out a borrowed apartment or some cheap rental where he might be lying low somewhere in the same city. Instead, you're telling me Yuri and Valentina are a moving target anywhere within over six million square miles of the biggest country in the world. Dozens of major cities to choose from. Massive mountain ranges. Forests the size of England. The longest rivers on the planet. A coastline that stretches from the Pacific to the Arctic Ocean. A lone operator couldn't cover that much ground in months, maybe years. Only the Russian authorities would have the resources and manpower to launch a nationwide manhunt on this scale. I don't even speak the language.'

'If it's a question of money—'

'It's not,' Ben said.

'I would spare no expense to find her. None whatsoever. My own resources are vast.'

'I know that, Auguste.'

'I am begging you, Major.'

'Ben.'

'I implore you, Ben. Go to Russia and find Valentina. Bring her back. There is nobody else I trust to carry out this job. My own men are amateurs by comparison to you.'

Everyone was staring at Ben. He lit another cigarette and took a long, slow drag. He washed that down with a long, slow drink of the red wine. Then he set down his glass. Gave a deep sigh. Looked straight into the eyes of the two desperate people sitting across the table from him. And said:

'I'm sorry. I think the two of you should waste no more time in reporting this to the police. For all their faults, they're the only ones who can help you right now. It's out of my league.'

Chapter 7

The octogenarian billionaire and his niece said little as they left the farmhouse, looking even grimmer in his case, and more inconsolably distraught in hers, than when they'd first arrived. Ben drove them back to the meadow where their helicopter was still waiting, the pilot patiently absorbed in the sports news. By the time the Land Rover rolled up next to the stationary aircraft Eloise had started gently sobbing. Kaprisky had uttered not a word, nor Ben. There seemed nothing more to say.

Ben stood and watched as they climbed aboard. Kaprisky managed a brief wave as if to say, 'No hard feelings', but it wasn't entirely convincing. The pilot pulled his switches and twiddled his controls, the turbine fired up and grew in pitch as the rotors began to spin, slowly, then faster, until they began to snatch at the air and the chopper danced and skipped on the ground. Then it rose upward, its downblast flattening the grass. The sunlight glinted along the KAPRISKY CORP company logo on its side as it spun around in the direction from which it had come, and sped off. Ben stayed where he was until it was just a red dot over the green hills of Normandy. He trudged back to the Land Rover, hauled himself up behind the wheel and drove back to the house.

The yard was deserted, no sign of Jeff or Tuesday or any of the trainees. Walking towards the farmhouse's door Ben heard the sound of running paws approaching, and turned to see Storm bounding towards him. Storm was a large German shepherd, black and tan with streaks of gold and silver across his shoulders and a thick mane that made him look like a wolf. He was Ben's favourite of the guard dogs that helped to protect Le Val's widening borders from intruders, and the feeling was mutual. He and Ben enjoyed a particular kind of entente. If Storm ever got annoyed at the way his master kept disappearing for periods of time, he never seemed to hold it against him. The dog licked his hand and looked up at Ben with amber eyes so full of intelligence that it would have been quite unsurprising if he'd broken into speech like a person. He frowned at his favourite human, seeing something wasn't right. Storm didn't miss much.

'Yeah, buddy, it turned out to be a pretty rotten day,' Ben said, smoothing his soft fur. 'Coming inside? I wouldn't mind the company.'

The shepherd bounded up the steps to the front door after him, and the two of them made their way into the kitchen. Still no sign of Jeff anywhere. The wine bottle, now half-empty, had been put back on the side and the four glasses were upside-down on the draining board by the sink. Jeff was gradually becoming more domesticated thanks to the influence of Chantal, though in this case Ben could have saved him the trouble of washing up. He grabbed one of the glasses and filled it back up with wine, slumped in his chair at the top of the table and began working on finishing the bottle with Storm lying glumly at his feet, having given up trying to cheer his master's spirits.

The bottle was empty by the time Jeff reappeared soon afterwards. Ben knew from his footsteps in the flag-stone-floored passage and the telltale banging open of the kitchen door that his old friend and business partner wasn't in the best of moods either. Jeff stalked into the room, saw Ben sitting there, stood with his arms folded and gave him one of his patented hard glares.

'Something on your mind, Jeff?'

Jeff glared a little longer, then said, 'Out of your league?'

Ben stiffened. Knowing a fight was coming. Jeff wasn't a man to hold back with his opinions, nor to back down in an argument.

'That's right,' Ben said. 'I've already explained why.'

If Ben had declared he was becoming transgender and henceforth wished to be known as Lolita, Jeff wouldn't have been looking at him with any more incredulity. 'Bullshit. What's the real reason? You getting old? Tired out? Not up to it any more?'

'I belong here now,' Ben said. 'You and I have a business to run, remember? We've got bookings coming in every day, more classes than we can handle and a waiting list as long as your arm, we're expanding all the time, mortgaged up to our eyeballs; and in case you've forgotten, we're in the middle of looking for a second location to grow the business even more.'

That idea had been on the cards for a few months. They'd looked at a couple of rural properties in the south of France, though no commitments had so far been made.

'To hell with the business,' Jeff spat.

'Oh, to hell with the business?'

'You heard the old man. You saw the look on that woman's face. They need help, and fast.'

'He's not going to hurt her.'

58

'He's not going to give her back, either,' Jeff said.

'Kaprisky can easily find someone else to do the job.'

Jeff shook his head. 'Kaprisky's going to hit the panic button, is what Kaprisky's going to do. He's liable to either bring in the bloody A Team, a bunch of trigger-happy numbskulls who think they're Dolph Lundgren. Or even worse, he'll take your advice and call the authorities. Either way he's going to drive Petrov even deeper underground, or something bad will happen.'

'That's the risk,' Ben agreed. 'But even if I still worked in K&R, which I don't, I can't be in two places at once. If I said yes to Kaprisky, there's no telling how long I could be away hunting for this guy.'

'I can draft in a couple of temporary replacements to cover for you. I could call Boonzie. He knows a million guys out there who'd come in at short notice.'

'I didn't realise I was so replaceable.'

'We'll muddle through somehow.' Jeff unfolded his arms, reached out and spun a chair out from the table and sat down, leaning towards Ben on his elbows and giving him an earnest, penetrating stare. 'Seriously. This is what you do, mate.'

'Did. We've moved on, Jeff. *I've* moved on. I'm retired from all that.'

'Start talking like that, pretty soon you'll be gathering moss in front of the fire with your fucking carpet slippers on, and a briar pipe in your gob, listening to Bing Crosby albums.'

'That'll be the day,' Ben said.

'Want my opinion?'

'Do I have any choice?'

'Nope. My opinion is that if you don't find this Petrov guy and bring that girl home, you'll never forgive yourself.

I've never known you to turn down a chance to help someone who needed it, and I'm buggered if I'm going to stand by and watch you do it now. If you're afraid of failing, you just need to look in the mirror, 'cause the guy looking back at you doesn't *do* failure. And don't you dare try to put this on me by talking about the sodding business.'

'I have responsibilities,' Ben said.

'Too right, you do.'

'I've already spent far too long away from home, running around the world doing too much crazy stuff.'

Jeff shrugged. 'You know what they say. When the going gets tough, the tough get going.' Jeff always had an appropriately hackneyed saying to hand.

'Maybe they do. But I wouldn't want you thinking I was the kind of bloke who'd just up and run off towards trouble at the first beat of the drum.'

Jeff craned his neck closer over the table, and his eyes bulged. 'Mate, I already know that's *exactly* who you are. So get the bloody hell out there and find that little girl and bring her home to her mother. Because you know you want to.'

And so it came to pass that, two hours later, Ben Hope was sitting behind the wheel of his silver twin-turbo Alpina B7 with his old green army haversack on the passenger seat next to him, Miles' *Bitches Brew* blasting on his speakers and a 180-kilometre-an-hour wind streaming in the windows as he tore southwards on the motorway towards Le Mans.

Persuasive, that Jeff Dekker. And incredibly perceptive, for all his rough edges. He could read Ben's mind as if his skull were made of glass. As usual, he was dead right. Because despite all his protests and refusals, Ben had known all along he wanted to do this. He was back in the saddle. Back doing what he did best. And the thought of a missing child was the only thing that could take the smile off his face.

Chapter 8

The home and reclusive sanctuary of Auguste Kaprisky was a seventeenth-century castle that had formerly belonged to the Rothschild dynasty. The security cordon its current owner had built around himself made entry into his private world something like accessing the Pentagon. If Ben hadn't called from the road and left a message with Kaprisky's PA to say he was coming, the armed guards on the gate probably wouldn't have let him in at all.

Once inside the perimeter, Ben drove for almost twenty minutes through the vastness of the chateau's landscaped grounds, past rolling green paddocks where magnificent Arab horses grazed and cantered; past hectares of carefully tended orchards and vines, and along the shores of a perfectly blue glass-smooth lake with boathouses and a jetty where a moored sail cruiser rocked gently in the late afternoon breeze.

Just as it seemed the grounds might go on forever, the fantastical chateau with its baroque architecture and columns and turrets rose up in front of him like a mirage. A classical fountain with a bronze statue of the goddess Diana the huntress dominated the circular courtyard, spouting jets of water that made rainbows in the air. Ben drove around it and crunched to a halt on the gravel, next to a row of cars.

Most men of Kaprisky's wealth would own a collection of the world's most expensive supercars, but Ben happened to know that his personal vehicle was the battered, ancient Renault 4 parked nearest the house. He was a strange fish, that Auguste Kaprisky, with his own peculiar sense of priorities. It was rumoured that he put artificial flowers on his wife's grave, so that he wouldn't have to replace them too frequently.

As Ben climbed out of the Alpina a pair of plain-clothes security guys appeared from nowhere and zeroed in on him. Neither was concerned about trying to hide the weapon strapped under his jacket, which their body language made clear they were ready to pull out at the first sign of trouble. They both had the fast eye and alert manner of ex-military men whose skillset had been bumped up to the next level. Ben knew how well trained they were, because he'd been the one who trained them: hence the failure of the attempt on their boss's life; hence Kaprisky's eternal debt of gratitude to all at Le Val, and to Ben in particular.

'Easy, boys,' Ben said to the pair. 'I'm expected.'

Recognising him, the guards smiled, nodded and backed down. One of them spoke into a radio. Seconds later the grand entrance of the chateau opened, and a butler in a black waistcoat and white gloves appeared in the doorway to welcome Ben as he climbed the balustraded stone steps. The butler was a small, gaunt man with oiled-back hair, who looked like Peter Cushing. He led Ben through a vast marble hallway that made their footsteps echo all the way to the frescoed dome of the ceiling. The Greek statues lining the walls were probably not plaster copies, Ben thought. The butler stopped at a door that King Kong could have walked through without ducking his head, knocked twice and then ushered Ben inside without a word.

Kaprisky was pacing by one of the tall windows at the far end of the magnificent salon, overlooking an endless sweep of formal gardens. The billionaire looked twenty years older than he had a few hours ago. Even from a distance the stress of the situation was visibly etched all over his face in deep worry lines. When he saw Ben he came rushing to welcome him with a pumping handshake and tears of gratitude.

'I was unsure what to make of your phone message. Dare I presume that you have changed your mind?'

'It was wrong of me to disappoint you, Auguste,' Ben said. 'I'm here now. Let's get your little girl back.'

'I'm so thankful. I have no words.'

'Any developments since we talked?'

Kaprisky shook his head gravely. 'We have heard nothing. The situation is unchanged, except that with every passing moment that brute could be getting further away with Valentina.'

The salon door burst open. Eloise. She was wearing a different dress from earlier, and had a matching handbag the size of a postage stamp hanging from one shoulder. Her face was mottled from crying, but lit up with sudden joy at the sight of Ben standing there with her uncle. She rushed into the room and hugged Ben so violently that she almost head-butted him in the face and he felt her ribs flexing against his chest. 'Dupont told me we had a visitor. I didn't want to believe it was really you. Thank you. Thank you.'

Ben said she was welcome and managed to detach himself from her death-grip without breaking any of her fingers.

'Now, let us make the arrangements,' Kaprisky said. 'Before we begin, we must talk about money.'

'You can keep your money, Auguste. That's not the reason I changed my mind.'

'Nonetheless, money is the oil that will make the machine

64

run smoothly and enable a happy outcome to this dreadful crisis. You will have every possible resource at your disposal. Anything whatsoever you may require, you only have to ask.' Kaprisky darted a hand inside his jacket, came out with a tatty old wallet and produced from it a shiny new credit card with the Kaprisky Corp logo emblazoned on its front.

'This is your expense account. It will work in any country or currency in the world. The limit is set at five million euros per week, but that can be extended with one phone call. Please make free use of it. You will of course be provided with an additional sum of cash in Russian rubles, for your convenience.'

Ben took the card. Five million a week. Unbelievable.

'One more matter. You indicated that your lack of familiarity with the Russian language was a concern; that will no longer be an issue. I am arranging for an assistant to accompany you at all times, to act as guide, interpreter, whatever you require. They will be entirely at your service.'

Ben wished now that he hadn't made a big deal of it. The last thing he really needed was a tag-along slowing him down. 'Who's that, your man Andriy Vasilchuk?'

Kaprisky shook his head. 'His skill is security, not detection. In any case my men will be standing down from the moment you depart for Moscow. Your guide will be the same local private investigator who assisted us previously, a partner in Moscow's most highly reputed detective agency. As you know, I must always have the best.'

Kaprisky allowed himself an uncharacteristic dry smile that showed his grey teeth, then glanced down at his watch. He seemed to delight in wearing the cheapest plastic Casio digital going. 'For the sake of expediency, we should delay as little as possible. When can you leave?'

'Are we forgetting the small matter of a travel visa?' Ben

said. 'As far as I'm aware, EU citizens still can't go just waltzing in and out of Russia without the right papers.'

Kaprisky gave a dismissive little wave of his hand, like brushing off a mosquito. 'Forget such piffling technicalities. It is already, as you British would say, sorted.'

'In that case,' Ben said, 'I'm ready to leave right this minute. I'm assuming the jet's standing by to take off at a moment's notice.' Kaprisky kept the aircraft at Le Mans-Arnage airport, just a few minutes' drive from the estate.

'Naturally. You will be familiar with your flight crew, I think, from your journey to Africa.'

There weren't many things Ben wanted to remember from that particular escapade, but he'd never forgotten the stalwart service of Kaprisky's chief pilot Adrien Leroy and his Number Two, Noël Marchand.

'Flight time to Moscow will be three hours and eleven minutes,' Kaprisky said. 'It will be evening by the time you arrive, and so my chef will be at your disposal to provide whatever you wish to eat. You will land at Vnukovo International Airport, twenty-eight kilometres southwest of the city. Your assistant will be there to meet you on landing, with a car to take you to your hotel. I hope you will be satisfied with the accommodation.'

'Just the basics, Auguste,' Ben said.

'Oh, it is nothing remotely fancy, I assure you. But then, a man of your experience is used to the rougher side of life.'

'Just a couple of things before I go,' Ben said. 'First, I'd like a photo of Valentina.'

Eloise unsnapped the tiny handbag, dug inside and pulled out a glossy print. 'This one is very recent.' It showed a pretty dark-haired child with lots of light and joy in her sparkling hazel eyes, pictured by the lake. Eloise said, 'There are more pictures in her room. Would you like to see it?'

Ben said yes, anything was useful. With her uncle in tow, Eloise led Ben quickly from the salon, through the gleaming labyrinth of marble and priceless rugs and furniture, and up a grand staircase to a bedroom on the first floor. Valentina's room was the size of a luxury penthouse apartment, with its own bathroom and dressing room and a walk-in wardrobe fit for Marie Antoinette. Everything was pink, from the silk on the walls to the canopy of the Cadillac-sized four-poster bed to the teddy bears clustered on the pillows, and the pillows themselves. There were books everywhere, a precarious stack of them piled on a pink bedside cabinet: Dostoyevsky's novel *The Brothers Karamazov*, a collection of short stories by the same author, *Eugene Onegin* by Alexander Pushkin and a volume of poetry by Mikhail Lermontov. Ben wondered how many twelve-year-old girls were so heavily into Russian literary classics.

Eloise saw him looking at the books and explained, 'She adores reading. And her goal is to become completely fluent in Russian before her father's fortieth birthday next April, so she can surprise him.' Eloise let out a deep, shuddering sigh and screwed her eyes shut, shaking her head in anguish. 'What has he done? What has he done?'

'She's a clever kid,' Ben said, to keep it light.

'A little genius,' Kaprisky weighed in, voice heavy with emotion. 'She already speaks Dutch, German and English and has come on greatly with her French since moving here. Naturally, she is also proficient in mathematics, and developing a strong interest in science. She could be anything she wanted. She is such a talented actress, too. She does the most incredible impressions of people.'

'But most of all she loves animals,' Eloise said. 'She wants to be a vet when she grows up.'

Which made sense, judging by the pictures on the walls.

Every inch of available space was crammed with framed photographs of a variety of dogs and cats and horses. Kaprisky held back tears as he told Ben what a keen little photographer his grandniece was, among her many talents, constantly snapping shots of animals everywhere she went. Other framed pictures that hadn't been taken by Valentina featured her hugging various puppies, kittens and ponies, each time with the same dazzling smile on her face.

Eloise couldn't look at the pictures of her daughter without bursting into tears once again. Wiping her eyes she went to a little pink chair and picked up a little pink gilet jacket that was neatly hung over its back. She caressed the material with a sob. 'She has another one exactly the same as this, which she was wearing when she left. Tailor-made especially for her. Pink is her favourite colour, as you might have noticed.'

'That's all good to know,' Ben said. 'What about her father?'

Eloise looked confused. 'No, he hates pink.'

Kaprisky's mouth gave a twitch. 'Please forgive my niece,' he said in French so that Eloise wouldn't understand. 'With such parents I can't begin to imagine where her daughter gets her intelligence from.'

Ben smiled patiently and said to Eloise, 'I mean do you have a photo of him?'

Eloise went from confused to blank, then her cheeks flushed. 'No, but I think Valentina keeps one in her bedside drawer.'

She hurried over to look. While she was rooting through all the usual paraphernalia that twelve-year-old girls keep in their bedside drawers, even academically brilliant multilingual genius ones, Ben added, 'It'd also be useful to know all you can tell me about your ex-husband.'

Eloise looked up with a frown. 'Like what?'

'Like who his friends are, where he hangs out, habits, hobbies and interests. I realise details of current girlfriends might be difficult, but the more information I have, the more it could help provide a clue to his present whereabouts.'

She chewed her lower lip and shook her head. 'I'm sorry, I can't help you. Even before Yuri moved back to Russia, I couldn't have given you the name of a single friend, or anyone he kept company with. He has no interests, no hobbies I know of, no activities outside of his work. Only his religion. He's Catholic, and attends church quite often.'

'That's handy information,' Ben said. As long as he could stake out every Catholic church in Russia on the off-chance of Yuri wandering inside to worship. There couldn't be more than a few thousand of them. He asked her, 'Would you happen to have his mobile number? That could be useful to me, as well.'

'I haven't spoken to Yuri by phone in a long time,' Eloise said, still rooting around in the bedside drawers. 'Not that I would want to, because it would only end in arguments. All I have is an email address. From what Valentina says, he's changed phones a dozen times since I last had a number for him. Ah, here it is.' She pulled out the photo she'd been looking for. It was obvious she didn't want to look at it, and quickly passed it to Ben with barely a glance.

The picture was an old family snap of when Eloise and Yuri were still together. Valentina was much younger and smaller, with gaps where her baby teeth had fallen out. Eloise had a different hairstyle, and looked rosy and happy. Yuri Petrov stood with his arm around his wife's shoulders, smiling broadly. He had lots of shaggy jet black hair, a broad, craggy but not ugly face, a solid jaw and pronounced cheekbones. His eyes were dark and not as stupid-looking as Ben might have expected, given Kaprisky's account of him.

'He has a bit more weight around the middle now,' Eloise said. 'And Valentina says his hair is longer, and he grew a beard.'

'What a deadbeat,' Kaprisky muttered in the background.

'Can I keep this?' Ben asked.

She shuddered. 'Please, take it out of my sight. I don't want to see his face ever again.'

Chapter 9

The Kaprisky staffer who drove Ben to the Aéroport Le Mans-Arnage appeared to be an ex-racing driver of some kind, with special dispensation from the French police to deliver his passenger to their destination as fast as possible, irrespective of public safety. By the time the black Mercedes S-Class had screeched to a halt at the private terminal, the Gulfstream G650 had already taxied out of the huge Kaprisky Corp hangar and was on the runway approach, fuelled and prepped for takeoff, its lights twinkling in the falling dusk.

Ben was greeted on the tarmac by a sombre Adrien Leroy and Noël Marchand. 'Every time we meet,' Leroy said as he shook Ben's hand, 'it's in unfortunate circumstances. I can't believe this is happening. Poor kid. Everyone adores her.'

'How well do you know Petrov?' Ben asked. With so few clues to go on, he needed to fish for all the scraps he could get.

Leroy shook his head, barely able to contain his anger. 'I've seldom even laid eyes on the bastard. He's never there to collect her. But I'll tell you, if I do ever see him again I'll smash his teeth down his throat.'

So much for fishing. Leroy went off to attend to his pilot duties as Ben boarded the jet.

The plane's luxurious interior offered a choice of nineteen empty plush leather passenger armchairs, all with marble-topped tables and a thousand gadgets to play with. Waiting for him on one of the seats was a designer travel bag containing his visa documentation and half a million rubles in large denominations, which equated to about six thousand euros for walking-around money. Kaprisky had thought of everything. Ben transferred the cash into his old green haversack and settled in a window seat.

Soon the jet was in the air. A ridiculously pretty Korean flight attendant with a smart uniform and glossy black hair appeared from the galley, sauntered brightly down the aisle towards her sole passenger and asked him in a California accent if he wanted dinner. 'We have a full à la carte menu. The butter poached lobster, caught fresh this morning, is one of Mr Kaprisky's favourites.'

'You can prepare me anything I want?' Ben said.

She beamed at him. 'Absolutely whatever you desire. Your wish is my command.'

'Great. I'll have a ham sandwich. Thin bread, white or brown, I don't care, light on the butter, just a smear of mustard. That's it.'

Her smile wavered. 'Can I offer you a glass of champagne with that? The Krug Private Cuvée is the finest in the world.'

'No, but you can bring me a triple measure of single malt scotch, no ice, no water. And an ashtray, please.'

Now she was looking at him as if he'd just run over her cat. 'I'm sorry, smoking is strictly disallowed on board.'

'Whatever I desire, eh?' Ben muttered to himself when she'd stalked off to convey his order to the chef. The whisky and the sandwich duly arrived. The chef hadn't been able to resist putting on a fancy herb garnish, as though it were beneath him to serve up anything so plain and unadorned. Ben ate quickly, savoured the drink slowly, then set his Omega diver's watch for the hour's time difference between France and Russia, closed his eyes and let the plane carry him through the night.

Two hours later, Ben opened his eyes and saw the huge sprawling lit-up expanse of Moscow far below as the Gulfstream overflew the city on its approach to Vnukovo International Airport. Ben gazed down at the glittering lights and wondered where among all that he was going to find little Valentina Petrova and her father.

Kaprisky's ETA proved startlingly accurate. The jet hit the runway at Vnukovo precisely three hours and eleven minutes after takeoff. Five minutes after that, they'd taxied to the business aviation terminal and the Korean stewardess returned, all smiles again, to say Ben was clear to disembark.

Moments later he was stepping down the gangway into the balmy summer night to set foot, for the first time in his life, on Russian soil. If Ben had stuck coloured pushpins in a world map showing all the places he'd travelled in his time, some countries would have been bristling with them and only a very few untouched. Should this prove to be his one and only visit to the Russian Federation, he could only pray that he would return home successful, and not empty-handed.

Ben walked from the plane with that dark thought in mind and his bag over his shoulder. Kaprisky had said his new assistant would be there to meet him – but nobody seemed to be around. Bright floodlamps lit up the tarmac and probed into the deep shadows between the private aircraft hangars. The screech of a jumbo jet coming in to land pierced his ears; then as the noise died away he heard the rev of an approaching car and turned. Strong headlights dazzled him momentarily, making him narrow his eyes and put up a hand to block out the glare.

The oncoming car veered in front of him and stopped directly in his path with a soft hiss of tyres. It was another black Mercedes S-Class identical to the one that had transported him to Le Mans-Arnage earlier that day. The windows were tinted, so he couldn't see anyone inside. The rear passenger door swung open and a black high-heeled shoe stepped out, followed by a long, slim but well-muscled leg and then the rest of a woman in a charcoal business suit. Ben didn't know her, but she seemed to know him.

'Major Hope?' Her English was marked with the unmistakable intonations of the Russian accent.

'I'm Ben Hope,' he said. The woman stepped towards him from the Mercedes. In her heels she was as tall as he was, an inch under six feet. She had the build of a model, but wide shoulders like a competitive swimmer. The eyes fixed on Ben could have been airbrushed aquamarine blue. Her blond hair was cut very short, which accentuated the angular contours of a face that would have been pleasantly attractive, except for the severe expression of hard purposefulness as she approached and stuck out a hand as rigid as a blade.

'I am Tatyana Nikolaeva,' the woman said. 'I am employed to assist you in whatever way may be required during your visit to Russia.'

Ben took her hand. Her grip was as strong as it looked. 'So I've been informed,' he replied. 'But I prefer to work alone whenever possible. If you'd like to show me to my accommodation and pass on any particulars I might need, after that you can feel free to stand down and let me take it from there, okay? I'll square things up with Mr Kaprisky, so there's no misunderstanding.'

'Regrettably, that is outside of my remit to decide,' she answered with a frosty smile. 'My orders are clear. I take my obligations very seriously.'

Ben returned the smile. 'Well, then, it appears neither of us has much of a choice, do we?'

The driver's door opened and the chauffeur unfolded himself from the car. The Mercedes wasn't a small vehicle, but at very little under seven feet in height, the guy would have been cramped in anything less than a Humvee. If Kaprisky's driver back in France had been a racing driver in a past life, this guy had been an ultra-heavyweight boxer. The broken nose, shaven head and cauliflower ear, he had it all. The hulk exchanged some quick-fire words of Russian with Tatyana that made Ben wonder whether having an interpreter might not be such a bad thing, after all, then stepped around the car and held out a girder-like arm to take Ben's bag and load it into the boot.

'You have no other baggage?' Tatyana asked, eyeing the tatty old haversack with an air of obvious distaste. 'You are a man who likes to travel light, I see.'

'Thought I'd leave the golf clubs at home this time,' he replied.

Tatyana Nikolaeva frowned. 'I do not think there would be time to play. There is work to do.'

Some people were too armoured for humour, obviously. Ben decided that would be his last attempt to break the ice with his new assistant.

She motioned towards the open rear door of the Mercedes. 'Please.' Ben got in. Tatyana climbed into the front passenger side. The chauffeur hefted his monstrous bulk back behind the wheel without another word, and they sped off.

Twenty-eight kilometres later, Ben was getting his first taste of Moscow. For the moment he had no idea what awaited him there.

Chapter 10

Deep into the night, the heart of the city was alive and in full swing. The driver carved fast and efficiently through the busy traffic while Tatyana gazed absently out of her window and ignored Ben's presence behind her. Now and then the two of them spoke in Russian and Ben listened, trying to pick out some of the words from the limited vocabulary he'd sifted from his memory of the language. Twenty minutes after entering the city, Tatyana said, 'We are here,' and the Mercedes pulled up outside their hotel.

Ben climbed out of the car and looked up at the towering facade of the building, light spilling from hundreds of windows across what he understood to be Neglinnaya Street in the heart of Moscow. So much for the basics, he thought. If the Ararat Park Hyatt was Auguste Kaprisky's idea of the rougher side of life, then he wouldn't plan on taking the old guy on a camping expedition any time soon.

'You are booked into the Winter Garden Suite,' Tatyana said to Ben. The chauffeur removed Ben's bag from the boot of the car and handed it to a hotel valet, who didn't seem all that perplexed by it. Maybe frayed, battered and faintly fusty-smelling army surplus could become the new chic, set to spark off a fashion craze among the super-rich. Ben and Tatyana followed the valet into the cathedral-sized atrium, which was bustling with activity. Ultra-modern steel and glass wasn't Ben's style, but then he wasn't the one forking out thousands of rubles a night for the room.

Ben was checked in without having to do anything, and Tatyana said, 'I will meet you here downstairs, in the Neglinka Lounge, in thirty minutes.'

The Winter Garden Suite offered panoramic views of the Bolshoi Theatre and Red Square, the Kremlin towers grandly silhouetted against the night sky and the colourfully striped domes of St Basil's Cathedral lit up like a gigantic, gaudily elaborate dessert. Ben had what he considered a silly amount of furniture for one person, an art collection that could have graced a small gallery, a bathroom with a marble bathtub you could swim lengths of, a separate guest bathroom in case he got tired of the main one, and a bedroom that compared size-wise with little Valentina Petrova's at Kaprisky's chateau, except it wasn't pink. As for the remote-controlled window blinds, forget it. Could people not close their own blinds any more?

The suite did, however, come with an Illy coffee machine, and that Ben could appreciate. Paying as little attention to the sumptuous decor as he would have to a drab-olive military barracks dorm, he showered, changed into fresh black jeans and a clean denim shirt from his bag, killed a Gauloise on his own private terrace while gazing down at the speeding traffic on Neglinnaya Street, then went downstairs to meet his assistant, who so far seemed to be calling all the shots.

Tatyana Nikolaeva was waiting for him in the bar, sipping some kind of vodka cocktail in a tall glass with an umbrella sticking out of it. The bartender spoke English, and Ben ordered a straight double scotch from the amazing selection of single malts. The battered old steel whisky flask he'd carried on many travels was getting low on its customary

Laphroaig, which had been Ben's favourite scotch for a good many years. He had the barman top it up with Macallan Rare Cask Black, a single malt that retailed for over £600 a litre back in the UK. Ringing the changes, and Kaprisky was paying.

Ben and Tatyana perched on a pair of bar stools. They were the last two guests in the place and the staff were starting to clean up in preparation for closing for the night, though an establishment like the Ararat Park Hyatt was far too classy to boot out the stragglers.

'I was told you are no ordinary kind of army major in your country,' Tatyana said, nonchalantly twirling her glass on the table and stirring it with the cocktail stick. Ben noticed for the first time that her fingernails were painted the exact same blue as her eyes, and immaculately polished. 'That you belong to a special regiment, something like our GRU Spetsnaz forces.' As she finished saying it, her eyes flashed up at him in a look he couldn't quite read.

Old man Kaprisky must have been blabbing about him, Ben thought. He replied, 'I thought we were going to discuss our plans for tomorrow, not indulge in idle chit-chat about me.'

'It is important for me to know something about the colleague I am to be working with. Are you saying it is not true?'

This wasn't Ben's favourite topic for discussion, but he could see she wasn't going to let it go. 'Technically, no, seeing as I've been retired for a long time. Prior to that, yes, it's true, I did serve in UK Special Forces, 22 SAS if you really want to know, and that I did reach the rank of major by the time I quit. But I no longer go by that title. Do those details satisfy your curiosity?'

'So I should not call you Major?'

'If you have to call me anything, call me Ben. That's my name.'

'I prefer a more formal address.' She scrutinised his face for a moment, then added, 'You are much too young to be retired.'

'I didn't say I stopped working.'

'Looking for missing people, is that the work you do now?'

'I've done a lot of K and R missions over the years. That's short for kidnap and ransom. But I'm sure you could deduce that, detective.'

She smiled. 'It seems an unusual career change for a retired soldier to become a person finder.'

'There are a lot of people in the world who go missing because someone stole them, usually for money, sometimes for other reasons. I wanted to do something about that, because I know how much pain and suffering it causes to the victims and their families.'

She watched him for a moment, looking deep into his eyes as if she could see unspoken secrets there. 'You have suffered from it too.'

'When I was in my teens, my younger sister was kidnapped by human traffickers in Morocco. The police never found her.'

'You never saw her again?'

'It's a long story.'

'But it explains why you do this,' Tatyana said. She paused, sipping delicately from her drink without taking those vivid eyes off him. 'Is there a Mrs Hope?' she asked, switching tracks.

The question brought more memories to Ben's mind. There had been a Mrs Hope, once upon a time, all too briefly. The vision of Leigh's face flashed through his thoughts for a moment. And Roberta's, and Brooke's, accompanied by the same mixture of emotions those reminiscences always rekindled. The best times, the worst times. He didn't share his deeper feelings, as a rule, and he wasn't particularly inclined to discuss the current state of his personal life.

'Is there a Mr Nikolaev?' he countered.

'I asked you first.'

'Not currently.'

'What about a girlfriend?' she asked him, leaning forward to plant both elbows on the table and curling one side of her lips in a teasing smile. 'Come now, I am sure you have many of those.'

Ben wasn't going to be drawn into mentioning Sandrine Lacombe. Not that she could have been considered a girl-friend, exactly. They'd met by chance a few months ago, back home in France. A few dates since then, hints of mutual attraction, no commitments made, nothing serious. He had the impression she'd been hurt before, as he had. It might grow into something; it might not. Either way it was no business of Tatyana Nikolaeva's, and he made no reply.

She frowned as a thought struck her. 'You are not *goluboi* – what is the English expression – a sodomite?'

'We in the West tend to use slightly more progressive terms nowadays.'

'But you are not one of them?'

'No,' he replied. 'I'm not one of them.'

She took a sip of her drink and looked relieved.

'Shall we get down to business?' he said.

'Of course.'

'Tell me what we know about Yuri Petrov.'

Tatyana replied that, in fact, they knew remarkably little. He didn't appear on the voter register and finding an address for him had been quite a challenge for her investigation firm. The easy part had been checking for a criminal record, which had come up blank – he had never been charged with anything in Russia, at any rate.

'Employment?'

She shook her head. 'Whatever he does for a living, he is getting paid only in cash. His bank account is almost empty and shows no activity within the last twelve months.'

Which, as far as it went, seemed to fit with Kaprisky's portrait of the man as a low-life ne'er-do-well, possibly involved in all sorts of petty criminal dealings for which he hadn't yet been caught. Ben couldn't be sure until he knew more. 'First thing I need to do is check out his apartment.'

'He is not there,' Tatyana said. 'I assumed you had been informed of this.'

'Tell me what you found.'

Tatyana seemed mildly irritated by having to repeat the same information she'd already told Kaprisky. 'It is all in my report. I accompanied the team to the address, where we found the door locked and the apartment empty.'

'Did you look inside?'

'Breaking and entering was not our purpose.'

'If it's an apartment block, there must be a caretaker or a concierge. You could have got the key from them.'

'Only the police have authority to demand access to a private property.'

'Okay,' Ben said. 'So if you didn't get to look inside, how could you be so sure the apartment was empty?'

'Petrov had been seen leaving, and not returned. I spoke to neighbours, who reported having not seen him for several days.'

'All the same,' Ben said, 'I'd like to see the place for myself, first thing in the morning. I'll need you to meet me here at eight o'clock on the dot.'

Tatyana seemed not to object. 'Any other instructions for me?' she asked.

He shook his head. 'None, other than try to keep up. I'm using to working alone, which means I go at my own pace and push hard. I don't believe this man intends to harm the little girl, but I don't intend to let him hold her hostage any longer than absolutely necessary. Fall behind, I won't wait for you, okay?'

'I am a professional,' Tatyana replied coolly. 'You do not have to worry about me.'

'Glad to hear it. The last thing to discuss is transport. Do you have a car, or are we using Kaprisky's? Because if so, I'd like to ditch that big lunk of a driver.'

'Car is a terrible way to travel in this city,' Tatyana said breezily. 'From early in the morning until late in the afternoon, Moscow is solid with traffic. It is worse than Los Angeles. But the public transport system is best in the world. That is what we will use instead.'

Ben wasn't sure about that idea. For the first time since he'd met her, Tatyana Nikolaeva smiled with enough warmth to melt away the icy severity of her face.

'I am a *МОСКВИЧКА*. A Muscovite. Trust me, Major Hope.'

Chapter 11

Ben rose early, out of old habit. As sunrise broke over Red Square and bathed his balcony in a flood of golds and magentas, he ticked off a hundred press-ups in sets of twenty-five, followed by the same routine for sit-ups. It wasn't much of a morning's exercise session for him; maybe he could go for a ten-mile run later, or abseil up and down the towers of the Kremlin just for the hell of it. He brewed up a pot of espresso on his coffee machine, the one luxury of his suite that meant anything to him, then walked through onto the balcony to consume it, along with the first Gauloise of the day, and watch the city rumble into life below.

After a pummelling in the cavernous marble shower room, he was back downstairs at three minutes to eight to meet Tatyana. She was three inches shorter in the flat shoes she was wearing in anticipation of walking about the city, and had exchanged yesterday's charcoal business suit for a double-breasted navy affair with heavy epaulettes a little reminiscent of Russian military dress uniform.

'Good morning, Comrade Major Hope,' she said briskly.

'And a very good morning to you, Miss Nikolaeva.'

Ben followed her out of the bustling hotel lobby into the buzz of Neglinnaya Street. Eight months of the year the place was icebound, but the summer sun felt warm. Then why wasn't everyone smiling?

'So what's the travel plan?' he asked. 'Are we getting a bus? Tram?'

'Neither,' Tatyana said. 'The Moscow metro system is the most efficient in the world. I have been to New York, Paris and London,' she added with a shake of the head, clearly not impressed with what the western world had to offer. 'Here, you often have to wait less than one minute for the next subway train. And our stations are far superior, naturally. We even have free wi-fi everywhere in the system. As for the architecture, prepare yourself to be amazed.'

'I'm so glad to have you as my guide,' Ben muttered, but she either missed the sarcasm or didn't give a damn either way.

Tatyana had certainly been right about the road traffic, which was so heavily congested that it could have taken them hours to get anywhere by car. As they walked through the fume-filled streets, Ben tried not to breathe in too deeply and gazed around him at the unfamiliar city in daylight for the first time. If he'd been expecting Moscow to be filled with the brutal relics of the old USSR, he'd have been disappointed. Streets down which Stalin's tank battalions had once rumbled in an intimidating show of might to the West were now transformed into a modern, vibrant space that had Starbucks and Le Pain Quotidien outlets on every corner and looked and felt much like anywhere else in the world, except that there wasn't a single non-white face in evidence anywhere.

He asked, 'Why are there so many flower shops?' He'd never seen such a proliferation of them before.

Tatyana replied, 'Because Russian men are the most romantic in the world, and they love to make their women happy.'

85

Ben wondered if Kaprisky's niece felt that way. Maybe Yuri Petrov was the single exception in all of Russia and she'd just been unlucky in her choice.

Five minutes' walk from the hotel, they came to Lubyanka metro. The subway station was in sight of a much more infamous building bearing the same name, with which Ben was familiar from his historical reading. The first real relic of the old regime he'd glimpsed so far, the Lubyanka prison had once doubled up as the headquarters of the feared Soviet secret police, the Cheka, later restyled as the no less notorious KGB. Lubyanka had been intimately connected with the worst atrocities of Stalin's Great Purge of the 1930s, and those that had followed all through the darker history of the USSR, involving many more horrific tortures and brutal executions than would ever be officially admitted.

As for the metro station that shared its name, Ben knew of it only as the scene of the 2010 bombing that had left a swathe of dead in its wake and been blamed on Islamic terrorists – although some independent news sources had claimed the attack to have been a false flag operation carried out by the Russian security forces to justify political ends. Ben had seen enough of covert dirty dealings to know such tactics were a reality, and not just here in Russia. The official versions of tragic events were often far from the truth, a truth known only to a tiny few.

They passed under the arches of the station's entrance and were quickly swallowed up in the throng of fast-moving commuters. Tatyana had a pair of prepaid contactless Troika cards that were the fastest way to negotiate the metro, and gave one to Ben. On their way down to the trains, without warning he paused to crouch down in the middle of the tunnel and retie his left bootlace. The river of foot traffic parted around him, jostling by with more than a few looks as Tatyana waited impatiently for him to finish. 'So you see, it is not me who slows us down,' she said acidly.

The slight delay caused them to miss the train, which departed as they were stepping out onto the platform. The short wait gave Ben time to decide that the station's Soviet-era architecture looked pretty much as plain and severe as he'd have imagined. 'Doesn't look any great shakes to me so far,' he observed.

'Just wait,' she said, smirking at the sceptical look on his face.

True to her promise, the next train came whooshing into the station within less than a minute. Crowds bundled out; more crowds piled on board. Ben and Tatyana's carriage was crowded, with standing room only. As they began to snake their way beneath the city, Ben was in for a revelation. Station after station offered a staggering display of vaulted ceilings and grand chandeliers, amazing murals and friezes, stained glass and gilt, marble arches and columns and great bronze statues of Socialist icons, each one designed around its own individual architectural theme and every inch as pristine and magnificent as London's underground was dingy and depressing.

'Stalin intended the metro to be a triumph of Communist ideology,' Tatyana said, keeping her voice low enough that only Ben could hear over the clatter and rumble of the moving train. Ben supposed that maybe mentioning Stalin's name too loudly in liberal Moscow was akin to referring to the unmentionable Adolf Hitler in public anywhere in modern-day Germany, a serious social misstep. Though he'd read that many Russians were still misty-eyed about their ruthless mass-murdering former dictator, which worried a few folks. 'While Khrushchev and later leaders condemned the luxuries of the old era,' Tatyana continued, 'resulting in many of the stations of the 1960s and 1970s being much plainer in style.'

'I see. Interesting.' Ben nodded and listened as she prattled on, while glancing around him at the sights. The truth, which he was keeping to himself for the moment, was that he was observing more than just the breathtaking architecture.

Almost from the moment they'd left the hotel, he'd become aware they were being followed. Ben had enough years in the field under his belt to have developed an extremely acute spider sense, which was the name soldiers gave to that feeling of being watched. Sure enough, he and Tatyana hadn't walked a hundred steps from the doorway of the Ararat Park Hyatt before he'd used the reflection in a shop window to spot the two goons shadowing them.

The pair were dressed casually, not tall, not short, well blended into the crowds and as instantly forgettable as all good shadows should be. They were doing a creditable job of hanging back and looking unsuspicious, and would have been perfectly invisible to most ordinary Joes; not, however, to a former SAS man trained in the delicate art of counter-surveillance.

Without having to turn around, Ben had been able to keep the two in almost constant view. When the goons had followed them into Lubyanka metro station, Ben knew exactly where they were. When he had deliberately paused to fiddle with his bootlace as a way of testing their response, they'd stopped moving and huddled to one side of the tunnel, pretending to be gawking at something terribly fascinating on a mobile phone. And when Ben and his companion had got on the subway train, the pair had slipped surreptitiously on board after them. Now they were loitering at the opposite end of the carriage, innocently chatting to one another and throwing the occasional discreet glance at their targets, obviously unaware that they, the watchers, had themselves been spotted.

Tatyana looked surprised as Ben bent close to her ear, interrupting her history lecture. Her cropped blond hair smelled of fresh apples. In a whisper just loud enough to be heard he said, 'Tell me, what's Russian for "Don't look now, but someone's following us"?'

She didn't look, but two small vertical lines appeared above her nose and her blue eyes narrowed. 'Who are they?' she whispered back. 'Why would this be happening?'

'Perhaps I should go and ask them,' Ben said. 'What do you think?'

'I am sure you are just imagining it,' Tatyana said. 'You are . . . what is the word?'

'Paranoid,' he said. 'Maybe. All the same, don't turn around and look for them. They don't know I'm onto them, not yet.'

'What are you going to do?'

'Make a phone call, for starters.'

'And then?'

'Maybe we ought to confront them, shoot them, dump their bodies on the track and then make a run for it before the cops arrive,' he said. 'Have you got a gun on you?'

Tatyana frowned. 'You are not serious.'

Ben had Auguste Kaprisky on his list of speed-dial contacts. Two taps, a couple of bleeps and a few moments' wait, and the old man's crackly voice came on the line. Hurtling through a tunnel deep beneath Moscow, and the signal from 1500 miles away was crystal clear. The benefits of superior Russian technology.

Ben spoke softly, in French. 'Auguste, I thought you said your guys were off the job.'

'They are,' Kaprisky replied, sounding taken aback.

'Positive about that? I seem to have picked up some company here.'

'I can assure you, it has nothing to do with me. Are you quite certain you are not——?'

'Imagining things? Thanks, Auguste. Talk later.' Ben ended the call. It was hard to know whether to believe Kaprisky. The wily old fox could be hedging his bets by keeping an eye on him. Maybe you didn't get to become a billionaire by being too trusting.

Tatyana was looking at him, an eyebrow raised. 'Well?'

Ben thought about all the places in a subway system he could lure the two goons. Men's toilets were always a good place for an impromptu roughing-up and forced interrogation of the 'Who are you working for?' variety. If indeed Kaprisky had sent them, the old man might not be happy to have Ben knock his hirelings around. If however they were someone else's guys, the use of forceful tactics could be stirring up a hornet's nest that Ben preferred to leave alone, for now. He decided he could worry later about who they were. For the moment, his priority was to give them the slip so he could get on with the job he'd come here to do.

'Next stop is ours,' he said to Tatyana.

'But we are not halfway there yet.'

'I fancy a little fresh air, don't you?'

The next station they arrived at was even more ridiculously opulent than the last. As Ben stepped off the train, followed by a confused Tatyana, he saw the two goons filter among the throng of disembarking passengers and drift along in their wake. Ben moved faster, forcing Tatyana to trot to keep up. The goons kept following, keeping their distance like before but moving with greater urgency. If they were working as part of a bigger surveillance team, it was time to put their organisation to the test.

Back up at street level, Ben saw they were still deep in the heart of the city. Traffic was heavy and pedestrians crowded the pavements. At a nearby taxi stand a line of yellow Ladas was waiting. Ben hustled over to the car at the head of the queue and got in the back seat. Tatyana piled in after him.

'Speak English?' Ben asked the driver.

'Sure.'

'Just drive. And step on it.' Ben thrust a sheaf of rubles through the gap between the seats, where they disappeared instantly into the driver's clutches.

'Twenty years I waited for someone to say that,' the driver said, gunning his engine with a grin. As the little Lada took off into the traffic, Ben turned to glance out of the window and caught a momentary glimpse of the two goons running out of the subway station and looking around in a panic for their disappearing targets. Then they were lost among the crowds.

Chapter 12

'This is a foolish waste of time,' Tatyana protested.

'Still think I'm imagining things?' Ben asked her. He glanced left, right and to the rear, looking for telltale signs such as motorcyclists in black visors slipping through the heavy traffic after them.

Tatyana said, 'Even if Kaprisky is having us monitored, what does it matter? He already knows where we are going, to Petrov's apartment.'

He looked at her. 'And if it's someone else?'

She shook her head. 'Like who?'

'I don't know,' Ben said. 'Whoever they are, I don't much like people breathing down my neck.'

'Welcome to Russia,' Tatyana said. 'Here, there is always someone watching everything you do.'

'Britain is no different. That's why I don't live there.'

The driver's high-speed sprint through the traffic had started well, but within a minute he was being forced to brake for an ugly snarl-up ahead. A truck had broken down in the middle of two lanes, provoking an orchestra of blaring car horns. 'Sorry, boss. Here we go again. Roads are very bad today.'

'The roads are always bad.' Tatyana turned a triumphant glower on Ben. 'I told you this was a terrible way to travel.'

'I'm all for diversity,' Ben replied. 'Let's try something else instead.'

They got out of the taxi and threaded a path on foot through the stationary queues of honking traffic. There was a tram lane with a red-and-yellow car going in the opposite direction. Ben quickened his step to chase it, and hopped on board. Tatyana had no choice but to follow. 'Now we are going the wrong way,' she complained. 'Petrov's apartment is to the east of here.'

The detour would give Ben a better chance of telling if they were still being followed. As the tram whirred along the tracks he additionally kept an eye open for places of worship, in case he might spot a Catholic church among all the onion-domed Russian Orthodox ones and the occasional mosque they passed. Maybe he'd catch Petrov in the act of attending morning mass. Probably unlikely, but right now Ben was feeling he needed all the improbable good fortune he could get.

After a few more kilometres, they jumped off the tram and hustled back to the nearest underground station to resume their journey to the eastern suburb where Petrov lived. This time, Ben and Tatyana reached the underground platform just as the train was departing, and had to sprint to catch it. Ben didn't want to hang around even for a minute to give anyone a chance to catch up with them again. 'I told you you'd have to keep up with me,' he said to Tatyana as she jumped aboard after him, flushed and a little breathless from the dash.

'You are crazy.'

'We haven't even got into any gunfights and car chases yet,' he said. 'This is easy, so far.'

Emerging back into the daylight several stops later, they collared another yellow taxicab to drive them the rest of the way. By the time they had arrived at Yuri Petrov's apartment building Ben was quite certain they'd given their followers the slip. Now was the test: if anyone was lurking in wait to observe them at Petrov's place, Ben could be sure Kaprisky had lied about his men standing down.

Even in the sunshine, Petrov's apartment block was grey and downbeat and depressing. The rundown suburb was a far cry from the vibrant heart of modern Moscow, with broken windows here and there, garbage piled in the walk-ways and sworls of graffiti adorning any bare patch of stonework. If not for all the signs in Cyrillic alphabet, it could have been just about any English inner city. No great surprise that Eloise Kaprisky wasn't too enamoured of sending her daughter here for visits.

Ben's spider sense had gone quiet. A few glances around him and at the windows of the surrounding buildings, checking for twitching curtains or the glint of binoculars, and he was pretty confident that nobody, whether Kaprisky's team or anyone else, was watching them as they approached the building. Had he been imagining the whole thing, after all? Possibly, but he wasn't in the habit of imagining things. Time would tell.

Tatyana led the way up a flight of dirty concrete steps and along a walkway with a rusty iron railing. They passed a number of identical doors, all painted the same drab green and made of the same flimsy plywood with rusty fittings. Tatyana pointed ahead and said, 'It's that one.'

'Let's see what's what,' Ben said, pushing past her towards Petrov's door.

'I do not see what the point of this exercise is. I already told you the place was empty.'

'And only the police have authority to take a look inside. I get that. But here's the thing. I don't recognise their sole authority.'

'Surely you would not break in, Major Hope?' Tatyana said, aghast.

'Needs must when the Devil drives, Miss Nikolaeva,' Ben replied. 'It wouldn't be my first time.' He'd never met a locked door that had stopped him, and going by his wide experience this one wouldn't take a lot of kicking in. He glanced left, glanced right, walked purposefully up to the doorway.

And then stopped.

Someone else had got there before them.

The door was open just a crack, maybe half an inch, so that from any distance it looked shut.

'He must have come back,' Tatyana whispered.

'Then he must have forgotten his key.' Ben pointed to where the flimsy lock had been forced. The doorframe was cheaply made and the only real damage was a slight buckling of the aluminium casing and a few deep scores where someone had let themselves in with a pry bar. Ben nudged the door the rest of the way open with his foot, then stepped aside quickly in case of an edgy occupant lurking within, clutching a sawn-off shotgun to greet unexpected visitors.

Nothing happened. Ben listened hard at the open doorway, and all he could hear was the sound of emptiness. If anyone was hiding in there, they were being extremely quiet. He waited ten seconds, then stepped into the apartment. With an anxious look around to make sure they weren't observed by any nosy neighbours, Tatyana followed.

The entrance led directly into Yuri Petrov's living room, which was as poky, basic and modestly furnished as might have been expected from the exterior. It had also been thoroughly and completely trashed. Furniture had been knocked over, drawers emptied all over the floor, TV gone, stereo gone, a bare patch in the dust on a cluttered work table from which an item roughly the size and shape of a laptop computer had been removed. All the classic signs of a burglary, or a fairly convincing attempt to make it look like one.

'When you left here, did Kaprisky's men all come with you?' Ben queried Tatyana.

'One or two of them stayed,' she replied. 'To watch in case Petrov came back.'

'That's what I thought.' Ben took out his phone and speed-dialled Kaprisky once more. 'Me again. Did you tell your guys to turn Yuri's place over?'

Kaprisky sounded as taken aback as he had earlier. 'Those were absolutely not my instructions. As I told you, they were only sent to observe and ask questions.'

'Any reason why they might have seen fit to ignore those instructions?'

'None. Please explain to me what is going on. Are you getting closer to finding Valentina?'

Right now, Ben felt as though he was getting further away from that goal with every passing moment. 'You'll have a progress report soon enough,' he said, and put the phone away. He spent the next few minutes scouting through the debris of the wrecked living room, then went up the narrow passage to inspect the rest of the empty apartment.

Yuri Petrov had not been living in the lap of luxury, that was for sure. The entire bathroom was about a third of the size of Ben's hotel shower, with cracked tiles and mildew and water stains everywhere. It took Ben very little time to verify that no toiletries, shaving kit or toothbrushes appeared to have been removed. Moving on up the dingy passage to the main bedroom, the few cheap items of clothing bundled into the wardrobe and chest of drawers had likewise apparently been left alone. A pair of reading glasses lay on top of a John le Carré novel in English beside the bed, and an empty suitcase had been stuffed below it.

The last room he checked was a poky spare bedroom with a bare floor, a narrow wardrobe, a cheap dressing table and no space for much else. Going by the little pink suitcase and items of pink clothing scattered on the bed, this had obviously been Valentina's quarters on her visits. Like her father's things, it seemed that most or all of the girl's possessions had been left behind when they disappeared.

Something crunched underfoot. Ben looked down, saw the small shards of brittle pink plastic he'd stepped on, and picked up the largest fragment to inspect more closely. It had part of a silver N embossed on it, from the NOKIA logo of a mobile phone. Lowering himself to peer under the bed, he found more fragments among the dust balls on the bare floor, and retrieved them. The fragments amounted to part of the casing of the phone; the rest of it was missing.

Ben slipped the biggest fragment into his pocket. Sensing a presence behind him, he turned back towards the bedroom doorway to see Tatyana standing there, leaning against the wall of the passage with folded arms.

'What are you making of it?' she asked.

Ben thought for a moment, then said, 'You know what, Miss Nikolaeva? Maybe you can be useful to me after all.'

Chapter 13

They left the apartment, closed the door behind them as well as its buckled frame would allow, then retraced their steps back along the walkway and down the concrete stairs. A narrow archway led through to a lugubrious, dirty courtyard where they found the apartment block's concierge emptying trash into a row of bins that had been left standing out in the sun and were swarming with flies. The concierge was a brassy-looking, blond-haired woman of around forty or forty-five, dressed in a grey overall and clumpy, oversized shoes.

'Did you talk to her before?' Ben asked, and Tatyana shook her head. 'I want to ask her some questions, and I need you to interpret for me.'

'I am happy to be of service.'

They walked up to the woman, who turned as they approached. She had too much makeup and eyes like a pigeon. She said something terse in Russian, which Ben took to mean, 'You want something?'

Tatyana spoke politely and showed her private investigator's ID card, which the woman scrutinised with great suspicion. After a lot of persuading, she agreed to answer a few questions. The flies buzzed around her as she talked. Ben kept waiting for one to disappear into her mouth, but she didn't seem to care about them.

With Tatyana interpreting, the conversation was painfully slow. The woman became defensive when quizzed about the broken-into apartment. She knew nothing about anything. No, she hadn't noticed the forced lock; now that she was learning of it, she wasn't very pleased about the hassle of getting it repaired. She was equally edgy when it came to discussing the apartment's tenant, Mr Petrov. With some effort, Tatyana was able to coax out of her that she'd last seen him eight, maybe nine, days ago though she couldn't be sure.

'He was home then?'

'He was on his way somewhere.'

'Alone?'

'Not alone.'

'Who was he with? A little girl?'

The concierge reflected, and replied that yes, she thought so. At that cue, Ben stepped forwards and showed her the photo of Valentina. Was this her? The concierge said she hadn't got such a good look at her, but it was probably the same child she'd seen leaving with Mr Petrov. What about it?

Had Mr Petrov by any chance mentioned where he was going? The concierge shrugged and replied that people came and went all the time. It wasn't any of her business to poke into people's lives, and she didn't care anyway. No, she couldn't remember if Mr Petrov had been carrying a bag, or luggage of any kind. She didn't watch everything that happened around the place, and why should she? All she knew was that she now had a terrible mess to clear up. She seemed anxious to know whether these two detectives would notify the cops about the break-in, and appeared not to want the law involved. Too much trouble, she kept saying.

At that point, another woman appeared from a nearby

ground-floor apartment. She was a few years older than the concierge, grey and skinny with a shawl wrapped around her bony shoulders, and it quickly transpired that she not only had been eavesdropping on the conversation but had an axe to grind, too. Within seconds, the two women had launched into a heated argument in quick-fire Russian, which Tatyana had to try to keep up with as she related it all to Ben. The older woman claimed that the concierge (who was a rotten bitch and a shameless tart) didn't want the cops involved only to protect her boyfriend (who was a filthy thieving crook and a drug peddler to boot). This drew an extremely vehement protest from the concierge, and soon the courtyard was echoing to the sound of their furious yelling. The older woman went on to claim that the same thing had happened to her twice last year, and everyone knew who was doing the break-ins in the neighbourhood, but that when she called the police this here dirty cow Rozalina Morozova – thrusting an accusing finger at the concierge, who glared back at her as though she wanted to rake her eyeballs out or kick her to death with those big shoes – stood up for the bastard by coming up with some alibi. He was probably cutting her in on the spoils of his burglaries, and that was why she was afraid of the police.

Tatyana kept translating at high speed as the argument raged on. Ben, getting all this with about a five-second delay, was in danger of losing the thread.

The concierge screamed, 'Nasty old witch, why don't you go tell your filthy lies elsewhere?'

'You're not fooling anyone, Rozalina Morozova. I saw Bogdan Lebedev coming out of there with a box *this big* in his arms. Just a few days ago, after Mr Petrov had already left.'

'Hold on,' Ben said, raising a hand to interrupt their stream at the mention of this new name. 'Bogdan Lebedev?'

That stopped the argument dead in its tracks, though not for long. The older woman explained, via Tatyana, that Lebedev lived across the way with his two brothers, Maksim and Artem. That was, when he wasn't shacked up with this one – pointing again at the concierge, who now started screaming and yelling all over again. Mercifully, moments later the concierge had taken enough abuse for one day, burst into tears and retreated to the safety of her little ground-floor office, from which the sounds of objects being furiously hurled and smashed could soon be heard.

'Where across the way?' Ben asked.

Tatyana asked, listened and then replied, 'She says he lives in one of the flats on the other side of the street, but that he is never at home because he and his brothers are always either riding around on their motorcycles, or hanging out at a local vodka bar, a place called the Zenit.'

'How would I know this Lebedev?' was Ben's next question. Tatyana related it to the woman, again listened and then translated: 'She says that unless you were blind, you could not easily miss him. He has a great big spider in the middle of his forehead and one ear missing from where someone slashed it off with a razor. She also says they should have cut his rotten throat while they were at it.'

'That's all we need to know,' Ben said. 'Please thank the good lady for her time.' He peeled another sheaf of Kaprisky's rubles from the wad of walking-around money, and offered it to the woman. She snatched the cash faster than the taxi driver had, muttered something in Russian and stalked back to her apartment.

'I do not understand,' Tatyana said.

'Come on,' Ben replied. 'I'll explain on the way.'

'On the way where?'

'It's almost lunchtime. Buy you a drink? I happen to know of a bar nearby.'

Chapter 14

Tatyana used her smartphone to locate the Zenit, which turned out to be just a few minutes away on foot from the apartment block. As they walked quickly through the streets, Ben took the broken fragment of pink plastic from his pocket and rolled it thoughtfully in the palm of his hand.

'You said you were going to explain,' Tatyana reminded him.

'Never worked a kidnap case before?'

Tatyana shook her head. 'No, and I am confused. Please tell me your thoughts on this situation.'

'When a man takes the fairly extreme step of abducting his own child and going on the run,' Ben told her, 'there's a certain amount of forward planning involved. At the very least, he'd pack a bag of clothing, in which he would probably have put various personal items like a toothbrush, razor, and so on. Petrov isn't fitting that pattern. His wardrobe and bedroom drawers are still full, and there's an empty suitcase under his bed. He left behind his reading glasses, too, along with the book he's halfway through. The same goes for Valentina's things. If they're travelling, they're travelling awfully light.'

'What about that?' Tatyana pointed to the pink shard of plastic in Ben's hand. 'It looks like part of a cell phone.'

'A *pink* cell phone. Therefore relatively unlikely to belong to Yuri Petrov.'

'Unless he were a—'

'*Goluboĭ*?'

She smiled. 'You are picking up Russian very well.'

'Safe to say the phone belongs to Valentina. Or used to, before someone smashed it.'

She pursed her lips. 'How do you know someone smashed it? Things break.'

Ben wasn't so sure about that. 'Mobile phone casings are pretty tough things. Designed to withstand everyday accidents, like being dropped onto a pavement. It takes a fair bit of force to shatter one. I know, I've killed a few phones in my time. Looks like this one's been hit with a hammer. Or a good hard stamp or two would do the trick. However it was done, it took more force than a young girl would normally unload on one of her valued possessions. Another kid with her pampered life might have turned out a spoiled brat, but she strikes me as the kind of child who takes good care of her things.'

Tatyana's lips downturned at the corners. 'So you are saying Petrov did this?'

'Or whoever broke into his apartment,' Ben said. 'But then it makes no sense for a burglar to deliberately harm an item that could be sold, even for a few rubles. So if it was Petrov, the question is, what would make a man want to go and smash his own kid's phone?'

Tatyana thought for a moment and said, 'Perhaps to prevent her from calling her mother to say what was happening, or to call for help? That would fit with the picture of a kidnapping, no?'

'It's a possibility,' Ben said. 'But here's another thing. If he stamped on it or hit it with a hammer, or whatever, the rest of the pieces should be here, scattered over the floor and under the bed. They're gone.'

'You are thinking the thieves have taken it?'

'Again, a possibility. If only the casing was broken, it could be replaced. The guts of the phone might still be intact, therefore salvageable.'

'Then they would have sold it by now.'

'Then we can ask Mr Lebedev very nicely for the name and whereabouts of the buyer.'

'Assuming Lebedev is the thief.'

'Which could be an assumption too far,' he said. 'Though we might get lucky.'

'But why go to so much trouble?' she asked.

'Because if we had the phone, and if we could verify that it was definitely Valentina's, we might find other numbers on it. Such as a mobile number for her father, which could be useful. Maybe even something that might give us an indication of where they've gone.'

'Perhaps,' Tatyana said, looking doubtful. 'If it has not already been erased.'

'These things are technically known in the trade as clues, Miss Nikolaev. And they're in somewhat short supply at this moment. Every little bit helps.'

They were getting close to the location of the Zenit bar. Ben had heard about the efforts of the Russian government to knock down entire rundown sections of Moscow for extensive redevelopment. This particular suburb had yet to be reached by the bulldozers, but its time couldn't be far away. The streets were almost deserted and the grey, crumbly buildings gave off an air of desolation and hopelessness.

Before the Zenit bar was even in sight they heard the muted thud of loud music from around the corner. The flat-roofed concrete block building stood in a wasteground surrounded by a rickety wire fence. If it hadn't been for the faded sign above the doorway, the place could have been a bunker. There were no windows Ben could see, and the door was protected by a galvanised steel grid. A row of a dozen or so large motorcycles stood outside, mostly chopped Harley-lookalikes with raked front forks and the kind of elevated handlebars that aficionados called 'ape hangers'. Great for aerating your armpits in the summer breeze. Three of the bikes were sprayed matt black, with hammer-and-sickle symbols, swastikas and skulls crudely hand-painted on their tanks.

'What kind of low life would ride a motorcycle like this?' Tatyana said.

'I'm guessing, maybe the kind with a giant spider tattoo on his forehead?' Ben suggested. 'Looks like we may have found our Lebedev brothers.'

'I do not think I would like to have a drink in there,' Tatyana said, eyeing the building.

'Nonsense. This is my kind of place.'

The steel grid in front of the door was unlocked. Ben swung it open, and they walked inside.

The volume of the music swelled about twenty times louder as they entered the Zenit. The heat and smell of stale smoke, booze and confined bodies in the airless space hit them at the same time. Flashing multicoloured lights washed over the murky scene within. The Zenit was dank and dark and every bit as seedy as any self-respecting bad boy could have wished for. A pair of strippers occupied a low stage at the far end of the room, wrapping themselves around poles and surrounded by drooling men clutching bottles of booze. Across the bare concrete floor, the bar was crowded with jostling punters all vying to get their next drink, many of them looking as though they'd been at it all through the previous night.

Ben gazed around him. To his immediate left, four drunken men at a table were openly doing a drug deal, a pile of cash and a bag of something illicit in the process of exchanging hands. To his right, seated at a corner couch behind a table loaded with bottles and glasses, three hood-lums ranging from about twenty-five to thirty-five in age and all bearing a slight facial resemblance to one another were laughing uproariously at some joke.

Ben caught Tatyana's eye and knew she was thinking the same thing he was. Here they were: the brothers Lebedev, exactly as described, enjoying life in their favourite hangout. The one in the middle was the eldest, lounging lazily with his arms and legs all spread out and taking up as much room as possible between his two younger siblings. He had yellow hair buzzed to a stubble, doing little to hide his missing right ear. He also displayed an enormous black tarantula in the exact centre of his forehead, as though the tattoo artist who had consented to permanently disfiguring him had measured out the dimensions with great care before applying the ink.

If that one was Bogdan, the other two must be Maksim and Artem, whichever was which. The youngest had more delicate features, almost good-looking if it hadn't been for the sneer on his face and the greasiness of his hair which, if he hadn't tied it back in a ponytail, would have been hanging about his face in rats' tails. The third was bald with a thick beard, as though his head had been turned upside-down. All three were hard at work on tall pitchers of beer, and judging by the number of empties crammed on the tabletop in front of them, it was at least their fifth or sixth each. It appeared that the brothers' breakfast was running into lunch, with no sign of slowing down.

Ben and Tatyana drew a few looks as she followed him over to the bar. Ben pushed his way through to the front, signalled for the barman's attention and, with a combination of English and sign language, ordered a whisky for himself and a vodka for Tatyana. The barman looked as much of a bruiser as the majority of his clientele. Ben figured that he probably knew most of them by name. As the guy was pouring out the drinks, Ben signalled for his attention again, pointed over to the three thugs in the far corner and said, 'Bogdan Lebedev, da?' The barman paused and scowled at Ben, then finished pouring without a word and thrust his hand out for the money. His unwillingness to talk was all the confirmation Ben needed.

Tatyana refused her drink, protesting that it was too early in the day. Ben shrugged and downed the rubbing alcohol that passed for scotch in this vicinity. 'We did not just come here to drink, did we?' she asked, tightlipped.

'Nope,' he replied.

'What are we going to do?'

'You're going to do nothing except hang back and watch.'

'While you do what exactly?'

'Just routine stuff,' he replied. 'Trust me.'

Then he slid his empty glass back across the bar, smacked his lips and headed over towards where the Lebedev boys were sitting.

Chapter 15

The brothers were cracking up at another incredibly funny joke as Ben approached. Suddenly aware of the stranger's presence, their laughter died away and all three pairs of eyes focused on him, as focused as they could be after so many beers.

Ben walked right up to the edge of the crowded table, stopped and peered down at the three. 'Bogdan Lebedev?' The elder brother was as forthcoming about his identity as the barman had been, but Ben had only wanted to get his attention.

Ben's strategy was a simple one. To get the information he wanted, he needed to talk to Bogdan on his own, which meant sidelining the brothers. And to do that, he first needed to get all three of them outside. There was only one way to make that happen.

Without breaking eye contact, he very deliberately reached down, touched two fingers to the rim of the tall half-empty pitcher in front of Bogdan Lebedev, and just as deliberately pushed it over. Glasses rolled and smashed on the floor. Beer sloshed across the tabletop and spilled off its edge into Bogdan Lebedev's lap. The Russian recoiled with an angry yell, stared down at the crotch of his soaked jeans that looked as if he'd wet his pants, and then glared up at Ben with a look of quivering fury.

In Ben's experience, the art of picking fights in bars was all about maximum provocation. The next phase of the plan was to add insult to injury. Still not taking his eyes off Bogdan he pointed a finger like a gun and came out with the most recent addition to his fledgling Russian vocabulary. A slight that was still more or less guaranteed, especially in that country but in pretty much any drinking men's barroom in the world, the real world, to elicit a strong reaction.

'*Goluboi!*'

Neither subtle nor politically correct, and all the more effective for it. All three brothers instantly jumped to their feet, ready for battle. A few punters gazed across, momentarily distracted from their drinks, the writhing strippers or their other business; but Ben hadn't expected the clientele of the Zenit to come racing to the aid of the Lebedevs, and he wasn't proved wrong. Fistfights were probably an everyday occurrence in the place, and if you couldn't look after yourself, you had it coming.

'This way, if you please, gentlemen,' Ben said, heading for the door and motioning for the three to follow. Tatyana was near the bar, staring at him as though he'd lost his mind. Ben stepped outside into the fenced-off patch of wasteland. As before, the street was empty. He walked towards the parked motorcycles.

The three Lebedevs stormed out in his wake, Bogdan leading the pack and virtually drooling in rage. They emerged into the daylight just in time to see him push the sole of his boot against one of their bikes and topple all three of them off their sidestands like a row of dominoes. Ben had learned at an early age that few things infuriated wannabe outlaw bikers like seeing their proudly displayed machines fall over in a mass of crunching, twisting, buckling metal. The provocation was complete.

Now the Lebedevs were itching to tear this impudent foreigner apart, and they formed a semicircle around him with clenched fists as he stepped calmly away from the fallen bikes. A few of their bar buddies lingered in the doorway, watching the spectacle with mild amusement. There were a couple of shouts of encouragement, the Russian equivalent of 'Get'm, Bogdan, sort'm out, kick his ass!'

Tatyana squeezed past the group and hovered uncertainly to one side.

The brothers came a step closer, shoulder to shoulder, Bogdan the eldest in the middle, with all the confidence of scrappers who'd done this a hundred times before and were certain of their victory. Three against one. How could they lose?

Ben didn't back away. His body was relaxed, his heartbeat slow and steady, arms loose by his sides. The brothers came on another step, and when Ben still didn't back away he saw a tiny flicker of doubt appearing on the face of the one on the right, the youngest: Artem or Maksim, Ben neither knew nor cared. His money was on Bogdan to make the first move.

Which Bogdan did, two seconds later. With a furious yell he lowered his head and crabbed his arms and rushed straight at Ben intent on ramming him with all his bodyweight. Ben stood motionless until Bogdan was almost on him, then quickly sidestepped out of his path and put out a foot to trip him. An opponent's power and momentum can quickly turn against him in a fight, a fact of life that Ben had known and exploited for many years. In Bogdan Lebedev's case, it was like derailing a fast-moving train. The Russian landed belly-down on the concrete with a wheezing grunt as the wind was knocked out of him. Ben kicked him lightly in the head, just enough to keep him down a while longer without doing any lasting damage. Whatever few brain cells the man possessed, Ben needed to keep intact for later.

The remaining Lebedevs stared down at their fallen sibling, exchanged a brief glance and then came at Ben in unison. Ben almost had to feel sorry for anyone so poorly schooled in the true craft of street brawling. He put an elbow in the youngest one's face and a boot in the bearded one's kneecap. The first went down backwards, the other forwards. The youngest brother hadn't been a bad-looking kid, but now his days of being pretty were behind him. He struggled gamely to his feet and put a hand to the pulped mess where his nose had been, gaped down at his fallen brothers and seemed ready to bolt. The bearded Lebedev stayed on the ground, writhing in agony and clutching his knee while braying at the top of his lungs. The noise was irritating, so Ben knocked him out with a harder kick to the head than his elder brother had received.

About four seconds in, the fight had now gone from three-to-one to even odds. The gathering crowd in the bar doorway had stopped offering yells of encouragement. Tatyana was still watching, as though transfixed. The last Lebedev standing wiped blood with his sleeve and circled Ben warily.

'We haven't got all day,' Ben said. 'Get on with it.'

Now out came the knife, a small stiletto dagger the younger Lebedev kept tucked in the back of his belt. Ben shook his head. People really shouldn't play with those nasty things unless they knew how to use them.

The young guy wagged the blade this way and that, slicing at the air as menacingly as he could, then made a determined lunge at Ben's chest. Ben deflected the strike and rolled the weapon out of his hand as easily as confiscating a lollipop from a child. Blood still pouring from his nose and horror in his eyes, the young guy stared at his empty hand, then back at his inert brothers, then back at Ben, before taking off like a startled antelope.

'Not so fast,' Ben said. As the younger Lebedev shot away he grabbed him by his greasy ponytail and yanked him backwards off his feet. Thump, kick, and it was over. Ten seconds, three knockouts, and Ben hadn't taken a punch.

The barman had other ideas, though. The gang in the doorway moved aside as he emerged and stalked towards Ben, burly and bristling and toting a pump shotgun. Maybe the fight wasn't over, after all.

Chapter 16

A pump-action twelve-gauge hunting shotgun, out of the box, would typically sport a twenty-eight-inch smoothbore barrel and a good heavy wooden buttstock for absorbing the strong recoil of the firearm. This one had been converted to make it the ideal under-the-bar concealment weapon, in case its owner needed to blow away armed robbers or stop a riot among the punters. It would have served either purpose admirably. Both ends had been hacksawed away, leaving a stub of a pistol grip and a barrel no more than a foot long. Much less accurate, but just as dangerous to the guy on the wrong end of it.

The barman angrily racked the pump. The metallic *crunch-crunch* of the machinery of death in motion. He stood planted with his feet apart, the weapon butted up against his right hip, the short barrel pointing Ben's way.

Ben was still clutching the stiletto knife. The question was, whether he could whirl it through the air accurately and quickly enough to plant the blade in the barman's eyeball before the guy launched an ounce and a quarter of buckshot down that sawn-off tube at something like fifteen hundred feet per second. There would be only one way to find out.

Tatyana had been standing frozen still throughout the fight. Now she suddenly came to life. Without hesitation and before any of the assembly could stop her, she strode up behind the barman and stunned him with a hard, blindingly fast blow to the back of the neck.

As he half-staggered, half-spun towards her she whipped the shotgun from his hands and whacked him under the chin with the cut-down buttstock with a crunch of wood against flesh that echoed across the urban wasteland. The barman flopped to the ground like a wet mattress and lay spreadeagled on the concrete.

In a flash, Tatyana turned the weapon on the gang in the doorway, who seemed about to get threatening. The sight of the chopped gun muzzle pointing their way was enough to dispel any such notions, and they retreated back inside, almost falling over one another in their haste to abandon their fallen comrades to their fate. When the door slammed shut, Tatyana shucked the shells out of the gun's receiver and lobbed all five of them up onto the flat roof of the Zenit, from where it would take a ladder to retrieve the ammo. She threw the empty weapon among the weeds at the side of the building.

'We should leave now, before the *politsiya* come.'

'If they do, that'll be their problem.' Ben walked over to the semi-comatose heap that was Bogdan Lebedev, grabbed him under the arms and hauled him upright. The Russian swayed on his feet, blinked several times and managed to focus on Ben. Recognising his tormentor, he staggered backwards in terror.

'Miss Nikolaev,' Ben said, 'please inform this gentleman that we'd like to be taken to wherever he keeps his stash of stolen goods, because we believe he has something we want back. Advise him that if he plays any silly games with us, he's going to get both his wrists very painfully broken and his brothers, when they come out of the hospital themselves, will be taking turns wiping his arse for the next several months.'

'You want me to put it exactly that way?' she asked, arching an eyebrow.

'You can improvise a little, if you prefer.'

'I understand English, motherfucker,' Bogdan Lebedev muttered in a croak. 'What is it you want?'

Ben took a step towards him and raised a hand. The Russian flinched like a beaten dog. 'Okay, okay, I take you to my place. Is not far.'

Ben looked at him. 'Bogdan, please tell me you're really not that stupid that you'd keep a load of stolen goods in your own home.'

Bogdan sort of shrugged, indicating that yes, he really was that stupid. But it would have been stupider still to refuse to comply with Ben's request. 'You can have what you want. You promise not to hit me again, agree?'

'We'll see about that. Move.'

With a last wistful glance at his toppled motorcycle and barely a look at his unconscious siblings or the barman, Bogdan led the way at a shuffling limp. Ben and Tatyana followed. Minutes later, they were walking along a dismal street just a pistol shot away from Petrov's apartment building, which, by comparison to the Lebedev residence, suddenly seemed about as upmarket as Ben's hotel. Bogdan managed to drag himself noisily up three flights of stairs, pausing now and then to rub his bruises and complain of the agony he was in. Finally he led them into a squalid, dingy flat that reeked of cheap cooking, body odour and the smoke from all manner of illegal substances.

The loot was kept in a spare room. Burglary was how the Lebedev boys seemed to earn much of their living, and stacked boxes of stolen goods covered nearly every square inch of the floor. 'You want TV, video?' Bogdan muttered, pointing to a crate full of equipment. 'I got Panasonic fifty-inch screen, almost new. I got lot of stuff here.'

Ben made him shove boxes aside and show him the stuff he and his brothers had raided from Yuri Petrov's place, then ordered the Russian to stand aside while he and Tatyana rummaged through the junk. It was hard to believe that any of it had value, even to a low-end thief.

'What are you, a friend of his? I get it. He send you to get his shit back, yeah? He got nothing worth having. Here, you want DVDs? I got hardcore, real hot shit.'

'All I want is this,' Ben said, finding what he was looking for. He fished the plastic bag out of the cardboard box in which it had been stored.

Bogdan pulled a face. 'What you want that for, man? I try fix it, but no chance. It is total fucked.'

Which was a fairly accurate account of the phone's condition, as Ben saw when he inspected the remains. The crooks had attempted to glue the shattered pink plastic casing back together, then obviously given up when they realised they didn't have all the pieces. The internal chassis and keypad of the phone were badly buckled, and the screen was cracked in three places. The power button appeared to be dead. Ben replaced the bits and pocketed the bag.

Bogdan Lebedev could hardly believe his good fortune. He'd been ready to part with a truckload of valuables in order to save himself from a beating, and all this crazy foreigner wanted was a worthless piece of junk phone that would never work again? He couldn't stop grinning. His two younger brothers, lying injured and bleeding on the concrete outside the Zenit bar, were quite forgotten. He said to Ben, 'You get what you want, now you leave me alone, huh?'

Ben had, in truth, been toying with the idea of breaking

a couple of minor bones and maybe punting Bogdan out of the window to teach him a lesson. Relenting, he replied, 'All right, Bogdan, you survived this one. But let me tell you something. Your burgling days are over. You won't see us, but we'll be watching you. Any hint that you're getting back to your old tricks again, you'll be getting a visit from my associates, and believe me, they're not half as touchy-feely as I am. You and your brothers will be hung up like deer and castrated with a blunt chisel. And that will be just the beginning. Tell me you agree with the deal.'

No longer grinning, Bogdan hung his head and muttered, 'Okay, man. You are the boss.'

Ben and Tatyana left. She waited until they were back out in the street before turning to him with a crookedly mischievous smile. 'I must say that I find your methods not unimpressive, Major Hope. Unconventional, but interesting.'

'Thanks, but all we have to show for them so far is a broken phone. If anything comes of it, you can congratulate me then. As for our friend Bogdan, he'll be back to his old ways within a week.'

'I am not so sure. Russian men are very afraid of castration.'

'They're not alone, I can assure you. By the way, I never thanked you for your help back there. That was a smooth disarming move you pulled on the barman. Where did you learn a trick like that?'

Tatyana gave a modest shrug. 'Oh, you know, it is just something I – how do you say it – picked up along the way.'

'I had no idea I was working with a lady of such talents.'

Chapter 17

Returning to the hotel was the reverse of the process of leaving it, undetected and unfollowed. The mystery of who had been shadowing them was still very much an open question and bugging Ben every moment, but would have to take second priority while he focused on extracting whatever information Valentina's phone might have to offer. He and Tatyana threaded their way back to the Ararat Park Hyatt by means of a succession of buses and trams, stopping en route to purchase a recharger for the damaged Nokia. The final leg of the return journey came courtesy of a mini-van-sized taxicab with tinted rear windows, whose driver Ben had take them around the back of the hotel so they could duck discreetly inside via a rear kitchen entrance. If eyes were still on the street side, the watchers would have little chance of knowing their targets had returned.

Avoiding the main lobby for the same reason, Ben found his way to the hotel's IT lounge, which offered the full range of technological bells and whistles as a perk for paying guests. He and Tatyana found an unused computer station in a secluded alcove of the room and pulled up two chairs. The IT lounge was as hushed as a public library, just the clicking of keys and the occasional cough from one of the other guests at their terminals.

'This facility is not very private,' Tatyana whispered, glancing around. 'Your suite has its own wi-fi facilities. I suggest we use those instead.'

Ben had already considered that idea, and dismissed it. He shook his head. Spider-sense, intuition, paranoia, whatever it was, a voice in his mind kept telling him that all was not right and the less anyone knew about his movements, the better. Anyone watching, given sufficient resources, could also be hacking. Anything that the Winter Garden Suite's wi-fi was used to search for online could easily be traced to its registered occupant. By contrast, the hotel's open network made him anonymous. And anonymity was a rare privilege these days.

He fired up the computer. Even he had to admit, these damned things had their uses. He would soon find out whether the morning's excursion had brought anything of value at all.

Tatyana watched as he took the plastic bag from his pocket and spread its broken contents over the desk. She shook her head and sighed. 'What a mess,' she whispered. 'If Petrov did this, he has really tried hard to destroy it.'

'Let's hope, not hard enough,' Ben whispered back.

Tatyana gave a nasty little smile. 'If the data is all lost, the Lebedev brothers have suffered for nothing.'

'Poor souls. I'll arrange to have roses sent to the hospital.'

Ben tore open the packaging for the phone recharger, plugged it in at both ends and tried switching it on. The dead device remained dark and lifeless. 'Of course, that would have been too easy,' he said. 'Let's move on to Plan B.' He flicked the computer mouse and the screen flashed brightly into life, ready for action.

'Have you done this before?'

'First time for everything,' he replied. Ben was no IT

wizard, but he had a rough idea what he was doing. The hotel broadband was the fastest he'd ever seen. Superior Russian technology, once again. It took only moments to whiz through the search engine and track down the correct data recovery software online, which quickly became his second purchase of the day with Kaprisky's expenses account credit card.

Once the software was downloaded onto the computer, Ben returned to the smashed phone. His hope was that the SD card, containing all Valentina's stored files, was still intact. The phone's chassis was the flimsiest kind of lightweight, paper-thin alloy and so badly buckled that the card was stuck fast in its port. Checking that nobody was looking, he took out the stiletto knife that the Lebedev brother had tried to stick him with earlier, and gently inserted its sharp tip into the edge of the port to try to pry the card out.

'Carefully,' Tatyana winced, peering over his shoulder. 'It is very fragile. You do not want to break it.'

'Thanks for the advice.' Ben dug the blade in as deep as he dared, gave it a little twist, and felt the card come free. He delicately slipped it out and inspected it for damage, of which he could see no external signs. Next he inserted the card into the matching port on the computer and ran the data recovery software to scan for lost files. This was the moment of truth. The card would either respond, or it would prove to be as dead as the rest of the device. Tatyana pulled her chair closer to the terminal, and her knee pressed against Ben's. He breathed her perfume as she watched the screen with bated breath.

After a pause, the computer did its work and a new window flashed up onscreen. The software had found a large number of data files on the card and was ready to download them to the hard drive.

'Excellent,' Tatyana said.

'So far, so good,' Ben muttered. 'Let's see what we've got.'

Not tall, not short, casually dressed and as instantly forgettable as all good shadows should be, the man standing on the far side of Neglinnaya Street took out his phone. He spoke without taking his eyes off the front of the hotel, constantly scanning between the main entrance and the windows and terrace of the Winter Garden Suite high above the street.

There had been no physical sighting of the subjects since earlier that morning, the unfortunate incident on the metro train when the man and his partner had allowed themselves to be spotted. But the GPS tracking device the man was carrying on his mission indicated their whereabouts to within a matter of inches. The team knew exactly where their targets were, the entire time.

'This is Number Four, reporting,' the man said into the phone, speaking his native Russian. 'Hope and the woman are inside the building. Situation under control and monitoring.'

On the other end of the line, the Mission Chief was reclining in a large, soft leather chair at a desk far, far away, inside a private and secure room filled with screens. The largest screen of all was the one on the wall opposite him, on which he was watching the real-time aerial feed of the Ararat Park Hyatt hotel as it was bounced down to Earth from a classified geostationary spy satellite some 250km up.

Such reports from his field agents were largely superfluous, but he tasked them anyway. The Mission Chief already knew exactly where the subjects under observation had been that morning and had a pretty good idea what they had been up to during that time. He knew to the exact second when they had returned to the hotel, and would be able to freely track their movements wherever they went when they left there. The Winter Garden Suite was fully monitored with audio bugging devices, and any online activity on the room's wi-fi connection would be instantly intercepted straight to his desk.

In short, the Mission Chief possessed all the same data as his operatives, plus a great deal more. The footsoldiers' role in this part of the mission was simply to keep pace down there on the ground, remain on standby, report any developing situations that might require their quick intervention, and in such cases respond accordingly.

So far, such intervention had not been necessary and all was going according to plan. Except, of course, for that one significant glitch that the Chief was not pleased about. He was a calm man by temperament. He wouldn't have achieved his position otherwise. But there were times when the urgency of a critical mission caused him to grill an operative, and this was one of them. He spoke slowly, Russian being not his mother tongue, but the menace in his words came over loud and clear to his underling.

'Remember who you're dealing with here, Number Four. Hope is not your normal subject. He's as expert in surveillance and counter-surveillance as all of you lot put together, and then a good deal more. Risk blowing this whole operation by letting him spot you again, and I'll have you replaced in a heartbeat. Understand?'

The agent knew that to be replaced was to be eliminated. He swallowed hard and tried not to let his fear show in his voice as he replied, 'He won't spot us again, chief. That's a guarantee.'

'Do not screw this up, Number Four. You and your team have your orders, and they are clear. Stay well back, keep the assets in sight and move in only if and when I give the command. They'll lead us straight to Petrov, and *that's* when you can put your talents to good use.'

The agent smiled at the thought. The one per cent of his job that wasn't brain-numbing surveillance work made it all worthwhile. 'Copy that, chief. Number Four, over and out.'

Chapter 18

Once the intact data files from the phone were all safely stored in the computer hard drive, Ben began opening them systematically. He was soon disappointed to find that the phone's stored memory of calls and numbers, which he'd hoped to retrieve, had not survived. What remained was mostly a mixture of text messages, image and video files.

Ben started with the texts, in case something there might offer up a clue as to Yuri Petrov's whereabouts. It was a long shot, as he was all too aware. But even long shots could sometimes hit their target.

As Ben now discovered, little Valentina Petrova was a prolific texter. 'This might take a while,' he warned, speaking softly to not be overheard by the other IT lounge users.

'We have nothing else to do,' Tatyana whispered back.

By the time they'd sifted through the first sixty or seventy texts, patterns were emerging, none of them remotely useful. Valentina's circle of friends included a dozen or so with whom she seemed to communicate more frequently, and one in particular, Adalie, who was her closest confidante. A brief detour to Facebook showed Adalie Beaulieu to be a resident of La Suze-sur-Sarthe, Le Mans, France, twelve and a half years old and a big fan of Demi Lovato, whom Ben had never heard of, but no surprises there. Valentina additionally kept in touch with a couple of friends back in Amsterdam, Britt and Danique, with whom she swapped messages in Dutch.

The texts were pretty much what any bright, life-loving young kid would send to her pals. A good number of them concerned a boy called Paul back home in France, on whom Valentina obviously had a bit of a schoolgirl crush. It was all perfectly innocent stuff, but Ben felt bad about prying into the child's personal life. There was loads of chatter about the usual pop stars and movie actors, with lively debates about who was the hunkiest and who was the creepiest. Something about a really cool birthday party for someone named Nicole and what a terrific time everyone had had; various ravings about a lovely bay pony that 'cher Grand-Oncle Auguste' had bought for Valentina as a Christmas present; and on, and on. Ben trawled doggedly through nearly four hundred useless texts and found nothing.

Maybe the poor Lebedevs had suffered needlessly, after all. Ben didn't know how he could ever forgive himself.

Next were the image and video files. Ben recalled the framed blow-ups plastered all over the walls of Valentina's bedroom back home, and Kaprisky's mention of his grandniece's love of snapping images wherever she went. It wasn't too much of a surprise that the aspiring little photographer had crammed her phone with an endless array of pet pictures. Dogs of all shapes and sizes, all manner of moggies; but most of all horses, horses and more horses. She must have photographed every equine in France.

'She is very fond of animals,' Tatyana observed.

'She wants to be a vet, apparently.'

'I was the same, at her age.'

Ben looked at her. 'That's amazing. You mean, there's a softer side to your personality that we haven't seen yet?'

Tatyana's eyes turned from the screen and flashed at him. 'You know nothing about me.' No smile this time.

'True,' he admitted, and went on clicking through the image files. Interspersed with the animal shots were ones of people and places: Ben recognised a few settings from Kaprisky's estate, the lake, the orchard and the palatial house. There were quite a few of her granduncle and her mother taken indoors and out, plus a variety of kids around Valentina's age who most likely included her best friend Adalie and her little beau, Paul. In one picture, Valentina's own shadow was visible where she'd snapped Kaprisky's Gulfstream on the tarmac at Le Mans-Arnage, Adrien Leroy standing by the plane in his uniform. Others showed the interior of the aircraft, and views of fluffy clouds taken from the windows while in flight. Ben kept clicking.

'I recognise that one,' Tatyana said, pointing. 'Vnukovo airport, the area where the private jets land.' Ben recognised it too, though it looked very different in the daytime. The Kaprisky jet had just landed and was parked outside its hangar, light snow on the tarmac. The file information dated the image to October 6 the previous year, during what must have been an earlier visit to Moscow.

More clicks. The images rolled onwards, and now what Ben and Tatyana were seeing was a visual travelogue of Valentina's trip to Moscow last October. A short video file, jerky and only a few seconds in duration, showed a scene of city traffic labouring through the icy streets, pictured from inside a scabby car with steamed-up windows and an interior that was unmistakably that of a VW Beetle, the old type with the rear-mounted engine that sounded like an outboard motor. The model of vehicle was confirmed in the

127

next photo, which showed the pale blue Beetle parked at the snowy kerbside outside Yuri Petrov's apartment building. Valentina had clambered on top of the car and was standing on its domed roof, arms spread wide, face rosy from the cold and split by an enormous grin. Her hair was sticking out from under a woolly hat and a thick scarf was wrapped around her neck. She had grown a lot in the months since the picture had been taken. Her mother would probably not have approved of such antics, but the kid looked full of joy.

'That car is not registered to him,' Tatyana said. 'We would have found it otherwise.'

'Wherever it is now,' Ben said, 'we know it's not at his apartment.'

The next video file, dated October 7, showed the scruffy and hairy figure of Yuri Petrov, posing with a stupid expression as he stirred a pot at the stove in his tiny kitchen, pop music blaring in the background. Dated two days later, in a snowy park somewhere in Moscow, was a photo selfie of Valentina hugging her father as the two of them beamed for the camera.

'That is Gorky Park,' Tatyana said, clinking a perfect sea-blue fingernail against the screen. 'See, the House of Artists and the Graveyard of Fallen Monuments are in the background.'

Not all that wildly interested in Moscow sights, Ben was scrutinising the faces of father and daughter and thinking you could see the love there. However much Valentina's father might look like Russia's answer to Charles Manson with the hair and the beard, nothing but tenderness showed in his eyes. A pathetic excuse for a human being. A worthless imbecile. A lying deadbeat. All that Kaprisky had said about Yuri might be true.

But a dangerous liability and a threat to his child?

And yet, according to everything Ben had been told and all the evidence so far, this man was supposed to have abducted his beloved little girl, taken her hostage, whisked her away from everything she loved and all the good things in her life.

Ben said, 'Hmm.' This case was starting to feel as if it were going upside-down on him. Something wasn't right. There were details he was missing here.

Tatyana looked at him. 'What?'

'Nothing,' he said, and clicked open the next file. Back to the VW Beetle now, a short piece of video footage filmed from the front passenger seat as the car travelled up a crowded motorway on the sleety ninth of October. A pair of pink-shod feet was visible in the shot, perched up on the VW's dashboard. A man's hand – presumably Yuri Petrov's – could be seen resting on the steering wheel.

'That is the Federal Highway M10,' Tatyana said. 'I have travelled it many times. It goes all the way to St Petersburg, seven hundred kilometres.'

Ben wondered where Yuri and Valentina's road trip might have taken them. By the time the kid had snapped the next image later the same day, her father had turned off the highway and the Beetle was deep in the sticks. The road looked like little more than a dirt track, winding through snowy countryside and woodland. The focus of Valentina's photo, taken through the side window of the car, was a great Gothic church standing alone and apparently abandoned in the middle of open fields. Even from a distance, the signs of sad decay were obvious. Part of the roof had collapsed and trees had grown up through the nave. It would probably have been vandalised to an even worse state, if vandals bothered to venture out into the middle of nowhere.

'I know that place,' Tatyana said. 'I was taken there once,

as a child. We had family living in the area, dead now. The church once belonged to the family of an old manor estate nearby, where nobody has lived for a hundred years. When I saw it, it was already falling to pieces. I remember my father telling me how, in the Soviet days, it was used as a grain warehouse.' She shook her head sadly. 'My father believed that everything would get better, now that the Communists were gone. He was wrong. Things change, but they do not get better.'

'Could you find it again?'

After a hesitation, she replied, 'I think so. It is a few hours' drive, maybe two hundred kilometres to the east of Moscow.'

Ben peered closely at the screen, trying to drink in the picture and understand its significance. 'Where are they going?'

'That region is a very empty place,' Tatyana said. 'Under the old regime many villages were abandoned and became phantoms.'

It took him a second to understand her meaning. 'Ghost towns?'

'Also many farms were left in ruin. There was much depopulation. It has taken years for the people to return but still there are thousands of square kilometres of nothing. This is a big country, you understand.'

And it looked as if Yuri and his daughter had taken a road trip into the empty heart of it last October. The subsequent images Valentina had taken were of forests and lakes and winding country roads that stretched over large distances with not a single other vehicle, let alone a human dwelling, in sight.

After that, there was a gap of two days before any new pictures or bits of video footage appeared.

The next one was something unexpected.

Chapter 19

'Those are *kozy*, goats,' Tatyana declared. As if nothing so exotic existed outside Russia.

'Yes, we have them too,' Ben said.

'Disgusting.'

'You don't like goats?'

'I hate them. They smell worse than rats.'

'I thought you wanted to be a vet.'

'At age ten I had not yet smelled a goat.'

'So you decided to pursue a career in detection. Makes sense.'

They were looking at a video clip filmed on what appeared to be a somewhat rundown rural smallholding in winter. The bottom left corner of the shot was a little hand, a child's hand, wearing a fluffy pink mitten that was curled in a fist to grasp a handful of some kind of dried animal feed. In the middle of the picture, a cluster of hungry-looking white goats with floppy ears and staring split-pupil eyes were scrumming up to a rickety barbed-wire fence to get the food she was offering them. Valentina was giggling off-camera and speaking Dutch to the goats as they barged past one another and pressed tight against the wire to lick the food from her outstretched palm, condensation billowing from their breath in the cold air. The camera was shaky in her other hand, and as the image swayed this way and that, the right edge of the frame offered a momentary glimpse of a stone farmhouse half-hidden behind snow-laden conifers. A dog barked in the background. A couple of chickens could be seen scratching at the frosty ground near the farmhouse. The camera flickered again and Ben thought he saw something else, right on the edge of the frame.

'There,' Tatyana said, pointing.

'Yup.' Ben rewound the clip a few frames, found it, paused the playback and clicked keys to zoom in on the frozen screenshot until it was as large as he could make it without losing resolution. There they were, two vehicles parked on a hardcore track near the farmhouse door. One was some kind of early-model Japanese pickup truck. The other was Yuri Petrov's dilapidated pale blue Beetle. There was no doubt that this place, wherever it was, marked the destination of the road trip on which Yuri Petrov had taken his daughter last October.

'They visited a farm?' Tatyana said.

'Either that, or the world's crummiest theme park.'

'The child is fond of smelly animals. Maybe she wanted to be taken to see the goats.'

'But why the need to travel so far?' he said. 'They don't have animals in Moscow? Like a zoo?'

'Of course. The Moscow Zoo is one of the finest in the world.' Naturally.

The next file was a posed photo of Yuri Petrov and another man standing outside the farmhouse. Up close, the building seemed in a neglected state, surrounded by the usual kind of countryside junk: empty feed sacks, firewood logs, rolls of chicken wire and rusty butane gas bottles. The two men had their arms around each other's shoulders, like old friends hamming it up for the picture. The stranger was a bigger guy, some five inches taller than Yuri and much broader. His hair and beard were even more unkempt and he had teeth missing. The boiler suit he was wearing was covered in old grease and mud and possibly goat shit too, but he didn't seem to care. Welcome to life in the sticks. Maybe he was regarded as one of the stylish trendsetters and eligible bachelors of the region.

'A relative?' Ben wondered out loud.

'According to the records, Petrov is an only child,' Tatyana said. 'A distant cousin, perhaps.'

'Do we have any details on former schoolmates? Friends from student days?'

Tatyana shook her head. 'None. Though I would not say this man is educated. A peasant like that does not keep intelligent company.'

'Some of my best friends are peasants,' Ben said.

'My point exactly,' she fired back.

'Funny.'

She motioned at the screen. 'Keep looking. There may be more.'

There wasn't, at least not of the mysterious goat farm nor of Yuri Petrov's unknown rustic buddy. There now followed a whole series of images and clips taken back in France. Christmas at the Kaprisky estate. Parties. More kids. More horses. Dozens of uninformative image files later, the season moved into spring, then finally into summer, bringing the record more closely up to date.

'Here we go at last,' Ben said. 'Full circle.' Just like before, Valentina had captured her most recent trip to Moscow on her trusty little pink Nokia – the trip from which she had unexpectedly and dramatically failed, so far, to return. Photos and video clips tracked her progress from France to Russia, except now it was summertime. More exterior shots of Yuri Petrov's building, more inside pictures of the apartment, more brief clips of father and daughter messing around and laughing in the immediate lead-up to the abduction and disappearance. The last file was a still image of Yuri, sitting over plastic food in a McDonalds, making a goofy face for the camera. It was dated the same day as the pair had vanished.

'And that's it,' Ben said.

Tatyana turned away from the screen to fix him with a quizzical look. 'What are you making of this?'

'You're the professional investigator,' he said. 'What's your take?'

Tatyana hesitated and glanced around the room at the other IT lounge users. Some had gone, some newcomers had arrived. Lowering her voice, she said, 'I am thinking about this farm.'

He nodded. 'And what strikes you about it?'

'That it must be very remote,' Tatyana said. 'A place where nobody could find you. How do you say? A hide?'

'A hideaway,' Ben said. 'A refuge. A safehouse. All of those things.'

'If he has taken Valentina there before, then he could possibly return there. No?'

'I'd say that's a reasonable assumption,' Ben said.

'He would want to go to a place where a loyal friend would help him to stay hidden. And with animals everywhere, so the child would feel comfortable and happy. It would seem like just another visit, part of the holiday. Her father could have told her he had arranged it with her mother. With no phone, she would not be able to know otherwise. The question is, what is the next stage of Petrov's plan? He may not wish to stay long in one place, and so it is urgent to follow this lead quickly before he disappears again.'

'We'll make a detective of you yet, Comrade.'

Tatyana smiled. 'Your idea about the phone was very good work.'

'That's why I get paid the big bucks,' Ben replied. 'And now we know where to go next.'

'How will we get there?' Tatyana asked as they were leaving the IT suite.

'Leave that to me.'

'It is a long drive.'

'If you want to freshen up before we leave, my room has a guest bathroom. Feel free to use it.'

'Thank you. I am hungry, too. We should have lunch before we set off. The restaurants of the Ararat Park Hyatt are among—'

'The best in Moscow. I know. But we'll grab a bite to eat once we're on the road. This place is a little too public for my tastes right now. Ten minutes, and we're out of here.'

'You think they are still watching us?'

'You don't?'

'Do you still believe it is Kaprisky?'

If it was, Ben was deeply disappointed in the old man. As far as Ben was concerned, he'd been hired as an expert specialist Kaprisky could absolutely trust to get the job done, based on his past record. However understandable the family's panic and anguish over Valentina's disappearance, he resented having his progress covertly checked on at every step. He also resented being lied to. That was, *if* Kaprisky was behind the surveillance.

'I don't know,' he told her. 'But we'll find out soon enough, if they show their faces again.'

'You would ask them nicely, I suppose?'

'I've always found that the gentlest methods work best.'

'So I am learning, Major Hope.'

Chapter 20

Ben had said ten minutes, and he held her to it. Once they'd sneaked up to the Winter Garden Suite with nobody following them, he finally found a use for the remote-controlled blinds by closing them without risking being seen from the window. Tatyana disappeared into the guest bathroom while he set the coffee machine going, then took the world's fastest shower and changed in the master bedroom. Not bothering to shave he gulped down a cup of fresh black coffee potent enough to keep him fuelled for the next few hours, grabbed his bag and was waiting for her in the corridor when she emerged. Her short hair was still damp and spiked from the shower, and she hadn't had time to reapply her makeup. She tutted at herself in one of the corridor's fancy mirrors. 'I look terrible.'

Women. Ben had long since given up trying to understand why they did these things to themselves. He said, 'You look a lot better without the face paint. Let's go.'

The unknown watchers could be lying in wait for them anywhere, but fortunately it was a big hotel with too many nooks and crannies for a surveillance team to cover completely. Ben led Tatyana downstairs via a fire escape staircase. They avoided the main lobby and repaired to an empty conference room on the ground floor, where at his request she made two calls: the first, to the driver who'd chauffeured them from the airport; the second to the taxi firm that operated the yellow minivans with the dark tinted windows.

With typical Muscovite efficiency, a minivan arrived around the rear of the hotel exactly seven minutes later and the two of them hustled aboard like a couple of celebrities trying to escape the paparazzi. The kitchen staff must have been starting to wonder who they were. As the taxi and its invisible passengers sped off down Neglinnaya Street, Ben was scanning the pavements for anyone obviously scoping the hotel, and the road for anyone in pursuit. Neither materialised.

Twenty minutes' hack through the dense traffic, and the minivan pulled up at their destination, a dirty concrete underpass near the Lefortovo road tunnel on the city's third ring road. Ben overpaid the taxi driver handsomely, and the minivan sped happily away, leaving them standing there in the shadows of the underpass with the sound of traffic rumbling overhead.

They weren't alone. The hulking chauffeur had got there ahead of them, as arranged, and was leaning against the side of his Mercedes S-Class with a cigarette. He'd obviously had little to do except polish the car since they'd last seen him. The black paintwork gleamed like a mirror, even in the shadows. He peeled his hefty frame off the S-Class and muttered something in Russian to Tatyana.

'What's he say?' Ben asked.

'He says this is a hell of a strange place for a rendezvous and where do we want him to take us?'

'I never said he was going to take us anywhere. Please inform him that he's just been given the day off, so he can go off and wrestle bears or whatever he does for fun. We won't be needing him, we just want the car. We'll call him when we're done with it.'

Tatyana relayed the message, which was not especially well received.

'He says what if we damage it?'

'Tell him I've never damaged a car in my life,' Ben said. 'But if we break it, Kaprisky will send him a new one.'

The hulk balked for a moment, clenched his fists as though he might want to start something, then took note of the serious look in Ben's eye and reluctantly handed over the keys.

Ben asked Tatyana, 'How do you say, "Now take a hike" in Russian?' Tatyana made it simple. A jerked thumb and a whistle work in any language.

'I didn't like him anyway,' Tatyana said as the big man skulked furiously away. 'He has bad attitude. And he asked me four times to go out with him.'

'I thought the two of you were getting along well.'

'How do you say? Not my style.'

Ben wasn't about to ask what was. He got into the plush leather cabin and handed her his smartphone, now containing the images of key landmarks downloaded from Valentina's phone.

'You navigate, I'll drive.'

She huffed. 'Of course. The woman never drives.'

The Mercedes purred smoothly into life, as silky quiet as an electric turbine. Ben snicked it into drive and they took off. 'Have you ever driven in Russia before?' she asked.

'Not that I know of.'

'There are some things you should know. First, anyone can buy a driving licence without passing a test. Most Moscow drivers do not follow the rules, even if they are sober. There are many more fatal crashes here than in any other country. Nobody ever uses their turn signals, obeys the speed limits or stops for pedestrians. But if you fail to stop at a red light, officers of the traffic police are authorised to open fire on your vehicle.'

'Any more tips for me?' he asked.

She shrugged. 'Drive as if everyone wants to kill you, and you will be okay.'

'I appreciate the advice. Now where to?'

'Around the third ring, and then take the tunnel,' she said, pointing ahead, and soon they were joining the lanes of traffic speeding beneath the Yauza River. 'The Lefortovo Tunnel is over three kilometres long,' she informed him as they plunged into the darkness. 'One of the longest built.'

'There's a longer one in Dublin,' Ben said, glancing at her. Her lips had gone purple in the tunnel lights.

'In Ireland?'

'My mother's home country. It's not all green fields and potatoes.'

'Really? They have motor cars there?'

'You'd be amazed.' And so was Ben. It appeared that Comrade Nikolaeva might have a sense of humour after all.

'Oh. Careful of the water,' she said, pointing ahead. The fast-moving traffic was slowing for the deep slick that covered part of the tunnel floor, reflecting the headlights. Ben dabbed the brake in time, and they hit the water with a spray that forced him to turn on the wipers. 'So much for superior Russian architecture. Your tunnel has a leak.'

'More than one,' she admitted. 'In winter the road becomes frozen and causes many fatal accidents. They call it "the Tunnel of Death".'

'Remind me not to visit during the coming Ice Age.'

She looked at him. 'What Ice Age? They say the planet is getting warmer, not colder.'

'My friend the solar scientist would disagree.'

'It sounds as if you have some strange friends.'

He smiled. 'You have no idea.'

They finally emerged back into the sunshine, and, guided by Tatyana, Ben escaped the city. As fascinating as Moscow was, it felt good to leave the concrete jungle behind. They soon picked up the M10 Federal Highway, following in the footsteps of Yuri and Valentina's excursion the previous autumn. Tatyana fell silent, scrolling through the images on the smartphone, and as the conversation lagged Ben was left alone with his thoughts.

His confidence that they were on the right track was variable – but the simple truth was that, at this moment, the few fragile scraps they'd found were all they had to go on. He distracted himself from his worries about not finding Yuri and Valentina by worrying instead about the strangeness of the case. Then when he'd exhausted that track, he switched his thoughts back to the perplexing question of who had been trying to follow them. As he drove he was flicking his gaze constantly up to the rearview mirror, now and then varying his speed to let other vehicles pass and watch for the ones that stayed behind.

Nothing suspicious. No helicopters tracking overhead in the clear blue sky, either. The car-switch ploy had seemingly done the trick. Or else maybe he'd imagined the whole thing and he was just going crazy. Certainly, he was beginning to feel he had no real handle on what was going on. He couldn't remember the last time he'd felt such unease on what had started out as a fairly straightforward job. It was hard not to let the doubts creep into his mind that he shouldn't have let himself be talked into taking it at all.

He could always blame Jeff Dekker for that one.

They made a quick pit stop at a motorway services, topped

up their fuel on Kaprisky's expenses account and sat in the car munching cold sandwiches and sipping a non-alcoholic brew called *kvass*, which Tatyana insisted was much better for you than cola. Something else Ben had already decided to avoid if he ever returned to Russia.

Soon afterwards, they turned off the highway. Ben had seen nothing sinister and was sure nobody was following them, but the worry wouldn't pass. He went on driving in silence, puffing Gauloise smoke out of his open window, as Tatyana checked the landmarks against Valentina's photos and guided their route. He kept asking, 'Are you sure?', to which she kept frowning and saying she thought so.

As they left the major artery of the M10 behind them, Ben began to discover the truth of the old saying that the country's terrible roads had done more to hamper the advance of Hitler's Wehrmacht in World War II than the efforts of the Red Army. He was glad of his off-road driving skills, because their luxury mode of transportation had most certainly not been built with such a patchwork of rutted dirt and broken asphalt in mind. The only other vehicles they passed were an over-loaded poultry truck with a mangy dog hanging out of one window, and a pre-war tractor held together with rust and baling twine. The occupants of both, including the dog, all stared at the Mercedes. Not many strangers would tend to come out this way, let alone in an executive limousine worth ten or twenty times more than the value of the average roadside homestead.

'Want a sip?' he asked, taking out his whisky flask.

Tatyana pulled a face. 'It stinks like gasoline.'

Ben shrugged and let a swig of £600-a-litre Macallan Rare Cask Black wash away the revolting aftertaste of the *kvass*.

The deeper they ventured into the countryside, the more obvious were the signs of poverty everywhere. They passed through semi-derelict and half-abandoned backwater settlements slowly being reclaimed by forest, where wild boars roamed freely, scavenging for food and apparently quite unafraid of the occasional passing vehicle. On the edge of a dismal village whose Russian name Tatyana translated as 'Black Dirt', Ben saw an emaciated old man with arms like sticks struggling to replace a tyre on a truck that looked almost as old as he was, and didn't have the heart to drive on without stopping to help. The old man might have been the archetypal square-jawed, thick-chested, uncomplaining Soviet worker back in his heyday, but now he was a worn-out empty husk in danger of being blown away by the next gust of wind. He kept jabbering toothlessly in Russian as Ben crouched by the roadside, twisted off the rusty wheelnuts, hefted the punctured wheel up onto the truck's flatbed and manhandled the new one into place. When the job was done, the old man gave him a solemn nod of thanks and offered him a swig of some kind of clear alcohol from a dirty bottle. Ben took a drink, so as not to offend him, and got back into the Mercedes wiping the grime from his hands and wondering what the hell the old man's moonshine was made out of. Tatyana was watching Ben with curious eyes as they drove on.

'What?' he said.

'You like to help people, don't you?'

'If they need it,' he replied. 'If I can.'

'You are a very unusual man.'

The endless route climbed and fell, twisted and turned, on and on. Ben began to wonder if Yuri and Valentina had come this way at all. Kilometres from anywhere, a lone woman with snow-white hair and skin like tanned rhino leather sat on an upturned bucket outside a dilapidated wooden chapel at the roadside, smoking a corn-cob pipe and looking as though she was waiting for God. But God seemed to have vacated the place long ago, along with most everyone else. After a dozen more disappearing settlements, Ben was seriously questioning whether they were on the right road – if indeed it could be called a road – when Tatyana suddenly pointed and exclaimed, 'There. We found it. Did I not tell you?'

In Valentina's picture the broken-down church had been clearly visible through the shedding October branches; in summer it was half hidden by foliage and they could easily have driven right by without noticing. A little more of the roof had collapsed in the intervening months, but there was no doubting it was the same landmark they'd been looking for. A short way further on, Tatyana had Ben slow the car, and they were able to glimpse the abandoned country estate mansion through a copse of trees, a sorry sight as it gradually crumbled away to nothing.

'Now what?' Ben said.

'I would expect we will pass this lake soon,' Tatyana said, holding up the smartphone to remind him. 'It will be on the right side of the road, down below us in a valley.'

'But which road?' Ben said. He pointed ahead at the fork that split their chances fifty-fifty. If only the kid had taken more pictures. Or brought a full film crew along to record the entire trip for posterity.

'That one,' Tatyana said, nodding in the direction of the left-hand fork.

'Reason or intuition?'

'You do not trust me?' she said, cocking an eyebrow.

He shrugged. Fifty-fifty wasn't the worst odds. In any case, if they drew a blank they'd just come back on themselves and keep scouring every lane and track across this whole godforsaken wilderness until they got lucky. Ben was used to doing it the hard way, though he'd have preferred going about his business alone. 'You're the tour guide. The left fork it is.'

Four kilometres later, Tatyana let out a laugh of triumph as they topped a rise and the lake suddenly came into view, stretching smooth and blue between steeply rising banks of forest in the distance. 'See? You should be glad that you trusted me.'

'What would I do without you?'

'It cannot be much further to the farm,' Tatyana said. 'Keep going on this road and I am sure we will find it.'

Ben kept going, though if he'd known better he would have turned back. Nine kilometres later, as dusk was beginning to fall, they found the farm. That should have been the end of the journey. As he was soon to discover, it was only the beginning.

Chapter 21

The track snaked along the crest of a hill, overlooking a vista of forest out of which maybe four or five acres had been cleared to make way for the smallholding. Ben slipped the gearbox into neutral, cut the engine and let the Mercedes coast down the slight gradient until a stand of trees hid it from view of the farmhouse below.

He brought the car to a silent halt, got out, opened the back door and reached inside his bag for a compact but powerful pair of night vision binoculars he had carried on many kidnap rescue missions. 'Stay low and out of sight,' he instructed Tatyana, noting the peeved look she fired back at him.

Ben crept through the trees to the crumbling edge of the steep hillside, rested himself against a fallen trunk and drank in a clear aerial view of the farmstead. The image was bright and clear even in the failing light, and the aerial view confirmed right away that this was definitely the same smallholding he'd seen in Valentina's video clip from last October. Free of snow, the haphazard beaten earth paths that crisscrossed the property were visible, and the rust that covered the tin roof of the farmhouse itself. The land stretched over maybe three or four acres, the smallest of hobby farms, partitioned into paddocks and small fields by rickety fences and the whole encircled by barbed wire. The smallest area contained a couple of ramshackle chicken coops, though the poultry ranged free and Ben could see a few of the shabby-looking birds foraging here and there. The largest enclosure housed the same meagre flock of white, floppy-eared goats Valentina had been feeding in the video clip.

The farmhouse lay to the right of where she'd been standing, closer to the entrance gate at the narrowest part of the property. Ben edged forward to get a view of the whole building. It was the simplest kind of country dwelling, a good century and a half old and showing every day of it; a single low-slung storey that had had bits added on here and there during the years, creating a strange rambling layout. The outer walls were blackened by soot washed down by the rain. The battered front door was so low that anyone of average height or taller would have to stoop to pass through, as though it had been intended for impoverished nineteenth-century country folks with empty bellies and stunted growth – which, Ben thought, was doubtless the case. The windows were even tinier, likely made that way because they'd had to wait until sometime in the twentieth century to be fitted with glass panes to keep out the winter wind. A single metal stovepipe jutted up from the middle of the rusty tin roof. The bare ground around the farmhouse was littered with all the same junk – crates and old feed sacks and assorted gas bottles – that had been there last October, only now it was all overrun with a fresh summer growth of weeds springing up everywhere. An elderly cat lounged on a broken rocking chair outside the front door, watching the loose gang of chickens scratch about the yard in the dusk but obviously not considering them worth going after. The chickens let out the occasional squawk. The goats bleated and milled about in their paddock. A dog was barking incessantly inside the farmhouse.

The animals were the only visible or audible signs of life about the place. But someone was at home, all right. The same beaten-up pickup truck sat parked outside the farmhouse, in the exact same place, as though it hadn't turned a wheel since last October.

Next to it was the pale blue Volkswagen Beetle.

Yuri and Valentina were here. Ben resisted the urge to jump to his feet and go clambering down the hillside, march up to the door and wrench it open. He took a breath. One step at a time.

He was eyeing the Beetle through the binoculars when he sensed a presence next to him, and twisted around. Tatyana had made no sound at all creeping up behind him. Impressive, and unsettling. He didn't like being sneaked up on.

'We found them,' she whispered at his shoulder, peering down at the farmstead with hungry eyes.

Ben whispered back, 'I've seen no sign of the kid yet. That's all I'm interested in.'

The daylight was fading fast. As Ben went on watching, the glow of a lamp came on in the nearest window, offering him a limited view of the inside of the farmhouse. He could make out the corner of an old rustic pine table in what must be a living room or kitchen. Someone walked past the window, too fast to make out details, but someone large and heavyset. That someone made their way around the table and plonked themselves down in a chair beside it.

Ben recognised the portly figure of Yuri's rustic buddy from the photo. He'd traded his dirty boiler suit for grimy, faded blue dungarees and a tatty khaki army-surplus jumper. He reached across the table and slid something square, flat and white towards him. It was a newspaper, and obviously of interest to him, the way he hunched himself over to stare at the front page. After a few moments he looked up from the paper and began gesticulating and talking to someone else on the other side of the room. The dog was still barking away, showing no sign of running out of steam. Yuri's pal seemed irritated by the noise. After a minute he hefted himself brusquely from his chair and disappeared from view.

A moment later, the low front door creaked open. Yuri's rustic friend reappeared briefly in the doorway, along with the dog which streaked outside into the yard, barking and baying loudly. It was some kind of hunting dog, gangly and lean. Ben didn't recognise the breed but he knew right away the thing was trouble. Some dogs will rip into an intruder without hesitation, and this was one of them. The hound went dashing about the yard, filling the air with its explosive noise. The old cat, obviously an experienced veteran of past conflicts with the brute, slipped off the rocking chair and disappeared into the weeds.

This was a problem. The SAS had spent decades trying to work out effective ways of defeating guard dogs, without ever finding a wholly satisfactory solution. They were the best kind of low-budget early warning system going, able to detect a potential threat from crazy distances. Once they started barking, they wouldn't stop until someone made them. You couldn't go up and pacify them; killing the poor beasts was a noisy business at the best of times and only made you feel rotten afterwards; and feeding them drugged meat to knock them out only worked in bad action movies.

The dog was barking even more loudly. In towns and cities, the usual first thing people did was to yell at them to shut up. They didn't generally go to see why the dog was barking. In the countryside, it was a different matter. Farmers with livestock to protect were more likely to follow up on the alert signal, to see what, or who, might be lurking out there.

As were jumpy folks harbouring fugitives. Or the nervy fugitives themselves.

The door opened again and now the fat guy in the dunga-rees stepped out into the yard. Ben's night vision binocs offered a green-hued daylight view of him in the falling darkness. He was looking edgy. Edgy enough to have brought a torch and a shotgun outside with him. The gun was a far cry from short-barrelled urban street sweeper the barman of the Zenit had been toting, but even a farmer's old-fashioned knockabout double-hammer gun was one of the deadliest close-range weapons a civilian could own, anywhere in the world. This situation wasn't getting any easier to deal with.

The fat man stalked about the yard, shining the torchbeam this way and that, over towards the goats that were now huddling inside a makeshift shelter, over at the cars, running the light along the perimeter fence.

Then someone else came out of the farmhouse to join him. A smaller guy, plumpish but not fat, dressed more for the city than the country in jeans and a baggy shirt. The hair, the beard, the whole urban hippy look. Ben's first sighting of Yuri Petrov, in the flesh.

Tatyana whispered excitedly, 'Is that him?'

'That's our man, all right. Take a look.' Ben passed her the binocs for a moment, let her get a peek at their quarry, then snatched them back from her.

Yuri seemed even more agitated than his buddy. He was also just as well armed, maybe even better. The weapon in his hands was some kind of old bolt-action military rifle left over from World War II. It looked from a distance like a

Russian Mosin Nagant. With over forty million produced back in the day, it was hardly surprising that a few remained in civilian hands, still as effective now as then. Yuri was pointing the thing all over the place.

Jumpy, all right. Invisible as they were from their hidden position among the trees, Ben instinctively ducked and pressed Tatyana down into the bushes as the gun momentarily pointed their way. These old battle rifles could still kill a man stone dead a mile away and sometimes had worn mechanisms prone to go off inadvertently, especially in the wrong hands.

Now Yuri was stepping over to his friend, and the two of them were talking. They were much too far away for Ben to hear, even if he'd understood Russian.

'What do you see?' Tatyana hissed impatiently in his ear.

Ben was about to let her have the binocs back for another glance when he saw someone else appear in the lit-up doorway of the farmhouse. The smaller figure of a twelve-year-old girl wearing a sleeveless pink gilet jacket, standing there clutching at the doorframe and looking uncertainly out into the darkness, clearly worried by the sight of the guns.

Ben felt the air go out of his lungs.

It was Valentina.

Chapter 22

'I see her,' Ben whispered to Tatyana. 'She's scared, but she's all in one piece.'

'Let me look,' Tatyana insisted, but Ben was holding on to the binoculars. He scanned his field of vision away from the farmhouse and back across the yard. The fat man was still shining the torch about but losing interest. The dog hadn't stopped barking the entire time.

The fat man called its name. 'Alyosha!' Then called it again when he was flatly ignored, his voice angry now. At the tone of his voice the dog stopped barking and came slinking back. The fat guy grabbed it by its collar, hung on for a moment while he and Yuri took a last look around the yard, then dragged the reluctant Alyosha back to the farmhouse. Valentina had disappeared from the doorway. The men went inside, bringing the dog in with them. The door creaked shut and the yard fell back into darkness and silence. Ben put down the binoculars and eased himself back from the edge.

'Well, you found them,' Tatyana said in a low voice that was breathy with excitement. 'Excellent work. I am most impressed, Comrade Major.'

'We haven't got him yet,' Ben replied softly. 'Now's where the fun begins.'

'A peasant, a beatnik and a little girl, and you are frightened?'

'I wouldn't say frightened,' he replied. 'It's just that there are these things called bullets, and they hurt. I don't fancy copping a load of buckshot either. Or you. It won't do if I have to drag you all the way back to Moscow full of holes. What would your agency say?'

'Thank you for your concern, but I thought that you SAS men were born to take risks.'

'No, we're the most cautious people you'll ever meet. That's how we live to collect all the medals the Queen gives us.'

Tatyana's eyes widened. 'You have met the Queen?'

'We're like this,' Ben said, holding up crossed fingers. He pointed down the hillside. 'Let's get back to business. It's at least a two-gun household. We have to assume they have ammo, and that the country boy at least has done his fair share of potting rabbits and crows and isn't afraid to pull a trigger. Plus they're scared, and scared people are prone to shoot at shadows that might turn out to be us. Plus they have the ears and nose of that dog working for them. Not an easy proposition.'

'You have done this before, I see.'

'Once or twice.'

'Then I presume you have a plan?'

'It involves you. That okay?'

'For the man who always works alone, you certainly need my help a lot. What do you require from me this time?'

'Oh, just the pleasure of your company,' Ben said.

'I think I can manage that.'

'Then let's get it done. I'd like to have this kid back on her granduncle's plane by dawn.'

'And her father?'

'Not my concern. He can stay here with the goats and chickens, for all I care.'

Ben knew he needed to deal with the dog first. Back in the day, one of the tricks the SAS had used when evading enemy K9 teams was to work on the handler. Ben had schooled his troopers not to waste effort on eluding the dogs' almost preternatural sense of smell; forget it, it couldn't be done. Instead he taught them: 'Once they have your scent, race for the nearest steep climb and get up it as fast as you can. The dogs might be able to follow, but the handlers are generally much less fit than their animals. They won't be so inclined to chase you up the hill and they'll be worried about what might be waiting for them at the top.'

And it worked. More often than not, the handlers would rather call the dog back and pretend to their officers that it had lost the scent. Exploit the human, defeat the dog, win the day. Psychology was a powerful tool of warfare. And Ben could use that tonight, in a different way.

He was thinking about the anger in the big guy's voice when he yelled at the dog. And about the dog's reaction to its master's tone. Ben sensed an established pattern there. Maybe the dog had a habit of sounding off at nothing, raising false alarms and getting its owner riled. Ben could use that, too.

Darkness had fallen completely now. Ben hung the binoculars around his neck, left his bag and the rest of his kit inside the car and locked it, then slipped down the hillside, Tatyana following. 'Do not make me go near those goats,' she warned.

'I wouldn't dream of it.'

They spent the next several minutes working their way around the perimeter, keeping a good distance between themselves and the farmhouse. If Tatyana minded getting her nice clothes dirtied and torn by brambles, she didn't show it. The wind had picked up a little, blowing their way, which would help prevent the dog from getting their scent. As they passed around the rear of the farmhouse Ben saw that it had no windows on that side, nor any back door.

One way in, one way out. For Ben's purposes, that was good too.

Thirty metres from the goat enclosure, Ben crouched and found a stone about the size of a golf ball. The animals' pen was a shadowy rectangle in the darkness. He lobbed the stone at it, and heard the clang and clatter as it hit the pen's makeshift tin roof. The goats began bleating and milling about nervously at the disturbance. The humans inside the farmhouse might not have heard their commotion but sure enough, as expected, the dog started up its furious barking once more. Ben and Tatyana withdrew into the bushes, to a spot where they could see the yard. Ben readied the night vision binocs.

'Always the man who has the toys,' she whispered.

'Jealousy is an ugly thing, Comrade,' he whispered back.

'I wish you would stop calling me that.'

'I will, if you stop calling me Major.'

Moments later, Ben heard the farmhouse door open, and voices, and the explosive barking of the dog as it was released and went charging straight for the goat pens, startling the poor creatures even more. Through his binocs Ben could see Yuri and the fat guy patrolling the yard with their longarms. Two minutes, three minutes, and their body language was changing as they began to understand it was a false alarm. The fat guy was getting grumpy. He shouted for the dog, was ignored again, repeated its name at twice the volume, and like before the dog came slinking back with its head low: canine sign language for 'Okay, okay, no need to get all riled up'. They returned to the farmhouse, the door closed and all that could be heard was the anxious goats shifting about.

'Come on,' Ben whispered. They continued working their way around the perimeter and within a few more minutes had circled the property, positioning themselves behind the wire fence directly opposite the front of the farmhouse where they could observe the door and windows. One window was curtained with only the faintest glow emanating from inside, while the other was brightly lit up and casting a yellowish shaft of light over the parked vehicles outside. Through the binocs, Ben could see no more sign of Valentina but her father was clearly visible, sitting at the table with a glum expression on his hairy face as he gazed pensively at the same newspaper that his buddy had been looking at earlier. There was a bottle of vodka in front of him, and a glass that he kept refilling and knocking down. The old Mosin Nagant was propped against a sideboard within easy reach. Portrait of the happy fugitive celebrating his successful escape.

'One more time should do it,' Ben muttered to Tatyana.

He picked up a stone from the dirt and threw it towards the parked vehicles. It pinged off the bodywork of the Beetle, kicking off the same routine all over again. The thunderous barking must have been deafening inside the farmhouse.

The door flew open. The hound burst out, filling the night with its noise and making straight for the vehicles. He was an excellent guard. Ben felt sorry for him, because he knew what was going to happen next.

Chapter 23

The fat guy had had enough. Storming from the doorway in a rage he propped his shotgun against the wall and seized the dog roughly by its collar. Yelling and cursing, he started dragging the poor animal over to a corrugated tin shed adjoining the house near the parked pickup truck and Yuri's VW Beetle. He yanked open the shed door.

Then the fat man froze as he heard the distinct *click-click* of the shotgun's twin hammers being cocked, five yards behind him.

Still clutching the dog, he slowly turned around to face the terrifying sight of a shadowy figure standing in the yard, pointing his own gun at him. The figure was joined by a second as Tatyana hopped over the fence.

Inside the farmhouse, Yuri Petrov had got up from the table. He returned to his seat a moment later and went on looking at the newspaper and drinking his vodka as the strains of an old Dr Hook number began to thump through the farmhouse. Anything was better than listening to dogs barking.

Not taking his eyes off the fat guy, Ben said to Tatyana, 'Tell him not to let go of Alyosha. If he does, what happens is on him.' Tatyana relayed the message in Russian.

'I understand, man. I speak English good.' Which the fat guy did, though with a heavy accent made even thicker by the quaver of fear in his voice. His arm was getting stretched as the dog strained furiously to be let go, but he had a solid grip on the animal's collar.

Ben said, 'Then be a good boy, do what you were about to do and close Alyosha in the shed. I don't want to hurt him. You're a different matter, so no tricks.'

The fat guy's hands were shaking so badly that Ben worried the dog would get away from him, but in the end he managed to close up the shed with its prisoner safely locked inside. Alyosha was in a frenzy in there, claws raking at the door. Ben wanted to take him home, as a fine addition to the guard pack at Le Val. The fat guy turned to face Ben, raised his quivering hands and managed to mumble the words 'Don't shoot me, man'.

Ben kept the gun aimed steadily at his chest. It had a trigger for each hammer and he had fingers on both. 'What's your name?'

'Grisha Solokov,' came the rapid reply.

'Where's the child?'

A look of mixed surprise and consternation came over Grisha's face. He pointed at the other window, the curtained one.

'She is just a kid. Please don't—'

'Shut up and do as I say, Grisha, or I'll blow you in half. Understand?'

Grisha was sweating and his legs seemed ready to buckle under him. 'W-what do you want?'

Ben had weighed the options. If he and Tatyana burst inside the farmhouse, Yuri might very well snatch that rifle he was keeping close by, and start blasting in all directions. Assuming he knew how to work it. Ben couldn't afford to assume differently. If that happened, there was no telling who might get hurt, including the child.

Ben had to find a way to get Yuri outside.

He said to Grisha, 'I want you to call your pal out here.'

Through the farmhouse window, the pal was still deeply absorbed in what must have been the world's most fascinating newspaper, and seemed completely oblivious of what was going on outside. He refilled his glass, drained it, refilled it once more. He was getting drunker but the rifle was still just as close to hand.

'You have come to kill him, yes?' Grisha quavered.

The question struck Ben as genuinely odd. Why would anyone want to kill Yuri? He covered his surprise and replied, 'You first, if you don't obey me.'

Grisha held out both palms. He blinked sweat from his eyes. 'Okay. Okay. Please. I will do it. What do I say?'

'You say, "Hey, Yuri, come and take a look at this." Keep it light. And remember, the lady speaks Russian. Warn him, and you're dead.' Ben turned to Tatyana. 'The thing you did at the Zenit. Think you can do that again for me? Without doing any damage?'

Her eyes sparkled in the light from the window. Delighted to be of service once again, she moved fast and silently past the door and pressed close to the wall beside the doorway.

Ben nodded to Grisha. 'Go.'

Grisha staggered towards the lit-up window, rapped a trembling knuckle on the glass, and inside the farmhouse Yuri looked up sharply from his newspaper. Grisha called to him in Russian, swallowing back the terror that threatened to strangle his voice. Nonetheless, Ben had known Yuri would be bound to sense something was up.

Yuri grabbed the rifle and darted away from the table, fully alerted. Now it was fifty-fifty as to whether he'd grab his daughter from the other room and try to hole up protectively inside the farmhouse, or act the hero and come storming outside to face whatever threat he clearly thought awaited him there. Ben was hoping for the latter.

Yuri acted the hero.

The front door opened and he jumped out, feverishly working the bolt of the old rifle. His eyes flew wide open in horror as he saw Ben standing there pointing the hammer gun at Grisha. Yuri's rifle barrel swung up and he rammed the butt into his shoulder in readiness to shoot; and then he was tumbling backwards and the weapon was torn from his hands as Tatyana came up fast and hard behind him.

Her disarming move was as slick as it had been at the Zenit. Maybe even slicker. Yuri Petrov landed heavily on his back and looked up to see the rifle turned on him, its muzzle pointing at his face twelve inches away. He opened his mouth to scream, but before any sound came from his lips Ben had rushed in and stifled it with a clamped hand so as not to alarm the child in the other room.

Yuri's eyes rolled wildly and he tried to struggle, but Ben forced him back down and pinned him to the ground.

'Yuri Petrov. You're not as hard a man to find as you think you are. Now I'm going to take my hand away and you're not going to yell. There's no need to scare the child.'

Yuri stared up at Ben. 'I . . . I . . . I'm not Yuri Petrov. You have the wrong person.'

'Come on, Yuri. You're found, have the guts to admit it.'

'Who sent you?' Yuri demanded, suddenly full of indignation. 'Bezukhov? Tell him I don't have it yet. Tell him to go and fuck himself. Tell him what you like.' Then his defiant act subsided again as fast as it had appeared. 'Just don't hurt my little girl. Please! I'm sorry I ran. I was scared. I—'

Ben was about to say, 'You don't have what yet? What are you talking about?'

Just then Valentina appeared, framed in the light of the

doorway as before, only now she looked much more distraught. Seeing these strangers threatening her father she let out a sharp cry and ran outside. She threw herself at Ben and started throwing wild punches and kicks. Tatyana grabbed her and pulled her away. Yuri was yelling 'Don't harm her!' Grisha was advancing with his fists clenched. Ben warned him back with the shotgun.

'I didn't come here to hurt anyone, Yuri,' he said. 'Not you, not your daughter. But there's something else going on here. And now you're going to tell me what the hell this is really all about.'

Chapter 24

They all went inside. Ben marched the two men at gunpoint into the farmhouse's tiny living room. Aside from the table, there were just a few flimsy sticks of furniture, a small TV perched on a beer crate, and a ratty sofa. He trussed their wrists behind their backs with cable ties, then made them sit side by side on the sofa. Neither tried to resist him. When the two men were effectively out of action, Ben laid both firearms on the table, where he could still get to them quickly if needed.

Yuri demanded, 'If Bezukhov didn't send you, who did? Are you the police?'

'Not a chance,' Ben said.

'Then who the hell are you?'

'When guys like you disappear off the face of the earth with someone else's child, I'm the guy they send to deal with it. You didn't stop to think whose grandniece you were making off with?'

Yuri Petrov's jaw dropped open. The news that he was suspected of abducting his own child was like a kick in the guts. 'She's my kid,' he protested, close to tears.

'I'll give you a tip, Yuri. Next time you smash your daughter's smartphone because you thought it'd cover your tracks, make sure nobody can put the pieces back together again.

Especially when there's a whole trail of photo and video files leading straight to your hidey-hole. You're not half as clever as you think you are.'

Meanwhile, Tatyana was doing all she could to quieten the tearful, near-hysterical Valentina. Ben had never seen an alleged kidnap victim so upset that their abductor had been apprehended by the forces of justice.

Turning to the child he crouched down to make himself less threatening, and spoke in a soft, calm voice, knowing she understood and was fluent in English. 'Valentina, I understand you're scared and confused. Calm down and let me show you something.' He reached into his jacket pocket and took out the photo he'd been carrying since Le Mans. Valentina peered at it, and he could see the understanding in her intelligent eyes. Nobody but Eloise could have given him the picture.

'Your mother asked me to come and find you. She's worried that you didn't come home when you should have.'

'I'm here with Papa! She knows that!'

'She's worried about your dad as well,' Ben said, shooting a glance at Yuri. 'So is your granduncle Auguste. They're afraid he might have got himself into some kind of trouble.'

'Stay away from her!' Yuri yelled. 'Valentina, don't listen to him!'

'I'm your friend, Valentina,' Ben said. 'And your father's, too, even if he doesn't realise it.'

Valentina looked at her father, then at Ben, then at the photo. She was no longer crying, but her eyes were red and her cheeks were flushed and wet. 'Are you working for Tonton?'

In France, 'tonton' was a child's familiar expression for 'uncle'. Ben had to smile at the thought of the great Auguste Kaprisky being called by that nickname. 'That's right, Tonton sent me here,' he explained in the same gentle tone. 'I flew over on his plane, just like you. And you and I are going to travel back to France together, and I'm going to take you back to your mummy, and that lovely house you live in, and your horse, and all your nice things, and you'll be able to tell Adalie all about the big adventure you had. Paul, too.'

Valentina was unable to resist blushing at the mention of her secret boyfriend. 'What about Papa?'

'Papa lives here in Russia. He can't come with us. You know that, don't you?'

'But I like being here with him.'

'You can come back and visit him anytime you want,' Ben said, knowing it was a wildly false promise.

'Don't listen to a word he says!' Yuri yelled from the sofa, struggling purple-faced against his bonds. 'He's working for them!'

Ben stood up and walked over to glare down at the pair. 'If I'd been sent to eliminate you, Yuri, do you think we'd be having this conversation? You and Grisha here would already be in the ground. So get that notion out of your head and talk to me.'

'Mind games,' Grisha growled. 'The old trick.'

Outside, the dog still hadn't stopped barking. The shed's thin wooden slats were doing little to muffle the commotion.

Ben shook his head. 'I don't really care if you believe me or not. My name's Ben Hope. I'm not a cop, never was, never will be. I'm a former British serviceman living in Normandy, France. The old man is a former security client and a friend of mine. As a favour to him, I'm here to fetch the child home safely to her mother, nothing more, nothing less.'

He paused to let those words sink in, then pointed at Tatyana. 'This is Miss Nikolaeva, a private investigator from Moscow hired to find you after you absconded from your apartment. You're in deep shit, Yuri. There's no telling what host of charges might be brought against you as a result of this little escapade. The moment Valentina's home safe and sound, you're a marked man. Kaprisky will bury you.'

'I didn't . . . I thought . . .'

'You didn't think,' Ben said. 'You didn't stop for one moment to consider the consequences of your actions, or what kind of shitstorm one of Europe's most powerful men would unleash against you in retaliation. You only reacted, without a second thought. Because when people are as frightened as you obviously are, logic goes out of the window. What are you so afraid of, Yuri? Who's Bezukhov? Who are you running from?'

Yuri stared up at Ben. His whole face was trembling with tension and his eyes were rimmed with red. There was absolutely no doubt in Ben's mind that he was being totally sincere.

'If you know Auguste Kaprisky even half as well as I do,' Ben said, 'then you know that when he's not being dear, sweet Tonton he's the most vengeful, ruthless, cold-hearted man you'll ever meet in your life. There are very few people he trusts, but I happen to be one of them. I can persuade him to ease off on you. In return, I need to know the truth. If you're in trouble, I might even be able to help.'

'Why would you help him, man?' Grisha spat. 'You don't even know him.'

'For the sake of the family,' Ben said. 'And for Valentina. There's been enough hurt already. So talk. You owe this Bezukhov money? It is over drugs? Gambling? It doesn't matter. He can be paid off, with interest.'

To Ben's surprise, Yuri Petrov suddenly burst out laughing.

'Oh, God. This is too much. You really have no idea, do you?'

'I'm on the level here,' Ben said. 'Help me to help you.'

The laughter stopped as abruptly as it had begun. Yuri fixed him with a look of the utmost intensity. 'You think you're so clever, finding me. But really you're so blind. You think you can take Valentina away, just like that?'

'It's my job,' Ben said. 'I aim to finish it.'

'You're going to look after her, huh?'

'She'll be safe with me. You have my word on that.'

Yuri sneered. 'Your word. Your *word*? Bullshit. You don't have a clue. You wouldn't even make it back to Moscow, let alone out of the country. They're watching, don't you see? They're watching everything.'

'They?'

'Yeah, *they*,' Grisha snorted. 'Who else?'

'They'll catch you,' Yuri went on. 'Before you even know it, they'll be on you. And they'll take her and use her to force me to come out of cover, and then that'll be the end of me. They'll torture me to death to find out what I know. Don't you fucking get it?'

Valentina had started crying again. She forced her way past Ben and flung her arms around her father's neck, pressing her face into his shoulder, tears streaming down her little cheeks. 'I don't want anyone to hurt you, Papa!'

'Cut me loose,' Yuri said. 'At least let me hold my little girl.'

Ben took the clasp knife from his pocket. Yuri held his bound wrists away from his back so that the cable tie could be slashed. When his hands were free he hugged Valentina for all he was worth and he began crying, too. 'Nobody's going to hurt me, baby. I promise.'

'This is called a sign of good will,' Ben said as he cut

Grisha's wrists free as well. 'Don't even think of abusing it.'

'Asshole,' Grisha muttered under his breath as he rubbed the circulation back into his hands.

At last, the dog had gone quiet outside. The silence of the night enveloped the remote little farmhouse, just the occasional bleat of a goat in the distance.

'Enough messing around,' Ben said to Yuri. 'Are you going to tell me what this is about, or am I going to have to torture it out of you myself?'

Yuri blinked away the last of his tears. 'Be careful what you wish for, my friend. Once you learn the truth, it can't be unlearned. Are you ready for that?'

'Don't trust this *ublyudok*,' Grisha hissed at his friend. 'I still think he's one of them.'

'I was born ready,' Ben said to Yuri, ignoring Grisha.

'And there are things you don't know about me that would surprise you, as well,' Yuri replied. 'And others.'

'Such as?'

'What if I don't want to tell you?'

'What if you really have no choice in the matter?' Ben said.

Yuri considered for a moment, fixing Ben with the same intense look. Then he ran his fingers through his little girl's hair and tenderly kissed the top of her head. 'Sweet Pea, why don't you go back to the other room and read your book for a while longer? We have some grown-up stuff to talk about.'

'Okay,' Valentina sniffed reluctantly. She wiped her face with her sleeve and peeled herself out from her father's arms. Tatyana gave her a smile, which was not returned. Valentina walked self-consciously past the adults, over to the rickety slat door that led to the bedroom, grasped the old iron handle and disappeared inside with a last doe-eyed glance at her father.

Yuri waited for the bedroom door to creak shut and close with a click of the latch. With the girl out of earshot he said to Ben, 'I can guess what the old man probably told you about me. He thinks I'm just a nobody, a waste of time. Right?'

'Those weren't his exact words,' Ben said. 'But it's fair to say you haven't exactly endeared yourself to him.'

'Yeah, well, maybe that's what I wanted him to think. Him and my dear ex-wife too.'

Ben stared at him. 'And why, pray, would you want your spouse and her family to think that about you?'

'To protect the truth,' Yuri replied with a flash of pride. 'Like I said, there are things about me that might surprise a few folks.'

'No kidding,' Grisha interjected.

Yuri nodded. 'It's true. For a long time I even kept the truth a secret from this guy here, my best friend. Because in my former profession we were trained to secrecy, and the training sticks.'

'You shouldn't tell him,' Grisha said, jerking his chin Ben's way.

'I need to,' Yuri replied. 'Then maybe he'll understand why I can't let him take my little girl away from me.'

Chapter 25

Slowly, deliberately, Yuri Petrov related to Ben the secret of the double life he'd been leading throughout his marriage to Eloise, and the reason for the lie. Ben didn't allow a flicker of astonishment to show on his face when Yuri revealed that he'd worked for years as an agent of the Russian secret service.

Yuri's story was frank and convincing in every detail, though that didn't necessarily make it the truth, as far as Ben was concerned. However, if Yuri was lying, he was putting on a fine show. As candid as he was about his former career as an intelligence operative and code-cracker, he was even more so when it came to describing the long, painful decline that had led to his wanting out.

'I came to hate that whole world. I was ashamed that I'd ever played a part in it. It felt so good to get away. I almost managed to forget what I'd once been.'

'We're all pawns of the New World Order, brother,' Grisha said sympathetically. 'It's like I always say. If they don't get us one way, they get us another.'

'They got me, all right,' Yuri grunted. 'No matter how much I tried to get away from them, there they were again. And there I was.' He sighed and shook his head as he retold the chilling moment when the agents had found him and taken him to meet his former chief, Antonin Bezukhov.

Ben found it hard to imagine this man as a spy. Then again, the perfect spy would be the man nobody could picture in that role. But what was an ex-spook for Russian intelligence doing holed up in a backwater hideout with a conspiracy nut spouting about the New World Order?

Ben asked, 'What did Bezukhov want from you?'

'To tell me a story. The story of a British spy who got caught in Moscow back during the Cold War, in the winter of 1957. He was posing as a Russian citizen under the false identity of Pyotr Kozlov. His real name was Ingram, Captain Ingram, of SIS, the British Secret Intelligence Service.'

Ben was listening intently but still thoroughly mystified. 'Am I to assume that this old tale has some relevance to today?'

'Oh yes. Keep listening, okay? Ingram was arrested by Soviet agents and detained in the old Lubyanka prison, where they tortured him and would have executed him, too, if he hadn't died under interrogation. They weren't able to extract much information about the nature of his mission. That was that. Just another forgotten horror story. Just another bunch of secret shit that lay hidden for years, decades. Until now.'

Yuri paused, sighed as though the weight of the world were crushing down on his shoulders, then continued. 'Not so long ago, some workmen were demolishing an old house in the crumbling section of the city where, it so happens, Ingram was arrested in 1957. They found a piece of paper. A cryptogram. Code, cipher, call it what you want.'

'And that's where you come in?'

'Bezukhov gave me the job of decoding it,' Yuri replied bitterly. 'Why me? Good question. Because I was so good, back in the day? Or because being off the reservation for so long made me so easy to get rid of, when the job was done? Take a guess. Whether I cracked it or not, they were handing me a death sentence. I was so stupid, I didn't realise that until it was too late. Some part of me wanted to relive those glory days, I suppose. I *had* to break that cipher. I worked at it night and day. Drove myself crazy over the damned thing.'

'But you beat it.'

'In the end, yes, I did. It was me or it. There's a winner and a loser.' Yuri paused to savour his moment of triumph, then his shoulders sagged again and he sighed. 'Some victory, hey? Crack the cipher, find out the truth, and Bezukhov would have me killed the moment I reported back to him. Fail, admit defeat, go back to Bezukhov and tell him it was too tough for me, I'd still have been a dead man.'

Yuri looked Ben in the eye. 'And if I tell the secret to you, so are you, my friend. Until that moment when you hear the truth, the only thing protecting you is your ignorance. Once you know what's in the cipher, and what it led me to discover in an old abandoned warehouse the night I finally cracked it, the death sentence is handed to you as well. Like some kind of ancient demon curse that damns anyone who comes into contact with it.'

'You must have been a cryptologist too long, Yuri. You're talking in riddles.'

'You don't believe me, do you?'

'Truthfully? I think you're full of shit.'

'Oh, you want to see some proof of what these people are capable of? Let me show you something.' Yuri pointed across the room, at the table. 'The newspaper.'

Tatyana stepped to the table and picked up the paper that both Yuri and Grisha had been scrutinising with such interest earlier. She frowned at it for a moment and then handed it to Ben, saying, 'It is *Metro Moscow*, a daily tabloid for local city news. The date is from last week.'

170

Predictably, not a word of the Cyrillic writing on the front page meant anything to Ben. He looked in puzzlement at Yuri, who said, 'See the picture?'

'I see a picture of some geeky Russian pop star with silly hair,' Ben replied.

'Not that one. The small one, below, with the sidebar article.'

'A priest?'

'A *dead* priest. Found hanging from a bridge the night before, having apparently committed suicide.'

Ben glanced again at the picture, a grainy head-and-shoulders portrait shot of a grey-haired, slightly chubby man in the garb of a Catholic priest. Nothing remarkable about it whatsoever, other than the circumstances of his death, the Church taking a somewhat dim view of suicide among its clergy. Ben understood that this was the newspaper article that had seemed to so fascinate both Yuri and Grisha earlier, but he didn't understand why. 'Okay, a priest killed himself. What's that got to do with us?'

'Only the fact that I was probably the last one to see him alive,' Yuri shot back. 'And that he's dead only because I did see him.'

'This secret of yours, you told him?'

Yuri shook his head. 'I wanted to, so much. Or did I? I don't even know. The stress of what I'd found out was driving me insane. I didn't know who else to talk to at that point. I needed to confess, to ask for help. But they were already onto me by then, and watching the church.' He clasped his hands in front of him as though praying, squeezing until the knuckles showed white. He closed his eyes for a moment, anguish etched into his face, then reopened them and fixed on Ben. 'The worst thing is knowing that poor old man died for no reason, except that he and I shared a few moments together. I wish I could have warned him. It was all happening so fast. Do you think, if I'd known they were onto me already, I'd have gone straight from the church to pick up Valentina at the airport and take her home to the apartment? It was only when I saw the paper, the next day, that I realised the danger we were in. We left Moscow the same day.'

'But not before stopping off at the apartment on the way,' Ben said, still highly sceptical. 'Do people fleeing from hired government killers normally take risks like that?'

'I could only hope I was still half a step ahead of them,' Yuri explained. 'I thought I'd been cautious. I was so wrong. Only by pure chance, we got away.'

Ben narrowed his eyes and waited for more.

'They tried to get us. Not once, but twice. The first time was shortly after we drove away from the apartment. There was a car following us, a black Mercedes.'

'It's always a black Mercedes,' Grisha said, shaking his head in disgust. 'Like they don't even try to hide any more.'

Ben might have pointed out that he and his companion had just driven there in the very same kind and colour of vehicle, but he decided to withhold that information.

Yuri went on, 'They must have been watching the place the whole time we were in there, seen us go inside, seen us leave, just waiting for the right moment to pounce. Why they didn't spring their trap when we were inside, I don't know. They might have thought I was armed and would start shooting. That's the only explanation I can think of, that they wanted to keep it quiet. I mean, not even they can get away with kidnapping a father and child in broad daylight.'

'You obviously managed to get away, or we wouldn't be having this conversation.'

'I didn't think we'd make it. As the car kept tailing us, I could see no escape. I just kept driving aimlessly around the city, terrified that we'd eventually run out of fuel and then they'd grab us and take me away to be tortured. What would happen to Valentina? That was all I could think about. I was so scared I could hardly see straight to drive or hold the wheel steady. Next thing I knew, we were entering the Lefortovo road tunnel. Then something incredible happened. I mean, things happen there all the time, but—'

'Stick to the point.'

'I was going about eighty kilometres an hour, foot to the floor, as fast as my car can go. Most of the other traffic was overtaking, but the black Mercedes was stuck right on our tail. I could see the shapes of the two agents in the front. Just then, a car came speeding up behind us, much faster than the rest of the traffic. A Porsche, I think it was. Some rich reckless maniac, but I remember thinking that if I'd had a fast car like him I'd have been going like a bat out of hell too. As he swerved to overtake, he hit a pool of standing water. The Yauza River leaks in from all over the place.'

'Just tell it,' Ben said tersely.

'The Porsche's wheels must have aquaplaned on the surface of the water and lost grip. Just as he was about level with the Mercedes, the driver spun out of control. He slammed into the Mercedes and the impact drove it into the side wall of the tunnel. Next thing, all I could see in my mirrors was cars skidding and piling into one another and wreckage flying everywhere. I just put my foot down and got out of there. It was terrifying.'

Yuri shook his head at the memory. 'We sped out of the city. No more sign of the Mercedes following us. As much as I wanted to believe we were home free, I knew they wouldn't give up so easily. They have eyes everywhere. The second attempt happened when we stopped for fuel, just before we left the Federal Highway. We needed some provisions for our journey, so I grabbed a few things. Valentina had to go to the bathroom and I was waiting for her to come back out when two men walked inside the building from the car park and approached me. Dark glasses. Short hair. More of Bezukhov's thugs. One said, "Mr Petrov, please come with us." I thought I was done. I thought maybe I could stall them for a moment, so I asked who they were, if they were police, if they could show me ID. Then the other one pulled out a gun. Held it close to him, like this, so nobody would see. There were too many people around. He said, "Let's go, moron," and waved towards their car parked outside.'

'How did you get out of it?'

'Valentina,' Yuri replied, as though he still could hardly believe it himself. 'She'd left the bathroom and was making her way back to find me when she saw them getting out of their car. She ran back to the bathroom, closed herself in a stall, climbed up on the toilet seat and managed to wriggle through a narrow window and sneak around the side of the service station building to their car without being seen. While I was stalling for time, convinced I was done for, she let down two of their tyres. Next, she started screaming at the top of her voice and pointing at the two men who were trying to grab me, raising a whole big commotion. A woman cashier saw the gun and started going hysterical, thinking an armed robbery was taking place, or Chechen separatists had come to kill everyone, or God knows what. Some young guy tried to intervene and the thug with the gun pistol-whipped him right in the face. People were running, yelling, pure chaos, in the middle of which I managed to break away and make a run back to the Beetle. Valentina was already there. We sped away. The thugs tried to chase after us, but they couldn't get far on two flat tyres. When we left the highway a few kilometres down the road, we stopped to switch the number plates from the Beetle for ones that I stole off an old farm truck. There was no way they could track us on these backroads. All the same, I didn't stop shaking until we got here. Two lucky escapes. More than lucky. I think it means God intended for me to get away. Do you believe in miracles?'

'I think you owe more to your daughter than you do to the Lord above,' Ben said.

'Then you accept that I'm telling the truth? You believe me now?'

'Let's run back through the facts. You're claiming that the Russian secret service murdered a man and tried twice to abduct you and the kid, with the intention of torturing you to death to find out what you discovered from a Cold War code they employed you to crack for them.'

'That's the essence of it.'

'It would help if I understood just what the hell you've got that's so valuable to them.'

Grisha was shaking his head, but Yuri reached into his pocket. 'I was coming to that. Here it is. The red pill moment. The point of no return. I warned you, but you wanted to know. Your funeral, my friend.'

Ben watched as Yuri produced an old tobacco tin, so speckled with rust that the manufacturer's logo was almost obliterated. It looked like an old piece of junk that had spent the last few decades slowly rotting in a damp corner.

Yuri said, 'I discovered this in an old warehouse in Moscow, exactly where Ingram, the British spy, had planted it all those years ago in 1957, not long before his capture. The cipher was simply a set of directions designed to lead his colleagues to its hiding place. Needless to say, they never found it.'

Ben asked, 'So what's inside?'

Yuri unscrewed the lid of the tin. Inside was a modern flash drive that was unlikely to have been left for fifty years in an old warehouse. Next to it was a tiny roll of what Ben thought looked like microfilm, though he'd never seen one before. But what Yuri wanted to show him was wrapped inside a folded square of rough cloth, which he spread open with his fingers to reveal a small metal object nestling within.

As though handling a precious stone, Yuri lifted it out and laid it delicately in Ben's outstretched palm. Ben ran a fingertip along its shiny metal surface. The object was just over half a centimetre in length, smooth and oblong like a medicine capsule, cold and almost weightless in his cupped hand.

'Congratulations. You just joined the exclusive club of people who have actually set eyes on one of these gadgets. With any luck, you may even live to regret it.'

'With any luck, you might actually tell me what this is,' Ben said.

'Evidence,' Grisha said.

Ben's eyes flicked from one man to the other. Both looked grimly serious. 'Evidence of what?'

Yuri replied, 'Of everything truth seekers have been saying about what these bastards are into, and have been for years. That little thing you're holding in your hand, it's the confirmation of all our worst fears.'

Grisha said, 'It's the fucking Holy Grail of conspiracy theories, man.'

Ben gazed down at the smooth, shiny object in his palm, then looked back up to meet the deadly earnest eyes of the two men.

Yuri and Grisha exchanged a brief conspiratorial glance. Grisha said, 'You really going to tell him?'

'We said we would tell the world about this,' Yuri replied to his friend. 'Why not let him be the first?'

'What about her?' Grisha asked, pointing a chubby finger at Tatyana.

Tatyana hadn't spoken a word for several minutes, just standing to one side of the room with a thoughtful look on her face. 'She's with me,' Ben said. 'What you say to me, you say to her.'

Yuri leaned close to Ben. His eyes were full of fear. They darted towards the window, as if he thought that enemy agents might be out there in the night, listening to every word.

He said, 'What do you know about mind control?'

Chapter 26

Ben's silence filled the room. Tatyana remained quiet, too, frowning at the two men on the sofa.

'What a relief,' Ben said at last. 'I thought maybe you were going to tell me this was an artifact recovered from the wreckage of an alien spacecraft that crashed in Soviet territory sixty years ago. The USSR's very own answer to Roswell and Area 51. And that this little metal bean was a special chip containing all of the aliens' knowledge, which could save humanity from nuclear disaster and global warming.'

'I told you not to show it to this prick,' Grisha said angrily to Yuri. 'He's not going to take anything we tell him seriously.'

'Oh, mind control is no joke,' Ben said. 'It happens all the time. Fifty million people are sitting watching a TV channel and an ad comes on, full of happy faces enjoying Coca-Cola in the sunshine and telling them how happy it could make them, too. Next thing you know, half of these idiots are guzzling the foul-tasting swill like there's no tomorrow. Mind control. That's about as sinister as it gets.'

'You're a pretty clever guy,' Yuri said, 'for such a fool.'

Grisha shot Ben a sneer. He said to Yuri, 'Let me talk to him, man. Maybe I can convince him.'

Ben looked at Grisha. 'So if your pal here is the runaway spy, what does that make you?'

'He's an expert,' Yuri shot back in his friend's defence. 'He's spent years studying this stuff. Nobody knows it like he does.'

'If I need a lesson in milking goats, I'll be sure to give the professor here a call.'

'You never heard of Truth Radio?' Grisha grumbled at Ben. 'Part of the Freedom Network, broadcasting on short-wave and across the internet to twelve million listeners across Russia and Europe?' He jabbed a thumb to his bulky chest. 'You're looking at its founder, host and CEO. The man the New World Order globalist elite lives in fear of, because one day the truth is gonna bring 'em down. I run the whole show myself out of my trailer, deep in the woods where the fuckers could never find it.'

'A trailer.'

Grisha nodded proudly. 'Oh yes. Got the works out there, all totally hidden. They've wanted to close me down for years, but I'm too clever for them.' He slyly tapped a finger against the side of his nose.

In his dungarees and holey jumper, chicken shit all over his boots, few people would have mistaken Grisha Solokov for a successful entrepreneur and media personality, let alone the scourge of power-mongering global conspirators or a major threat to any sovereign country's national security. A large part of Ben wanted to get out of this madhouse, grab the girl and speed back to Moscow, jump on Kaprisky's jet and go home. Another part of him was too intrigued not to listen to what crazy Grisha had to say.

Ben would later curse himself for his curiosity.

'Mind control,' Grisha repeated. 'Brainwashing. Coercive persuasion. Psychological programming. Re-education. Call it what you like, man, it's real and it exists, and it ain't just about selling you Coca-Cola. Look it up on Wikipedia or wherever. First thing you'll see, they're telling you it's a *non-scientific concept*, therefore something phony and suspicious that you should avoid, like fake news.' He spat. 'Bullshit! That's mind control right there, instructing you what to think, persuading you not to consider for one moment what's actually happening all around us in the world. See, when you control people's thoughts, you control everything. Tell 'em what to believe, what to do, who to vote for, who to support and venerate, who to boo and jeer at. Tell 'em it's okay to shovel genetically modified food down their throats and pump toxic vaccines into their kids and old folks. Tell 'em how lucky they are to live in a nice police state and give up all their personal freedom. Most importantly, drum it into their heads never, ever, ever, to question anything for themselves. What does that sound like to you?'

'I'd say it sounds much like the modern world we live in,' Ben conceded.

'A society of brainwashed zombies. But what if it went even deeper than that? What if you could take a person, even a very smart and capable person, and turn them into a total robot you could literally program to do anything you wanted them to do?'

'Anything, like what?'

'I need a drink,' Grisha said in a cracked voice. Ben allowed him to pause in his narrative while more vodka was served into four shot glasses that looked like egg cups. The Russians muttered their toast of '*Zazdarovje*' and emptied their glasses, Tatyana included. Ben swallowed his in silence. It was like jet fuel. He couldn't remember the last time he'd tracked down a den of kidnappers, only to end up having a drink with them. But then, nothing about this case had been normal so far.

'All right,' Grisha said, helping himself to a refill. He launched back into his narrative by firing a question straight at Ben. 'Tell me, man. Who's the perfect assassin?'

After a moment's pause to wonder why on earth he was being asked this, Ben replied, 'Someone picked at random, without any apparent motive, whom nobody would suspect. Someone expendable, who if they get caught doesn't even know who they're really working for.'

'Wrong,' Grisha said. 'The perfect assassin is someone who doesn't even *know* they're an assassin, not even after the deed is done, because they have no memory of the event.' He gave a dark smile. 'That's just an example of what this is all about. Forget everything you think you know about the "non-scientific concept" of mind control. Because the science is very real, man, and the secret rulers of our world have been perfecting it for decades. Let me tell you all about it. We start from the beginning. Psychotronic warfare 101.'

'I didn't come here for a history lesson,' Ben said. 'I asked you what this thing is.'

'None of what I tell you is gonna mean shit unless you know the background first,' Grisha insisted.

'Listen to him,' Yuri said. 'He's the man.'

Ben sighed. 'All right, I'm listening.'

Grisha shifted to the edge of the sofa, fixing Ben with his big, intense eyes. 'You have to understand, my friend, that the quest to develop effective mind-control methods goes back decades. Right from the start it became a race between world powers, just like the space race and the arms race. But for a good many years, before the electronic age, the lack of technology meant they had to focus on using drugs. The Brits, the Frenchies and the Krauts were all secretly experimenting with drug-induced interrogation techniques in the 1930s. The Nazis even devoted a whole section of Dachau concentration camp to mind-control experiments. Which afterwards led to the Nuremberg Code of ethics that banned using these experimental techniques without the participant's consent. Of course, the Nuremberg Code was completely flouted and pissed on by everyone after 1945, and especially when the Cold War got underway. The CIA spent years messing around with drugs like LSD for their MK-ULTRA mind-control program. They drove a lot of people crazy and caused a lot of deaths.'

'Tell him about Cameron,' Yuri chipped in.

Ben said, 'Cameron?'

Grisha nodded. 'Right. In the fifties, the head of the US Psychiatric Association, a guy called Dr Ewan Cameron, came up with this idea of "depatterning" the mind as a way to cure mental illness. It was a simple theory. You use the available methods to wipe the diseased mind clean to the point where you can "repopulate" it' – Grisha wiggled bunny-ear fingers to simulate quote marks – 'with healthy thoughts and behaviour. Erase the old personality and replace it with a new one, basically. His experimental test subjects were mostly ordinary citizens suffering from mild depression and other everyday psychological issues. Cameron's system was to reduce these poor people to a vegetative state by overdosing them for days and weeks on end with LSD, combined with super-aggressive electroconvulsive therapy.'

'Which meant you strapped them to a metal bed and fried their brains with high voltage,' Yuri explained helpfully.

Grisha went on, 'The idea was to roll back the clock on these adults and return them to some kind of infant state, like babies. A totally blank sheet, literally washed clean of any memory of their previous life and waiting to be rewritten. Theoretically, once you reduced them to such a state, you could get them to do anything you wanted. Stick a loaded pistol in their hand and tell them to blow their own brains out with it, they'd go right ahead without a second thought. By the same token, if you ordered them to assassinate someone else, whether it be a stranger or a loved one, they'd obey unquestioningly.'

Ben gazed at the metal object in his hand. 'But this isn't about drugs any more.'

'You're dead right,' Grisha said. 'The researchers all eventually began to realise the chemical approach just wasn't working. It was too labour intensive and crude. Blasting people's minds with cocktails of hallucinogens was not the most sophisticated way of achieving their goal. That's why other researchers had already started turning to alternative technologies. By the time of the Cold War they were messing about with hypnosis, thinking maybe here was the magic system they could use to create some kind of super-spy, a whole new concept in espionage, who could carry out missions with no risk of confessing valuable intelligence secrets if they got caught and interrogated, because they had no conscious knowledge of why they were there, who or what they were spying on, who they were working for, or even who they were. You could torture that person until they died, and they wouldn't reveal anything useful. That was the dream, the gold standard. And it was here in Russia, back then the Soviet Union, that the idea of combining hypnosis with other techniques like sleep deprivation and drugging developed into the concept of "brainwashing". Do you know about the Moscow show trials?'

'Stalin's answer to Hitler's Night of the Long Knives,' Ben said.

Grisha nodded. 'In the late thirties, during the Great Purge, when our illustrious leader was systematically wiping out all opposition from inside his party ranks. They created a trumped-up court in which subject after subject came forward to confess all manner of treason against the state. The fact is, they'd all been reduced to such a state of mental confusion that they'd have confessed to anything even if it meant their execution, which it did of course. By the time the Cold War began, we Russians had fine-tuned the brain-washing methods to a point where men could be turned into virtual automatons, tools for espionage, assassination, whatever their controllers desired. But things were just about to get really interesting, because a whole new technological revolution was just around the corner and the era of using crude mind-control drugs was history.'

'Are we getting close to the truth now?' Ben asked.

'We're almost there,' Grisha said.

Chapter 27

Grisha paused, still fixing the same intense stare on Ben. 'You know what an EEG is?'

'Of course. It's an electroencephalogram, a recording of electrical activity in the brain.'

'Smart guy,' Grisha said. 'So was Hans Berger, the German dude who invented it in 1924. He was the first scientist who detected the rise and fall of alpha and beta waves in here.' He tapped his head, took another slurp of vodka and continued: 'By 1969, another extremely smart dude called Eberhard Fetz, American biophysicist and neuroscientist, had created the first brain–machine interface technology by connecting a neuron in a monkey's brain to a rotating dial, which the monkey learned to operate just by the power of thought. So, for the first time it became possible for the brain to remotely control a machine. That's technically known as bio-medical telemetry, if you really want to know. But the question was, what if you could reverse the process, and get a machine to remotely control the brain? Of course, scientists were quick to get in on the game. By then, you had guys like Delgado already figuring out how to make it work.'

'Delgado?'

Grisha rolled his eyes at Yuri as if to say, 'This guy really doesn't have a clue about anything, does he?' He looked back at Ben. 'José Delgado was a neuroscience researcher at Yale, way back in the fifties and sixties. A very strange and dark character, kind of like Mr Spock's evil twin. He wrote a book called *Physical Control of the Mind: Towards a Psychocivilised Society*. The title kind of says it all, no? Years before Fetz had started messing about with monkeys, Delgado was putting wireless radio receivers into the brains of animals and controlling their behaviour. His most famous experiment was in 1963 when he faced a charging bull armed only with a remote control handset, and stopped the damn thing right in its tracks before it could touch him. The video's all over YouTube. I guess you never got around to watching it. Anyway, before long Delgado stopped with animals and started applying his technique to humans. Which of course had been the goal from the start, and you can be sure the CIA were paying very close attention to his work. Hell, they were probably funding him.'

'So Delgado turned people into his robots?'

Grisha shook his head. 'Not quite. He was never able to create specific behaviours in human subjects, like, say, if I wanted you to get up and walk across the room, pick something up and bring it to me without even realising you were doing it. What he did succeed in doing, with hundred per cent efficiency, was to control aggression levels in the brain. His methods could calm a raving psycho into a quiet little mouse, or spark off violent behaviour in a totally peaceful person. In one of his demonstrations, a brain-implanted woman quietly playing the guitar suddenly, at the flick of a switch, went nuts and smashed the instrument to pieces.

'Needless to say, this was all seen as very progressive and important for psychiatric science. Being able to subdue a violent mental patient without having to hold 'em down and pump sedatives into them could only be a good thing, right? But Delgado was pretty forthright about the social engineering implications of his work. He wrote that "Man does not have the right to develop his own mind. We must electronically control the brain. Some day armies and generals will be controlled by electronic stimulation."'

Ben was perplexed that he'd somehow managed to go all his life without hearing any of this stuff, whether it was true or not. Grisha seemed to read his expression. 'Freaky, huh? And what's even more amazing is that so few people've even heard about this crazy shit. Not that it would change a thing if they did. Before Delgado died in 2011 he wrote that you couldn't stop the technology from developing on and on, despite ethics, despite anyone's personal belief in how evil and wrong it was, despite everything. We can only guess at how far it's secretly come.'

Ben held up the shiny metal pill between thumb and forefinger, rolling it between his fingertips. 'So this is what exactly?'

Both Grisha and Yuri fixed eyes on it. Their faces showed all kinds of mixed emotions, as if their minds were torn between terror of whatever it signified to them, and a kind of awestruck reverence.

'That, my dumb-ass friend,' Grisha said, 'is Объект 428. Otherwise known as Object 428, the legendary lost first-generation psychotronic weapon prototype of the Special Projects Division of GRU Generalogo Shtaba, the Main Intelligence Directorate of the Soviet Union. Its date of manufacture is classified, but we now know it to have been 1955. Way ahead of its time, like totally revolutionary. Its experimental and possible deployment history, also classi-fied. As was the codename of the research project that gave birth to it.' Grisha gave it its Russian name. 'Операция кукольный мастер. Translation, Operation Puppet Master.'

'Pretty lousy tradecraft for the operational codename to hint at its purpose,' Yuri said. 'I suppose they thought it sounded cool.'

Grisha went on, 'None of these facts would have ever been known, except for intelligence leaks after the collapse of the Soviet Union. The official version was, and remains, that neither Operation Puppet Master nor its brainchild ever existed. The real version is that Object 428 disappeared from a secret GRU laboratory in Moscow in early 1957, causing a huge panic for the Kremlin and a bunch of officials to be sent to the Siberian salt mines as punishment. Object 428 was never seen again. Until now.'

'Tell him about the microfilm,' Yuri said.

Grisha nodded. 'Oh, yeah. Our other little piece of evidence. Only the entire set of original blueprints for Object 428, along with all of the plans, research notes, secret case studies, the whole deal. It's copied onto the flash drive that's inside the tin.'

Ben was slowly piecing together the strands of all this, and still just as unsure whether he should believe a single word. 'So it was the British SIS agent, Ingram, who stole this material from the lab?'

'There was a network of agents dedicated to obtaining and smuggling it across to the West,' Yuri said, picking up the baton from Grisha. 'Nobody knows for sure how many, or what their identities or exact roles might have been. The agents themselves were probably kept much in the dark, for the usual reasons of the espionage community. They must have known little about their mission objective, even, because no one could be sure that the very existence of Object 428 was anything more than a wild rumour.'

'Kind of like Saddam Hussein's supposed weapons of mass destruction at the time of the Iraq War,' Grisha muttered. 'Except that story really was made up.'

'However they succeeded in getting hold of Object 428,' Yuri said, 'we'll never know. My guess is that they had contacts inside the lab. Maybe someone managed to smuggle it out, perhaps substituting a fake copy in its place. But they did succeed. Getting it out of the USSR was an even more dangerous part of the mission. The KGB were everywhere, nobody could be trusted and the risks were enormous. Ingram planned on passing it to a fellow agent by means of a dead drop, creating a chain of links to smuggle it out of the country.'

'And the cipher?' Ben asked.

'All it said was "Operation Puppet Master is real",' Yuri replied. 'As though they couldn't believe themselves that it was true. Along with that message Ingram encoded the location of the dead drop, which was where I found it, undisturbed after all those years. The chain had been broken. It's pretty certain that Ingram wasn't the only operative who paid with his life when the mission fell apart.'

'Of course,' Grisha grunted, 'if the SIS *had* managed to get their hands on Object 428, nothing would have changed. They weren't trying to unmask the evils of the Soviet regime, they just wanted the technology for themselves. Our wonderful mind controllers were years ahead of theirs. It took decades for the West to catch up.'

'So our boys are still producing these little gadgets, is that what you're claiming?' Ben said.

'No way, man,' Grisha snorted. 'This is prehistoric technology compared to what they're using now. Object 428 is the great-grandfather of today's mind-control devices.'

'But if you exposed the great-grandfather to the public

eye, it would still cause quite a stir,' Ben said. 'At least, that's the idea, correct?'

'You bet your ass it would,' Grisha said.

'I've come this far,' Yuri said. 'I risked my life, and my daughter's, for this thing. There's no going back for me now, you understand?'

'Here you go. It's all yours.' Ben reached out a cupped hand and dropped the little metal pill into Yuri's eager palms. 'There's only one problem with your story, gentlemen,' he said after a pause for reflection. 'It's all pure conjecture. Not a single hard fact or detail. That little gadget could easily be a fake, and so could this microfilm you claim to have. Why should anyone believe a word of what you just told me?'

'Then let me tell you another story,' Grisha said.

'Will it change my mind?'

'Only if you're alive, man. With ears to hear with, and a brain to think with.'

'Then try me.'

Chapter 28

The tale that now unfolded was the peculiar case history of a person Ben had no reason for ever having heard of before, a Czech national named Jan Wolker. It was one that dated back many years, to before Ben had been born. With nothing else to do except try to understand why Yuri Petrov had risked everything to escape to this isolated hiding place, Ben listened.

Back in the troubled days of the late sixties when revolution had been in the air across much of the world, few parts of Europe had been in as much turmoil as Czechoslovakia, a country deep in the shadow of the looming might of its neighbouring USSR and its then president Leonid Brezhnev. The so-called Prague Spring had been a short-lived period of protest against what the Czechs angrily regarded as dictatorial Soviet domination. In the spirit of the times, nationalistic reform campaigners had kicked up strong protests in the hope of freeing their country from the shackles of Russian might. Jan Wolker had been a prominent member of the movement. If things had worked out differently, he might have become a Czech hero.

They hadn't. When Brezhnev's response to the trouble-makers was to roll the tanks into Prague in August 1968 and crush the protests with an iron fist, the reformers were scattered and many went into hiding, Wolker among them. He tried to get on with his life, keeping under the radar. He was forced to re-emerge, however, when in March of 1969 medical surgery was needed to address his worsening stomach ulcer condition. And it was during what should have been a fairly routine operation that all his problems really began.

Wolker left hospital feeling fine, and happy that his ulcer had been fixed after plaguing him so long. Within a few weeks, though, he began to experience strange symptoms: altered thought patterns, loss of memory, impaired capacity for logic; as well as physical symptoms like visual disturbances, somnambulism and peculiar changes to his heart rhythms. It all seemed to be coming from inside his head, though he could find no possible explanation.

The symptoms continued and in fact worsened. Wolker began to believe he could hear sounds similar to radio frequencies emanating from inside his skull, which he found deeply disturbing. The conviction began to dawn on him that something bizarre had happened to him in the hospital, while under the general anaesthetic. The effects of the drugs on his brain? When the symptoms continued he consulted the doctors who'd performed the operation only to be assured that nothing was wrong, and he'd soon settle back to normal.

Refusing to accept such a brush-off, Wolker sought a second opinion and visited the Prague clinic of a Dr Miloš Brodský who carried out an X-ray of his skull. To both men's shock, Brodský detected the presence of a foreign body inside Wolker's head. The small object was apparently cylindrical in shape, definitely of artificial manufacture, measuring about 7mm in length by 4mm in width. Described unequiv-ocally by Brodský as 'an intracranial implant', it was situated slightly anterior to the frontal bone, in a part of the brain that suggested it had been inserted via the nostril with no need to drill or cut into the skull itself: hence, no marks of the procedure showed externally.

Wolker panicked and demanded the thing be removed. An extremely perplexed Brodský urged caution for the moment, promising to write a full report which he planned to take to the highest level of the medical authorities.

When Wolker heard nothing after a few more weeks, he returned to Brodský in late May 1969 – only to find the doctor had changed his story, denied all knowledge of the conversations they'd had, and was no longer prepared to make a report, claiming that the X-rays of Wolker's brain were completely normal. Sure enough, the suspicious X-ray photographs clearly showing the presence of the object seemed to have vanished from the files, replaced with images of a perfectly healthy and unimplanted brain. The men argued. Wolker stormed out of the clinic, threatening all manner of legal action. But there was little he could do, and his worsening symptoms were making it hard to think straight. He began to drink heavily and would bang his head against the wall to switch off the thing in his head, to no avail. Nightmares, suicidal thoughts and terrifyingly violent urges began to take him over.

'This is all on record?' Ben asked.

'Hold on,' Grisha said. 'It gets wilder.'

On June 8th 1969 there was an assassination attempt against a man named Elmar Gödel, another prominent Czech activist who had been very vocal against the Soviets and complicit in setting fire to a Russian tank during the invasion of Prague. Wolker and Gödel had been close friends back in 1968, before things had turned bad.

On the night in June 1969 that Gödel was shot twice in

the stomach at his home, witnesses reported seeing a man answering Wolker's description fleeing from the scene clutching a pistol. Wolker awoke in a ditch the next morning, fully dressed, his clothes dirty and torn, and a loaded revolver in his pocket that he was certain he'd never seen before, with two chambers fired. He had no recollection of having been anywhere near Gödel's home the previous night, nor of having seen or even spoken to him for several months prior to that. He later stated that he would never, in a thousand years, have dreamed of harming anyone, let alone his old friend Elmar.

Tipped off that the police were coming to arrest him, Wolker fled Czechoslovakia. He was able to get to Frankfurt, Germany, where, now convinced that the thing inside his head was making him do things against his will and without his conscious knowledge, he found a sympathetic surgeon called Stefan Mandelbrot who was prepared to surgically remove it.

The device was removed on September 13 1969, six months after it had been implanted and just three and a half months since the Czech doctor, Brodský, had strongly denied the existence of any foreign object inside Wolker's head. Dr Mandelbrot confirmed the description from the original X-rays, stating that the device was 7mm by 4mm in size, metallic and of unknown origin, like nothing he'd ever seen before. On examination, it appeared to be some kind of high-frequency electromagnetic transponder, or a miniature radio receiver. There was no power cell; the device seemed to run on phantom power from the radio frequencies entering the host's brain, operating between 17 and 24 kHz.

Unlike Brodský, Mandelbrot was willing to go on the record and do whatever it took to expose the bizarre conspiracy by which his patient had been violated. In the meantime, still wanted by the police back home, Wolker next tried to escape to the safety of Switzerland. En route he contacted a German journalist named Heinz Krüger who was a writer for the magazine *Stern*. Wolker told Krüger the whole story, said he could prove it and promised to get in touch again when he made it to Zürich. Krüger was to travel there to meet him, whereupon Wolker was going to show him the device that had been removed from his skull, along with photographs of it being removed and a verifying letter from his physician Dr Mandelbrot. An excited Krüger planned on blowing the whole story wide open with a sensational feature in *Stern*.

'But things didn't work out that way,' Grisha said. 'Wolker got arrested before he reached the Swiss border and was whisked back to Czechoslovakia to face trial for the attempted murder of his dear old pal Elmar Gödel. Remarkable East-West collusion for the time, don't you think?'

Somewhere between his imprisonment and deportation back to Prague, the brain implant, the key piece of evidence that would have proved Wolker's story true, mysteriously vanished, never to resurface again or be mentioned in any report. Meanwhile, within hours of Wolker's arrest, Dr Stefan Mandelbrot was cycling home through the streets of Frankfurt when he was mown down by a six-wheeler truck and killed instantly. Any and all evidence of the operation he had performed on Wolker, including any copies of his letter and photographs of the device, was removed from his office. The nurse who had assisted with the operation was suddenly transferred to another hospital, and disappeared shortly thereafter.

'When Heinz Krüger decided to go ahead and write the story anyway,' Grisha said, 'his editors fired him from the magazine without explanation. Over the next few months he researched and wrote a book called *Minds in Chains: The Tyranny of Tomorrow*, which you won't find anywhere now. He was found drowned in his swimming pool in August 1971.'

Elmar Gödel had passed away in 2013 at the age of eighty-five, maintaining to his dying day that his friend Jan Wolker would never have tried to murder him. No matter what witnesses or forensics might say, poor Jan had somehow been set up to take the fall for a crime he did not commit.

'Which begs the question,' Grisha said. 'If someone hijacked your mind, took over your body and made it perform terrible acts that you would never have carried out of your own volition, can anyone say you were guilty of the crime?'

Ben had no answer for that one.

'Here's another question: did the powers that be really want Gödel dead back in 1970? If so, why didn't they try again and finish the job? Maybe the answer is that killing him wasn't their aim; rather, maybe all they wanted to do was retest the effectiveness of their mind-control technology, using a couple of expendables as their lab rats.'

'If you can manipulate a man's mind to kill his own friend,' Yuri said, 'you can turn anyone against anyone. The whole thing could have been just a sick experiment.'

'What about Wolker?' Ben asked.

Grisha replied, 'He spent the next year in Pankrák Prison, in Prague. When he kept on protesting his innocence and raved on about the implant that had been put inside his brain, prison doctors declared that he was insane, psychotic, paranoid and in need of psychiatric treatment. He was transferred to a mental asylum, where a course of drug and electroshock therapy was begun. Within a week of his admission, a staff member accidentally turned up the patient's voltage too high and induced a fatal heart attack. That was the end of Jan Wolker.'

'But it's not the end of the story,' Yuri said, clutching the metal pill in his fist. 'Not now that we have this.'

'So you want to continue where Heinz Krüger left off, is that it?' Ben said. 'Use your Freedom Network to blow the whole story back open to the world media? Hope that major news outlets will pick it up or that it goes viral on the internet?'

'Sure, why not?' Grisha said.

'That's what needs to happen,' Yuri echoed.

'And then what?' Ben asked them both. 'The story gets buried in a ton of conspiracy hokum that only a handful of weirdos will look at. Your sole market would consist of the kind of people who believe that there's a monster in Loch Ness and that alien lizards are walking among us. Is that what you call being taken seriously?'

'Hey, watch what you say about the alien lizards,' Grisha rumbled, pointing. 'Maybe they are.'

'I rest my case,' Ben said, shaking his head. 'But let's say what you've told me tonight is true. Let's say it's even a tenth true. You break this story just like Krüger tried to do, and a month later, a year later, however long it takes for Bezukhov or whoever to find you two clowns, the pair of you will end up floating face down in whatever you've got around here that might pass for a swimming pool. A slurry pit, maybe. Those things will dissolve a dead body as fast as feeding it to pigs.'

'I was hoping for a little more understanding,' Yuri said, flustered. 'Don't you see how important this is? We have the decrypted cipher, we have the name of the operation, we have the device itself. It's dynamite.'

'And dynamite is liable to get you blown up,' Ben said. 'All the more reason why I need to get Valentina out of here and home safe. That's the job I came here to do.'

'Haven't you been listening to a word?' Yuri yelled. 'You won't make it!'

'I'll be the judge of that,' Ben replied calmly. 'Whatever you've got yourself mixed up in, it's not my business. And you shouldn't have brought the kid into it either.'

'I didn't plan it that way,' Yuri protested, waving his arms in frustration. 'If I'd known they were going to try to kill me, would I have let my daughter be exposed to danger? Do you think I'm nuts?'

'Nuts, maybe,' Ben said. 'Stupid, definitely.'

'Don't blame me, blame Eloise. That bitch forced my hand with her legal bullshit about terminating my parental rights. This could be the last time I see Valentina until she's grown up.'

'If what you say is true, Yuri, you might not live to see her next birthday. But that's your problem. I'm taking her home to her mother.'

Yuri glowered at him. Ben saw his eyes flick across to the table, where the firearms lay. Assessing whether he could get to them before Ben did. Calculating his chances. Gambling on a wing and a prayer.

'Don't even think about it,' Ben said. 'This is no time for foolish and desperate measures. This is a time for you to sit nice and easy and consider what's best for Valentina.'

'To let her drive off into the night with you? I don't even know you.'

'Call Kaprisky,' Ben said. 'He'll confirm who and what I am, and my qualifications for the job.'

'You must be kidding, man,' Grisha said. 'Kaprisky is one of the New World Order. I wouldn't be surprised if he was a fucking Bilderberg Group member, takes vacations at Bohemian Grove and all that, performing satanic rituals with Merkel and Obama and all the other Illuminati scumbags. He'd track our location in a heartbeat and send a hit squad to wipe us out.'

Ben ignored him and looked at Yuri. 'You have my word that she'll be safe. The jet will be on the tarmac by the time we reach Moscow. She'll be back in France within a few hours. This is the only way it's going to go down, Yuri. It would be much better for her if you cooperate.'

They'd been talking for almost an hour. In the heavy silence that now followed Ben's words, he heard a tiny creak of the bedroom door behind him and turned to see Valentina half-hidden in the doorway, peeking anxiously through the gap.

'How long have you been standing there listening, Sweet Pea?' Yuri asked her in a soft voice.

She pushed the door fully open and burst into the room, head hanging, her little shoulders slumped miserably, her lower lip sticking out and trembling as she struggled not to burst into tears. She ran to her father and flew into his embrace, locked her skinny arms around him as if she never wanted to let go. Yuri's face contorted with emotion as he hugged her tightly.

'*Ik wil niet gaan!*' the child sobbed, reverting to Dutch. '*Laat ze me niet nemen, Papa!*' I don't want to go! Don't let them take me away, Daddy!

'Maybe it's for the best, baby,' Yuri replied, holding back his own tears. 'Mummy's so worried about you. She can't wait to have you home safe. You've got to try to understand, Sweet Pea. Papa made a mistake bringing you here.'

'But I want to be with you and Uncle Grisha!'

Ben heaved a sigh and exchanged glances with Tatyana.

199

This isn't going to be easy, her look said, and he was inclined to agree.

Yuri was stroking his little girl's hair and trying his best to quieten her tears as she pressed against him for comfort, her little body racked with sobs. The confined Alyosha had started up his barking again, barely muffled by the thin walls of the shed. Grisha looked towards the dark window and pulled an irritated grimace at the racket coming from outside.

Ben took out his cigarettes and was about to light one up when Tatyana frowned, pointed at the child and shook her head. He heaved an even heavier sigh and put the Gauloises away and reached for the vodka instead. Anything to soothe the nerves while Valentina calmed down. The least Ben felt he could do was let her and Yuri have a few moments together before they had to part for what would probably be quite a while. He knew the kid would probably hate him forever, but what choice did he have?

'I wish that dog would shut up,' Grisha muttered, rubbing his beard. 'He goes off at shadows, the wind, chickens farting, anything at all.'

Nobody had a reply to make to that. And it was during that lull in the conversation, before anyone spoke another word, that a sudden loud percussive blast from outside flared across the night sky and rattled the farmhouse window panes. At almost exactly the same moment, the farmhouse door burst in and three armed men in black tactical assault gear stormed into the hallway.

Then the lights went out, the farmhouse was plunged into darkness. Amid the screaming and chaos, the gunfire began.

Chapter 29

The insertion of the commander and a twenty-man assault team into the vicinity of the target had had to be carried out fast and covertly, using a hastily scrambled trio of Kamov Ka-226T utility helicopters carrying seven troops apiece. Once the exact position had been pinpointed, the Mission Chief back at base had established a suitable drop zone 4.5 kilometres to the north: close enough for the commander and his team to make their way cross-country once on the ground, far enough away for the helicopters to make their pass unheard by the occupants of the farmhouse. A survey of the local topography had revealed a ridge of forested hillside that would mask the lights of the aircraft from view, if the pilots made their final approach to the DZ at sufficiently low altitude.

The drop had gone without a hitch. Moving silently in seven squads of three men each, the team covered the four and a half kilometres like the skilled, experienced operatives they were. Once they reached the target zone, every man knew his role. For this mission they had been issued a mixture of non-lethal weaponry in the form of the latest extended-range wireless Taser guns intended for the capture of Petrov and the girl, as well as the more usual hardware associated with their work: 9mm Glock pistols for the Taser crew, and compact AEK-919K Kashtan submachine guns as used by Russian Special Forces, fitted with silencers, tactical lights and lasers, for everyone else.

The lethal firearms were primarily intended for the purpose of eliminating the British ex-soldier called Ben Hope who posed the most significant threat to the success of their mission and had been the sole reason for deploying such a large force of men in the first place. If not for his presence, the idea of sending three helicopters loaded with twenty-one combat operatives to take care of two amateurs and a little girl would have seemed like madness. But Hope's involvement, whatever the reason for it, changed everything. The team had been briefed on his background and level of ability. What they had been told about this man made them rightly nervous. Nobody would hesitate to shoot to kill on sight.

Arriving at the target zone, the team had spread out to more closely reconnoitre the operational area from various angles and finalise their assault plan. Other than a barking dog and a few nervous goats, all seemed quiet and calm at the farmstead. The team leader had been in frequent radio contact with the Mission Chief who, sitting in his command centre far away, was watching the entire show via live satellite feed on his big screen. It was the satellite that had picked up on the dark shadow on the rise overlooking the farmstead from the south. When the commander sent a squad to investigate, they confirmed that it was the same black Mercedes they'd been looking for.

The remaining troopers, meanwhile, carried out a final weapons check and prepared themselves for the breaching entry of the farmhouse. One unit of three had been selected as the point men, whose responsibility it would be to take down Hope in the opening few seconds of the surprise attack and secure the building as the rest of the team moved in and rounded up the prisoners.

The backup units took up their positions around the farmyard, ready to move at the signal. Everyone was wearing the standard issue military night vision goggles. One man carried a belt pouch containing syringes loaded with powerful sedative drugs in doses ready prepared for two adult males and one twelve-year-old child.

The countdown was tense. Nobody spoke. Clutching the radio remote in his gloved hand the commander pressed the button that activated the explosive device attached to the fuel tank of the Mercedes. The percussive blast of the explosion shook the trees and a fireball lit up the sky. An instant later, the entry squad breached the front door at the same moment that a secondary explosive device rigged to the power transformer outside the farmhouse took out the electricity.

The unexpected fusillade of loud gunfire that rang out from inside the farmhouse was the first sign that the assault was going bad. The team's silenced automatic weapons made little more than a clattering sound. The commander froze just an instant too long when he heard the crashing double BOOM – BOOM followed by the sharper crack of a high-velocity rifle going off inside the building. The troopers still outside all looked to him, eyes wide behind their masks, awaiting his order. He yelled, '*Go go go!*' and led the way inside the farmhouse, illuminated an eerie sea-green by the night vision goggles. He swung his weapon left and right in search of his target but could see nothing except an empty room. The toe of his combat boot touched something heavy and soft on the floor of the hallway and he looked down to see the bodies of the point men, all three of them, sprawled at his feet.

Stepurin and Orlov had each had his head partially removed by a shotgun blast. Vasiliev had made it about a metre further inside the room before he'd hit the floor dead from a gaping hole in his throat, an inch above the edge of his bulletproof vest. His submachine gun was gone.

But the commander had little time to survey the damage to his men as the remainder of the assault team swept into the building in his wake, pointing their guns in all directions.

Suddenly their tactical plan was all awry. Where moments earlier all five of their targets – Hope, Petrov, Solokov, the child and the woman Nikolaeva – had been inside the room, they were all gone as though vaporised. All that remained of their presence was a rumpled newspaper, an empty vodka bottle and four glasses, and a rustic double-barrelled shotgun and a World War II battle rifle lying on the floor with wisps of smoke still trickling from their muzzles.

Getting a grip of his frazzled nerves the commander remembered that there was no back door to the farmhouse. That meant the targets were still inside. 'Find them!' he yelled to his men.

In Ben's way of seeing things, when a bunch of heavily armed men come storming into the house with the obvious intention of hurting someone, you shoot first and keep shooting until they're down. That lightning reaction time and unflinching response had been instilled into him as a young warrior until they were completely second nature to him, and he'd only become faster since.

Still, getting the drop on the surprise attackers when his own guns were lying on the table next to him hadn't been easy, even for him. Ben had taken down the first two with Grisha's old hammer gun and the third with the Mosin Nagant rifle, before the damned ejector had snapped off leaving the chamber blocked by the fired shell case and the weapon about as useful as a baseball bat. That had left Ben about one and a half seconds to rearm himself and get Yuri, Valentina, Grisha and Tatyana out of the room before more attackers came bursting inside the farmhouse.

Where they were going, he had little idea and no time to consider, just as now was not the moment to try to understand what was happening, who was attacking them, and how anyone could have found them so fast. *Survive the moment and figure it out later . . . if you live that long.*

The house was pitch black around him, save for the thin beam from the tactical light mounted to the weapon he'd taken from one of the raiders. Bursting through a door at the end of the narrow passage through which they'd come, he shone his light around a poky kitchen that looked filthy even in the dark. Next in was Yuri, clutching Valentina in his arms with a hand over the child's mouth to stifle her terrified cries. Then Grisha, stumbling through the doorway like a blind-drunk bear. Tatyana came last. Ben closed the door, which had an old-fashioned lock and key that he twisted home.

No way a nineteenth-century iron lock would keep anyone at bay for long. There was an ancient electric stove on the other side of the kitchen. Ben grabbed it and heaved it away from the wall, ripping the electric cord from its socket, and dragged it quickly across the greasy linoleum floor to barricade the door. He glanced around him. The kitchen had no windows and no other door. That was very, very good, because it eliminated points of entry by the attackers. And it was very, very bad, because it meant the five of them were trapped here inside.

As Ben's mind raced for a way out of the situation, he heard thundering boots in the passage. Something hard and heavy thumped against the door, and then again, with enough force to flex the timber frame. The attackers would be inside the kitchen in no time. Ben stalled things by rattling off a couple of three-shot bursts at the door, his bullets ripping clear through the wood. A Kashtan submachine gun chambered for the short, stubby and less powerful 9x18mm Makarov cartridge was ballistically inferior to the classic 9mm Parabellum he'd relied on for most of his life. But it did the job just fine. The thumping stopped.

Ben grabbed Yuri and shoved him away from the door, fearful that the attackers would return fire through it. When that failed to happen, Ben remembered what Yuri had said about his enemies wanting to take him alive. Maybe there was something in his crazy tale, after all. They might not risk firing through the door. What would it be instead? Gas? A stun grenade? Ben's old SAS unit would not have been defeated by a simple wooden door barring their way. Nor would these guys.

Valentina was in a wild panic and struggling like a little eel in her father's arms. Yuri was as terrified of hurting the kid as he was of letting go of her in the darkness. Ben caught a glimpse of Grisha in the darting light beam and could see the big guy was losing it too. Grisha staggered to the kitchen counter, groped about until he found a carving knife and started waving it around like a lunatic, yelling Russian curses that were probably something like 'Come and get a piece of this, you bastards'. Ben had seen the effects of shock overcome better-trained men than Grisha, and if someone didn't do something fast he was liable to harm someone, or himself. There were enough people already trying to harm them from the outside without a deranged slasher in their midst.

Ben was on the big guy in two strides, dazzling him with the weapon-mounted light. He twisted the knife out of his hand and stuck it deep into the kitchen worktop. Pressed the gun muzzle hard up under Grisha's chin and said, 'Be calm or I'll kill you.'

Grisha became suddenly much quieter and stood there, breathing hard, white froth bubbling at the corners of his mouth. If he collapsed of sudden heart failure, at least Ben wouldn't have to worry about him. There was enough to worry about already.

The enemy seemed to have fallen back from the door, but he could be certain they were planning their next move and it would come very soon. Ben had already used up about a third of his one and only magazine. When the bullets ran out they would be down to pots, pans and cutlery to use as improvised weapons.

The walls were solid brick. The ceiling above them was planked with heavy boards. The floor was paved with stone slabs. If there was a way out of this, he couldn't think of what it might be.

Yuri said, 'Grisha – your prepping cave.'

Chapter 30

At first, Grisha seemed to have no more idea what his friend was talking about than Ben did. Then, like a man woken out of a trance by a bucket of cold water splashed in his face, the big guy got a hold of himself. 'My prepping cave!' he repeated.

'His what?' Ben demanded. There wasn't a lot of time for discussions here. He could feel the seconds ticking by before the attackers stormed their puny defences.

Grisha stumbled across the dark room, his movements lit only by the thin bobbing beam of Ben's tactical light. Ben watched, mystified, as the Russian crouched awkwardly in front of a cupboard by the sink, opened a drawer and groped about inside with his arm buried up to the elbow. There was a click. Grisha scrambled back to his feet, and grabbed hold of the cupboard unit with both hands. The hidden latch he'd undone released the entire thing from the wall, allowing it to swing away freely on hinges. Quite what this DIY modification was all about, Ben had no idea, until he saw the hole in the floor that the unit had been concealing.

An area of flagstone flooring had been laboriously chiselled away. In its place was a sliding metal trapdoor lid covering whatever was below. Grisha yanked it aside to reveal a circular hole dug through the compacted earth beneath the house. The cavity was easily wide enough for a man of his bulky girth to fit through, extending downwards like a manhole for a metre or so before it apparently opened out into a much wider space. The first few rungs of an aluminium ladder glinted from the light of Ben's beam.

Ben was about to ask where the hell the hole led to, but didn't bother as the answer could only be: a better place than up here. 'Okay, let's go,' he said. He kept the light shining on the mouth of the hole as Yuri released Valentina from his clasp and urged her to clamber down. Wide-eyed and too bewildered to argue, the girl started shinnying like a monkey down the ladder. Yuri went after her, then Grisha, slow and ponderous, causing the ladder to creak with his weight and Ben to tense with impatience.

'I don't like it,' Tatyana muttered, shaking her head.

'No choice,' Ben told her. 'Move.' When she had reluctantly disappeared downwards through the hole, Ben swung his legs over the edge and slid down the ladder to join them inside the space beneath.

Grisha pressed past Ben to where a length of rope dangled down at the side of the hole. The big guy tugged on the rope and the kitchen unit swung back into place overhead. He grabbed a handle on the underside of the trapdoor and slid it across to seal off the hole. Once two heavy bolts had been shot into place, they were firmly closed inside.

Inside what, Ben was about to discover. 'Let's have some more light,' Yuri said, and suddenly the darkness was filled with the glow of a gas-cartridge camping lantern. Ben peered about him and saw they had climbed down into what appeared to be a dug-out space within the foundations of the house. The walls were solid earth and stone. Thick wooden posts rested on concrete slabs and supported the weight of the kitchen floor above.

'You built this?' he asked Grisha. The big guy nodded and held out both hands as if to proudly display the many calluses such a Herculean task must have cost him. It had to have taken months, if not years, to dig this place out by himself. It was as big as a wine cellar – except other things than wine storage had been on Grisha's mind when he built it. Rack shelving filled every available inch of wall space, crammed with emergency supplies for the coming apocalypse, impending disasters or whatever the evil tyrants of the New World Order had in store for mankind. He'd been stockpiling tinned food by the truckload, stacked to the ceiling as well as barrels of drinking water with dates labelled by marker pen. Crates were overflowing with survival gear and purification tablets and firelighting equipment and batteries and tools, even a hazmat suit and an assortment of gas masks. As long as their enemies didn't lob a nuclear weapon down on their heads, they should survive all right, for a while at least.

They had made it down into the makeshift cellar just in time. From overhead, strangely far away as though they were deep in a mineshaft, came the muted crash of the kitchen door being rammed in. Muffled footsteps thumped about as the assault team burst into the room, only to find that their quarry seemed to have done a magic disappearing act.

But the attackers weren't stupid. It wouldn't take them long to inspect every inch of the kitchen and work out where they'd gone. Next thing, they'd be tearing up the flagstones and trying to batter and tunnel their way through.

In other words, as Ben now realised, Grisha's hidden disaster-prepping room might have just bought the five of them a little bit of time, but they were still well and truly stuck.

'Rats in a trap,' Ben said. 'Unless you have another trick up your sleeve.'

'What, you think I would have gone to all this trouble without giving myself an escape route, man?' Grisha said, pointing into the shadows. He snatched another gas lantern from the clutter of a shelving rack, turned it on with a little *whoof* of flame and angled it towards where he'd pointed.

Ben suddenly realised where all the countless tons of earth and stone excavated from the hole had gone. Grisha couldn't possibly have disposed of them via the kitchen, wheelbar-rowing them one at a time through the house. Old houses like these, Le Val included, had often been built up on the ground on which they stood without the benefit of modern foundations, and this place was no exception. Where the dug-away earth met the base of one thick stone wall, Grisha had created an opening beneath the skirt of the building, with a length of iron girder acting as a lintel to bear the weight of the wall. During the long, arduous dig the opening must have resembled the Lefortovo road tunnel while he made innumerable trips with barrow-loads of earth to dump about the property. Once the job was finished Grisha could have partly filled in the hole and built it up to appear like a culvert or a drain that from the outside would hardly be noticeable once the weeds had grown up around it.

On the inside, Grisha had equipped his secret escape route with heavy metal doors that looked as though they'd been forged by a medieval blacksmith and could withstand a direct hit from a rocket. He wiggled open an iron bolt the size of a scaffold pole, and heaved. The heavy doors creaked open, letting in the first breath of fresh air the cellar had probably known in years. 'Never thought I'd really have to use it,' Grisha muttered.

Still shaking his head in astonishment at the big guy's ingenuity, Ben went first because he had the only weapon. The escape hatch tapered to a narrow opening just beneath the outer wall, partly covered with a pile of old sacking and empty goat feed bags that Ben pushed aside, careful not to make the slightest sound as he emerged into the night. Outside, the commotion of the assault team in their quandary was loud and clear. There were voices and the spit and crackle of a radio. Running shapes of armed men flitted here and there. The dog was in a greater frenzy of barking than ever.

Ben clutched his submachine gun and peered cautiously around the corner of the house. The acrid smell of burning fuel and rubber was in the air. To the south, up on the rise overlooking the farm, he could see the glow of the blazing Mercedes and a tower of black smoke that blotted out the stars. That accounted for the first of the two explosions that had immediately preceded the team's breaching entry. The second, he guessed, had been what had done for the power transformer whose remains were burning in the yard near the farmhouse door, live wires throwing off showers of sparks.

Ben felt a wistful pang as he gazed back up the hillside at the burning Mercedes. His bag had been inside that car, containing all his kit and Kaprisky's half million rubles in cash. Ben was less concerned about the money than the bag itself. Another old faithful companion bitten the dust.

One by one the others crawled out after Ben, and the five huddled unseen in the shadowy lee of the farmhouse wall. All the activity was centred inside the house and around its sole doorway. The assault team had only to send a man to skirt around the corner and things would get interesting very fast. Had Ben been alone in this predicament, he'd have been less worried. To be in charge of a motley crew comprising a frightened child, a couple of jumpy conspiracy nuts and a silent, tense female detective whose mood he was

212

having trouble reading, didn't inspire a great deal of confidence.

He was relieved that Valentina's panic had left her. The kid was showing the same determined grit she'd made evident when she'd saved her father from capture at the service station on the M10 Federal Highway. Kaprisky genes, or Petrov? Valentina clutched her father's hand tightly and rolled her anxious eyes up at him. 'Are these men here to hurt us?' she asked in Dutch.

Yuri put a finger to his lips. 'Shhh. But we won't let them.'

'What about Alyosha?' she whispered.

'We can't leave the dog closed in the shed like that,' Yuri said to Ben.

'He'll dig his way out eventually,' Ben said, wishing they would shut up and let him concentrate on a plan to get away from here.

Grisha tapped Ben on the shoulder. He pointed westwards, past the goat pens, in the direction of the woods. 'We can make it to my trailer,' he hissed.

'How do you know they haven't already found it?' Ben hissed back.

'Not a chance, man. It's safe.'

Ben weighed up the idea. Making a break for it in that direction would entail crossing a portion of the yard in full view of the farmhouse doorway. With the electricity cut off the house was in darkness, but by the fiery glow of the burning car and electrical transformer any running target would be easily spotted by the men milling around the entrance. Only luck would prevent them from being seen. Then again, staying here was totally out of the question. Unless they went and hid in the chicken coops, Grisha's suggestion might just make the most sense.

Ben considered the option for only three or four seconds

before making his mind up. But that was three or four seconds too long for Grisha, who with a grunt of impatience shoved past him and broke away from the house at a lumbering run.

Chapter 31

Ben lunged to stop him, but Grisha knocked his hand away with a determined snarl and kept moving, waddling out into the open as fast as his chubby legs could carry his weight.

Almost instantly, there was a shout from the doorway as Grisha was spotted. Two of the assault team burst into a sprint after the big guy, who threw a panicked look over his shoulder and tried to lumber faster, moving with all the stealth and agility of a baby rhinoceros.

Before Ben could react, there was a sharp crack and something that glinted in the firelight flew through the darkness towards the fleeing Grisha, as fast as an arrow from a bow. Even before it hit him, Ben realised what it was.

A normal Taser gun had a range of only about fifteen feet, its twin darts connected to the launching device by wires through which a pulsing 50,000-volt electric charge would incapacitate the victim with involuntary muscle twitches. Ben had heard of the longer-range models being issued to police forces and the military, but never seen one in action before now. They were considered the ultimate in 'non-lethal' weapons, even though Tasers had caused more than a few fatalities in their time.

The dart struck Grisha in the left buttock. He let out a yowl and went straight down on his face in the dirt, jerking and convulsing like a landed fish as the powerful electric current made his muscles spasm out of control.

A silenced submachine gun was decidedly less non-lethal in its ways, but Ben had no problem with that. Stepping away from the house, he pinpointed the hovering red dot of his laser sight onto the upper body of the nearest man, aiming for the spot between his throat and the top of his bulletproof vest, and pulled the trigger. Three-shot burst. The silenced Kashtan chattered like a sewing machine, its muzzle report suppressed so well that Ben could hear the rapid clicking of the bolt as it hammered back and forth, chambering rounds and spewing out the empties. No sooner was the first man down, but the second was getting a burst of 9mm copper-jacketed lead that scythed him backwards off his feet.

Ben muttered, 'Shit.' Now the fight was on for real, any attempt to slip away unnoticed well and truly blown. He dashed over to Grisha and removed the high-voltage dart from his rump with a well-aimed boot. The big Russian immediately stopped convulsing and began struggling to get up, but he was dazed and disorientated from the electric shock. Ben signalled and shouted to Tatyana and Yuri to make a run for it. Every split second was critical. More men were streaming from the house. Five down already, but Ben could only guess how many more he might have to deal with. Any number of them could have been dropped by helicopter at a safe distance and hiked overland to the farm.

In which case, he thought, he'd best get started whittling them down further, if he and the others were to have any chance of getting out of here alive. The first dark figure to come running from the doorway was met with the red dot of Ben's laser sight, instantly followed up with a triple-stitch of bullets that punched his flesh from throat to temple and dropped him like a wet sandbag.

Muted muzzle flashes lit up from the dark doorway. While Ben had only vague shadows to mark as targets, he himself was a lit-up ghostly yellow-green figure in the eyepieces of the assault team's night vision goggles. He kept low, moving fast. Bullets skipped off the ground by his feet and smacked into the hulk of a derelict tractor whose final resting place was across the farmyard. Ben swept his laser left and right and returned fire at anything that moved, squeezing off bursts, chewing through the ammunition supply in his one and only magazine. He saw another dark flitting shape stagger and fall.

Seven down. Two more he sent scurrying for cover along the front wall of the house, where they dived into the relative safety of the space between Yuri's parked Beetle and the tin shed. Ben's shots punched through the car's side and the driver's window shattered. No way to treat a classic.

There was a brief lull in the shooting as the forces still inside the house fell back and regrouped; how many of them remained, Ben couldn't say. Grisha was trying to get up but was still on his hands and knees, groaning. Ben lashed a kick to his ribs and yelled 'Move it!' When that didn't motivate the big Russian, Ben reached down and grabbed a fistful of his scrappy beard, yanking him sharply to his feet. Grisha howled more loudly than he had when the dart had perforated his rear end, but now he was at least upright. Ben gripped his thick arm and half-steered, half-dragged him in a stumbling zigzag across the yard towards the southern perimeter fence and the woods in the distance.

Shots whistled by, missing them by pure chance, though as the larger target Grisha was the luckier of the two. Ben rattled off a few more rounds one-handed, then let go of Grisha's arm and sent him at a wallowing run towards the fence. Whether he could even climb it was uncertain, but

Ben was more concerned about the others, especially Valentina, still huddled behind the shelter of the farmhouse's side wall. His intention was to lay down a covering fire to enable her, Yuri and Tatyana to follow Grisha's escape route to the woods – but now his submachine gun was almost empty. The way these damned things chewed through their ammo supply was a perennial problem no military mind had ever been able to solve.

Ducking across the yard to the hulk of the old tractor he took cover behind one massive rear tyre. Every bullet counted with his magazine running perilously low, so he switched the weapon to single shot and let off two carefully aimed rounds towards the house. One of the men firing at him from over the bonnet of the perforated Beetle slumped and slid backwards out of sight. Another, hidden in the doorway, pushed his luck a little too far by stepping out where Ben could see him, and collected a bullet that caught him under the chin and exited through the top of his head. Nine men down, by Ben's count. Not bad going.

But now his gun was empty. Cursing, he glanced around him. The nearest of the dead men, one of the pair who'd come after Grisha, was lying slumped a few yards away, loose fingers still curled around the pistol grip of his firearm. Ben had no choice but to make a run for it across the stretch of open ground and grab the weapon to resume his covering fire.

Ben broke away from the tractor, clutching the empty gun as a ploy to make the enemy think he was still in play. The deception failed. Two of the shooters hiding behind the Volkswagen jumped out, jostling each other to be the first to gun down the foreigner who'd messed up their neat assault plan.

Ben was caught in the open with several paces to go before he reached the dead man's weapon. But in their haste to slaughter him, one shooter made the other stumble against the shed door. He must have caught the latch lever with his elbow, because now the door swung open and Alyosha, driven wild by all the noise and commotion, burst out ready to sink his fangs into anything warm-blooded. The man scrambled into the shed and kicked the door shut to escape the dog. His companion was raising his weapon to line the sights up on Ben.

Ben was almost on the fallen weapon when he saw the red dot of the guy's laser suddenly appear on his chest.

He was done.

Then a tawny blur erupted out of the shadows with gaping jaws and sharp teeth that clamped onto the shooter's upper arm and dragged him to the ground. His weapon flew out of his grasp as he thrashed desperately to free his arm, but Alyosha's fangs were clenched tight. The dog began to shake him, the way a wild canid breaks the neck of his prey. The man struggled and screamed, kicking out wildly to get the dog off him but instead hitting one of the tall propane bottles by the house, which toppled over and rolled across the yard. Still the dog clung on. The guy could do nothing to defend himself, and at this moment none of his comrades were going to help him.

Ben reached the body of the dead man and snatched the fallen gun free from his limp grasp. He fired a burst through the door of the shed, to take out the guy hiding in there. Then he ran back to the shelter of the tractor, pinned himself firmly into place and resumed his covering fire to drive back the attackers and let his remaining companions make their break for the woods.

Grisha had somehow managed to clamber over the perimeter fence and was now nowhere to be seen. From the corner of his eye Ben glimpsed Yuri grabbing Valentina's hand and the two of them running madly across the yard. He couldn't see Tatyana, and thought she might have jumped the wire into the animal enclosures to make her escape by a different route.

That was when things began to unravel.

Ben hadn't noticed the two men creep around the back of the house. When they unexpectedly appeared by the side wall where Yuri, Valentina and Tatyana had been sheltering moments earlier, they had an unimpeded field of fire towards the fleeing targets and Ben suddenly found his position open to a new angle of attack that forced him to scramble further behind cover, from where he couldn't shoot back. The silenced reports of enemy gunfire came thicker and faster. Bullets pinged and bounced off the engine block of the tractor, inches from his head. One huge tyre burst and the machine sagged at one corner.

The assault team might be under orders to take certain targets alive, but that didn't mean they weren't authorised to shoot to wound. Ben heard Yuri yell out and turned just in time to see him stumble and fall, still clinging on to Valentina's hand. He took her down with her, but she hit the ground like a parachutist and rolled nimbly back up to her feet.

'Papa!' Her cry was a shriek of pure anguish at seeing her father hurt, blood leaking out from between his fingers as he clutched his right leg below the knee. Yuri shouted in Dutch, 'Run, Valentina, run!' For an instant the girl hovered indecisively, torn between wanting to stay close to her stricken father and to bolt for her life. But it wasn't her decision to make. There were men sprinting towards her, intent on catching her. She wailed in terror and took off like a deer.

More black-clad figures burst out of the house, spitting muzzle flashes as they came. Ben belly-crawled out from beneath the tractor and fired back. He saw one fall; then another. The enemy were now a dozen men down, plus the one mauled by the hound. How many more were there? They seemed to keep coming and coming. It wouldn't be long before his replacement gun was empty, too.

He wasn't in a good place. Bullets struck the ground much too close for comfort, kicking dirt into his face and half-blinding him.

Yuri was trying to hobble to his feet. He'd managed to get up on one knee when a Taser dart nailed him squarely in the back. Like Grisha before him, he was instantly overwhelmed with the tremors and convulsions as the voltage seared through his muscles. The man with the Taser came running up, ready to fire another dart into Yuri. The man's comrade was close behind, clutching his submachine gun. Spying Ben emerging from beneath the tractor he sprayed a burst his way, only to collect a return burst that punched him diagonally from chin to cheekbone. He dropped his weapon, clutched at his face and toppled over forwards, dead before he hit dirt.

The one with the Taser wheeled around and fired his dart at Ben. Ben ducked. The dart flew over his shoulder. His magazine was down to its last four rounds, but there were other ways to use a firearm. Ben's opponent was a large and powerful man, at least six-two, at least two hundred and thirty pounds. But Ben had fought much bigger men. Before the guy could fire another Taser dart Ben charged, reached him in three long strides and clubbed him viciously in the face and throat with the butt of the empty gun until he was down and senseless, blood streaming from his smashed lips and nose.

Yuri was still in the throes of the electric shocks from the dart stuck between his shoulder blades. It was in too deep for Ben to swipe it out with the butt of his gun, so he grasped it with his fingers and plucked it out, wincing at the residual shock that sent a painful tremor up his wrist and arm. He could see the blood soaking Yuri's right trouser leg where a bullet had taken him in the calf. The Russian was in no state to run very far, even if he hadn't been rendered half unconscious by the Taser. Seizing his collar Ben started dragging his limp form to safety.

He glanced back at the house and his mouth went dry at the sight of yet more men spilling from the doorway. To send so many, just to capture one fat country bumpkin, one ex-spook and a twelve-year-old child, made no sense.

Ben felt that cold chill in his bones that comes with the growing certainty that one's chance of survival is slim to zero. He'd experienced that chill plenty of times before and lived to prove it wrong. But one day it would be right. One day, he wouldn't make it out alive.

That day might just have come.

Chapter 32

Ben could either let go of the half-unconscious, injured Yuri and abandon the guy in order to save himself, or he could stand his ground and let himself get shot to pieces. Neither option appealed to him. He kept hold of Yuri's collar, hauling him one-handed away from danger. With the other hand he trained his near-empty weapon on the stream of men emerging from the house.

Four rounds left. Four rounds to make the difference between living and dying. *Here we go*, he thought, and squeezed the trigger.

No submachine gun ever made was going to be much of a target weapon. Firing one-handed backwards over his shoulder while at a run and simultaneously struggling with a hefty dead weight made it even less conducive to accuracy. His first shot took off a man's earlobe and smashed a window of the house. His second hit another man in the arm. His third went nowhere at all.

But in the next fraction of a second Ben had one of those crazy ideas that were known to make Jeff Dekker, and others who'd seen him in action, go pale.

The flicker of the still-burning electrical transformer and the showers of sparks from the severed high-voltage line were gleaming off the cylindrical surface of the propane bottle that had been knocked over and rolled across the yard. It was lying at just the right angle, so a bullet fired from where he was standing wouldn't simply ricochet off its rounded side.

Would the underpowered 9mm Makarov round penetrate the thick steel? Only one way to find out.

Ben thought *fuck it* and fired. Last shot. He heard the *clack* of the silenced weapon's bolt and the simultaneous solid *clank* of the bullet punching cleanly through the metal of the bottle's curved flank and out the other side.

In the movies, firing at vehicle petrol tanks, propane canisters or anything remotely volatile was always guaranteed to make them go up like a ton of TNT, killing all the bad guys in the vicinity without harming the hero. Ben usually fell asleep watching those kinds of films, and he'd seen enough bullet impacts in his life to know that such things just didn't occur in real life.

And this was real life, not cinema. When he shot the steel bottle, as expected, nothing happened except a rapid and hissing escape of pressured gas from the two holes his bullet had made on its way through the bottle. In itself, quite harmless.

But that was without accounting for the flames of the burning transformer just a few feet away. Flammable gas is at its most dangerous when mixed with air. The hissing gas jetted into the flames and ignited.

The explosion happened so fast that the men running from the house had no warning. The fireball expanded across the yard, lighting up the night and swallowing up Yuri's Volkswagen and Grisha's pickup truck, which immediately caught light and blew up in a staggered sequence as their tanks ruptured and detonated. The pressure of the burning gas inside the propane bottle blew it apart like a bombshell. Jagged fragments of steel flew outwards in a deadly rain. A man who hadn't been close enough to the fireball to be engulfed was hit in the belly by a piece of shrapnel that tore him almost in half and spilled his intestines onto the dirt.

The heat of the explosion seared Ben's face and drove him back. He dropped his empty gun and grabbed the prone Yuri with both hands, manhauling him to his feet and yelling '*Move!*' in his ear. Yuri's shot leg buckled under him. Ben went down on a knee, let Yuri topple across his shoulders, raised him up in a fireman's lift and ran. He'd no idea how many of the enemy had survived the blast, and he had no intention of hanging around to do a headcount of survivors. The time to get out of here was now or never, while the wall of flames raged and could have held back a regiment.

Bent under Yuri's weight and thankful he hadn't had to carry Grisha instead, Ben hurried towards the darkness of the woods. He was half blinded by the sunspots that the propane blast had imprinted on his retinas and had to keep blinking to get his vision back. Behind them, the farmyard looked like a battlefield. A couple of bodies lay burning. The whole front of the house was ablaze and the inferno would soon take over the entire building.

Reaching the perimeter fence Ben turned to look in all directions and called, 'Valentina!' He'd last seen her taking off after her father was hit. Where had she gone? He called her name again, as loudly as he dared. Then saw the figures of armed men skirting like ants around the edges of the fiery farmyard and ran faster before they spotted him and gave chase.

Ben struggled over the perimeter fence and kept moving through the darkness towards the trees, stumbling over the rough ground, bushes tearing at his legs. He spun around at the sound of a voice.

'Psst! Over here!'

It was Grisha. He was hiding at the edge of the woods, still panting hard from his flight. The flicker of the distant fire reflected in his eyes as he glanced around and then looked ashen-faced at Ben. 'Where's the kid? Where's Valentina?'

Ben had to admit, 'I don't know. I lost sight of her back there.'

'Oh, no. No, no.'

'She must know every nook and cranny of the farm,' Ben said, trying to sound more assured about it than he really was. 'She'll be hiding somewhere. I'll go back for her. First I need to get him to safety.'

Grisha touched Yuri's arm, tentatively, as though he might be dead. 'Holy shit. Is he okay?'

'He will be,' Ben replied. 'Once we get the bullet out of his leg. He took a nasty zap from a Taser.'

'I know the feeling. What about the chick, what's-her-name?'

'Tatyana?' Ben shook his head. He was perplexed about her. Why had she vanished so suddenly?

Another explosion sounded from the direction of the farm, making Grisha jump. Another propane bottle had just gone off.

'Oh man, what happened to my house?'

'It was a tip anyway,' Ben said. 'Now why don't you shut up and lead us to the trailer, or do I have to find it myself?'

The lumbering Grisha led the way into the dense forest. They kept moving for several hundred yards, until the burning house was just a dim orange flicker through the trees. While Grisha trampled through the bushes like a water buffalo, Ben moved stealthily and quietly even with the weight of an unconscious man over his shoulders.

Suddenly Ben tensed at the sound of crackling twigs. Fast footsteps, coming up behind him.

He whirled around to meet the threat.

Chapter 33

But it was on four legs, not two, that they'd been followed. Alyosha trotted up to Ben and dropped to his haunches, tongue lolling. Ben breathed a sigh of relief and patted the hound on the head. He seemed to have come away from the battle uninjured, and none of the blood that matted his tawny fur was his own.

'You helped me out a lot back there, Alyosha. How'd you like to come and live with me in France?'

The dog made no reply. Maybe he needed time to think about it.

With Grisha in the lead, Ben's new best friend bringing up the rear and nobody else in pursuit, they kept moving through the dark forest. Just when Ben was becoming convinced that the big guy had lost his way, Grisha stopped up ahead and pointed. His breathing was so laboured that he could barely wheeze out, 'Here it is.'

At first Ben could see nothing but shadows. As his eyes got used to the darkness he was able to make out the solid black shape among the foliage. He stepped towards it, reached out and his fingers felt the mesh of the camouflage netting with which Grisha had draped his trailer, carefully blending it into its surroundings. If the assault team had come this way from their drop zone, they could have stalked

228

within a few yards of it in the darkness, and not known it was there. For the second time that night, Ben had to confess that the company of a paranoid conspiracy nut brought certain advantages.

Grisha pulled aside some netting, fumbled with keys and managed to find the trailer door lock in the darkness. Between them they manhandled Yuri's limp form up the steps and laid him down on the floor. Grisha bolted the door shut behind them and groped about for a light switch until he remembered there was no power, and reached instead for another of his gas-powered survival lanterns.

'No lights,' Ben said.

'All the windows are blacked out, man. Nobody will see it.'

'Keep it low.'

The dim light shone about the trailer. Grisha's hideout was some forty feet in length. Two thirds of the space was devoted to his internet radio setup, enough equipment piled everywhere to sink a boat. Every bare horizontal surface was crowded with mouldy coffee mugs and the remnants of meals and snacks. The walls were plastered with peeling conspiracy posters in Russian and English. A recent US president with airbrushed demon eyes and goat ears. A UFO overflying a Cyrillic slogan that probably said 'I WANT TO BELIEVE'. Electric cables covered the floor like a nest of snakes. 'Watch you don't trip,' Grisha warned.

'How do you run all this stuff?' Ben asked, looking at the mountain of computers and assorted gear.

'Power supply runs all the way from the house. The wire is buried four feet deep. I keep a couple of backup generators, too.'

'Know something, Grisha? You're even nuttier than I realised.'

'That's what it takes to elude the New World Order, man.'

'Says the guy who just had his home destroyed by a tactical raid team. You're going to need to have a real think about how the hell they found you out here in the middle of nowhere.'

'Oh, I'm thinking about it, man. And it beats me.'

'Me too. For now.'

Alyosha curled up in a heap of old clothes covered in dog hair. Ben and Grisha heaved Yuri into the narrow aisle between the trailer's bench seats. Yuri stirred. His eyes flickered open, then rolled back shut. Blood from his gunshot wound was leaking all over the carpet. Crouching beside him Ben ripped the blood-soaked trouser leg to the knee and inspected the wound. The bullet had torn right through the muscle without touching bone, but had left a nasty exit wound that was going to need sutures. 'Got a first-aid kit in here?' Ben asked Grisha.

'Sure.' Grisha tossed aside a pile of old magazines and dragged out a plastic box, which turned out to be a comprehensive piece of kit that any survivalist prepper would be proud of. First Ben reached into his jacket pocket for his flask and splashed whisky on the wound, which had the effect of bringing Yuri much more to life. The kit contained local anaesthetic spray and antiseptic cream, both of which Ben applied liberally to the holes in Yuri's leg before wrapping him up from knee to ankle in a makeshift field dressing that would do for now. Yuri's pain eased, but nothing could allay his distress about Valentina.

'I'll find her, Yuri,' Ben promised him. 'I'm going back.'

'I want to come too,' Yuri groaned.

'Not a chance.' Ben turned to Grisha. 'If I'm not back after thirty minutes, it means you're not safe here and you need to get away. Is there a place you can go?'

'Screw that, man, I'm not going anywhere.'

'We'll have that conversation when I get back. Thirty minutes.'

Ben left the trailer and scouted back alone, silent and fast, just a shadow flitting among the trees. As he reached the edge of the woods, he paused and heard the distant rhythmic pulse of helicopter blades. At least two choppers but more likely three, judging by the sound. They were incoming from the north, still some distance off but approaching fast.

Ben kept moving and soon reached the perimeter fence. The goats were bleating in agitation and milling around their pen. He slipped over the fence and let himself inside their enclosure, crouching low behind the wire to observe the scene. There was no sign anywhere of either Valentina or Tatyana. Grisha's farmhouse was still burning out of control, nothing to save it from total destruction. The air was thick with the stench of smoke. He could see the remnants of the assault team silhouetted against the fiery background, at least half a dozen men that he could count. They were busy collecting their equipment and gathering up all the dead bodies of their comrades they could find, the ones that hadn't been burned up in the blaze. One man was speaking on a radio. A couple more were hobbling about or sitting nursing their injuries.

But the walking wounded could still maim or kill an unarmed enemy, as long as they still had a trigger finger to shoot with. Ben could get no closer.

Above, the blinking lights of the approaching choppers were becoming visible through the smoke. As he'd guessed, there were three, flying close together in a V-formation. They hovered over the farm and began to descend at a safe distance from the flames. The deafening hurricane from the combined blast of their rotors was whipping the fire into an even

231

greater frenzy and beating back the smoke, which swirled and roiled in the bright white shafts of the searchlights sweeping the ground. For an instant the goat pen where Ben was crouching was lit up like daylight, before the dazzling beam quickly passed over and he could breathe again.

As the helicopters came down, Ben recognised them as Kamovs, a type in service to the Russian military. All three were painted black, with no identifying markings. Special Forces, or something else? Whoever this enemy was, the resources being deployed against Yuri Petrov and his partner in crime were all the proof anyone needed that something much bigger was happening here. The wild conspiracy tales that Ben had hardly been able to swallow earlier that night now all seemed deadly plausible.

The worrying question now on his mind was whether the enemy was about to drop a fresh contingent of men on the ground, to search the whole area and finish the job they'd come here to do. But as he watched, he saw with relief that they were pulling out. The wounded clambered aboard, while their able-bodied teammates slung their dead in after them like sacks of rice.

This wasn't over, by any means. Ben knew they'd be back, and probably in larger numbers. For the moment, though, they were beating a retreat. Someone would be wondering how the hell a crack squad of over twenty men, bristling with all the firepower they could muster, had managed to be repelled by such a tiny force. There would be a lot of questions, explanations, recriminations. He'd have loved to be there to see it.

If some part of Ben was able to derive grim satisfaction at the sight of his decimated enemy retreating from the field of battle, what he saw next made his heartbeat shudder to a halt and his blood turn to ice in his veins.

Grasped tightly in the arms of two men, a smaller figure was being loaded aboard the chopper. Smaller, and all too familiar, and kicking and struggling and screaming in a terrified little voice that Ben could hear over the noise of the rotors and turbine.

Valentina.

In that moment, all hope of finding her hiding somewhere in the vicinity of the farm was lost. They'd found the poor kid. She was now their prisoner. Their hostage.

Ben shot up to his feet, every muscle tight as steel cables. Even if he'd had a weapon, he couldn't have dared open fire for fear of accidentally hitting the child. He wanted to run to save her, but knowing he would achieve nothing except to die trying. How he was going to tell Yuri this news, he couldn't begin to think. Or Kaprisky and the girl's mother.

The last of the men clambered aboard the chopper after their captive. The pilot increased his revs. The turbine screeched and the rotors became a blur. The helicopter went light at the nose, then the tail. Firelight glinted along its fuselage as it lifted off and climbed.

Ben watched helplessly as the helicopter, and Valentina with it, disappeared into the smoky night sky.

Chapter 34

As he was leaving the ruin of Grisha's farm with a leaden heart and a sick feeling in his stomach, Ben paused by the goat pen. The animals were stampeding around their enclosure in a blind panic in the darkness, bleating wildly and butting the wire in their desperation to escape. The farmstead was lost now. The trapped livestock wouldn't survive long penned up without food or water, so Ben flipped the latch of their gate and let it swing open to free them. At least he'd have helped to save *someone* that night, he thought miserably.

That was when he heard the low groan from nearby, a sound definitely not made by a goat.

It was the raider he'd battered unconscious earlier with the butt of his weapon. On coming to, the guy must have managed to drag himself as far as the fence of the enclosure before he'd passed out again and slumped in the shadows where his comrades had failed to notice him. He was splayed out on his belly, all six foot three of him, slowly returning back to the painful reality of consciousness.

Ben rolled him over with his boot. The man's lips and nose were a mess of blood. His Taser gun was lying in the dirt nearby. Ben thought of using it on him and watching him twitch a while, just out of sheer savage nastiness and to get back at the men who'd taken Valentina.

The raider's eyes fluttered open a glimmer, then widened all the way as he registered Ben standing there over him. Suddenly fully awake, he made a grab for a pistol on his utility belt. Ben stamped on his wrist and kicked the hand away from the weapon, got to it first and drew it out of its holster. From the feel of the pistol in his hand he knew without looking that it was a Glock 17. From its weight, that it was fully loaded up. He pointed it in the guy's face. The guy put up his hands to shield himself, in that irrational moment when even trained soldiers have to believe their palms could stop a 9mm bullet. But Ben had no particular intention of killing him, not yet anyway. He had a better purpose to which to put this fellow.

'Looks like your friends gave you up for dead,' Ben said. 'Which makes tonight your lucky night, because now you're mine.'

Still holding the gun on him, Ben grabbed one thick wrist and with some effort hauled his prisoner upright. He twisted the arm behind the man's back and shoved his bulk roughly towards the perimeter fence, keeping the pistol poked into his side.

'Speak English?'

There was a slight nod.

'Good. Then you'll understand what "one stupid move and I'll shoot you through the liver" means. Let's go.'

They marched through the darkness, Ben maintaining enough leverage on his prisoner's arm to hurt. The man stumbled over the fence, tripped and fell on the other side, and Ben saw a trick coming and kicked him hard in the ribs, extracting a yowl. 'That was your warning shot, Boris. Don't be a silly boy.'

'You think you will make me talk,' the prisoner said, as best he could through his broken lips. 'But you are wasting your times. I know nothing.'

'Maybe I don't want to make you talk. Maybe I have absolutely no interest in anything you have to tell me, and all I want is to take you somewhere I can pull you apart, nice and slow, piece by piece. What do you think about that?'

'I was only following the orders.'

'That's what they all say, Boris.'

'My name, it is not Boris.'

'I don't give a hoot what your name is,' Ben said. 'And I'll call you Doris if it pleases me. Keep moving.'

Soon they had reached the woods, the burning house just an orange glow far behind them and the trailer just a couple of minutes' march through the trees ahead. Ben was still keeping up the painful pressure on his prisoner's arm, forcing him to walk hunched over and wincing at every step. Twigs crackled underfoot. Twice the man stumbled again and nearly broke his own arm. 'Go ahead and cry out,' Ben said. 'Your friends are long gone. Nobody's going to hear you.'

Then Ben stopped, hearing a movement close by. He turned, thinking it was Alyosha again. Why had Grisha let the mutt out of the trailer to go mooching about on his own?

But this time, it wasn't a four-legged creature wandering about the forest. As the figure stepped closer from between a pair of pine trees, the dim moonlight fell across her face.

'Tatyana!'

She had blood on her face from a gashed lip, but otherwise seemed unharmed. 'I didn't know where you'd gone,' Ben said. 'You had me worried.'

'There was so much shooting. I . . . I just ran. One of those men caught me, but I hit him and kept running.' Her voice was low and husky and faraway, like someone not quite fully engaged in the present moment. Ben noticed that her breathing seemed a little laboured. The moonlight gleamed in her eyes, which were moist and appeared somehow distant, detached. Those were all signs of shock.

Ben motioned with the pistol. 'Grisha's trailer is just up ahead. When we get there I'm going to look you over and examine that cut, okay?'

'Who . . . who is that man?' she asked, apparently only now noticing the prisoner in Ben's grip.

'Meet Boris,' Ben said. 'Our new recruit.'

Moments later, five bodies instead of three were crowded together inside the trailer. Grisha had helped Yuri to the tiny bunk area at the far end, where Yuri was sitting slumped and pale, nursing his bandaged leg.

'Where did she pop up from?' Grisha said. 'And who is this fucker you brought into my trailer?'

Ben roughly dumped Boris's muscular mass on the floor. 'A contender for the Russian Bodybuilding Federation championship who lost his way in the woods. What do you think?'

Tatyana blinked in the light and seemed disorientated. Ben helped her over to a bench seat and sat with her. He checked her pupil reflex and pulse, which seemed okay. Examining the cut on her lip he said, 'It looks worse than it is. You won't need stitches.' He spoke gently, even though he was full of questions about how she'd managed to get away from the attackers. This was no time for an inquest.

Yuri opened his pain-racked eyes and stared at Ben. 'Where's Valentina? You said she was hiding. You said you were going to bring her back. You said—'

Ben heaved the deepest sigh of regret, turned to him, and told him the unhappy truth. 'They have her, Yuri. I'm sorry. I couldn't have stopped them.'

Yuri sank his face into his hands.

'You have any idea what they'll do to her, man?' Grisha demanded angrily.

'They won't harm her,' Ben replied. 'She's a bargaining chip, and that will keep her safe. It's her father they want. But I'm not going to let them have him.'

'So what's the plan, smart guy? You gonna march in like Rambo and take her back, just like that, on your own?'

'One way or another,' Ben said. 'Whatever it takes to get her out of there, that's what's going to happen. But right now we need to get away from here.'

'We're okay right where we are,' Grisha said, shaking his head. 'Nobody can find this trailer.'

'I wouldn't count on that, Grisha. We might have beaten them back, but that was only the first wave. More will come, and soon.'

'"Beaten them back,"' Yuri echoed in a ghastly voice. 'They took my girl. You call that a victory?'

'It's not over, Yuri.'

'I'm not leaving here,' Grisha insisted, waving his arms around him. 'This place is my life.'

'And you can die here just as easily,' Ben said. 'Face it, it's over. They know where you are now. You can't ever come back, understand? What you need to do is focus on not getting caught again.'

Ben slipped the pistol out of his belt. Popped the magazine. Seventeen rounds plus the one in the chamber. The shiny new 9mm cartridges were copper-jacketed hollow-points, designed to expand into little mushrooms inside their target, for maximum damage. He wondered how much more damage he was going to have to do before this was over.

Grisha muttered, 'It's like they knew exactly where to find us. But how?'

'I don't know,' Ben replied. 'That's what I'm hoping our friend here is going to help us figure out.' He pointed down at Boris on the floor.

'I tell you, I know nothing,' Boris groaned, gingerly touching his bloody, broken nose and glowering up at his captors.

Grisha directed a stream of Russian obscenities at the prisoner. 'Bullshit he knows nothing. Let me have five minutes alone with the son of a bitch and he'll soon talk, trust me.'

Ben found that hard to believe. A broken nose and a couple of loose teeth wouldn't have hampered big Boris from ripping the chronically unfit Grisha apart with his bare hands.

'You can make yourself more useful by coming up with ideas of where we can go from here,' Ben said. 'There's got to be a village nearby, or a trading post. Supplies, and a vehicle. Our first priority is to establish a secure base.'

'The nearest village is an hour's drive away. We're in the middle of nowhere. Why else would I have chosen to live here?'

'This isn't Siberia,' Ben said. 'The place can't be completely empty.'

Grisha reflected. 'Well, there's old Georgiy's farm. It's about six, seven kilometres through the forest.'

'Will your neighbour be happy about us landing on him in the middle of the night?'

'He won't complain,' Grisha replied. 'Old Georgiy died in March. His wife's been dead for fifteen years, and it was just him. He must've been a hundred when he croaked. Now the place is empty, as far as I know.'

'You're sure?'

'As sure as I can be, man. They had no family, no kids, and I can't see anyone queuing up to buy the place.'

'Then here's our plan,' Ben said. 'We fall back to the neighbouring farm, where I'll attend to Yuri's leg. There might be some kind of supplies we can scavenge, maybe even some kind of vehicle we can use to widen the distance between ourselves and whoever comes looking for us. We'll find a properly safe place to hole up in. Then I'll go after Valentina. Okay?'

Yuri was too distraught to speak. Tatyana was sitting dumb, as though she'd barely registered any of what was being discussed. The debate was between just Ben and Grisha, and Grisha wasn't liking Ben's plan one bit.

'It's a hell of a long trek through the woods to old Georgiy's farm. We got a spaced-out chick who looks like she just swallowed half a bottle of zombie pills, a grieving father with a chunk of leg shot away and this *ublyudok* here who'll bolt back to his masters the instant any of us turns our back on him. How the hell do you propose we can make it even halfway?'

Ben couldn't do much about Tatyana except hope she soon came out of the strange, silent, almost dreamlike state she'd fallen into. As for the other two, he'd already hit on a secondary plan that cancelled out both problems.

'Boris is a strapping big bloke. He'll make a fine pack horse. Yuri's going to ride cross-country to Georgiy's in comfort.'

Chapter 35

The night-time hike through the woods seemed to take forever. The reluctant Grisha led the way, his lantern bobbing as he trudged wearily at the head of the line and casting menacing shadows of branches that looked like hooked claws. Grisha was not always sure of his path, stopping now and then to rethink their direction as the trees seemed to thicken and the terrain seemed to grow rougher with every kilometre.

Yuri, who'd at first resisted the idea of being carried even more strongly than their prisoner had objected to piggy-backing the injured man all that distance, had finally relented and now rode along slumped like a sack of potatoes on Boris' shoulders. Ben walked close to Tatyana, watching her and wondering about the odd change that seemed to have come over her.

Now and then Alyosha, tagging along in their wake, would freeze and let out a low growl directed at the darkness, as though sensing some other presence observing them from the depth of the forest. Ben had read somewhere that wolves were on the rise throughout much of Eastern Europe. But whatever was out there, it kept its distance and they saw and heard nothing. They stopped only once, to let Boris rest for a couple of minutes. Yuri sat propped up against a tree and petted the dog, as though seeking comfort from his company. Tatyana was still weirdly silent and detached, in a world of her own.

An arduous ninety minutes after abandoning the trailer, as the first glimmers of dawn were beginning to streak pink and purple above the tree line to the east, they finally came across old Georgiy's farm. The abandoned homestead lay in a wide forest clearing, deathly still and as quiet as a grave-yard. It consisted of a scattered collection of ramshackle buildings, towards the largest of which Grisha led them across an overgrown wasteland. The house was perhaps a quarter of the size of Grisha's former home. By the light of dawn it looked like the dwelling of a tenth-century hermit who made his living by hunting and gathering. The walls were insulated with dried manure and the roof was made of thatch.

'Careful,' Grisha warned as they approached. 'The porch steps are kind of rotten.' Which was an understatement, as even Alyosha's weight was too much for the decayed wood to bear.

The tiny house was cluttered with junk, and every bit as damp and uncomfortable on the inside as it looked from the outside. Georgiy and his wife had obviously lived all their lives without electricity. One room served as the main living quarters, in which the old man had slept, eaten and most likely died. There were candles in every corner, which Ben lit with his Zippo. His next priority was to secure the prisoner. By candlelight he used a length of dirty nylon baling twine to truss up the sullen and fuming Boris, and propped him up in a mouldy corner away from the others. 'I haven't finished with you,' he said as he left him.

Next, Ben set about lighting the ancient cast iron range, the only form of heating in the house, to get some of the damp chill out of the air. The firewood logs were damp and gave off a lot of smoke. Ben had to open the window so everyone could breathe. Then it was time to attend to his patient, who was in a lot of pain. Glad he'd brought the first-aid kit from the trailer as old Georgiy certainly hadn't possessed such items, Ben sprayed more local anaesthetic on the gunshot entry and exit wounds in Yuri's leg, waited for the painkilling effect to kick in and then packed each hole with antiseptic and stitched up the wounds with the suture kit. When he was done he said to Yuri, 'You'll never win the lovely legs competition, but that should sort you out reasonably well until we can get you to a doctor.'

'You know what, I don't even care if it rots off. I don't care if I live or die. I've lost my little girl.'

'You're wrong. I will find her. I will get her out of there. I swear to you, Yuri. Valentina's going to be okay.'

'You shouldn't make promises you can't honour, my friend,' Yuri said.

The Russian would never know how deeply those words lanced through Ben, more keenly than the sharpest knife.

Ben touched his shoulder. 'Get some rest.'

Leaving Yuri in peace, Ben went over to Tatyana. She seemed to have grown steadily even quieter and more withdrawn with every passing hour. Now she was curled up in a battered armchair that had been one of old Georgiy's few items of furniture, and was staring unblinkingly out of the open window at the pale sun rising over the forest. She barely appeared to be breathing. Ben crouched next to her and studied her for a moment. He noticed that Grisha, sitting against the wall opposite, kept looking at her too.

Something strange was definitely up.

Ben whispered to her, 'You okay?'

'I'm okay,' she mumbled semi-coherently back.

'You want me to see if there's any coffee or tea in this place?'

'No. Leave me alone.'

Ben stood up and did as she asked. Grisha caught his eye, shook his head doubtfully, and Ben shrugged in reply.

As the unelected leader of the group, it was on him to take charge of their needs. Finding a couple of expired tins of some kind of Russian meat stew in Georgiy's primitive kitchen he dumped their lumpy contents into an old tin pot and heated them up on the range. He doled portions of stew out on five mismatched plates and handed them around. Forks for everyone except Boris, who couldn't be trusted with anything pointier than a wooden spoon.

'What are you wasting food on that piece of shit for?' Grisha challenged as Ben untied Boris's wrists so he could eat.

'Because we don't let our prisoners of war starve in this army. Not while they're still useful to us.'

'I say shoot him.'

'You shoot him.'

'Hey, I don't shoot people. That's your job, friend.'

'I forgot,' Ben said. 'You're the brains of this operation.'

Yuri barely touched his meal, and let Alyosha guzzle most of it off his plate. Tatyana didn't even look at hers. Grisha and Boris both wolfed theirs down faster than the dog. When the prisoner had finished, Ben trussed him tightly up again and sat next to him. He said, 'We can do this the easy way. Tell me what I want to know, and I'll play fair with you.'

Boris said, 'What is play fair?'

'Maybe I let you walk away from this alive. Or else we do it the unpleasant way. Which you don't want to know about, Boris.'

'You do not scare me,' Boris said.

Ben had been giving a lot of thought to what he should do with his prisoner. Rank and file men did what they were ordered, end of story, no questions, no explanations. Boris was a tough nut, as well as a low-down player who might not know a great deal. If he wouldn't, or couldn't, reveal anything useful, there was a limit to what Ben could do with the guy. What then?

'If you are gonna shoot me,' Boris said, glancing at the pistol in Ben's belt, 'then do it. You think I am afraid to die?'

'No. But there are worse things than a bullet, Boris. Much worse. You should know that. You were a soldier once, weren't you? I can tell.'

'Spetsnaz GRU. Forty-fifth Guards Special Purpose Brigade. Fought in Abkhazia and Chechnya.'

'I was a soldier too,' Ben said. 'For a while. British Army. But they kicked me out. Know why?'

Boris's eyes anxiously searched his. He said nothing.

'Because of what I did to a couple of insurgents my unit picked up one day in this little backwater province in Afghanistan. We happened to know they had information on where some of their Taliban pals had a fort, but they wouldn't talk. So, I sneaked into the cell where we were holding the two of them. Afterwards, I got a nickname. Understand "nickname"?'

Boris nodded slowly.

'They called me Sausage Man. Because that's what those two guys' entrails looked like after I'd pulled them out and spilled them all over the floor. Next I lit up my Jetboil stove and dumped a few pounds of their guts into a mess tin, while these poor bastards were still alive. Fried them until they were sizzling and popping like chipolatas. Never forget the smell. Know what I did then? Have a guess.'

Boris looked away.

Grisha was staring at Ben from across the room with a look in his eyes that said, '*Sausage Man?*'

'Picture it,' Ben said. Which he could barely do himself, stretching his imagination to the limit to conjure up such an insane tale. But Boris seemed to be buying into it. He was definitely picturing the nightmare scene in his mind, vividly enough to make his jaw clench and the sweat pop out on his brow.

'You'll talk to me,' Ben said. 'I promise you'll talk to me.'

Boris clenched his eyes shut and was silent for a drawn-out beat. Then he opened his eyes, gazed fearfully at Ben and muttered, 'I work for government.'

'Now we're getting somewhere. What branch? What agency?'

Boris shook his head, pouring sweat, fear in his eyes. As if the worst psychopathic horrors inflicted by Sausage Man were nothing compared to what his own people would do if he ratted them out. Or perhaps he simply didn't know. A lot of these ex-military guns for hire would work for cash, get picked up by a van, do their job, come home – or not – and drink beer until the next anonymous call came in. From their perspective, the less they knew the better.

'You work for Bezukhov?' Ben prompted him.

'Maybe. I don't know. I just do what I am told,' Boris said. 'We are told there are terrorists in that house. Our job is to strike the target. That is all I can tell to you, I swear.'

'Terrorists,' Ben repeated. 'A twelve-year-old girl and her father, on the run and scared half to death. And what about this tub of lard here?' Ben pointed at Grisha. 'You think he looks like a terrorist? He couldn't terrorise a three-legged gerbil.'

Grisha, who for a moment there had actually looked quite

246

pleased at the idea of being considered so dangerous, scowled. 'Hey. Watch it, asshole.'

'They tell us there is one guy,' Boris said. 'Real badass. Mercenary, something like that. They say to us, this is a real hardcore motherfucker. Killed a shit load of people. They say he will fuck you up good, in a heartbeat. They say we will need many men to kill him.'

Ben's eyes narrowed. 'Did they say this person has a name?'

Boris turned to look at him. 'Yes. They say his name is Hope. And I think you are him.'

Chapter 36

'Wait a minute,' Grisha said, wrinkling his face up into a deep frown. 'How did they know—?'

'That I was at the farm?' Ben finished for him. 'Good question.' And a baffling one. Now he understood why such a large force had been deployed to attack the house. But he could think of no way the enemy could have anticipated his being there in the first place. He glowered at Boris for an answer.

'I tell you everything I know,' Boris quavered, his eyes full of the terror of Sausage Man. And Ben believed him.

'Where are you going?' Grisha asked as Ben stood up.

'To sharpen my knife,' Ben said. 'Watch him until I get back.'

The truth was, he needed to think. Nothing was adding up and his head was almost spinning with confusion. Stepping outside, he filled his lungs with the fresh morning air and listened to the chirping of the birds. Maybe they knew what was going on.

Nothing would be gained by standing there racking his brains like an idiot. He began to explore the farm. *Lugubrious* was the word for the place. Adjoining the tiny house were a few old sheds filled with the same kind of agricultural junk as Grisha's place, but even more neglected. A bunch of old tools lay about, disintegrating into rust. Rats were nesting in the straw bales and had been eating into sacks of decaying animal feed. The livestock were long gone, their deserted pens all dilapidated and overgrown. Ben peered into a barn that looked as though it was about to collapse, and thought better of going in.

Still no ideas had come to him. He was about to head back to the house when he glanced under a ramshackle lean-to next to the barn, and amongst all the heaped-up junk his eye picked out a shape hidden by a plastic tarp.

Under the tarp was old Georgiy's VAZ station wagon, about as ancient as its owner had been. Probably just as dead, too, he thought. To his surprise, it coughed into life after a few reluctant heaves of the motor. The car might actually be serviceable, except one tyre was hopelessly flat.

While he worked to change the wheel, Ben was thinking about a lot of things. How he'd been inexplicably tracked to Grisha's farm was one of them. How he ever hoped to get Valentina back was another. And the perplexing matter of Tatyana was yet another.

More than a couple of times since he'd landed in Russia, Ben had found himself not entirely disliking his travelling companion. After that frosty start, he'd warmed to her quite a bit. Maybe that was why, until now, he'd chosen to turn a blind eye to the oddities about her that had been slowly stacking up almost from the beginning of their acquaintance.

For a partner in a top detective agency that was the pick of a billionaire accustomed to always getting the very best of the best, Tatyana Nikolaeva appeared to be curiously inept at her job. Ben remembered the way she'd relied heavily on his lead back at Yuri's apartment in Moscow. How she'd admitted to a lack of experience in missing persons cases. Then there was the fact that she hadn't thought to question the apartment block's concierge before he came along. Ben had almost felt as though he was working with a rookie detective.

Yet Tatyana seemed to possess a high level of other skills, ones that seemed out of place in her line of work. Such as the ability to disarm a gun-toting opponent, at which she was far more proficient than a lot of the experienced police and military guys who came to Le Val for training. And the way she'd been able to sneak up on Ben in the darkness while watching Yuri's place, which had struck him as odd and even a little unsettling. Those were weird talents for a detective, more like things a soldier would be good at. And she certainly talked like a soldier, too, familiar with a lot of military facts and coming out with expressions like 'Comrade Major' that seemed to trip just a little too easily off her tongue.

On top of all that, now there was this bizarre change that had come over her yesterday. Shortly after they'd all gone inside Grisha's farmhouse and begun to talk, Ben had noticed the way Tatyana had gone increasingly silent. Now her behaviour was that of someone suffering from a bad case of post-traumatic stress, even though she'd apparently escaped virtually unharmed and without too much trouble from such a concerted and violent attack. She wouldn't talk about it. Wouldn't talk at all. The whole thing was a little too vague and hazy for comfort.

Ben could no longer ignore the conundrum that was Tatyana Nikolaeva, or the fact that he knew virtually nothing about this woman. Something was not right about her, though he couldn't put a finger on it. He had the impression that Grisha was suspicious of her too – although, admittedly, what *wasn't* Grisha suspicious of?

Ben tightened up the last wheelnut, wiped his dirty hands

on an old bit of rag and took out his smartphone. He had to walk nearly two hundred yards from the buildings before he was able to get one bar's worth of reception. In rural France, he wouldn't even have bothered trying. Russian technological superiority to the rescue, once again. The mobile signal lasted long enough for him to run a quick internet search on her detective agency, using her name as a keyword.

The Grendel Detective Agency had a suitably austere and no-frills website, readable in both Russian and English. A side menu tab popped up the names of its half dozen partners of which, sure enough, Miss Tatyana Nikolaeva was one. Fishing for all the detail he could get about her, Ben clicked on her name.

A new page opened up on his screen, showing a short bio of Miss Nikolaeva along with a picture of her in a business suit and scraped-back hairdo. The professional bio described her as one of the firm's most senior partners with an impressive body of experience. It was no surprise why Auguste Kaprisky would have picked her out. Nothing but the best.

There was just one problem.

Unless it had been taken on a very bad day indeed, the picture next to Tatyana's name was of a totally different person. The Miss Nikolaeva on Ben's screen looked at least fifteen years older. At least thirty pounds heavier. To resemble her in any way whatsoever, the woman Ben knew would have had to spend six hours in a movie makeup trailer receiving the full-on ugly treatment, warts, jowls, facial hair and all.

So who *was* the woman Ben knew?

He leaned against a tree, took a couple of deep breaths and then looked at his watch. It wasn't yet office hours, but the contact mobile number on the agency's site might lead him to an early bird. Ben dialled it. Four rings later, a scratchy male voice answered in Russian. Ben asked if he spoke English. Who didn't, these days? Ben apologised for the early hour, and asked if he could speak to Tatyana Nikolaeva.

'I am sorry,' the scratchy voice said, sounding suddenly morose and guarded. 'May I ask what this is regarding?'

'A confidential client matter,' Ben said. 'It's very important that I speak to her.'

'Tatyana is no longer with us,' the voice replied.

'I see. Is she with a different agency now?' Ben said, even more confused. 'Perhaps there's another number where I could reach her?'

'No, I mean she is *no longer with us*,' the scratchy voice repeated with more emphasis. 'It happened several days ago. So terrible. She . . . she is . . . We are all in shock here. The office is closed for the week.'

Ben's blood had chilled a couple of degrees. He said, 'What happened?'

'Nobody knows. The *politsiya* cannot say yet. She was found at her home. Perhaps she tried to stop a thief. Perhaps it was a crazy person.' The man's voice sounded genuinely upset. 'I am sorry to be the one to tell you, if you knew Tatyana. We all loved her. We cannot believe it. I have not had the heart to update the website . . .'

Ben offered his condolences, thanked the man for his help and ended the call. He stared into the distance for three long minutes, seeing nothing, his head churning, the ice in his blood turning to fire.

Then he ran back to the house.

Chapter 37

The woman Ben had until a few moments ago known as Tatyana Nikolaeva hadn't stirred from the armchair. Nor had she touched her plate of stew, which was being noisily gobbled up by Alyosha. Her glazed-over eyes were still fixed on the window.

Ben glanced around the room. Yuri was hunched up in one corner, apparently sleeping. Grisha hadn't budged from his position either. Nor had Boris, who had less choice in the matter.

'Look who's back,' Grisha said. 'Sausage Man.'

Without a word, Ben tossed the smartphone into Grisha's lap. The internet connection was broken but the screen still displayed the detective agency webpage with the real Tatyana's picture and bio. Grisha picked it up, stared at it, then gaped up at Ben with huge eyes. 'Just as I thought.'

Yuri gave a lurch and woke up from his slumber. 'What's that?'

Ben strode over to the fake Tatyana and grabbed her arm. He jerked her round to face him, but her eyes seemed to register nothing. He waved a finger an inch in front of her face. There was barely a flicker of reaction.

'Oh, man,' Grisha said.

'What's going on?' Yuri asked, straightening up and

wincing from the pain in his leg. Grisha tossed him the phone. Yuri caught it and stared at the screen. Same astonished reaction. Only Boris seemed uninterested in the turn of events, for the moment.

'She's one of them,' Grisha said.

'She's *what*?'

'I knew it the whole time,' Grisha said.

'You did?'

'Of course I did. This is all your fault, man,' Grisha snarled at Ben. 'You brought this bitch right to our door.' Catching the look Ben threw back at him, he shut up very quickly.

Alyosha had finished licking the empty plate clean, and now went over to curl up contentedly in a corner. Dogs didn't need to concern themselves with foolish human affairs.

Ben turned back to the fake Tatyana and lowered himself to her eye level. 'Tatyana Nikolaeva of the Grendel Detective Agency in Moscow is dead. I want to know who you are and who you're working for, and I want to know now.'

She said nothing. Her face was blank. If not for the fact that she was breathing and warm to the touch, she might have been as dead as her genuine namesake. Ben slapped her cheek to elicit some response, not hard, but not too softly.

'Understand this. I'm not gender discriminatory. Which means that if you don't tell me what I want to know, what I'll do to you will be a lot more painful than the little nick one of your buddies back there gave you to make things look real. I'll hurt you, Tatyana, or whoever you are. I'll hurt you very badly.'

Now Boris did start to pay some interest. He didn't mind seeing a bit of bloodshed, as long as it was a pretty woman getting sliced up and not him.

Ben's threat was no less of a bluff than the Sausage Man story. But the fake Tatyana didn't know that. The problem was, at this moment she didn't seem to know anything or have the least understanding of what was happening to her.

Ben drew the pistol from his belt and pressed the muzzle against the soft flesh of her neck, below a shapely ear. 'You have three seconds to talk,' he said. 'One.'

No response. Not a twitch. She remained perfectly still and composed.

Ben said, 'Two.' In another second, his bluff would be exposed, but the gamble was worth taking to get her to open up.

Or perhaps not.

He said, 'Three.'

And pulled the trigger.

The report of the gunshot was extremely loud in the confines of the tiny house. Yuri, Grisha and even Boris all jumped three inches in the air where they sat. Alyosha tensed and huddled deeper into the corner. Only the fake Tatyana didn't flinch as the bullet passed over her head and punched a hole in the roof. Dust and bits of thatch showered down and landed on her head and shoulders.

Grisha let out a long stream of Russian. Yuri's mouth was hanging open and he pointed at the unresponsive 'Tatyana'. 'That can't be normal,' he managed to stammer to Ben.

Ben's bluff was well and truly called. Short of shooting her in the leg which might only result in her bleeding to death, there was no more he could do except shake her violently by the shoulders and repeat loudly, 'Who are you?'

Tatyana's cool blue eyes gazed impassively at him for two, three, four more seconds. Then something happened that Ben couldn't have expected. Her eyes suddenly rolled over white and she slumped sideways in the armchair, as limp as a corpse.

'What the *fuck*?' Grisha yelled.

Ben quickly checked her pulse. It was steady and strong. She was breathing normally. Her skin was still warm to the touch. Nothing was wrong with her, except that she seemed, inexplicably and without warning, to have fallen into a complete catatonic state. He'd never seen anything like it before.

'You shot her,' Yuri said.

'Don't be stupid. The bullet missed her by a mile.'

'Then she fainted,' Yuri said. 'From the shock.'

Grisha shook his head vehemently. 'No way, man. This is something else. This is far out.'

'Then she's faking it,' Yuri said. 'That's all else it can be.' Dragging himself over with a wince of pain he grabbed the fork from her empty plate and jabbed it hard into her leg. No response. He did it again, stabbing it into her hand. The tines broke the skin, leaving five little bleeding holes. No response.

If she was faking, she was very good.

'You try,' Yuri said, thrusting the fork at Ben.

'What am I supposed to do with that thing?'

'I don't know, poke her eye out or something.'

Ben pointed the pistol at Boris. 'Tatyana, if you can hear me, best drop this act right now. Because otherwise I'm going to shoot your comrade here.'

Boris tried to shrink away. Ben grabbed him, shoved him hard down on the floor and jammed the pistol to his head. 'You hear me? The death of an unarmed prisoner won't be on me, it will be on you,' he warned her.

No response. Boris was struggling like a trapped animal. Ben whacked him hard on the skull with the butt of the pistol, and he went limp. Bluff number two called.

'She's not faking it, man,' Grisha said. 'She's gone and there's not a damn thing you can do to bring her back.'

Yuri was shaking his head, his injured leg all but forgotten. 'What the hell is happening here?'

'They shut her down, is what's happening here.'

Ben stared at him.

Grisha spread his hands. 'It's so obvious it hurts me to have to explain it, but here goes. She's got a chip inside her head. An implant, like happened to Jan Wolker and probably a thousand others walking around as we speak.'

'You can't possibly know that,' Ben said.

'It's the only explanation. Come on, man. Look at her. Her brain was already half shut down by the time you found her in the woods. She hardly even knew where she was any more. Then when you confronted her just now, it was like pressing the auto-destruct key. That's how it works. Like a switch inside the brain. They're programmed to deactivate under hard questioning, or if specific keywords tell the computer the asset's been captured and instructs it to pull the plug. It turns off sections of their mind like interrupting a circuit. If you were to do an MRI scan on her right now, you'd see that whole section of her brain is as dark as an aerial shot of North Korea at night.'

If Ben hadn't been looking at it right this moment with his own eyes, he wouldn't have believed it. He was beginning to realise that Grisha's idea, no matter how crazy it might sound, was the only possible explanation for what was happening here. If so, they were up against a powerful enemy, one with eyes and ears everywhere. The machinery had gone into motion the instant Yuri had gone on the run. No sooner had Kaprisky made contact with the Grendel Detective Agency in Moscow to hire the real Tatyana, than the poor woman's fate was sealed and the impostor took her place.

As if reading Ben's thoughts, Yuri asked, 'So what happened to the real Tatyana?'

'They killed her,' Ben said. 'The police think it's a burglary gone bad or a random murder.'

'Now you're talking,' Grisha said. 'See? She was taken out and this bitch was inserted to play the part. She's a remote control intelligence spook, sent to recover Object 428 before we can expose the truth to the world.'

'Then why didn't she just pull out a gun, shoot us all and take it when she had the chance?' Yuri said.

Grisha shrugged. 'Who knows? Maybe she was biding her time, waiting for the right moment. Looks like she missed her opportunity.'

Yuri said, 'All right, so *now* what?'

Grisha seemed morbidly fascinated by the shut-down 'Tatyana'. He crept closer to her on his knees, like a dog sniffing around a caught squirrel that might only be playing dead and about to jump up. He tentatively reached out and prodded her in the side with a finger. His eyes were running up and down her body and Ben could see all kinds of thoughts going on in his mind. 'Oh man, we could do anything we wanted to her. She'd never know a thing.'

'You can get that out of your head, for a start,' Ben said.

Grisha took his hand away, sat back and scratched his beard. 'There's an idea.'

'What's an idea?'

'When you said, "Get it out of your head." We could, like, literally cut it out of her.' Grisha dug in the pocket of his grimy dungarees and came out with a penknife. Opening out the rusty blade he brandished it as though it were a scalpel. 'The thing's got to be in there somewhere. I have a rough idea where to dig for it.'

Yuri looked at him as though he'd gone mad. 'Grisha, are

you telling us you intend to cut this woman's skull open with that knife?'

'Okay, so we might need some extra tools,' Grisha said. 'Old Georgiy must have had a saw and a hand drill kicking about somewhere.'

'But . . . but . . . you'd be *killing* her,' Yuri said.

'So? She's already worse off than dead. Look at her.'

'Put the knife away,' Ben said. 'Before it ends up somewhere you won't like it, pointy end first.'

Grisha's shoulders sagged with frustration. 'Come on, guys, don't you see? This is our golden opportunity to see how far the technology has come since the fifties. Think how freaking awesome that would be, to have not just one but two of these things, the old and the new, side by side.'

Yuri shook his head mournfully. 'I hate to tell you, Grish, but I don't have the other device any more.'

Now it was Grisha's turn to stare at his friend as though he'd taken leave of his senses. 'What? You mean you lost it?'

'No, I sort of hid it. The microfilm and flash drive, too. Between here and the trailer.'

'In the woods?' Grisha looked ready to run back and start scouring their trail.

'I'm not saying where. Somewhere nobody could ever find them. Not even you, Grish.'

Grisha started waving his arms around, purple-faced. 'Are you nuts? That was our evidence! That's what this whole thing was about! You risked everything to get it!'

Yuri said, 'And if they catch me with it, they'll just take it and put a bullet in my head. I have to stay alive for my little girl. She's all I have.'

His friend was so enraged he could barely speak. 'No, Yuri, you threw away all you had. I thought you were my partner in this, man!'

'I am,' Yuri replied. 'But my daughter is my whole life.'

'Jesus,' Grisha spat, 'you don't even see it. Your daughter's taken. You won't be seeing her again.'

Yuri's expression was resolute. 'Ben will get her back. Like he says.'

'Oh, so you believe that now, all of a sudden?'

'Yes,' Yuri said. 'I do.'

'Fuck!' Grisha yelled. 'Fuckfuckfuck!' Then he yelled it again in Russian, several times over. 'I can hardly believe you'd do this to me! Tell me where you hid the stuff!'

'I can't tell you,' Yuri said. 'Sorry, Grisha. If they catch us, you might crack and tell them. Then we're both dead.'

Grisha shook his head in disgust. 'To hell with you, Petrov. You just fucked us. But guess what. I don't need you any more. And I don't need Object 428 either. Not after I chop open this bitch's head and find what they stuck in there.'

Grisha made a lunge for the inert Tatyana, knife in hand. He hadn't moved more than a few inches before Ben levelled the pistol at him.

'I still have seventeen rounds in this. I only need one for you. Cut her and you're dead.'

'What the hell is she to you, man? You in love with the bitch or something?'

'Last warning, Grisha,' Ben said. 'Put the knife down.'

The Glock in Ben's hand was aimed squarely at Grisha's head, which at this range was a pumpkin-sized target Ben couldn't have missed with his eyes shut. And at this range a single 9mm hollowpoint bullet was all it would take to blow it right apart. Ben's finger was on the trigger.

'You're bluffing,' Grisha said. 'You already bluffed twice before. You won't shoot.'

'Try me,' Ben said. His finger tightened a fraction on the

trigger. His eyes were locked on Grisha's. He was prepared to fire, even though he didn't want to.

But then Grisha's head exploded anyway.

Chapter 38

Right before Ben's eyes, Grisha's skull separated into several pieces and flew apart like a ripe watermelon. The Russian's bulk was kicked backwards and he hit the floor with a heavy thump. Blood painted the wall behind him.

For about an eighth of a second Ben froze as he tried to compute what had just happened. The pistol in his hand hadn't fired. Even if it had somehow managed to go off by its own will, no 9mm handgun in the world, no matter at what range, could have caused such devastation. But that, as Ben understood another eighth of a second later, was because the shot had come from a high-powered rifle.

The sniper shot had come from behind him, way back among the trees. It had passed through the window he'd opened earlier because of the smoke, gone over his left shoulder and caught Grisha full in the middle of the forehead.

Then suddenly, there were more. Lots more. Gunfire smashed the remaining windows and thunked into the walls and floorboards of the house. One struck Boris in the chest, ploughing a furrow in him from heart to navel. Another hit the already dead Grisha in the thigh and laid it open to the bone.

Ben dived across the floor and grabbed Yuri, trying to

haul and shove him into a blind spot where no bullets could reach him. Yuri let out a cry, pain and fear intermingled. Ben shoved him into a craggy recess of the stone walls. Glanced back through the window. The gunfire had ceased for the moment, but the attack was only just getting started. He saw men running from the trees, many more of them than before.

Once again, the enemy had found them; once again, Ben had no idea how. Then it hit him, in a flash of sickening realisation. He glanced across at the prone body of the woman he no longer had a name for, and understood.

But there was no time to hang around thinking about it. Ben grabbed hold of Yuri again and heaved him towards the door. Their only chance lay in escape. If they could make it outside to where old Georgiy had kept his station wagon . . .

Yuri could hardly hobble two steps on his injured leg without collapsing. With one arm around Ben's neck he was a dead weight. Ben wrenched the door open and was almost tripped by Alyosha as the dog, driven into a panic by the noise and chaos, hurtled between his feet and out onto the broken-down porch. Alyosha leaped down the rotted steps and bolted away towards the outbuildings, barking like crazy.

The black-clad figures of armed attackers were swarming from all directions across the forest clearing towards the house. Ben was surrounded in broad daylight with very little cover and only a pistol in his hand.

Still clutching Yuri to his side he snapped off a couple of shots, but in the next moment the two of them were driven back inside the house by a volley of gunfire that tore up the porch and cut off all hope of escape. At least eight men, approaching in an arc, had Ben and Yuri in their sights and could have mowed them down.

Ben kicked the door shut. They fell back.

'We're trapped!' Yuri cried out. 'They're going to kill us both!'

'Not you,' Ben said. 'They want you alive.'

And Grisha too, except that hadn't worked out quite so well. Ben was pretty certain that the bullet that had killed the big Russian had been intended for him. The attackers would be more careful when it came to Yuri Petrov, the man they believed was still in possession of the stolen item someone so badly wanted back.

'What about you?' Yuri yelled.

'We all have to go sometime,' Ben said. 'It's just a matter of when, how and what you can make it mean when your time comes.'

With fifteen rounds still left in his pistol, he had every intention of making it mean a lot to the fifteen dead men he would leave on the battlefield before they finally took him down.

Last stand. So be it. He felt quite calm. He'd been mentally prepared for this moment for more years than he could remember.

'Get behind the stove,' he said to Yuri. 'Any moment now there's going to be a lot of bullets flying around and it wouldn't do for you to catch one by accident.'

'I'm staying right beside you,' Yuri said. Ben shook his head, grabbed Yuri's wrist and twisted his arm and shoved him into the nook between the wall and the cast iron range. 'Get your head down and don't move, or I'll shoot you myself. Understood?'

Ben stood in the middle of the room. He took a deep breath and aimed the pistol towards the door. He said to himself, 'Right then.'

The door burst open.

Chapter 39

Ben fired twice. The first man to come through the door went down. So did the second. More were coming. Shots cracked out.

Ben stood his ground, feet planted, eyes on target. He fired twice more. Saw two more of the enemy fall. Once he'd piled enough of them up in the doorway like sandbags, they'd have to come in through the windows.

And they would.

Smoke trickled from the muzzle of the Glock. He had eleven rounds left. His heartbeat was slow and steady. *Come on*, he thought. *Let's get this done.*

That was when the pair of 40mm grenades sailed in through two windows at once, hit the floor at Ben's feet and detonated.

The blinding white flash and ear-shattering blast obliterated Ben's vision and hearing. He felt himself toppling, the pistol falling from his hands, his body hitting the floor.

Flash-bang. Thunderflash. Stun grenade. Whatever designation they went by, they all worked on the same principle and did exactly what their name implied. The combination of a multi-million candela magnesium flare and an ammonium nitrate explosion producing some 180 decibels of noise were enough to momentarily neutralise the strongest and most determined opponent. Ben knew all about their use. The SAS had virtually pioneered the damn things and he could testify personally to their effectiveness. Especially now, being on the receiving end for the first time.

He fought to stand up, but the shock to his eardrums had destabilised his sense of balance. His head was spinning. All he could hear was the high-pitched whine filling his head. He could see nothing except the bright white afterimage of the flash, as if he'd stared too long at the sun.

But he knew what was happening all around him. He could feel the vibrations and the flexing of the floorboards as the attackers came flooding inside the house. Next, a boot was pinning him down hard on his front and strong hands were grabbing his arms, yanking them painfully behind his back and binding his wrists. He sensed the commotion nearby as the same treatment was doled out to Yuri. Then he was being hauled to his feet, the cold steel of a rifle muzzle being prodded against the base of his neck.

His captors frogmarched him through the doorway and outside, which Ben registered only as a slight brightening of the fuzzy halo that had obscured his vision. The effects would mostly wear off after just a few minutes and his senses would gradually return, leaving him with nausea, dizziness and slightly impaired balance for a few hours afterwards. For the moment, though, he was helpless, barely able to stand let alone fight.

Through the harsh ringing in his ears he could make out fragments of voices around him. Then the rasp of a diesel engine, something large and heavy like a truck. After a lot of jostling and shoving he felt himself being loaded aboard. He wondered whether Yuri was being put on the same vehicle, or another. 'Where are you taking him?' he managed to mumble, the sound of his own voice distant and muffled inside his head. The faint reply was something that sounded like 'Worry about yourself, comrade,' followed by a nasty laugh.

Then he was alone. He sensed more than heard the slamming doors that closed him in. Felt more than saw the bare metal walls of the back of the truck. There was a lurch, and then the long, uncomfortable journey began. He sat on the hard floor with his feet braced out to support him as the truck swayed and pitched for what seemed like interminable miles of farm track. By the time they'd reached what felt more like a proper road, Ben's hearing, vision and balance were about ninety per cent recovered. The remaining ten per cent would probably take the rest of the day to come back.

In any case, he had nothing to do except sit there and be consumed by his dark, bleak state of mind.

He had fallen short on every possible count. Been sold a completely false narrative right from the start of this mission. Been tricked by an impostor. Fooled into even having sympathy for her. Now both his charges were prisoners. Not only the child he'd been tasked with bringing home safe, but the innocent man who loved her more than life itself.

He'd failed to protect them. He'd let them down.

And there was only one way he would ever be able to make it right.

The road trip took hours. The monotonous droning thrum of the engine and transmission reverberated around the bare metal cage. Now and again, the truck would slow, as if they were passing through a village or encountering traffic. Ben had no idea whether the vehicle was travelling alone or in convoy with another truck carrying Yuri. But he could hazard a guess where they were going: back to Moscow, where he'd soon find out what would happen to him next.

The most obvious prospect was that they'd take him out somewhere and put two bullets in him, roll him into a ditch and goodbye. But then, if they wanted him dead, they could have taken care of it at the farm. Had they another purpose for him? He'd just have to wait and see.

The journey smoothed out. Ben was pretty sure the truck had now joined the Federal Highway, coming back the same way he and the fake Tatyana had travelled from the city. Then, at last, the truck felt as though it was reaching the outskirts of Moscow, all stop-start as they hacked through the suburban traffic. Ben's ears were still ringing from the stun grenade but he could make out sounds through the bare metal walls. After a few more minutes the traffic noise diminished. Then the truck paused and he heard voices outside, and the rattle of what sounded like a heavy wire-mesh security gate opening for them to pass through. The truck lumbered on a short distance and then rolled to a halt.

The back doors opened. Ben blinked in the sudden light. His vision was still not fully recovered, and all the detail he could make out of the two men who hauled him out of the back of the truck was that they were both squat and muscular, wore black jackets and had shaven heads. They seized his arms and walked him across a concrete yard of some kind; squinting about him Ben could make out tall metal fencing and brick walls. The place could have been a prison, or a military base, but it seemed deserted.

Wherever they were, it was far out on the edge of the city, well away from roads and traffic. And witnesses.

'This isn't my hotel,' Ben said. Neither of his escorts seemed amused by his brand of humour. Maybe that was because they didn't speak a word of English.

They marched him inside a block building with a sign in Cyrillic that he couldn't have deciphered even if he could see clearly. The stun grenade had knocked his sense of balance out of kilter, and he was weaving down the corridor like a man trying to walk along the deck of a ship in stormy seas. Up a long, narrow corridor, they led him into a processing room where one of his escorts produced a knife and none too gently slashed the cable tie that bound Ben's wrists. Next he was deprived of his jacket and its contents, along with his belt, watch and boots. Thankful he at least hadn't been strip-searched and made to put on an orange jumpsuit and leg irons, Ben was then taken deeper into the bowels of the featureless building until they stopped at a plain door with no window. One of the men rattled a ring of keys. The door was unlocked and swung open. Ben was shoved through it, into a small, plain, bare room with no windows and only a hard wooden bunk for furniture, not counting the metal toilet in the opposite corner.

'Thanks, boys. Now tell me, what time's dinner served around here? I'm starving.'

All he got in response was a smirk. Then they left without a word, slamming the door behind them. It had no internal handle and all the edges wcrc flush with the wall. Ben couldn't have forced or pried it open even if he'd had the tools.

With nothing else to do, he sat on the bunk under the cold, hard glare of the neon strip light, and waited for whatever was about to happen next.

Chapter 40

It was a long wait. As the hours passed, Ben's vision slowly returned to normal and whatever had been knocked out of tune inside his inner ear healed itself so he could pace the length and breadth of his tiny cell without losing his balance. The tinnitus would take a while longer to go away, but you couldn't ask for everything. No cameras were visible inside the cell, but he was sure there was probably one tucked away somewhere, through which his captors were monitoring him.

Out of bravado as much as to pass the time, he ticked off set after set of press-ups, then hooked his toes under the edge of the bunk and forced enough sit-ups out of himself to make his abdominal muscles cramp. All the while he was keeping track of the clock inside his head. How long were they going to keep him cooped up in here?

Finally, he heard the rattle of keys outside his door. He was standing ready for the pair of shaven-headed guards when they walked in, eyeing him warily. One was holding a pistol. It was an MP-443 Grach 9mm, current standard Russian military issue. A heavy and chunky weapon, all carbon and stainless steel, eighteen-round magazine. Reliable, highly effective, and not something to argue with. It had a stubby tubular silencer screwed to its muzzle. For those times when you might just have to blow out a troublesome prisoner's brains in a confined space without hurting your hearing too badly.

The other guard was clutching a bag containing Ben's jacket, boots, belt and watch. But something told him they weren't about to let him go just yet. He took his time doing up his boots, toying with possible ways he could overpower both guards, garrotte them with the bootlaces and make off with the Grach 9mm. It wasn't the best of plans. He let it go and decided to let things play out a little longer.

Once his boots were on, they made him stand up. The guy with the pistol kept it aimed at Ben's head from a safe distance while the other one produced a pair of handcuffs and stepped closer to snap them onto Ben's wrists. Ben allowed him to do it. Breaking the guy's neck wasn't much of an option right now, either.

From his cell the guards took him through a maze of identical bare corridors. He made a mental map as they went, memorising the sequence of left and right turns, until they arrived at another plain door. One of the guards knocked and opened the door, then unclipped a ring of keys from his belt and found the one for the cuffs. The other kept a steady aim at the back of Ben's head while his wrists were being unlocked. Then they shoved him into the room and closed the door behind him.

Ben now found himself inside a large room that contrasted starkly with the small, naked cell where he'd just spent the last few hours. If the building was a disused military facility of some kind, then this would have been a mess room, or perhaps a reception lounge for greeting visitors. The blinds were drawn over the windows, just a glimmer of fading daylight peeking through, and ceiling lights cast a soft glow. The flooring was yellowed linoleum tiling that had seen better days. A pair of blue sofas straight from an office furniture catalogue were gathered around a low table to one side, in a weak attempt to create a cosy space. Everything about the room gave the impression of its having been prepared in a last-minute rush. An old Formica-topped table had been shunted up against one wall, its surface bare except for a tray on which sat a pair of crystal tumblers and a matching decanter filled with amber liquid, a highly incongruous-looking addition. There was a faint musty smell in the air, as though the place had been closed up and out of use for a long time.

A tall, slender man in a well-tailored light grey suit was sitting primly on a sofa facing the door, and stood as Ben entered the room. The man appeared to be in his early sixties, of faintly aristocratic bearing with thinning silver hair neatly parted away from a high brow. His posture was very erect and he looked extremely fit. His shoes were black patent leather. So highly polished the toecaps were like mirrors. The overall package was unmistakable. Ben instantly knew he was in the company of a former military officer.

'Pleasure to meet you at last, my dear fellow,' the man said breezily, as though they were making their acquaintance at a summer garden party. 'Please, come in and make yourself comfortable. It's been a long day.'

'You're English,' Ben said, hiding his surprise. He'd been expecting Chief Bezukhov, the Russian intelligence boss Yuri was so terrified of.

'And I must apologise for the crudeness of your accommodation,' the man said. 'It was the best they could come up with at such short notice. This is Russia, you know.' He glanced at his watch, then motioned over at the glasses and decanter on the side table. 'Care for a drink, Major? I understand you're partial to scotch?'

'Never on an empty stomach,' Ben said, untruthfully. 'And never with strangers, that's my rule. I don't believe you introduced yourself.'

'The name's Calthorpe. Colonel Aubyn Calthorpe.'

'Now you're going to tell me you expect me to sir you.'

'Not at all. Like you, I don't tend to make much of my former rank, but the Russkies like it. They have respect for authority. Something sadly missing in much of today's world.'

'In my book, respect is something you earn,' Ben said.

'You don't think your rank qualifies you?'

'I was given my rank by killing men I didn't know on the orders of other men I didn't know, for reasons I didn't know.'

'And now?'

'Now I just kill the ones who have it coming,' Ben said.

'I admire a man of integrity. You sacrificed a promising military career for the sake of principle. Simply walked away from it all.'

'You've seen my record, then.'

Calthorpe smiled. 'Oh, I know all about you, Major Hope. I know you better than you know yourself.'

'So what are you, the head honcho around here?'

Calthorpe walked over to the ersatz drinks cabinet, plucked the stopper from the whisky bottle and poured himself a modest measure. 'Officially, I'm the Mission Chief. Another meaningless and arbitrary title to add to my collection. Then again, officially, neither I nor any of what we do actually exists. But we'll get to all of that later. You and I need to have a little chat.' He motioned to the sofa opposite the one where he'd been seated. 'Won't you sit down?'

'I've done plenty of sitting around the last few hours, thanks,' Ben said.

'Suit yourself,' Calthorpe said cheerily, returning to the sofa. He sat, took a sip of scotch and then leaned comfortably back, hooking one leg over the other as Englishmen of genteel breeding, or at least the semblance of such, are given to do. 'I've been looking forward to meeting you. You're not an easy man to get hold of.'

'Another rule of mine,' Ben said, 'is that I don't generally engage in polite conversation with people who've been trying to kill me.'

Calthorpe smiled. 'Then you'll be delighted to hear there's been a change of plan in that regard.'

'That was obvious enough, from the way your sniper missed me by a cat's whisker this morning. Call me silly, but I got the distinct impression that the bullet that took out Grisha Solokov was meant for me.'

'Sorry about that,' Calthorpe replied with a chuckle. 'Case of the old itchy trigger finger, I'm afraid. Even a Mission Chief can't guarantee that things will always go according to plan. There's invariably an element of luck involved, as you know. Anyhow, here we are, safe and sound.'

'I suppose I should be counting my blessings that you brought me here to this delightful place. I gather you have your reasons?'

'Indeed. We'll come to them soon enough.'

Ben said, 'I can't wait. What about Yuri Petrov and his daughter Valentina? I'd like to think they're somewhere nearby, and in good condition.'

'We're not animals, old boy. The child is being cared for by expert personnel. As for her father, we do have a bone or two to pick with him. There's a lot of history there.'

'I've already heard it.'

Calthorpe took another sip of scotch and smacked his lips. 'I'm aware of that. You're fairly well informed about a lot of things, thanks to Messrs Petrov and Solokov. Other things, not quite so much.'

'Informed enough to know that Yuri Petrov worked for *Russian* intelligence,' Ben said. 'Which either makes you the new Kim Philby, or I'm missing something. Who's "we"?'

Calthorpe waved his hand in a casually dismissive gesture. 'Oh, Russians, Brits, Yanks, Chinese, what does it matter any more? The concept of nations, of "them and us", is no more than a public relations exercise these days. The rivalry that existed between our countries all those years ago, the space race, the arms race and all those other silly areas of conflict, we long ago agreed were getting us nowhere. Russia and the West being a case in point. We all work together now, in the interests of global stability. The rest of it's nothing but a puppet show. A very well-orchestrated – and very expensive, I might add – puppet show, whose purpose is to keep the populace entertained, make them believe they actually have some role to play in how the world is run. Keeps the little children happy, by and large.'

'So nice to know you're looking after their wellbeing,' Ben said. 'I take it you must be one of the guys holding the puppet strings. I'm sure I should be honoured to be in your presence.'

Calthorpe gave a modest little shrug, as if to say, 'Someone has to do it.'

Ben continued, 'As you're so tight with your Russian pals, I daresay you know the real identity of the woman who was passing herself off as Tatyana Nikolaeva. I'm curious to know her present condition.'

'That would be Agent Yakunina. You'll be pleased to hear that she appears to be recovering nicely from her trauma. In fact she has no memory of what happened. And may I say, I find your concern for an enemy agent rather touching. I had no idea you were so sentimental.'

'That's me, all heart,' Ben said. 'Am I allowed to know her first name?'

'Why, of course. It's Katya Yakunina. *Captain* Katya Yakunina, in point of fact, to give her her proper title. Putin's female military officers are far more than just the miniskirt army they're often made out to be. She's been a great asset to us thus far. A very capable lady indeed.'

'That didn't stop you from planting one of your little devices inside her head, though, did it?' Ben said. 'Grisha was right. If I'd let him dig around in her brain, we'd have found something. The modern version of Object 428, whatever kind of new toy you sick bastards have been concocting in your secret labs all these years.'

'There you are,' Calthorpe said, obviously amused. 'I need say no more. You've got it all worked out, Major.'

'And a few other things besides. Such as the fact that the gadget you implanted in her brain was more than just a way to control her. It was a homing device. That's how you were able to direct your goons to find us so easily, not once but twice, and even before that. You were tracking her the whole time.'

Chapter 41

'Not particularly advanced technology, really,' Calthorpe said. 'Not when you consider that every civilian mobile phone on the planet contains a chip that intelligence agencies can activate to track and pinpoint the whereabouts of its owner to within a few square metres, should they become persons of interest for any reason. But you're quite correct. We were onto you from the moment Agent Yakunina first met you on the tarmac at Vnukovo airport. We knew exactly where you and she were, at all times, first while you were running around Moscow and later when you set off on your little escapade into the countryside. Not to mention, we were listening in on every word of your conversation the entire while. I thought we detected a certain rapprochement between the two of you. Seemed like it might get really interesting at a couple of points; sadly, that wasn't to be.'

'The marvels of modern technology,' Ben said. 'And that's why she didn't try to snatch the evidence when Yuri showed it to us. Because it wasn't part of her programming to take it. Only to lead her controllers straight to it. That was when she changed. The chip in her head was flicking switches inside her brain, shutting her down like a machine. Am I close?'

'Remarkably close,' Calthorpe said, smiling. 'Her mission

was simply to locate Petrov and Object 428, nothing more, while allowing us to monitor your own efforts to do the same. An entire network of agents was on standby to close in the moment either of you succeeded in locating the target. As it turned out, the remoteness of the location caused a delay in mustering the necessary personnel, which I now much regret. I missed an opportunity to have Agent Yakunina take possession of the item, by force if necessary.'

'Easy as pressing a button, is it?' Ben said, staring at him and thinking how much he'd love to tear this man's head off.

'A simple matter of resetting her command parameters, which I could have done from my control room in an entirely different part of the world. You'd be amazed at how far the technology of brain–computer interaction has come since the days of Object 428. As revolutionary as it was back then, it's an antiquated old relic now. It should really be in a museum – that is, if we could allow the public to be aware of its existence.'

Calthorpe paused, eyeing Ben with a curious expression. 'You're one of the very few people to have ever physically come into contact with it, you know. Something I should very much like to do myself. I was rather hoping you might be able to clue me in on its current whereabouts. It would appear to have been, shall we say, mislaid, along with the microfilm.'

'If I knew the answer,' Ben said, 'you'd have to persuade me to divulge that information.'

'I would have expected no less,' Calthorpe said. 'But bear in mind that persuasion is something we're rather adept at.'

'I'll bet you are. I'm sure you have a gang of your best persuaders working on Yuri Petrov right now to make him tell where he's hidden the loot. But they're obviously not getting results, or else you wouldn't have asked me the same question.'

Calthorpe gave an inscrutable smile. 'Let's just say your Russian friend is helping us with our enquiries. Chief Bezukhov's men are highly experienced at this sort of thing. I'm told Petrov's being a little stubborn, but he won't hold out forever. Nobody does.'

For all Calthorpe's display of smooth, calm confidence, Ben sensed that the man was being eaten up with worry. 'Object 428 really has got you in a flap, hasn't it? You're absolutely terrified that your filthy little secret might come out.'

'Damage limitation is a priority of ours,' Calthorpe said. 'We have whole departments devoted to flooding the airwaves with all the usual fake news and disinformation to muddy the waters, should the worst happen. We would do all we could to pass all this mind-control malarkey off as empty conspiracy theorising, while at the same time convincing evidence would emerge to show that the so-called Object 428 was in fact a medical device designed to treat seizures, psychosis, memory problems and suchlike. By the time we were done, the ordinary citizen in the street would be persuaded there was nothing remotely sinister about it.

'In any case,' Calthorpe went on, 'Object 428's workings are so radically different from the latest models that there's little to be gleaned from it about what we're doing now. It bears as much resemblance to the primitive technology of the 1950s as the laser-guided wonder the modern soldier carries to war does to the crude flintlock musket of the eighteenth-century British infantryman.'

'But your disinformation smokescreen wouldn't fool everyone,' Ben said. 'You're getting people wrong if you think there aren't a lot of folks out there who can tell a big pile of steaming bullshit when they see it. If the evidence was out that mind control was a reality, there'd be a lot of folks in power facing some pretty uncomfortable questions. This would be hanging over you like a dark cloud for a long time.'

'Well, certainly, I'd much rather not see Object 428 making its media debut on YouTube for all the world to see,' Calthorpe admitted. 'Containment is a far preferable option, not just for me but for my superiors, to whom I'd much rather not have to explain what went wrong. Why do you suppose I went to all this trouble to locate Mr Petrov in the first place?'

Ben couldn't quite believe that he was really hearing this. 'I have to say, Calthorpe, you're being remarkably candid. Anyone would think you were actually confessing the truth.'

Calthorpe laughed. 'Seems that way, doesn't it? Does it surprise you?'

'What I find surprising is that you chose to tell me, of all people.'

'No mystery there. You're a man who appreciates transparency,' Calthorpe replied. 'It's why you fell out with your military superiors, when you took a dislike to the way mid-rank SAS officers were being kept in the dark with regard to the real purpose of certain operations. I don't want you to regard me that way. That's why I'm being completely honest with you. Full disclosure. You have my word.'

'Why? You're not planning on letting me walk out of here.'

'Oh, please. If I really wanted you dead, Major, this meeting would never have taken place.'

Ben had an uneasy feeling he was being offered an option, but what?

'All right, full disclosure,' he said. 'How about you start by telling me where Yuri and Valentina are?'

'Gladly. Mr Petrov is being kept at a separate facility, where his hosts are best served in their efforts to take care of him. The little girl is right here in this very building, in a room just down the corridor. And as you very gallantly expressed concern for the welfare of Agent Yakunina . . .'

Calthorpe raised a hand and motioned past Ben's shoulder in the direction of the doorway. 'Why, here she is now.'

Chapter 42

Startled, Ben turned to look in the direction Calthorpe was pointing. The door opened. The same pair of shaven-headed guards stood outside in the corridor, as though they hadn't budged the whole time. With them was a familiar face. And yet, a total stranger.

Tatyana, or Katya as Ben would now have to make an effort to think of her, was brought into the room. The guards closed the door and took up positions either side of it, standing in that relaxed-but-ready position, feet slightly braced and arms loosely crossed, that armed security guys and close protection personnel adopt when trouble might be just instants away.

She walked into the room, slowly, paying no interest to her surroundings. She had changed into a plain dark outfit, like a jumpsuit. Her short blond hair had been shampooed and neatly brushed. The cut on her lip had been cleaned up and there was just a little bruising that would soon heal. The only other damage was the redness and slight swelling to one cheek where Ben had slapped her.

But it was her eyes Ben was staring at. Though she appeared to be walking and moving normally, the faraway emptiness of expression that had come over her after the raid on Grisha's farm now seemed to have grown deeper and more vacant. Her pupils, so vivid and full of colour before, were faded like dead butterfly wings and her facial muscles were slack, as though she'd been fed some kind of powerful mind-numbing drug like they gave to dangerous mental patients. Her cheeks were the colour of chalk.

Calthorpe made no attempt to greet her and didn't move from his seat, cradling the remains of his drink. Ben turned to glare at the man and demanded, 'What've you done to her?'

'Her mind has been purged,' Calthorpe explained casually, as though purging people's minds was the most normal and routine thing in the world. 'As I said, she has no memory of the last few days. It's all been taken out.'

'Taken out? What the hell do you mean, taken out?'

'It's much the same as removing files on a computer,' Calthorpe said with a little wave of his hand. 'A familiar enough concept for most people. When you delete a data document, it's binned but not permanently erased, able to be restored at any time. Likewise, the former contents of her mind are still complete and unharmed, but they've been electromagnetically ring fenced and isolated, as though they'd been relocated to a sort of cerebral recycle bin. At this point she has little idea of who she is, her name, history, where she grew up or who her parents were. *Tabula rasa.* A clean slate. In fact, at this moment she's not really processing any conscious thought of any kind.'

Ben's hands were shaking. This woman was his enemy. She'd tricked and betrayed him, and he'd no doubt she would have tried to kill him if ordered to do so. Perhaps she would have succeeded. Yet how could you feel animosity towards a foe who had done nothing to you by their own volition, and whose actions were totally controlled by an outside influence? He was disgusted by the cruelty of what they'd done. 'You lobotomised her.'

'Dear me, what a horrible notion,' Calthorpe said. 'As though we would stoop to anything so crude. Not at all. Not a single cell of her brain has been harmed. Don't think of it as damage. Think of it as modification. Enhancement, even. Agent Yakunina is the lucky recipient of one of the most fabulous pieces of modern scientific biotechnology ever created.'

Ben glanced at the guards by the door. Their jackets were partially unzipped, giving quick access to the concealed weaponry that was creating the bulges below each man's left armpit. One was completely poker-faced, the other watching proceedings with a look of wry amusement. Calthorpe had been right to bring them inside the room, for his own safety. Otherwise, Ben would have punched his trachea out through the back of his spine.

'And what do you call this gadget?' Ben said to Calthorpe. 'Object four-two-nine? Five hundred? Two thousand?'

'Its operational name is classified. Let's just say that it's the pinnacle, the Rolls-Royce of cerebral implants. We've come an awfully long way from Delgado's remote-controlled bull, I needn't tell you. Had you allowed Mr Solokov to perform his little impromptu brain surgery on Agent Yakunina, I doubt whether you'd have found anything in there. While Object 428 measured 7mm in length by 4mm in width, requiring a substantially large hole to be cut into the patient's skull, every generation since has become progressively smaller. Thirty years ago the implants had already shrunk to the size of a grain of rice, made of silicon or gallium arsenide crystalline semiconductor material rather than metal. The latest generation are tiny enough to be injectable via hypodermic needle, as well as being infinitely more sophisticated.'

'So nice to see the citizens' tax pennies being put to good use,' Ben said.

'You can be as sarcastic as you wish, but you can't deny the brilliance of what we've developed. This little "gadget", as you call it, puts us fully in charge of the human brain via an alternating magnetic field that applies specific inputs to specific neurons, causing them to fire at our will. It's really a triumph of micro-bioengineering.'

Calthorpe got to his feet, delicately set his empty glass down and began to pace up and down, looking for all the world like a benevolent university science professor educating a roomful of eager students.

'You see, Major, we are electric creatures. Our bodies run on electrical currents. So does the living computer we call our brain. Every thought and reaction we experience, everything we see or hear, causes a tiny spike in the neurological patterns of the brain's electromagnetic fields. Every individual brain has its own unique bioelectrical resonance frequency, in the same way we all have unique fingerprints and irises. Today's computers can decode and analyse those patterns, those minute fluctuations, into thoughts, sounds and images just like a brain can. For instance, thanks to research done at the University of Berkeley in the last couple of years, we can actually hook up a sleeping subject to a monitoring device, record their dreams and play them back as video images. One day people will be able to re-experience last night's dreams on a screen as they sit having breakfast.'

'Know what I'm dreaming of right now, Calthorpe? You wouldn't want to see it.'

Calthorpe gave a little smile. 'By the same token, the process also can be reversed. That's when a computer sends electromagnetic stimulants encoded as signals to the subject's brain, giving rise to thoughts or sense reactions that are experienced exactly as though they were the brain's own natural responses. We can influence a person's dreams when they're asleep, inducing anything from the most wonderful fantasy to the worst mind-bending nightmare imaginable. When they're awake we can cause them to see things that aren't actually there, hear voices inside their heads, do anything we want them to do. We can make them run faster and perform better, by instructing the brain to flood the bloodstream with adrenalin and endorphins. Another command can turn off their fear response. Yet another can shut down the pain receptors in the brain. For espionage purposes, should an implanted agent be captured, they can be rendered impervious to torture. Strictly for humane reasons, of course.'

'That's very decent of you.'

'And all operated remotely. The electromagnetic impulses can be directed from satellites, from the subject's mobile phone, an anonymous-looking van parked outside their house. An implanted person can even be triggered by electromagnetic waves coming from their television. Alternatively, where appropriate, we can use one of these handy devices.'

Calthorpe paused for a moment while he reached into his inside jacket pocket and slipped out a slim black device that looked like a standard TV remote control, but half the size and with only a few buttons. He held it up to show Ben.

'Impressed? You should be. This clever little box of tricks has been specifically attuned to Agent Yakunina's individual brain resonance patterns and pre-programmed with a range of specific stimulus commands that are emitted as an electromagnetic pulse. At the touch of a button I can manipulate her thoughts, direct her movements, or if desired cause her to completely lose control of her bodily functions. Which I will refrain from doing. Switch off the field entirely and she will return more or less to normal. Right now, as you can see, she's in standby mode.'

Ben took a step closer and looked at her. He waved a hand in front of her face, like he'd done before. 'Katya?'

Calthorpe said, 'You can call her Tatyana if you prefer. She couldn't tell the difference either way, even if she could hear you. Her mind is completely disconnected from present reality, like an epilepsy patient undergoing an absence seizure. She'll stay that way until I release her.'

Ben touched her hand. She gave no response. Just like before, not the slightest twitch. Like a living mannequin. Cold fingers ran down his spine and made him shudder. It was as though she were a robot, stripped of everything that made her human.

He looked back at Calthorpe. 'You know what I think? I think you make the most dangerous nutcase I've ever met in my life look sane and normal.'

'Of course you do,' Calthorpe said. 'That's just your natural psychological response to something too incredible and radically advanced to comprehend. I really don't take it personally. And now, if you'll permit me, I'd like to show you something.'

Calthorpe flipped aside the hem of his jacket, revealing his trim waist and a slender belt to which was clipped a small walkie-talkie handset. Unclipping it he pressed the talk button and said into the radio, 'Dr Arkangelskaya, please be so good as to bring in our young guest.'

Chapter 43

Moments later, the room door opened again. Two more black-clad guards had appeared outside. One of them was about Ben's size, a shade under six feet, fit and well built. The other was slight and sparrow-legged, standing no taller than five-two or so. Maybe Calthorpe's team were running some kind of equal opportunities non-height-discriminatory employment policy. Or else maybe the little guy was a small but extremely mean taekwondo master recruited for his fighting skills. Ben wondered if he'd ever get to find out.

The pair were accompanied by a thin woman in a white lab coat. She was almost exactly midway between them in height. Her hair was buzzed short, military-style, and greyed to the colour of dull steel. Her features were pinched and severe and she bore the wrinkles of an excessively heavy smoker that made her look older than she probably was. Ben could smell the stale tobacco across the room, as though her clothes and skin were permanently imbued with clouds of the nastiest and roughest cigarette smoke imaginable.

Standing very reluctantly by her side, and fighting to struggle free of the grip the woman had on her arm, was Valentina. The last time Ben had laid eyes on the child, she was being stolen away by armed men aboard a helicopter and there had been times since that terrible moment when privately he'd seriously doubted whether he would ever lay eyes on her again. Seeing her now brought a flood of emotions, his relief tempered only by the circumstances of her, and now his, predicament. She was still dressed as he'd last seen her, the little pink gilet zippered up to her neck and jeans dirtied and torn at one knee from the aborted escape from Grisha's farm. Her rosy cheeks had turned ghostly pale, her hair was dishevelled and her eyes were red from crying, though she was putting on a brave face and shooting looks of defiance at the woman in the white coat.

'Perfectly unharmed and all in one piece,' Calthorpe said. 'As you can see, Major, we've been taking good care of her.' He smiled at Valentina. 'Haven't we, my chick? Except that she refuses to eat a bite. You're far too precious to let waste away, aren't you, dear?'

'*Va te faire foutre, vieux connard!*' Valentina yelled at him in French, still wriggling to get loose of the doctor's grip.

'Such a foul tongue for one so young and pretty,' Calthorpe said, shaking his head in mock disapproval. 'She should put her talent for languages to better use. It's a good thing she doesn't speak Russian, or she might have given offence to our hosts. Thank you, Doctor, you may leave us.'

The tall, severe woman let go of Valentina, pushed her into the room and shut the door in the child's wake, closing herself and the guards outside in the corridor. The two flanking the inside of the doorway were as still as statues but Ben could sense from their body language that something was about to happen. His mind raced, but he couldn't guess what.

Valentina looked at Ben and said, '*Où est mon papa?*'

Ben shook his head. 'I don't know where your father is, kid. I'm sorry.'

She could slide between French and English like a train switching tracks, so effortlessly that she barely seemed conscious of it. 'I don't like it here. I want to go home.'

'Me too,' Ben said. 'And we both will. Soon.' Another promise that he could only hope he'd be able to keep. He turned back to face Calthorpe. 'Mind telling me what your game is, *Colonel?*'

Calthorpe smirked. 'Why, let me show you.' Flourishing his little black remote control device as though he were changing TV channels, he aimed it at Katya and pressed a button.

The effect kicked in as fast as it took for the electromagnetic signal to pulse across the room at something near light speed, hit the microprocessor inside her head and trigger off a lightning sequence of snapping neural connections within the brain. In a heartbeat, Agent Yakunina seemed to snap right out of her bizarre trance. She rocked on her feet, shook herself a little, then her eyes regained their focus and swivelled around the room as though she was suddenly taking in her surroundings for the first time since she'd arrived. Her gaze passed blankly over Valentina without any apparent sign of recognition. Then over Ben, showing a similar lack of response. As though they'd never met before.

'The reason I invited our young friend here to join us,' Calthorpe said, motioning at Valentina, 'was to enable a demonstration of the full power of this technology. Chiefly for your benefit, Major Hope.'

'That's not necessary, Calthorpe.'

''Fraid I must insist, old chap.' Calthorpe aimed the

remote and pressed another button. 'I've just sent her a new command. Now watch. I assure you this will be most interesting.'

As he spoke, something was happening to Katya. Her body seemed to go rigid. Whatever processes were taking place inside her head, whatever images she was seeing or voices she was hearing, it was all playing out through her expression. Her eyes darted and rolled wildly. Her facial muscles were twitching as though a hundred random electric pulses were being fired through them. It was eerie to watch. Almost frightening.

But what happened next was far worse.

Katya's eyes stopped rolling, and a strange light came into them as they turned on Valentina. Her lips drew back from her teeth in a mirthless smile that grew into a snarl.

And then she took a step towards the girl. Then another. The tics and twitches were gone. Now the look on her face was like a shark's. Blank, unemotional, void of compassion, empty of anything except pure predatory intent.

Valentina shrank away in terror, instinctively moving to Ben for protection in the absence of a father to look after her.

'Call her off, Calthorpe,' Ben warned.

'You don't want it, then stop it,' Calthorpe replied.

Katya came on another step. Her teeth were still bared and the veins were standing out horribly on her forehead. Her hands came up, clenched like talons. Valentina let out a whimper and backed further away, but she was running out of space to retreat.

Ben had seen enough. He grabbed Valentina by the shoulders, whisked her behind him and stepped protectively into Katya's path. 'No.'

291

It was like stepping between a tigress and her kill. Katya instantly dropped down into a fighting stance, reverting back at some unconscious level to military training that had been instilled so deeply it was second nature. Without hesitation and as fast as any karate black belt, she launched a savage blow at Ben's face.

Ben was faster, though only just. He rolled the blow harmlessly aside with the flat of his palm and shoved her back, making her totter on her feet. He could have trapped her wrist and snapped her arm in at least two places, but he couldn't bring himself to.

That would soon have to change.

Ben had never seen a human being look so demented. Her wild eyes flicked back and forth between him and Valentina, the target her programming had instructed her to destroy. Valentina was cowering behind Ben for protection, whimpering.

'We get the message, Calthorpe. Turn it off.'

'Sorry, old chap. Can't do that.'

'Tatyana. Katya. Please stop. Don't make me hurt you.'

Ben didn't even know if she could understand him. With a scream of fury she charged, and this time he knew she would leave him no choice.

Many times, he'd found himself pushed into combat against desperate men. Men so highly trained and motivated to survive that they would fight through their pain and fear, and keep fighting until either they or their opponent were out of commission. This enemy was different. She was like a machine. There was no fear to cloud her judgement. No pain through which to lever the body into submission. She would keep on coming until her target lay dead at her feet or until every bone in her own body was broken, without caring either way. The only way to stop her would be to take her apart.

Ben had been made to witness, and carry out, a lot of ugly things in his time. But the next few minutes would be the ugliest of his life.

Chapter 44

The guards had stepped closer, watching and waiting in hungry anticipation of a good show. Calthorpe's face wore a smug grin that Ben would dearly have loved to wipe off with something hard, heavy and blunt, if he hadn't had his hands full at this moment.

Katya attacked. A storm of unbridled fury, maximum violence, rushing him like a crazy person. But without guile. Deception and trickery are what decide the outcome of fights between well-matched opponents, rather than brute strength that can be converted into momentum to work against you, or blinding speed that can be redirected to trip you up. Like a bar-room brawler blinded by irrational rage, Katya wasn't thinking consciously – and that was her weakness.

Ben saw the throat-crushing strike coming and stepped out of its trajectory, snatching her right wrist out of the air and twisting it as he moved. It was Katya's own speed and power that pushed the joint past breaking point. He felt the sickening crackle and pop, felt her right hand go limp in his. He could have held on, twisted the arm behind her back and snapped it at the elbow while driving her face down to the floor and stamping on the back of her neck.

He let go. Still couldn't do it.

'Katya. Please. You know me. Stop this.'

Her lack of any reaction to the broken wrist made the hairs stand up on the back of Ben's neck. Right hand flapping loose at her side, she came back at him with an animal scream and a white-knuckle left fist. This time, Ben just dodged it without doing any more hurt to her, and backed away. Desperate to think of something, anything, he could do to avert this disaster, he said, 'You're Katya Yakunina. You were an army captain. You used to have family living out in the countryside near the old church we passed, and when you were little you were taken to visit them. You love romantic Russian men and vodka cocktails but you're not keen on whisky, and you hate goats even more.'

And you can handle yourself in a fight, he might have added.

'Nice try, Major,' Calthorpe commented from the sidelines. 'But it'll take more than a few unearthed memories to appeal to her better judgement. She can't even begin to process what you're telling her.'

Ben had to try. But Calthorpe was right.

Katya regained her momentum and attacked once more, this time aiming for Ben's midsection with a lightning strike that could have punched out a man's spleen. Ben had to call on all of his speed and agility to evade it. He spun outside of the blow's trajectory, hooked her left arm with his and twisted his body hard, feet braced solidly apart, using his rotational movement to yank her off balance and send her crashing to the floor. He kept hold of her left arm, exerting hard leverage on her shoulder joint and hoping the force of pressure would keep her down; but she barely touched the floor before leaping up again like an uncoiling steel spring, letting her shoulder dislocate itself rather than be pinned down. The awful searing crackle and crunch of cartilage was a sound usually accompanied by a shriek of agony, even from the toughest battle-hardened warrior. She didn't even flinch. There was nothing in her expression as she sprang back and away from Ben, tearing her dislocated arm out of his grip.

Now both hands were hanging limp and useless at her sides. It was insanity to go on. But there could be no sanity in this fight. Eyes ablaze, she came at him with a wild round-house right kick aimed at face height, the kind of kick that could floor a horse or smash a door off its hinges. Ben trapped her ankle, wrenched her foot clockwise through a hundred degrees of twist to unbalance her, then pushed hard and launched her violently backwards, sending her into the wall behind her. The back of her head impacted against painted brickwork with a meaty crunch. She collapsed to the floor, leaving a smear of blood and hair on the wall.

For a second, Ben thought he'd killed her. He should have known better. Katya scrambled to her feet, breathing hard and making low noises from deep inside her throat. Her skull was cracked. Dark blood was welling up through her short blond hair and spilling in crooked rivulets down her forehead, pouring into her eyes and mouth.

But still she came back, with a murderous left-footed kick that would have caved in his ribs if he hadn't dodged it. Then he threw out a sideways stamping kick of his own that connected with the side of her right knee and shattered the joint. Collateral ligaments and articular cartilage ruptured, patella displaced, the connection between femur and tibia totally disintegrated. A six-hour operation to repair, and even then she'd have been lucky to ever walk again. Her left leg buckled the wrong way under her and she went down without a sound.

'Katya, for Christ's sake stay down,' Ben implored her, even though he knew it was useless to reason with her. Her eyes were rolling in a mask of blood, bared teeth stained red as she growled and struggled desperately to regain her feet. She tried to push herself up with her hands, but neither was working. She tried to lash out at Ben with her last remaining unbroken limb, to heave her body closer to him so she could bite him. She was the only person in the room with no awareness whatsoever that this fight was now over.

'Finish it,' Calthorpe said. 'Break her neck.'

Ben shook his head. 'No.'

'Kill her.'

'I will not. I'm done. And this is on you, Calthorpe, you piece of—'

'Come now, Major. Surely you're not getting soft in your old age, are you?' Calthorpe teased, smiling.

'You want to find out?' Ben asked him. 'There's one neck in this room I'd love to break. And maybe I will.'

'No matter.' Calthorpe signalled to the guards. The two shaven-headed guys exchanged a brief glance. One motioned to the other, who drew a Grach automatic from inside his jacket and stepped towards the fallen, writhing and bloodied Katya.

Ben couldn't have stopped it. He could only watch as the guard put his pistol to her head and executed her right there on the floor like putting down a rabid dog.

He looked down at her broken body. Her mouth was open in a last gnashing gape of hatred. The pupil of one eye unnaturally distended, the other shrunk to a pinpoint. The catastrophic neurological event that had taken place inside her brain was like a hand grenade going off in there.

Ben's memory flashed on the night the two of them had sat talking until late in the Neglinka Lounge bar, not so very long ago when she'd still been Tatyana Nikolaeva and he was still looking for a little girl abducted by an errant father.

He pictured Tatyana, the low lighting of the cocktail bar reflecting in her eyes as she sipped on her drink, teasing, mocking, probing to know more about him, her conversation sometimes seeming to border on flirtation.

Now here she was lying in a pool of blood at his feet, a deactivated piece of meat waiting for some anonymous clean-up crew to cart her away like so much trash for disposal.

Ben badly wanted to throw up. Moisture stung his eyes, and he blinked it away. Valentina had flung herself behind a sofa at the edge of the room and was curled up on the floor, racked with sobbing. Children were not meant to witness such things. Ben had a bad feeling she would see more before this was over. Her went over to the girl, crouched beside her and held her as she put her arms around his neck and squeezed tightly, her tears wetting his neck.

'It's okay,' he whispered. 'You're going to be all right.'

'*Je veux mon papa.*' I want my daddy.

'He's not far away. You'll see him soon.'

'*I want Papa!*'

The guard who had shot Katya reholstered his pistol and returned to his position by the door. Calthorpe was watching Ben with a curious expression. 'Well, Major. It appears that the age of chivalry lives on in you. You really did like her, didn't you? Interesting. I trust you were satisfied with the practical demonstration, however?'

Ben let go of the weeping child, stood and took three fast steps towards Calthorpe. His hate for this man was boiling over so violently that he could barely speak. But there were plenty of other things that would come naturally to him. 'You made me do that. Now it's your turn.'

Instantly, both guards had their pistols drawn and pointing straight at Ben.

'I really wouldn't, if I were you,' Calthorpe said, still smiling.

Ben looked at the drawn guns, and for a second he truly didn't give a damn. It would be worth it, just to hear the sound of Calthorpe's neck snapping like a rotten stick of celery. Then he thought of Valentina, and Yuri, and what would surely happen to them once he was taken out of the picture. He was their last hope, if they had any at all. He balled his fists by his sides and breathed slow and deeply to control his anger.

Calthorpe said, 'In actual fact, you made it happen, by compelling me to persuade you by more forceful means that everything I've been telling you is the perfect truth. I also knew that you would do whatever was necessary to protect the child.'

'I hope you enjoyed the show, you sick bastard.'

'The exercise served a purely practical interest, I assure you. Firstly, Agent Yakunina had reached the end of her useful service life and it would have been time to decommission her anyway, so you needn't feel too bad. Secondly, it also shows me that I made a good choice in withdrawing the order to terminate you. Congratulations, Major Hope. Consider what just happened as the final stage of your audition. One that you have passed with flying colours, as anticipated by everyone on the committee. It's been agreed that you're just the man we need.'

Ben blinked and said nothing, taken aback.

'Take a seat, Major. We have some more talking to do.' Calthorpe clicked his fingers, and one of the guards opened the door. The woman in the lab coat was standing outside in the corridor as though she'd been there all along. 'Dr Arkangelskaya, you may take the child back to her quarters now.'

The woman and the second pair of guards entered the room, stepping around the pool of blood. The guards laid a thick plastic sheet on the floor, grabbed Katya's body by the ankles and wrists and dumped her on it, then began dragging her away as the mysterious Dr Arkangelskaya took Valentina's arm and forced her to stand up and come with her. The terrified girl protested and cried, to no avail. Ben was powerless to help her.

Then Ben and Calthorpe were alone again, except for the guards watching from the doorway with their weapons still drawn and ready.

'So, Major, are you ready to resume our conversation? Not that you have much choice, with guns pointing at your back.'

'What if I don't really feel much like talking?' Ben said between gritted teeth, still fighting to control his boiling rage.

'Then all you have to do is listen,' Calthorpe answered calmly. 'Because, as an astute fellow like you may have guessed by now, I have a proposition to make.'

Chapter 45

'A proposition,' Ben echoed.

'Indeed. Why else would we be having this discussion? I would be well on my way back home to London, in time to enjoy a pleasant dinner with the lovely Mrs Calthorpe. And you, my dear fellow, would have taken up permanent residence at the bottom of a very deep hole somewhere in the Russian countryside. So I'd say my proposition works out very much in your interest. That is, if you have sense enough to accept.'

Calthorpe ambled over to the makeshift drinks cabinet, helped himself to a top-up of scotch and then settled comfortably on his sofa. 'Now, let's get down to business. I won't ask you if you've ever heard of something called Operation Stairway, Major Hope, because I know you haven't.' He sipped his drink, letting the pause invite Ben to say something. When Ben remained seethingly silent, Calthorpe went on:

'You certainly wouldn't be alone there. It's a project so deeply classified that none of the elected so-called leaders of Russia, the United States, Great Britain or anywhere else are even vaguely aware of its existence. And yet it does exist, and has for many years, thickly veiled behind many layers of what we like to call "plausible deniability". In a nutshell,

Operation Stairway is a joint international psy-ops initiative that involves players from all the major superpowers. US Army Field Manual 33-1 defines psy-ops as "Any form of communication in support of objectives, designed to influence the opinions, emotions, attitudes or behaviour of any group in order to benefit the sponsor, either directly or indirectly". Which is their rather woolly way of describing what my particular department specialises in, the practical application of mind-control science. Post-Cold War, the purpose of Operation Stairway was to usher in a new era where, rather than spend precious resources finding ways for one nation to use the developing technology against another as in the past, we could work instead to cement our united vision of the future, creating a peaceful, stable world.'

'You mean a New World Order,' Ben said.

'Now you sound like the late, lamented Grisha Solokov and his misguided ilk. What's wrong with a new world order? What on earth could be less sinister than aspiring to bring about a new global era in which all human beings will be equal and co-exist in a spirit of harmony? In which war would be a thing of the past, and tanks and planes and bombs would be rendered obsolete forever? No more pain, no more unhappiness?' Calthorpe beamed at this beatific vision of peace. 'The wolf will live with the lamb, the leopard shall lie down with the goat, the lion and the calf and the yearling together; and a child shall lead them.'

'Isaiah, Chapter eleven, verse six. Last time I heard anyone quote that, it was a bunch of naive kids in theology class. Next thing you'll be getting out your guitar and bringing Dr Arkangelskaya in here to bang a tambourine while you sit cross-legged on cushions and sing "Kumbaya" together.'

Calthorpe's face darkened a shade. 'I can't fault your bible knowledge, but I can assure you that the deep thinkers behind such grand future visions are anything but naive. Such stability can't be achieved simply by declaring it to be so, and expecting the world to follow suit. Given the unrelentingly bloody mess that is the human history of the last umpteen thousand years, it's clear that populations have to be artificially controlled into achieving lasting peace on earth. In other words, it is necessary to exert force to make people think and act in ways conducive to the greater good.'

'Doesn't sound quite so benign now you put it that way, does it?'

'Now who's being naive, Major? You know as well as I do that human beings can't function without strict frameworks to govern how they lead their lives. Our species is simply too volatile, too complex, too prone to a host of psychological and behavioural dysfunctions, to be left unguided, unmonitored. In order to create any sort of lastingly peaceful, stable global civilisation, those negative psychological traits have to be ironed out.'

'Like the psychiatrists with their depatterning theory,' Ben said. 'Take out the nasty thoughts, wipe the slate clean and put in good ones in their place. Now you're talking about the human race as though every one of us were mentally ill.'

'It's not as sweeping a generalisation as most of us would like to believe,' Calthorpe said. 'If an alien observer were to view mass human behaviour from a distance, they could easily be forgiven for thinking the species was largely insane. *We* are the good guys. The last line of defence in the quest to restore and maintain the sanity of the human race.'

'You actually believe that, don't you?'

'If the individual is the problem, then individuality must be suppressed. If the source of dysfunctional behaviour is the mind, then the processes of the mind need to be simplified and harnessed for the greater good. And it's a fight we are slowly winning,' Calthorpe went on, warming to his theme. 'Look at the incredibly turbulent history of the twentieth century. The anti-Vietnam riots in America that nearly overturned the establishment. The madness of 1968, when it seemed as though the entire civilised world was about to disintegrate into Marxist revolution. The anarchy of the 1970s. The Red Brigade. The Baader-Meinhof gang, hellbent on subverting the fabric of Europe's social order with their bombings and shootings. Where are they all now? When did you last hear of a white European terrorist? Nobody could argue that our western nations, for all their upheavals and unrest, are far more quelled and passive than in the past. More contented, more stable, more accepting of their lot. And who do you suppose is behind that change?'

Ben said nothing.

'Do you ever wonder why today's general public ask so few questions and seem so unperturbed by even the most pressing issues of our times? Nobody cares about anything any more. You can tell them the planet's about to be destroyed, and they barely bat an eye. There's no rioting in the streets when governments persist in unpopular wars or impose new laws that crush what's left of their citizens' liberty. Ordinary members of the public are no longer moved to action to take a political stand, unless of course we want them to. With few exceptions, apathy rules almost every aspect of their lives. Why? Why do so few people seem to care, for instance, about the fluoride in their drinking water or the poisonous neurotoxins such as mercury and aluminium that are routinely injected into newborn infants in the name of medical science, intended to reduce their future adult capacity to think for themselves? Why, despite unprecedented access to the vast library of information that is the internet, does the public at large remain so sheeplike and not rise up in fury at these practices, and the many hundreds of other obvious lies their rulers – their real rulers, that is – feed them daily through the media? And they *are* crying-out-loud obvious, because in fact they're designed to be. The whole thing is a test, to gauge the level of non-reaction among the public and thereby measure how successful the program is.'

'So your mission objective is to brainwash the entire planet into zombie slaves?'

'I can't say I'm particularly keen on your choice of words there, Major. Neither "brainwash" nor "zombie" are terms I would use. But in essence, yes, we're working on it. The goal is to continually limit the population's ability to regulate their own thinking, or to have any opinions and ideas that we haven't already put into their heads. We're not there yet, by a long shot. Operation Stairway's founders knew that psycho-social engineering on such a mass scale was going to be an immense task, and they were right. Today's infowar goes way beyond the reach of mere state propaganda, which is yesterday's technology. Nowadays we call it "perception management". And to make it successful requires far more than just bashing a load of lies into people's minds through their television screens or internet news feeds. The runaway growth of the mobile device phenomenon was no accident. It has been one of the primary channels for directing pre-programmed electromagnetic wave signals straight into the brains of the masses. More specific targets require more specific and intensive approaches.'

'Let me guess. That's where your sick little implants come in.'

Calthorpe smiled. 'And that's also where you come in.'

Chapter 46

'You can imagine all the ways that my peers have devised for making use of the developing behaviour modification implant technology,' Calthorpe said. 'Entire think tanks have been devoted to it for decades. Billions invested in coming up with ideas. Everything from contriving assassinations to controlling what comes out of the mouths of certain politicians. I could give you names, but you wouldn't believe me.'

'I think I might,' Ben said.

'Anyhow, none of that is my department. Let me tell you what is. If there's one thing in the world more highly classified than Operation Stairway, it's a corollary initiative that goes by the codename "The Ploughshares Program". That is the project my employers have tasked me with. Ploughshares is run by a committee of very important people, though you wouldn't have heard of them. Few people have, despite the fact that they are among the senior elite who make far bigger decisions and carry far more influence than any elected ruler in the world. The man at the top – well, let's just call him the Chairman. In many ways the Ploughshares Program is one of the most essential initiatives of Operation Stairway, even though it's still in the early phases of its development. It's going to take a great deal of money and manpower to achieve its goals.' Calthorpe chuckled. 'Money, well, that's the easy part. Our budget is virtually limitless. But recruiting suitable personnel – now that's a little more challenging. I pride myself on being able to spot talent, but it's not every day I come across the right stuff. Purely by chance, and thanks to Comrade Petrov and his little escapade with our stolen property, you just happened to appear on our radar. Hence, my proposition.'

'The answer is no,' Ben said.

'I haven't even told you what the job entails.'

'Still no. To whatever you have to say. *Niet*. Or I could put it more bluntly, if you like.'

'I pray you'll change your mind, if you'll hear me out.'

Ben glanced at the guns. 'Go ahead and talk, Calthorpe. Much as I'd love to, it appears I can't stop you right now.'

'You and I were soldiers,' Calthorpe said. 'We've both seen and done things that ordinary men would never be called upon to endure, and that has formed our outlook on life. As warriors, we've learned that a lesser evil is often necessary to combat a greater one. That violence can be justifiable when it's used to end violence. And that's precisely what the Ploughshares Program is all about. Its purpose is to aid in bringing in the new era of peace on earth by the total eradication of private arms across the world. Some parts of the world are more problematic in that regard than others. The toughest nut to crack is North America, where gun violence has been responsible for the deaths of hundreds of thousands of innocent people. It must stop.'

'I can see why it would fit with your strategy to have private citizens disarmed and powerless to defend themselves.'

'If we had our way, there would be nothing for them to defend themselves against, hence no need to be armed,'

Calthorpe countered. 'It's a vicious circle that has to be broken. Desperate times call for drastic measures, and that's what we can provide. An orchestrated, sustained campaign of engineered situations involving prepared subjects that will knock this social cancer on the head once and for all.'

Ben stared at him. 'Did you just say "engineered situations"?'

'And I think you know exactly what I meant by it. The United States isn't the only country to be plagued by the phenomenon of random mass shootings involving significant loss of life, but it's way ahead in the leagues. Which presents us with a rich environment on which to focus, and a golden opportunity to exploit.'

'I can't believe what I think you're about to tell me, Calthorpe.'

'Let's be realistic. These kinds of incidents represent excellent value for money, so to speak, offering fabulous media traction and public outcry in return for minimal collateral damage. Thirty thousand US citizens killed annually in road accidents and nobody ever calls for a ban on cars. But a lone lunatic with a rifle takes a comparative handful of casualties, and you have every anti-gun lobbyist in Washington marching on the White House to mandate instant nation-wide disarmament. Quite rightly, too. Such tragedy.'

'Oh, I can tell you're all broken up about it,' Ben said. 'You're really quite the altruist.'

Calthorpe paused for a contemplative sip of his drink. 'The problem is, if you leave matters to run their natural course, there simply aren't enough lone lunatics with rifles out there to create the kind of stir that would really bring about change. To topple the powerful pro-gun lobby and bring down the Second Amendment of the United States Constitution we need to boost the number of mass shootings to such a degree that every armed American will voluntarily turn in every weapon they possess out of sheer disgust for what's happening to their society. See where I'm going with this?'

'In Technicolor. Now I'm guessing we come to the part about "prepared subjects".'

'That's the real crux of the matter,' Calthorpe said thoughtfully, rubbing his chin. 'The militant Islamists seem to have no problem recruiting sufficiently motivated chaps to strap on an explosive belt and blow themselves to smithereens for their cause. But it's a damned difficult thing to persuade your average secular Anglo male to hole up on a shopping mall rooftop with an AR15 and a few spare magazines, litter the street below with bodies and then blow out his own brains before the police can nab him and start asking questions. Suicide just doesn't seem to come naturally to them.'

'What a bummer.'

'So, as the saying goes, "If the mountain won't come to Mohammed, Mohammed must go to the mountain." It's a simple matter of locating suitable candidates, taking charge of their thought processes and, ah, *influencing* them to carry out one's intentions.'

'And you want me to be one of your recruiters.'

'Seems to me you'd be ideal for the job. You're intelligent, tough-minded and resourceful, a keen observer. You've spent many years of your life assisting, and very ably, in the process of war and destruction. Now let us enlist your talents to help us move towards a future of peace and harmony for all mankind. Not to mention the fact that you really don't have the option of refusing.'

'Sounds like an irresistible deal.'

'You would quit your current business in France and

relocate to the States. Somewhere nice and warm, with white beaches and swaying palms. We have a number of bases across the country, with which you'd be in constant contact as you travelled about locating potential candidates. Ex-military personnel would be a good source of likely subjects to choose from, as they often fit the right profile, are already familiar with the weaponry, and as soldiers were used to having all kinds of mysterious procedures done on them without asking questions. Once the subject was selected by you and approved by us, our teams would move in and take charge of the rest. The subject would be taken to a secure location where trained staff would administer the procedure. The implant takes only minutes to install, and the patient remembers nothing afterwards. Once in place . . .' Calthorpe waved a hand in the direction of the blood pool that was slowly congealing on the floor. 'Well, you've already seen how effectively it works.'

He went on, 'We also aim to target members of the public, in the interest of diversity. Implant them with ideation that gives them the desire to kill at random, while removing their natural inhibitions about ending their own lives when the task is complete. Then put a gun in their hand, and away they'll go, ready and willing to commit the perfect crime. It's a no-lose situation for us, because even if they managed to get themselves caught before they could terminate themselves, we can shut them down remotely prior to interrogation. In any case they'll be quite incapable of consciously revealing any information that might compromise the program, simply because they'll know nothing whatsoever about it.'

'You've thought of everything, haven't you?'

'All we have to do at this end is let things run their course, watch and wait for the fireworks as the media pick up the baton. Neighbours of the lone gunman will say on CNN, "Oh, but he seemed such a nice man." Friends and family will express justifiable shock, while the internet conspiracy brigade will spin their false flag scenarios as usual.'

'Where do they get these crazy notions?'

'But the public reaction is always the same, and it will ramp up until the policy makers, and eventually the gun manufacturers themselves, cave in under the pressure. How many incidents does it take to break the dam? Ten in a year? Twenty? Thirty? How many dead bodies of innocent men, women and children stacking up in morgues across the country? It's simply a matter of numbers; the more the better. The conclusion is inevitable.'

'Tell me, Calthorpe. Has this program already started? Are you already using brain-controlled patsies to murder innocent victims?'

Calthorpe smiled. 'Well, now, that would be telling, wouldn't it?' But the twinkle in his eye was all the answer Ben needed.

'You know, I thought I was already used to dealing with the lowest scum on earth. You've opened my eyes to a whole new realm.'

'Come, now. Don't you want to come on board the winning side once again? I haven't mentioned the pay. A lot of zeroes. Perks, too.'

'I already have a job, thanks.'

'Doing what, training the Keystone cops to plink at paper targets on a firing range and running errands for your billionaire chums on the side?'

'I'd scrub sewers in Bangladesh before I'd work for you.'

'You don't consider peace and harmony to be worthy enough aims?'

Ben said, 'I love peace and harmony more than anything.

311

But not at the expense of taking away the last real freedom people have.'

'The freedom to kill and maim one another?'

'No, the freedom to think and judge for themselves what's right and what's wrong.'

'Even if that freedom is the source of so much suffering and unhappiness in the world?'

'Human nature is flawed. We're doomed to unhappiness and uncertainty, from the day we're born until the day we die. But that's the way we're made. To force change on our species would be to play God. And no man can be God. Because then, who oversees him?'

'Back to the theology class,' Calthorpe said. 'But we're not singing "Kumbaya".'

'Nothing like a stimulating philosophical conversation.'

'The very last one you're ever likely to have, unfortunately,' Calthorpe said. 'Sadly, this job offer doesn't come with a get-out-of-jail-free card. If you still persist in turning it down, you walk away from more than just a great opportunity.'

'I get the idea. Then it looks as if you'll just have to kill me. Or get one of your ghouls here to do it for you, if you haven't got the guts.'

'When you told your superiors you were quitting the SAS, they didn't want to let you go so easily.'

'They gave me a week to think about it. But they could have saved themselves the trouble. My mind was made up, just like it is now.'

'But back then it didn't mean losing your life. This time is different.'

'At least I'll be able to live with myself, for as long as I've got.'

Calthorpe frowned at him in silence for a beat or two, then nodded.

'One hour. That's how long you've got. I suggest you use it to come to your senses. I have some business to attend to. We'll speak again in sixty minutes, on my return. If you still refuse, Major Hope, you'll be dead in sixty-one.'

Chapter 47

Calthorpe made his exit from the room, pausing a moment to mutter a few quiet words of Russian to the guards. Then Ben was alone with the shaven-headed pair, who seemed pleased at the prospect of maybe getting to kill him in an hour's time.

For the moment, they had their orders to keep him alive and locked up. Following the same routine as before, one guy kept his silenced 9mm Grach unwaveringly aimed at Ben's head from a safe distance, while the other guy stepped closer and fastened the cuffs back around his wrists, before he stepped away and pulled out his own identical pistol.

They escorted Ben outside into the empty corridor and began walking him back through the twisting passages towards his cell, the one in front setting the pace, the one behind keeping the gun aimed somewhere between Ben's shoulder blades. Staying well back. Doing the sensible thing, observing the proper protocol for escorting a highly dangerous prisoner who wants you dead more than most things in the world at that moment, and has a better idea how to achieve that result than the vast majority of humans who ever lived.

Ben walked slowly with his chained hands dangling loosely in front of him, measuring his step against the guy in front.

The corridors were narrow and featureless under cold neon light. The floor was smooth tile, grimy and dusty. The walls were whitewashed brick. He didn't need to test the handcuff chain to know it was strong. Slim and lightweight, four links in length, probably made of titanium or some kind of aircraft-grade aluminium. Impossible to break free. A bullet might not even do it. But that kind of strength could be made to work both ways, for him as well as against him. It was just a matter of opportunity.

As they entered the final stretch leading up to the cell door, Ben slowed his pace a little and turned his head, watching out of the corner of his eye to see if the guy behind was catching up. All Ben needed was for one of them to venture just a little too close. But the guy behind seemed to understand he was being tested. He maintained the safe distance between himself and Ben and gave a gruff command. Ben smiled to himself and kept moving.

As they reached the door to Ben's cell, the guy behind snapped out, '*Stoy*', and Ben obediently halted. The one in front tucked his pistol into his shoulder holster, and from his belt loop unclipped his key ring. He spent a moment jangling keys, head bent in concentration as though this were a difficult task for him. Which perhaps it was, because the first key he tried in the lock wouldn't work. He muttered irritably to himself. The guy at Ben's back said something in Russian, like 'What's up?' To which the guy with the keys muttered something back, shaking his head in annoyance as he searched for the right one to open the lock.

Ben watched closely, savouring their distractedness. Anything that diverted their attention from him was good. Even for a split second. A split second would be all he'd need. While their eyes were off him, he inched forward. Then another inch. They didn't notice. He smiled to himself again.

315

The second key worked. The cell door opened outwards into the narrow corridor, as all cell doors should do in order to prevent the inmate from barricading himself inside. As it swung open, the guy with the keys moved back a step to allow for its arc. And in so doing he made a terrible mistake. He entered Ben's space. Stepped right into the zone of maximum danger.

Protocol: momentarily forgotten.

Caution: foolishly allowed to slip.

Life: fast running out of time.

Before he could react, the slim, strong chain connecting Ben's wrists was up and over his head and locked back hard against the softness of his throat and he was being yanked violently off his feet, gurgling and choking and clawing at the metal links digging deep into his flesh. Ben pivoted backwards, using his hips and lower back to draw the guy's weight against his chest and use his momentum to swing him around in an anti-clockwise semicircle. Straight into the guy behind, who was caught off guard and failed to get a shot off in time.

Speed and surprise were everything, and Ben was a master of both. In two short steps he had the second guy jammed hard up between his choking, rasping human shield and the opposite wall. The second guy's gun arm was pinned sideways, his hand still clutching the weapon and desperately trying to grapple it around to bear on Ben so he could shoot him. Ben momentarily released the backward pressure on the first guy's throat and used his forearms to ram their heads together. He lashed out with his foot and crunched the second guy's gun hand against the wall. With a sharp cry the guy let go of the pistol and it clattered to the floor. Another swift kick, and it was spinning away across the dusty floor tiles. Ben crashed their heads together once more, feeling the solid impact of skull on skull. Then he whipped the chain out from under the first guy's chin and let his weight fall backwards. As he went down, Ben's hands were darting inside the guy's jacket and ripping the 9mm Grach from the shoulder holster. Ben danced backwards, clutching the pistol. The first guy slumped to the floor at his feet, fingers raking at his crushed throat as he battled for air. He was less of a threat than his buddy, who was still on his feet against the opposite wall, streaming blood from a broken nose. Ben dealt with him first.

In the confined space of a brick-walled corridor, even a sound-suppressed pistol would make a bang plenty loud enough to draw attention. But there were other effective, and more discreet, uses for a kilogramme-heavy lump of carbon steel and polymer. Ben laid into the two guys, hard and fast and brutal. The one still standing didn't remain on his feet for long. The one already on the floor put up even less resistance. Moments later, both men were stretched out in the corridor, pistol-whipped stone cold unconscious.

Ben froze for a few seconds, listening out for the sounds of voices and running footsteps that would mean the alarm had been raised. There was only silence, apart from the beating of his own heart. He quickly retrieved the second Grach, checked both weapons' magazines and stuffed them crossways through his belt, like a pirate of old. One at a time he dragged the unconscious bodies through the open cell door by their ankles, and dumped them side by side and face down. He pulled off one guy's shoe and jammed it in the door to prevent it from closing all the way. Then he stood over the bodies and thought about what needed to happen next.

The unconscious guards were both bleeding profusely from several head-butts and a fresh set of scalp wounds. If they were ever to wake up, they'd have headaches for a month. But Ben would be sparing them that discomfort, as well as the inevitably nasty punishment they'd receive for letting their prisoner escape. Their troubles were about to end.

Cold as ice, Ben knelt over each man's body in turn and strangled him with the handcuff chain. A true strangle, as opposed to a simple choke-hold, is the way a lion kills its prey by clamping the blood vessels in the neck to shut off the supply of oxygen to the brain. Ben maintained an even pressure for four minutes for each guard. When they were both clinically brain-dead, he calmly retrieved the keys from the cell door lock and went through the ring until he'd found the one for the handcuffs. Once his hands were free he spent a few moments checking the bodies for whatever he could find. Both were wearing slim bulletproof vests under their jackets, the kind of lightweight Kevlar weave that could turn a standard pistol round or a knife blade, if perhaps not a full-power rifle. Tools of the trade for guys in their profession. Unsurprisingly, neither man was carrying any form of ID, not even a wallet. Just two more anonymous dead foot-soldiers. And there would be more. As many as it took to finish this.

Ben had already decided to save Calthorpe until last. Some people deserved special treatment.

He stripped the bulletproof vest off one of the bodies and put it on under his own jacket. It wasn't a bad fit, and it made him feel better. He closed the bodies inside the cell along with the keys, then drew one of the Grachs from his belt and set off at a run back the way he'd come. He was ready to encounter more guards at any moment, but the corridors were empty. So was the lounge room where Ben's meeting with Calthorpe had taken place. The only trace that remained was the smear of Katya Yakunina's blood on the wall and floor, already turning russet-brown as it oxidised and congealed. Ben gazed at the blood and his anger and nausea returned threefold.

He sincerely hoped that he and Colonel Aubyn Calthorpe would meet again.

First, he had to find Valentina. Where they'd been keeping her wasn't far away. He slipped out of the room, snicked the door quietly shut behind him, and began making his stealthy way through the corridors. He met nobody, heard nothing. The building seemed deserted.

He came to another door. Paused, listening, pistol ready. He could hear nothing. He reached down and slowly, slowly, turned the handle. The door eased open a crack. He swung it open the rest of the way and stepped in.

A rush of stale air greeted him. The room was empty. Shadowy. Silent. Cold. Nobody had been here for a long time.

Ben moved on. He came to another door, and tried that one too. Same result.

And now he could feel the tension rising inside as doubts began to grip him. What if Valentina was no longer here? What if they'd taken her away? Then he would never find her.

It was when he came to the third door that he knew immediately that he was in the right place. It wasn't anything he could hear. Like before, there was nothing in the air but flat silence. But it was another sense that was telling him what lay behind the door.

He could smell something.

He gripped the pistol in his right hand. Reached for the door handle with his left. Counted *three – two – one.*

And went in.

319

Chapter 48

Its present users called the building 'the old hospital', which indeed it was, or had been in its time. More correctly, the abandoned and semi-derelict facility in the North-Eastern Administrative Okrug, a few minutes' drive off Prospekt Mira, had served for the latter part of the nineteenth century and much of the twentieth as a particularly harsh and repressive psychiatric clinic for mentally retarded children. The place had finally been closed down in 1976 when the full scale of its outdated and barbaric practices had come to light, and never repurposed. For more than forty years it had stood empty and unseen from the street in a weed-strewn wasteground behind tall rusty gates, slowly rotting, parts of its roof falling in, a silent and sombre monument to the many innocents who had lived and suffered there.

But some old traditions never die.

Antonin Bezukhov had been using the abandoned psychiatric clinic for years. It was conveniently situated not too far across the city from his headquarters, but most importantly it was secluded enough to keep what went on there strictly unseen and unheard. Many of the interrogation subjects his men had brought here for torture had never left the place. The clinic's two acres of overgrown grounds had a lot of graves in them.

Up three flights of stairs and along a dingy hallway where damp plaster littered the floor and toadstools sprouted from the mildew-blackened walls, there was a door; and behind that door was a room with boarded-up windows that had once been a dormitory for some of the facility's most profoundly disturbed inmates. Not all of the children had been so disturbed when they'd arrived, but the horrors of their new existence had quickly bent their minds. The rows of iron-frame beds were long gone now, though the anchor points where many of the kids had been chained to the walls remained, along with a few more added since. They were an occasionally useful feature for the purpose to which the room was put nowadays.

Chief Bezukhov was sitting on a wooden stool, smoking a cigar. To his left and right stood two of his main men, Vankin and Smyrnoi, who'd worked with him for years. Also in the room were a handful of the chief's other agents, there to assist with the torture under the expert supervision of Vankin and Smyrnoi. The pair had fine-tuned their skills back in the early 2000s while employed at the secret federal concentration camps set up to incarcerate and 'process' captured rebels during the Chechen insurgency. They'd perfected a variety of tortures, like the so-called 'wolf canines' method which involved prisoners having their teeth sawn to bloody stumps while forced to bite down on a wooden rod; the 'Chechen table' around which the victims were made to sit with their tongues nailed down to the tabletop; and other techniques still less savoury, some of them designed to extract information but mostly, in truth, just for the fun of watching someone being degraded and mutilated until they begged for death.

The situation had not yet reached that point for Yuri Petrov, but there was no telling how far things might progress before they were done that night. Yuri was manacled by his wrists and ankles to a metal chair. Several wires were attached to the tubular frame of the chair using car battery connectors, and ran across the floor to a voltage control box that could rack the current up high enough to cause extreme agony. To ensure maximum electrical conductivity, an assistant wearing thick rubber gloves and boots stood by with a bucket of water, which he sloshed over Yuri every few minutes.

'Hit him again,' Bezukhov said calmly between puffs of his cigar. Vankin's small, piggy eyes glowed as he twiddled the red rotary dial on the control box a little higher. Yuri let out a sustained shriek and squirmed desperately in the chair, trying to peel as much of his drenched skin and clothing away from the electrified metal as possible. To no avail. After five full seconds of tormented twitching and convulsing, Bezukhov nodded to Vankin, who turned the dial back down again. Yuri sank into his chair, gasping, his eyes bloodshot, his face ghastly.

'It's not pleasant, is it, Yuri? Is this really what you want? Of course not. Then answer the question.'

Yuri gritted his teeth and he stared at Bezukhov in hatred. 'I already told you a hundred times, I don't have it any more,' he croaked.

'Then tell us where you hid it,' Bezukhov said wearily. 'Or else . . .' He signalled to Vankin. 'Again.'

Vankin happily obliged. He cranked the knob even higher. Yuri's scream filled the room.

'You can make it stop, Yuri,' Bezukhov said when the agony subsided. 'All you have to do is utter those few simple words.'

'In the woods!' Yuri bellowed.

'What woods?'

'Near Grisha's place. I could take you there!'

'Think I'm stupid, Yuri? That I can't see you're just playing for time? What good do you think that'll do you, eh?' Bezukhov waved his cigar in the direction of a large packing case that stood by the far wall. 'See that crate over there? That's Vankin and Smyrnoi's little box of tricks. They've got all kinds of toys inside. It's just a question of time before one of them loosens your tongue. If we have to cut off your fingers and toes, you know we will. Other things, too. But it really doesn't have to go that far. Come on, Yuri. Make it easy on yourself. None of us is going anywhere until you give me what I want.'

Which, at least as far as Chief Bezukhov was concerned, wasn't strictly true. Evening was fast falling. He had tickets to the new production of Prokofiev's *Obrucheniye v monastīre* at the Teatr Bolshoi that night and he was already in danger of running late if he didn't get out of here in the next forty minutes, tops. Mrs Bezukhova was actually the opera fan of the family, more than her husband. She'd have his guts for garters if he made her miss the show.

Bezukhov exchanged glances with Vankin and Smyrnoi, who both shrugged. They'd been at this for ages; he should have cracked by now. They could press him much harder, but physical mutilation was a risky option. With Grisha Solokov dead, the last thing Bezukhov wanted was for Petrov to bleed out or die of a goddamn heart attack before revealing where he'd hidden Object 428 and its plans. There had to be another way to get him to talk.

'Let my child go,' Yuri croaked. 'Send her home. And I'll tell you where it is. Then you can kill me if you want. I don't care.'

Bezukhov crushed out the stub of his cigar and took out his phone. Yuri had just given him an idea.

'Who're you calling, chief?' Vankin said, a trifle disappointed that he might not get to start lopping off body parts after all.

'I'm calling Arkangelskaya. Let's get them to bring the kid over here. Something tells me that when we start opening her up in front of her loving daddy here, he'll change his tune. Won't you, Yuri? We'll soon have you singing like a sparrow.'

Yuri's cry of furious protest was lost in his scream as Vankin cranked the current once more.

The chief stood up and walked out of the room, so that he could talk without being drowned by the victim's noise. On the dark, dingy landing outside he dialled a number and waited impatiently. The phone rang several times before he got a reply. There was a silence on the line. 'It's Bezukhov,' he rumbled. 'Is that you, Arkangelskaya?'

Another silence. Then a woman's voice, deep and croaky from too many rough cigarettes, replied, 'Yes, this is Arkangelskaya.'

'We need the brat over here,' he said. 'I'm sending some guys to pick her up.'

Chapter 49

Ben stood motionless outside the door. The scent he could smell coming from behind it was the same stink of bad tobacco that he'd noticed hanging around Arkangelskaya earlier, as though she'd been smoking dried horse dung when she wasn't playing doctors and nurses.

This was the holding room. It might now be empty, or it might not. There might be a dozen armed men waiting just inside the door, ready to shoot him to pieces. Or both Arkangelskaya and her hostage might be long gone. Only one way to find out.

Ben held his breath. As slowly as he could, fighting his impatience to just fling the door wide open, he turned the handle. Pushing ever so gently, he saw a thin strip of light appear around the edges of the door. Someone was in there, for sure. The acrid tobacco scent from within was suddenly stronger in his nostrils.

Ben pushed the door open wide enough to peer through the gap. The first thing he saw was the white-coated beanpole figure of Arkangelskaya. She was standing with her back to the door, gazing out of a window at the falling dusk outside. One arm folded across her waist, the other poised with a cigarette dangling from between her long, bony fingers. A thin stream of smoke curled upwards and dissipated where it met a draught from the cracked window pane. There was a silent walkie-talkie handset protruding from one pocket of her lab coat. She seemed far away in thought and hadn't heard the door open behind her.

Arkangelskaya wasn't alone in the room. A few feet from the window, Valentina was sitting bound and gagged in a chair while the doctor lady puffed away in her brown study. The child looked completely exhausted and drained of emotion, slumped against the thin cord bonds that held her little body tightly in the chair.

Ben slipped silently into the room. Arkangelskaya still didn't turn around. Her radio made a little chirp, which she ignored. He took a step towards her. Valentina's puffy red eyes shot open wide as she saw him. He put a finger to his lips, signalling her to stay quiet. Took another step.

That was when Arkangelskaya sensed the new presence in the room and turned suddenly, her mouth opening to cry out in alarm. Before she could make a sound, Ben had closed the distance between them and clubbed her hard over the head with the butt of the pistol. Her eyes rolled back in their sockets and she slumped unconscious to the floor.

Ben hurried over to Valentina and pulled away the gag that covered her mouth. She stared at him in amazement, blinking, then looked down at the rumpled shape on the floor. '*Elle est morte?*' she asked him in French.

'Not dead,' he replied as he got to work loosening the cord holding her to the chair. 'Just sleeping.'

'I wish she was dead. I hate her so much.' She pulled a face. 'My arms are all numb.'

'Wiggle them like this, get the blood going again. Did she hurt you, Valentina? Did anyone harm you?'

Valentina shook her head.

'All right, now listen. I need to know where those other

guards are. One about my size, the other one not much bigger than you?'

'They were here before. They come and go. I don't know where they are now.'

Ben finished untying the child's bonds, then hurried back over to search Arkangelskaya. The channel her walkie-talkie was tuned to was inactive, apart from the occasional chirp and crackle. He tossed it aside and went through the rest of her belongings. In the pockets of her white lab coat he found a mobile phone, which he kept for himself, and a small zippered pouch. The pouch contained a pair of syringes, each with its own little vial of liquid. The labels were in English, and both were printed with names he recognised. One was pentobarbital, a powerful sedative of the type used to knock out patients before surgery. The other was potassium chloride. A highly versatile drug, one of whose uses was as the finishing touch in executions by lethal injection, to stop the heart.

'What's that?' Valentina asked, frowning at the pouch.

'Nothing you need to worry about,' he said. 'Not any more.'

This woman with the name of an angel was really some kind of demon. Once they no longer needed Valentina, they were planning on putting her down like an unwanted kitten.

Ben wanted to beat the good doctor's brains out. He wondered whether he'd find one of Calthorpe's micro mind-control chips inside, if he did. Maybe; or maybe she was just naturally evil and didn't need a little voice inside her head telling her what terrible things to do. He dragged her scrawny carcass over to the chair, propped her up and used the thin cord to truss her, none too gently.

When she was securely bound up and definitely not going anywhere, he glanced about him. A small door opened up into what turned out to be an empty storeroom to the side, little more than a cupboard.

'Are we going now?' Valentina asked.

'In a minute.'

'I hate this place. Horrible things happen here.'

'I don't like it much either,' Ben replied. 'But before you know it, you'll be home safe and sound, and this will all be over.'

'Are we going to fetch Papa and take him home too?'

'First I need to know where they've taken him,' Ben said. 'That's why I need to talk to the doctor here, in case she knows something. And that's why I need you to go and stand in that cupboard for a minute, while I have a chat with her. Okay?'

'I don't want to go in there.'

'Valentina,' he said, looking at her.

'I can help. Really.'

'No, you can't.'

'But I can! I—'

Before she could say any more, Ben grabbed her and shoved her in the cupboard. 'Put your hands on your ears and sing a song or something. Do not come out until I tell you, all right?'

'Why?'

'Because I say so.' With a stern warning look, he closed her in. He sighed. Kids.

Arkangelskaya was coming round. Ben slapped her lightly on the cheek. Her eyes fluttered open, focused and hardened into pinpoints of fear. Up close, the skin of her face was coarse and heavily lined, creases and pores packed with makeup like masonry cracks repaired with filler. 'Now it's just you and me, Doctor,' Ben said. 'I know you understand English, so let's not mess around. Tell me where Yuri Petrov is.'

'I do not know where he is. I do not know this person.' Arkangelskaya's voice was low and harsh and croaky from too many years of puffing those foul things. It was enough to make a person think seriously about giving up smoking.

'I was afraid you might say that,' Ben told her. 'I wouldn't like to have to give you a taste of your own medicine, *Doctor*.'

He picked up the pouch. Took out a syringe and the vial marked POTASSIUM CHLORIDE. Removed the protective cap from the needle and poked it through the silver foil of the vial. As he worked the plunger, the syringe filled with the whitish liquid. Arkangelskaya's eyes bulged as she watched him. She swallowed hard.

'Still don't know where your friends have taken him?'

She gasped and shook her head violently from side to side.

Ben stepped closer to her. 'Doesn't feel so great when you're on the wrong end of the needle, does it, Doctor? I'm a nice guy who normally doesn't do nasty things to people. But even nice guys can have a really, really bad day when they might suddenly forget themselves.'

'I do not know! I swear!'

'You're wasting time on that silly old cow,' said a voice behind him.

He turned. 'Valentina, I thought I told you to stay in the cupboard.'

'It smells in there.'

'Get back inside, please.'

'What if she really doesn't know?' Valentina said, matter-of-factly, then pointed at Arkangelskaya and added, 'Pump the horrible old witch full of poison and let's get out of here.'

Ben stared at the kid and privately swore never again to disparage anyone who complained about how hard parenting was. 'Are you trying to tell me my job now?'

She shrugged. 'No, I'm trying to tell you, but you wouldn't listen—'

'What?'

'That I *know* where Papa is.'

'*What?*'

'I heard the guards talking. They were speaking Russian, and they didn't know I could understand.'

Ben's mind flashed back to the memory of himself in the girl's room back home in Le Mans, seeing her collection of Russian literature. Her mother telling him how she'd been secretly learning the language, wanting to become fluent in time to surprise her father for his fortieth birthday. As far as Calthorpe and his crew were concerned, she was just a little Dutch girl now living in France. Foxed by a twelve-year-old kid.

'Tell me exactly what they said, Valentina.'

'The old hospital. That's where they've taken Papa.'

'What old hospital?'

'I don't know, that's what they called it,' she replied all in a rush. 'It must be somewhere in the city. They said they were taking him there to work on him. I'm not stupid, I know that means they're doing awful things to him. It's that horrid man called Bezukhov. I remember the name because of Count Pierre Bezukhov in *War and Peace*. I heard Papa telling Grisha about the things he does. Papa used to work for him, I think, but then he stopped because he didn't like it any more and now they want to hurt him.' Her face filled with strain. 'I can't stand thinking about it. We have to stop them.'

At that moment, Arkangelskaya rolled her head back and let out a long, rasping, ululating shriek, so piercingly loud that anyone in the building must surely be able to hear. The high-pitched cry was still coming from her mouth when

Ben silenced her with a short, sharp punch to the head. She slumped limply in the chair with her eyes shut and her tongue sticking out.

'Is she dead now?' Valentina said, peering at her.

'Haven't you seen enough dead people today already?' Ben shook his head and wondered at a twelve-year-old's concept of death. Had he understood what it really meant, at that age? Maybe not. That was a lesson he'd come to learn later, in spades.

But two things that all children certainly did understand were pain and fear. Both were etched all over Valentina's little heart-shaped face. Ben grabbed her shoulders and shook her, gently but firmly. She didn't resist his grip.

'Tell me more about the old hospital. We need to know where it is, Valentina. You have to try and remember if they said anything else, anything at all. That's the only way we're going to be able to help Papa.'

Valentina's eyes filled with tears as she shook her head. 'I'd remember if they'd said anything more. But you can find it, can't you? Like you found us before? You're someone who can find people, aren't you? That's why Tonton sent you, isn't it?'

Ben's heart was sinking as fast as his hopes had risen. 'Valentina, it could be anywhere in Moscow.'

'But you have to find it! Those men are going to kill Papa!' Her voice was rising. Ben suddenly clamped his hand over her mouth, stifling her words.

He'd heard something. The sound of voices and running footsteps somewhere within the empty building. Still some way off, but approaching fast. Next, Arkangelskaya's radio started crackling with urgent Russian voices. The damned woman had alerted the guards with her cry for help, and they'd be here any second.

Ben turned off the walkie-talkie. He said, 'Valentina, turn around with your back to the door. Eyes shut. Fingers in your ears. Now.' Whether it was the authority in his voice or her fear of what was about to happen, the girl obeyed. Ben whirled around to face the door.

In the next instant, two things happened. A pair of black-clad thugs burst through the door and charged into the room.

And Arkangelskaya's phone suddenly started ringing and vibrating in Ben's pocket.

Chapter 50

They were the same two guys who had accompanied Arkangelskaya and Valentina earlier. The bigger of the two about Ben's size, a shade under six feet, the other not much over five-two, whippy and mean-looking.

Stopping dead in the doorway, they stared bug-eyed at the trussed-up and unconscious shape of Arkangelskaya in the chair where the child had been before. Then they turned their astonished gaze towards Ben, the very last person they'd have expected to find running around free. Hence the fact that their weapons were still clipped inside their shoulder holsters under their jackets. Which gave Ben a distinct advantage, as his two Grach pistols were in his belt, butt-forwards and ready to hand for a fast cross-draw. And Ben wasn't so sporting that he wouldn't make the most of such an advantage at a time like this.

The moment of surprise lasted no more than three-quarters of a second before the two guards simultaneously fell into a combat crouch and reached inside their jackets, clawing out their pistols. Too slow, too late. Before either one had cleared its holster, Ben had yanked both Grachs from his belt, one in each hand. Silk-smooth and snake-fast, lining up on target without conscious thought. Their twin reports sounded like a single muted shot. A small red hole appeared in each man's forehead, dead centre, as the jacketed 9mm bullets drilled neatly through their skulls and exited to the rear, spraying the wall either side of the doorway with blood and brains. Their knees crumpled and they hit the floor with their weapons still half drawn.

Valentina had opened her eyes, taken her fingers out of her ears and turned to stare numbly down at the corpses with her mouth hanging open. 'Don't look at them,' Ben said. But she kept staring. The doctor's phone was still ringing in Ben's pocket. He hesitated, then pulled it out and thumbed the reply button.

A gruff, gravelly Russian voice spoke in his ear. He quickly held the phone close to Valentina's, snapping her out of her trance at the sight of the dead guards. The girl's face was pale and taut as she listened to the voice on the line. She cupped her hand over the phone and whispered, 'It's him. It's Bezukhov, calling the witch!'

Ben's thoughts whirled at light-speed. He remembered something else he'd been told: skill at languages was just one talent the kid possessed. Another, according to her doting granduncle, was doing impressions.

'Talk to him,' he hissed. 'Pretend you're her.'

Valentina's eyes widened as round as dessert plates. 'What shall I say?'

'Just talk.'

Valentina took a deep breath and replied into the phone. '*Da, eto gavarit Arkangelskaya.*' Yes, this is Arkangelskaya. The way she lowered her young voice into an impression of a much older woman's, deep and raspy from smoking too many horse-dung cigarettes, was beyond uncanny. Despite the urgency of the moment, Ben had to smile. This kid was every bit as smart as her granduncle and her father had made her out to be.

The rumbling voice on the line spoke again. Valentina listened, her face rigid with concentration, then quickly covered the phone with her hand and looked back up at Ben with the same huge, bewildered eyes.

Ben whispered, 'Well, what did he say?'

She whispered back, 'He said he's sending some men to pick up the brat.' From her look, it was clear she understood perfectly well that the brat in question was herself. 'What do I tell him?'

Ben had to think fast. Very few options were open to him and it was a stark, grim choice to have to make. But he knew it was the only way forwards. He said, 'Tell him she's ready whenever he wants her.'

Valentina flashed him a look of fearful confusion, then put Arkangelskaya's voice back on to relay the reply in the same perfectly croaky Russian, even though she didn't yet understand the reason for it. Ben had to smile again at the faultlessness of her impression. On the other end, Bezukhov seemed to be completely taken in.

After a couple more passes of conversation, Bezukhov ended the call. Valentina handed the phone back to Ben and puffed out her cheeks. 'Phew. That was really intense.'

'All right, Valentina. We're going to have company. I need you to be really brave and grown up for just a little bit longer, all right?'

'What do they want with me?'

'Don't worry, I'll be with you every step of the way.' He could see the deep apprehension in her eyes. He dropped the phone in his pocket, lowered himself into a crouch and grasped both of her hands in his. They were cold. As reassuringly as he could, he said, 'I know how scared you are, kid. But there's a good side to this. Before, we didn't have any way of knowing where your dad is. Now they're going to take us straight to him. And we know he's all right.'

She nodded, but the fear in her eyes hadn't melted. 'Do we?'

'These are bad men, Valentina. Really bad. But your father has a secret that they care about more than anything. They can't hurt him too much, because what they're most afraid of is that he wouldn't tell. That's why they want you there, because they're hoping the sight of you will persuade him to talk.'

He could see her thinking, working through the logic of what he'd said and understanding its dreadful implications. After a moment's silence she said, 'Are they going to hurt me?'

Ben clasped her hands more tightly, looking deep into those frightened hazel eyes. 'No, Valentina. I swear that won't happen. I'm here to protect you. You stay close to me, do what I say and everything will be fine. I promise.'

She sniffed, blinked away a tear, and then nodded pluckily. 'So what's going to happen now?'

Ben gave her hands a last reassuring squeeze and let them go. He took Arkangelskaya's mobile back out. 'First, I'm going to make a quick phone call.'

'And then?'

'And then we're going to get Papa, and take him away from the bad guys.'

Valentina blinked. 'How do we do that?'

'Tonton says you're a pretty good actress. From the way you fooled Bezukhov just now, I'd say you're a movie star in the making.'

'Maybe, I don't know,' she replied with a blush.

'A lot better than me, anyway. So, now's your chance to do a bit more acting. Are you okay with that?'

She shrugged her shoulders under the pink gilet. 'Okay, I suppose. And what then?'

'And then we're all going home,' Ben said. 'And we're all going to live happily ever after.'

'Papa too?'

Ben playfully ruffled her hair, and for all her apprehension she gave him a beaming smile that touched his heart. He said, 'Yep. Papa too.'

If only things could be that simple.

Chapter 51

Ben's call to Kaprisky was short and sweet, and Ben did all the talking. He kept his back to Valentina and his voice low. If the kid knew Tonton was on the line, she'd want to speak to him. Big emotional scenes could wait. When Kaprisky picked up, Ben said, 'It's me. Send the plane. We're coming home.' He ended the call before Kaprisky could react, and turned off the phone so the old man couldn't call back at an inopportune moment. There might be plenty of those ahead.

'Now let's get started,' he said to Valentina.

They didn't have long to prepare before Ben heard the sound of an approaching vehicle outside, and glanced out of the window to see headlights cutting through the dusk.

'Ready?' he asked Valentina, giving her a thumbs-up.

'Ready,' she replied from the chair she was sitting on, but her voice sounded nervous.

At any rate, they were as ready as they could be. Arkangelskaya was trussed up tighter than a Christmas turkey, securely gagged and stuffed in the tiny storeroom with the two dead guards for company. Ben had mopped the blood off the floor as best he could, then exchanged his denim shirt and brown leather jacket for the black polo-neck sweater and black nylon jacket he'd taken from the dead guard his size. Under Valentina's pink gilet she'd donned the bulletproof vest that Ben had stripped from the smaller of the two corpses. The wiry little guy had stood only an inch or two taller than she was, and with her gilet zipped up to the neck the thin but effective armour was invisible and added barely any noticeable bulk to her shape. At first she'd flatly refused to put it on, but Ben had explained that it would make her safe.

He was all too aware that was wishful thinking on his part. The idea of walking a child into the very heart of danger filled him with horror. But it was either that or leave Yuri to his fate in the fairly certain knowledge that Bezukhov's people would torture the poor guy to death. Had Ben been forced to take that grim option, he'd have had to kidnap Valentina himself and drag her out of Russia kicking and screaming while her father met his awful end, alone and abandoned. He couldn't have forgiven himself for such a thing, any more than she would.

It was a tense few moments as they waited, hearing the sound of doors and voices and footsteps growing louder. Ben patted Valentina's shoulder. 'Remember what I told you. Stay close to me but don't talk to me, and act scared. They have to believe that I'm one of the bad guys.'

She nodded. 'I will.'

'You'll be fine.'

'I trust you, Ben.'

It was the first time she'd addressed him by name. Those words placed such a heavy burden on him that they were hard to hear. The prospect of what lay ahead chilled him to the core, but nothing was more heart-warming than a child's trust. He smiled. 'It's all going to be okay,' he repeated, forcing himself to believe it. It was when you stopped believing that you started dying.

The footsteps reached the door, and an instant later it swung open. Ben held his breath. He was betting on the theoretical supposition that Bezukhov's thugs and Calthorpe's thugs were on separate teams and didn't know one another. Now was the moment when he'd find out.

Three unfamiliar faces of Bezukhov's guys looked in. At a glance they were pretty much what Ben had expected, the usual run-of-the-mill gorillas, not fabulously bright and perfectly suited to this line of work. The one who seemed to be in charge glanced around the room and frowned. He'd clearly been expecting to see Arkangelskaya. Maybe more than just a single guard watching over the kid, too. At least, that was Ben's interpretation of his grumbled query, to which Ben responded with a noncommittal shrug as if to reply, 'How the hell do I know where everybody is? I'm just doing my job, mate.'

The three came into the room, as brisk and businesslike as a haulage crew come to pick up a package for delivery. The leader walked up to Valentina's chair and made as if to grab her by the arm, but Ben stepped in between them and shook his head. With a stony expression and one hand on the girl's shoulder he drew out one of his Grach 9mms and pressed the muzzle to the side of her neck. Pointing a loaded firearm at a child was one of the hardest things he'd had to do in his life. But the unspoken message was clear, and it was one Ben needed to establish immediately with Bezukhov's delivery boys. This one's in my charge.

They seemed content to let Ben assume the role of the kid's minder, sparing them the ignominy of having to play baby-sitter themselves. Nothing more needed to be said, which suited Ben fine as they left the building and crossed the empty, unlit concrete to where a plain black minivan was waiting with its engine ticking over. The evening air was cool and damp and the moon was rising behind a drifting veil of fog.

Ben had been anxiously watching the clock for the last several minutes, because the hour was almost up and Calthorpe was due to return at any moment. If he appeared now, Ben's plan would explode disastrously before it had even begun. He felt a peculiar mixture of relief and apprehension as they reached the van. So far, so good; but the wave of luck Ben was riding could collapse at any time. All it would take was for someone to recognise him. Or to ask him something complicated in Russian and get suspicious when he failed to reply with more than a grunt or a shrug. He lit up one of Arkangelskaya's cigarettes and puffed clouds of the foul smoke around him to ensure nobody got too sociable.

The van was a GAZ Sobol. Manufactured by the Gorky Automobile Plant, virtually identical to scores of others Ben had seen going about Moscow in various configurations. This one was fitted with three rows of seats, like a minibus, and a sliding door at one side. Ben sat in the rear by the window with his young hostage next to him, the pistol resting in his lap. Valentina was acting her part well and looking suitably terrified of him. The others clambered in. Doors slammed. Nobody said a word. The driver set off through the gates and hit the road, wipers slicing away the sprinkles of mist on the windscreen, headlamps carving into the murk.

The short journey took them around the edge of the city, then carved towards the heart of Moscow through a twisting night-time maze of streets and junctions that soon stripped Ben of any kind of bearings. In a quiet, dark and austere-looking suburb with virtually no traffic, the van pulled up at a tall gate set into a rusty iron-railed fence, its headlights throwing long shadows into the badly overgrown grounds of what looked like a rundown old mansion house from a bygone century, barely visible through the trees. The driver waited as a pair of men appeared, unchained the gates from inside and hauled them open for the van to pass through. Both men had submachine guns dangling on straps. Ben could feel the odds stacking up against him already, and it wasn't a reassuring sensation.

The gates were closed and rechained behind them as they drove down a short avenue of trees and pulled up in a weedy forecourt in front of the tall, long, once grand building, whose state of creeping dilapidation was even more apparent up close in the headlights. Ben guessed that the 'old hospital' had been some kind of private clinic back in the day, perhaps a sanatorium or rest home. On the outside, it gave the impression of having lain totally disused for many years. Its windows, many of them broken, were almost completely in darkness; only a faint chink of light peeped out from a couple of boarded-up panes on the third floor.

But there was no question that someone still had a use for the place. It looked exactly like the kind of handy out-of-the-way spot where a guy like Chief Bezukhov and his thuggish Russian intelligence pals would bring people to torture and murder them. In the olden days of Lubyanka prison, they'd have been able to do these things more openly. Modern progress was of little comfort to their victims, however.

The shadowy figures of two more armed men stood by the door, to add to the two working the gates and the three in the van, plus the driver, plus whoever else was inside. Ben's headcount of opponents he'd have to deal with that night was growing fast. The men climbed out of the van, along with the driver, who plucked the keys from the ignition and tucked them in the back pocket of his jeans after blipping the locks. Ben couldn't blame him for wanting to lock his vehicle. A lot of crooks around.

Ben took Valentina's arm and followed, treating her just roughly enough to look the part without hurting her. As they reached the entrance, one of the figures by the door stepped forward and said something in Russian while reaching out to take Valentina from him. Like before, Ben gave the guy a dead-eyed stare, shook his head and dug his pistol muzzle against the side of the girl's neck. The universal sign language for 'Uh-uh, hands off, she's mine'. The van driver pointed at Ben and made a comment in Russian that sounded lewd, causing a ripple of coarse laughter among his pals. Ben turned his stare on them and they quickly shut up and looked away. The one at the door shrugged, like 'Whatever, dude,' and backed off.

Valentina glanced nervously up at Ben. Unnoticed by the others, he broke his stone-faced act for a brief moment to give her the world's smallest wink. It was all he could do to reassure her. No child should be brought into a place like this. No child should be made to witness the things she had seen, and would see. But that was the way it was. There was no turning back. Ben kept his hand on her shoulder all the way.

The four men from the van led the way inside the half-derelict building. Its interior was every bit as lugubrious as the outside, smelling strongly of mould and decay and dimly illuminated by a few naked bulbs crusted with dust and dead bugs. Ben kept a firm hand on Valentina's shoulder as the six of them climbed a sagging, creaking wooden stairway that went up three flights towards, he presumed, the boarded-up windows whose light he'd seen from outside. Halfway up the second flight the lights flickered and dimmed for a few seconds, and a desolate wail of pain sounded from somewhere upstairs.

It was Yuri's voice. A couple of the Russians laughed at the sound of torture. Ben felt Valentina go rigid and falter in her step. She let out a whimper. He urged her on with a push, worried that she might turn around and say something that would give the game away. If she did, he'd already decided he would shoot the four men before they had a chance to react. Then as the alarm was raised upstairs and downstairs, he'd find a safe room in which to hide Valentina while he faced whatever odds came at him and hoped for the best. It was a dangerous proposition that came with a very high chance of Yuri getting killed, if not all three of them.

Ben's tension was rising with every step. This was turning out to be the strangest, probably the riskiest and without a doubt the most unsettling rescue mission he'd ever been involved in.

And it was about to get worse.

Chapter 52

Yellow light glowed from around the edges of a closed door at the end of a dingy, mouldy landing on the third floor. As they walked towards it, the door suddenly opened and a large, hefty man stood framed in the doorway. Ben guessed his age at somewhere either side of sixty-five. He was grizzled and ugly, a steely-silver stubble covering his scalp and unwinking eyes set deep into a wide, florid face with broken veins laced across his cheeks. And very obviously in a foul mood. He made a big show of looking at his watch, and growled something in Russian that to Ben's ears was most likely something like 'You fucking well took your time getting here.'

Ben instantly recognised the gravelly voice as the same one he and Valentina had heard on the phone. So this was Chief Bezukhov, Yuri Petrov's nemesis and former employer, in the flesh. And a big mound of flesh it was.

Valentina was frozen in fear at the sight of him. Bezukhov's gaze took her in as though she were just an urgently awaited parcel turning up on his doorstep, then flashed up at Ben. The small hard eyes narrowed for an instant as though he were trying to place Ben's face and wondering why he wasn't succeeding. Ben's heart stopped beating momentarily. The chief might very well be one of the few individuals who

345

could flag him as an impostor. Or worse, as himself.

But then the moment passed. Bezukhov was too agitated and in a hurry to worry about a forgotten face. He motioned impatiently for Ben and the others to bring the girl inside the room.

And they stepped into hell.

Ben had seen rooms like this before, and long hoped in vain that he'd never have to set foot in one again. The torture chamber seemed to physically reek of the agony of all the nameless, faceless victims who had suffered and sweated and bled and died here. Men, perhaps women too, who had hung manacled from the iron rings set into the walls while their interrogators got to work. Throughout all of human history the application of severe pain, or even just the threat of it, had been the preferred method out of all the ways a person can extract secrets and confessions from another. If prostitution could be said to be the oldest profession, that of the torturer came a close second.

There were nine people already inside the room, including Bezukhov, his gang of men, and their guest. The four from the van filed in behind Ben, blocking the doorway. Still tightly in Ben's grasp, Valentina let out a cry of horror and despair when she saw her father. Yuri was sitting chained up to the legs and frame of a metal chair in the middle of the room. His head hung limply at a downwards angle so that his chin touched his chest but his face was visible, terribly ashen and gaunt, like that of an old man. His eyes were shut, a smudge of dark circles around them, and his clothes and hair were soaked and dripping.

Ben took in the entire scene at a glance. The wires that were hooked up to the chair by large crocodile clips ran across the floor to a splitter box connected to the mains and a control unit in the hands of one of Bezukhov's heavies, a shifty-eyed weaselly-looking fellow who looked as though he'd been richly enjoying himself. One of his comrades stood beside a wooden packing case that literally overflowed with torture implements like bolt croppers and blowtorches and ice picks, the sight of which made Ben feel sick. Another sadistic-looking individual with a beefy face and a moronic grin hovered behind Yuri, wearing thick black rubber gauntlets and clutching a bucket of water he'd been sloshing over the victim to keep him wet. Ben guessed the water was heavily salted, to allow the current to zap poor Yuri through the metal chair and his drenched shirt and trousers.

The rest of the room's occupants were spectators, clustered around their chief or lounging against the walls, smoking and idly watching the show. Everyone was armed, as if somehow they expected a man half-dead from hours of electric shock torture to jump up, break his chains and violently attack them. A few short-barrelled shotguns and submachine guns stood propped against the walls or hung from the backs of chairs. A pall of cigarette smoke hovered and curled around the single bare light bulb. Evidently the show had been going on for quite some time and most of the assembly were getting bored.

Which, given the contents of the crateful of torture implements and the potential for horrific damage they offered, told Ben that his guess had been correct. They'd been hurting Yuri, but holding back from inflicting too much harm. He wasn't a hard man. Their greatest worry would be that they'd too easily push him over the edge and he'd take his secret to his grave.

Which was in one way a good thing, because it had preserved Yuri's life thus far.

And in another way a bad thing, terribly bad, because Valentina's presence now gave Bezukhov a whole new kind of leverage over Yuri Petrov. One neither the chief nor his crew would hesitate to implement. And it was going to start happening any time now. They would cheerfully fillet her like a fish in front of her father to make him talk, and only Ben could prevent the unthinkable from unfolding right there in front of him.

Voices echoed in his mind. '*Are they going to hurt me?*' she'd asked him.

'*No, Valentina, I swear that won't happen. I'm here to protect you,*' he'd replied.

'*You shouldn't make promises you cannot honour, my friend.*' Yuri's words lanced through Ben once more.

Ben pushed all doubts and fears aside. His resolve tightened. A racing stopwatch began counting down inside his head, ticking off the seconds. He felt his heart slow and his body relax, the way it always did in the moments when battle was imminent and he was primed for action.

Valentina began struggling to break away from Ben's grip and go running to her father, but Ben couldn't let go. The tears flooding down her cheeks wetted his arm as he pinned her tightly against him. There were a few laughs among Bezukhov's men at the sight of her extreme distress. Anticipation was rising. The spectacle was about to become much more entertaining for them and they couldn't wait.

Yuri's eyes fluttered open. The look on his face when he saw his daughter was one of far worse pain than anything his torturers could have inflicted, no matter what they'd done to him. He began struggling wildly in the metal chair, calling her name. He looked to Bezukhov in desperation and shouted words of Russian whose meaning was easy for Ben to guess. 'Please! No! Don't harm her! You can't do this!'

'You left me with no choice, Yuri,' Bezukhov said calmly. 'Now it's too late.'

Yuri howled with rage and grief. Then his ghastly dark-ringed eyes turned on Ben, and the strangest look of bewilderment came over his face as he recognised the black-clad guard clutching Valentina with a pistol pressed to her. He blinked, as if he thought he was hallucinating. His mouth opened and closed soundlessly.

But none of Bezukhov's men noticed the odd change in Yuri's expression, because all eyes were now on the girl. The chief snapped a command at the weaselly-looking man holding the voltage control box, calling him 'Vankin'. Ben could easily guess what the order was, too. And Vankin seemed only too happy to abide by his boss's wishes. He set down the control box. Stepped towards Ben and Valentina, putting out a hand to grab the child's arm.

Bezukhov motioned to the man standing near the crate of implements. 'Smyrnoi.' Smyrnoi needed little prompting, and like Vankin he appeared delighted to obey the command. He reached inside the crate and pulled out a large pair of secateurs, the kind gardeners used for clipping hedges. The handles were padded with soft foamy rubber. Extra grip, for when the blood started flowing and things got slippery. He snapped the blades a few times for effect. His eyes twinkled.

The ticking stopwatch inside Ben's mind had now become a fast-burning fuse wire, its sparkling white flame hissing and crackling wildly as it raced towards the stack of dynamite that was about to go up like a volcano. This was it. Any moment now.

Vankin snatched Valentina's arm and tugged her harshly away from Ben. He started pulling her towards the middle of the room. She screamed and thrashed in Vankin's steely grip. No longer acting. Her terror was dreadful to watch.

Yuri was going berserk and would have rocked over the metal chair if its feet hadn't been screwed down to the floorboards. Smyrnoi stepped closer. Snapping the secateur blades. *Clack. Clack. Clackclackclack.* His eyes were burning bright and his teeth were bared in a leer of sadistic pleasure at what he was about to do.

Or what he thought he was about to do. Ben had no intention of letting anything remotely like that happen. All he'd wanted was to be in the same place as Yuri and the whole gang of his tormentors. Now here they were. *And here we go*, he thought.

Unnoticed by anyone around him as they were all too intent on watching the fun, he slipped the second Grach pistol out of his belt.

Between them, the pistols had fired three shots since their last reloading. One for the guard Ben was impersonating. One for the small guy who'd posthumously donated his bulletproof vest to Valentina. And one for the unfortunate Katya before that. By Ben's count, he still carried a combined payload of thirty-three rounds in his magazines, plus two in each chamber. It wasn't exactly enough to kick off World War Three.

But it would do to be getting on with.

Ben thought, *fuck it*, and raised his right-hand pistol and shot Vankin in the back of the head. Then he raised his left-hand pistol and put a bullet smack through the centre of Smyrnoi's forehead.

And then, all hell started breaking loose.

Chapter 53

When Aubyn Calthorpe had said he had business to attend to for an hour that evening, what he'd really had in mind was a speedy dinner in the classy, old-world surroundings of his favourite Moscow restaurant. His driver had whisked him from the disused military facility, one of several dotted around the edges of the city, to Café Pushkin on Tverskoy Boulevard. There he enjoyed a beautifully presented, if somewhat rushed, meal of grilled trout with fennel and lemon accompanied with a light salad, which he washed down with a glass of fine Sauvignon blanc before he had to hurry back to work.

Throughout dinner and in the car, Calthorpe had been musing over his mixed expectations as to whether or not Ben Hope would agree to the deal he'd been offered. Whichever way it went tonight, so be it. It would be a pity to have to eliminate such a promising potential recruit, but Calthorpe was confident he would find a suitable replacement. As for the girl and her recalcitrant father, there was no way out for them, no escaping their fate. Whether or not Antonin Bezukhov succeeded in learning the whereabouts of Object 428 and the microfilm, the pair would be dealt with as planned. Calthorpe felt little compunction at the thought of killing a bright, beautiful little child. She wouldn't be the first.

And whether or not Ben Hope opted to become an agent of the Ploughshares Program, a rogue ex-SAS killer offered the perfect patsy for the murders of Yuri Petrov, his twelve-year-old daughter and his friend Grisha Solokov. The evidence would be overwhelmingly conclusive, showing that the deranged and semi-alcoholic former soldier, possibly suffering from deeply repressed post-traumatic psychosis stemming from his past military experiences, had tracked Petrov to a remote farmhouse deep in the countryside, attempted to blackmail him in return for letting him go free, then brutally slaughtered the two men along with the child and burned the house to hide the evidence of his horrific crimes. The murderer had been shot by police while trying to escape Russia. If indeed Hope was dead by then, the circumstances of his death would be contrived to fit neatly with the story. If it so happened that he was still breathing, by then he would be working for Calthorpe under a fabricated identity, shackled to his new employers by the threat of exposure and unable ever to return to his former life.

And so, with the prospect of most, if not all, of the loose ends being neatly tied up and a more or less successful end to his mission, Calthorpe returned from his dinner break in a relatively cheery state of mind.

It didn't remain that way for long. As the Colonel strode back inside the building, ready to get back to business, it quickly dawned on him that something was terribly wrong. Where on earth were the bloody guards? Where was everyone?

With a mounting sense of dread and a thumping heart, Calthorpe rushed to the room where Dr Arkangelskaya – not her real name, needless to say – had been minding their young captive. He found an empty chair, and a cupboard containing two dead men and the "doctor" bound and gagged. His worst fears weren't fully realised until he ran to the cell where Hope was supposedly under lock and key, only to find it occupied solely by two more Russian corpses. One had been stripped of his bulletproof vest. Both had been beaten about the head and then efficiently, very professionally, strangled to death. He instantly recognised the hallmarks of a seasoned SAS veteran.

Calthorpe turned white and let out a groan, partly in pain as acid washed over his stomach ulcer and partly in dread at the thought of the wrath his superiors would unleash on him if he screwed up. He swallowed a handful of pills, vented some of his anxiety by cursing and yelling, then ripped out his phone. To stand any chance of extricating himself from this nightmare, his only option was to go right to the top of the tree, come clean and pray for leniency.

Very few people had the privilege of a direct, very secure, line to the man known only as 'the Chairman'. Calthorpe was authorised to contact him only in the very direst of emergencies. This was definitely one of those.

'Sir, I'm dreadfully sorry to disturb you at such a late hour. But it would seem that our plans have a hit a slight, ah, *snag* . . .'

'I had been given to understand you had this situation under control, Colonel Calthorpe,' the Chairman replied after listening in grave silence to the details.

'I'm afraid we may have underestimated our man' was the best way Calthorpe could describe his predicament without sounding like a complete failure.

'It would certainly appear so' came the Chairman's slow, measured tones, a little buzzy over the long-distance line. Calthorpe could picture him sitting in the splendour of his secluded English country home.

'Then he must be a special individual indeed,' the Chairman continued. 'More so than you anticipated.'

'Requiring special measures to deal with this contingency,' Calthorpe said. 'I'm going to need reinforcements, and fast. All that we can spare.' It daunted him to speak with such audacity to the Great Man.

The Chairman considered the request. 'Unless I'm mistaken, Colonel, we've already expended far more of our local assets on this situation than you had led us to believe would be necessary.'

'But we still have some reserves,' Calthorpe said, working hard to eliminate the squeak of desperation that threatened to creep into his voice. 'Don't we?'

The Chairman breathed a heavy sigh and pondered in silence for a further moment or two, before he replied, 'This is turning into quite a mess, Calthorpe. I have to say, I'm extremely disappointed in you. And I believe the rest of the committee will share my sentiments.'

Calthorpe gritted his teeth as a fresh torrent of stomach acid burned another hole in his belly. 'I can make it right.'

'Then shut up and get the bloody hell on with it,' the Chairman said, and the call was over.

Chapter 54

The firefight on the third floor of the old hospital was as brief as it was furious. In its opening salvo Vankin and Smyrnoi collapsed dead to the floor, rapidly joined by the moron with the rubber gauntlets and the bucket as Ben's follow-up shot plugged him between the eyes.

Ben quickly stepped in front of Valentina, shielding her with his body the way he'd told her he would do. She did as she'd been instructed and clasped herself as tightly as she could against his back, hanging on like a little limpet. They'd have to shoot through him to get her. He was less concerned about a stray bullet finding its way to Yuri, who was safely out of the crossfire.

After a stunned instant's delay, the rest of Bezukhov's men exploded into action and were reaching for their pistols or making a grab for the weapons they'd propped against the walls and hung off the backs of chairs. Ben took down two more men before they could snatch up their guns. Then the four from the van, blocking the doorway to his right. Wielding dual handguns against multiple moving targets that were shooting back at you really required two brains and two pairs of eyes, one for each pistol. Failing that, an awful lot of practice. That was something Ben had had plenty of. Firing alternating shots with each hand he could rake the room with a rate of fire not far short of a machine gun.

Chief Bezukhov's big florid face was a mask of incredulity. He'd frozen like a lamped rabbit in the first few seconds of the battle and now was stumbling backwards in his haste to retreat out of the field of fire, while groping inside his jacket for a shiny nickel-plated pistol that he fumbled getting out of its holster. That was the problem with seniority. You didn't get enough range time to keep your combat skills fresh. Or maybe the chief was just too old and fat for this kind of thing. Ben swivelled his right-hand Grach at Bezukhov and his left-hand Grach at the guy standing beside him, who was swinging up a pump-action twelve-gauge ready to fire, and squeezed both his triggers. The guy with the shotgun went down with a hole where his right eye had been.

Ben's aim with Bezukhov had been just a little off. The chief tumbled back with a roar, dropping his gun and clasping at the spurting wound that had opened up under his jaw. Ben was about to shoot the big man again when an impact slammed into his chest and made him stagger. One of Bezukhov's crew was hunkered down behind an overturned table, using it as cover. The big black pistol in his hand boomed again and Ben felt the .45 calibre slug smack into him with the force of a punch from a heavyweight boxer.

It hurt. A lot. But bruises and cracked ribs were better than being dead. Ben clenched his jaw and stood his ground, feeling the child squeezing tightly against his back like an infant clutching a parent for protection. He was about to fire back at the shooter behind the crate, but now the guy had ducked down out of sight. Ben dropped his point of aim twelve inches and sent three fast rounds into the side of the flimsy wooden box. BLAMBLAMBLAM. The first two glanced off solid objects inside and didn't make it all the way through. The third one penetrated both sides of the crate and hit its mark on the other side. Bezukhov's guy screamed and sprawled out sideways from behind the crate, letting go of his gun and clasping both hands to his right thigh to stem the crimson jet from his ruptured femoral artery. A probably fatal wound; but Ben sped things up for him with a shot through the skull.

More shots snapped out from around the room. Ben felt the scorching heat trail of a bullet that passed an inch from his face and smacked into the mouldy plaster of the wall behind him, and he heard Valentina cry out as its splashback sprayed harmlessly against her. Another bullet punched into the Kevlar vest, thumping him hard in the left pectoral muscle right over where his heart was, but he no longer registered the pain. He stayed on his feet and kept on firing, his pistols in constant motion as they tracked from target to target. Totally in the zone. His conscious mind almost completely shut off. Another one down. Then another. Then there was nobody firing except him, because he was suddenly the last man standing in the room.

He lowered his hot, smoking guns. The one in his left hand had locked back empty. He let it drop. The one in his right had maybe three rounds left in it. The decayed, mouldy room was suddenly still and strangely silent, strewn with prostrate bodies like zonked-out meth addicts in a derelict squat. Yuri Petrov's panda eyes were staring at Ben in speechless amazement. Valentina was still clutching him tightly, burying her head against his back. He pried her hands away from his waist and stroked her cheek. 'You were brave,' he said.

'It is over?' she asked in a small voice.

It wasn't. Ben could hear the shouts coming from below, and the thunder of footsteps hammering up the rickety stairs. He snatched a fallen chair and wedged it at an angle against the door. It wasn't much of a barricade. Next Ben stepped over dead bodies to the collection of torture implements, fished inside the crate and pulled out a pair of bolt croppers. Just the job for snipping off fingers and toes, but Ben preferred putting them to their original purpose. He carried them over to Yuri's chair and made short work of the chains holding him to its metal frame. Yuri needed to be helped from the chair. His exhausted brain was so full of questions, he didn't know where to begin. He kept murmuring, 'I can't believe it. I can't believe what you did.'

'You didn't think I'd leave you to your old boss's tender mercies, did you?'

Yuri fell to his knees and hugged his daughter with all the strength he had left, tears streaming down his face. But there was little time for an emotional family reunion. The urgent footsteps on the stairs had reached the third-floor landing. The door shook from heavy pounding; then bullets punched through as one of Bezukhov's sentries tried to take out the lock or inside bolt they thought was holding it shut. Ben picked up the pump-action shotgun that had been in the hands of one of the men he'd shot. He levelled it in the direction of the door, and the room filled with its numbing, ear-splitting blast as he sent an ounce and a quarter of buckshot ripping through the wood to pulverise whoever was standing too close on the other side and warn off anyone else who got ideas about forcing their way inside the room. That would buy them a little more time, but not much.

Ben asked Yuri, pointing at his injured leg, 'Think you can walk on that?'

'I can hardly stand, my friend. But I'll try.'

Ben stripped off the black jacket. Underneath, the bullet-proof vest was marked by the gunshots that had peppered him. His chest would bear a few marks, too. It hurt to breathe, almost as much as it hurt to move. At least one cracked rib in there, but he could worry about that later. He winced as he removed the vest. Yuri said, 'What are you doing?'

'You two are my charges, and you come first,' Ben said firmly. 'Put this on, Yuri.'

'I have one already,' Valentina said, part-unzipping her pink gilet to show her father the black garment hidden underneath. 'Ben got it for me. He thinks of everything.'

But there was one detail Ben had overlooked, which was that Antonin Bezukhov was still alive. Coming to, the injured chief groaned and tried to roll his thick body up onto his knees in the midst of his dead associates. His face and thick neck were shiny with blood in the dim light. He gazed around him, as though he couldn't believe what had just happened. Then he collapsed onto one elbow, and let out a deep, rasping moan. His red-spattered hand inched like a huge, pale, wounded spider towards his fallen Smith & Wesson.

Yuri's face twisted. Gasping at the pain it caused him, he stooped and snatched up the gun before Bezukhov's stubby fingers could close on it. He aimed it downwards at his former employer, teeth bared, eyes bulging with all the pent-up loathing he felt for this man. The words Yuri spoke were in Russian, but their sentiment was perfectly clear to a non-speaker like Ben. 'You would have harmed my baby girl, Bezukhov. You're an evil piece of shit. Now you're going to hell where you belong.'

Before Yuri could pull the trigger, Ben stepped in and twisted the gun from his hands, then tossed it away. Yuri turned towards him, eyes full of betrayal and confusion. A wave of pain and exhaustion washed through him and his face creased. He wobbled on his feet as though he might collapse, and Ben gripped his arm to steady him. 'You're a better man than that, Yuri. Don't tarnish yourself with his murder.'

'He needs to pay for all the things he's done,' Yuri said.

'He already is paying. He won't last long.'

Yuri's pain-racked eyes looked deep into Ben's. He opened his mouth to say something more. His words were drowned by the sudden gunshot that rattled their eardrums and made both men flinch.

Bezukhov sank to the floor with a final moan. He stopped moving and the last vestiges of life ebbed from his body.

Valentina stepped back, the big gaudy nickel-plated automatic huge and heavy in her small hands. She let it fall back to the floor where she'd picked it up. A tear rolled from her eye. But it was a tear of pride and vindication, not one of sorrow. 'Nobody hurts my Papa.'

Ben and Yuri both stared at her, neither able to speak.

And that was the moment when Bezukhov's phone began to ring.

Chapter 55

Bezukhov's mobile ringtone was the opening bars of the old State Anthem of the Soviet Union, belted out by the massed chorus of the Red Army Choir. Easy to tell where his allegiance had remained all these years.

Ben dug the phone out of the dead man's pocket and held it for a moment, uncertain whether or not to answer it. Two thoughts flashed through his mind: first, that information was power and the more he knew about Bezukhov's business the further it might take him and his charges from harm; second, that the call would be in Russian and he just happened to have a pair of multilingual interpreters to hand right beside him. He put the call on speaker so that Yuri and Valentina could hear.

Ben might not have understood what the caller was saying, but Aubyn Calthorpe's English-accented tones were instantly recognisable. As was the urgent note in his voice. And the mention of Ben's name. Calthorpe was calling to alert Bezukhov that Hope was free and there could be trouble.

Yuri whispered in horror, 'Who—?'

Ben had heard enough. He dropped the phone to the floor and smashed it with a stamp of his heel. Calthorpe would be quick to figure out that his warning had come too late. He'd be no less quick to mobilise whatever force of men he had left. And it wasn't such a long way from the deserted base to the old hospital.

Ben said, 'We don't have a lot of time. Let's go.'

'I didn't really want to hang around here much longer anyway,' Yuri muttered.

'Home now?' Valentina said.

'No stopping, no U-turns,' Ben replied. He scooped up Bezukhov's gun and jammed it in his belt. Then the pump-action, which he slung over his shoulder after topping up its underbarrel tube magazine from the spare cartridge carrier on the folding stock. Whatever hellfire Calthorpe might be about to rain down on them, he'd at least be ready for it.

'How are we getting out of here?' Yuri asked.

'Preferably not by Shanks's pony,' Ben replied. He kicked over a few corpses until he'd found the driver of the van, and the ignition keys in his pocket. Their magic ticket out of here, as long as Calthorpe's guys didn't land on them first.

'What pony?' Valentina said.

With Yuri supporting himself by an arm wrapped around Ben's neck and Valentina staying close behind, the three of them made their cautious way out of the awful room and into the dark, dingy landing beyond. A dead man lay sprawled outside the door where Ben's shotgun blast had laid him flat. A scattered trail of fat, penny-sized blood spots glistened in the shadows of the passage that led back towards the stairs. It looked like Ben had winged another of Bezukhov's crew through the door – how badly, and how much of a threat he still was, remained to be seen.

Someone had turned off the lights below, plunging the stairway into murky gloom. The stairs were quiet. Too quiet, full of potential hidden lurkers waiting to open fire. On his own, able to move like a ghost through the twisting passages and interconnecting hallways, Ben would have found another way down, whether by climbing from a window or abseiling from the damn roof if need be. But hampered as he was by a wounded man and a child in tow, the stairs were his only route out of this place. He slipped Bezukhov's fancy Smith back out of his belt and pointed it ahead, finger on the trigger, senses straining for the slightest sound or movement from the darkness that engulfed them more deeply with every downward step.

Oh so slowly, anxious not to let the stairs creak underfoot, they crept their way down to the second floor. Then the first. Whatever the darkness contained, Ben could only rely on the fact that his night vision would be at least as sharp as, and his reflexes considerably sharper than, any of Bezukhov's remaining men. That was, if they hadn't all fled the building.

Which, by the time Ben, Yuri and Valentina had reached the ground floor and retraced the way to the exit, appeared to be the case. Nobody tried to stop them. No shots came from the darkness. The faintly gleaming blood trail terminated in the foyer, where the guy Ben had winged lay dead. The rest of them had taken off and vanished.

'Bunch of miserable cowards,' Yuri grumbled. 'Take down their leader and they scatter like a pack of rats instead of fighting.'

'Be careful what you wish for,' Ben said. 'Isn't that what you once said to me?'

The black van stood abandoned in the grounds, just where its now-dead driver had left it. The whole place seemed deserted. So far, so good. Ben blipped the vehicle locks open and propped Yuri against its wing while he opened up the side sliding door and peered inside. They weren't out of the woods yet, and the child's safety was his top concern. In his experience, most modern civilian vehicles appeared to be manufactured out of some kind of soft cheese that offered zero protection against anything more potent than a pea-shooter. This van was no different, but Ben noticed that the rearmost seats were bolted to a raised section of the floor whose vertical face made a pretty solid bulkhead. He tapped it with his knuckles. Sheet steel. Not too flimsy. It would have to do. 'Valentina,' he instructed her, 'I want you to huddle as tight as you can into this little nook in front of the seats. Keep your head down and don't move, okay?'

She nodded. 'Yes, Ben.' Nothing in the world like a biddable, tractable child.

'And try not to shoot anybody else tonight,' Ben said. 'It's not the kind of thing little girls do.'

'I'm not a little girl,' she snapped back at him. Maybe not so biddable after all. She flashed Ben a resentful look before clambering in.

Ben helped Yuri into the front passenger seat, then stashed the shotgun in a nook behind the driver's seat, settled himself at the wheel and fired up the engine and lights. The GPS was all in Russian. He quickly twiddled with the language settings. Once it was reset to English he punched in the destination: VNUKOVO INT. AIRPORT. The airport was just sixteen kilometres away. So near, yet so far. But with any luck Kaprisky's plane would soon be there waiting for them.

'Ready to go home?' Ben said.

'I would be, if I still had one to go to,' Yuri replied.

'Then we'll just have to find you a new one.'

Ben slammed the van into first gear, hit the gas and slewed hard around to face the way they had come. As the van roared towards the street entrance, he saw that Bezukhov's surviving thugs had left in such a hurry that they'd clambered over the spiked iron gates without undoing the padlock and chain.

'We're shut in!' Yuri groaned.

'No, we're not,' Ben said. 'Yuri, you might want to fasten your seat belt. Valentina, hold on tight.'

He revved the engine harshly and accelerated straight for the tall, solid gates, aiming for the weakest spot in the middle. Yuri snapped his belt in place, covered his eyes and prepared for death.

The van hit the gates with a bone-jarring, rending crash, ripping one of them off its hinges and flattening it under its wheels as Ben drove right over the top of it and skidded out into the street, trailing wreckage and showering sparks in his wake. He floored the pedal and kept going. One headlight had gone dark and the front bumper was hanging in pieces and scraping the road, but all the van had to do was carry them a few short miles to the airport. Ben would drive it on its bare wheel rims if need be.

'We made it!' Yuri yelled with a triumphant whoop.

But Yuri had spoken too soon. There was a loud crack as a bullet hammered through the back window and embedded itself somewhere in the plastic fascia of the dashboard. Ben glanced in the mirror and saw the fierce headlights gaining on them from behind.

Calthorpe's men had arrived.

Chapter 56

'Who are they?' Yuri said, squinting at the mirror.

Ben replied, 'You don't want to know.' He hit the gas and spurred the van as hard as it would go, forcing a tortured yowl from its underpowered diesel motor. The lights in his rearview mirror kept gaining, and fast, bright and dazzling. He could hear the roar of powerful engines growing rapidly louder over the whiny rasp of the van. Whatever Calthorpe's men were driving was a lot more useful than a mild-mannered GAZ Sobol.

But high-performance saloon cars weren't the only toys they'd brought to play with. A dark figure leaned from the window of the lead vehicle, clutching something that spat a crackling yellow-white halo of muzzle blast as a burst of automatic gunfire raked the back of the van and blew out what was left of the back window. Ben heard Valentina's muffled cry of terror from where she huddled hidden between the rows of seats. He yelled, 'Stay down!' He had his foot all the way to the floor. The rev counter was soaring and the whole van was filled with noise, but the damn thing was giving all the power it would give.

Their pursuers had plenty to spare, by contrast. The two cars drew up parallel to one another in the van's wake, gaining rapidly and coming up so close that Ben could make out the Mercedes Benz badges on their radiator grilles. Suddenly they peeled apart like fighter jets and came swooping up on either side. Ben anticipated the flanking move before it happened. They were planning on closing in to block the way ahead and force the van to a halt. But he wasn't about to let these guys stop him so easily. Not without a fight.

Just as he expected, the instant the cars had shot past on either side of him, they swerved into a V-formation. Ben didn't lift his foot from the gas, and didn't touch the brake. Yuri let out a cry of alarm just before they hit.

The van slammed its way between the incoming cars with a crunch of buckling metal and crumpling plastic and splintering glass and a screech of scraping bodywork as the two cars were forced apart. Ben kept going, jamming his foot down even harder to milk the power he needed from the straining engine. The van's remaining headlamp was now pointing upwards at a cock-eyed angle and something was scraping badly on a front tyre. They'd lost momentum in the impact, and if he didn't make it up again fast the chase would be over as quickly as it had begun.

A stolen glance at his rearview mirror told him that the cars were on the move again. Three dazzling headlights where before there had been four. Growing steadily larger as they gained on their prey with discomfiting speed and ease.

More gunfire rattled in the night air, bullets punching through the flimsy sheet metal of the GAZ Sobol as though it were a tin can. Or a tin coffin. Which it could all too easily become if Ben didn't get them out of this. Calthorpe's people were obviously less interested in keeping Yuri alive than the late Antonin Bezukhov had been. Heading for the airport was out of the question. Ben knew he'd have to shake them off before he could get back on course.

The tree-lined iron railings of the old hospital were far behind them now. The street ahead had tapered into a narrow avenue flanked by looming white stone buildings. Ben was hammering the van for all it was worth, and more, steering a wild zigzag to present a harder target for the shooters on their tail. Bullets splatted off parked cars, buildings and the road. But most of them were hitting the van. It was taking heavy fire. Ben glanced sideways and saw the anxious gleam in Yuri's eyes. Yuri seemed about to say something when another snorting rattle of gunfire punched through the Sobol's bodywork and his face screwed up in pain and shock. He let out a grunt and slumped forwards in his seat. For an instant Ben thought he'd taken a fatal hit; then Yuri's eyes snapped back open, wide as an owl's. 'I'm okay, I'm okay. The vest stopped it.'

But it was only a matter of time and chance before someone was less lucky. The situation couldn't be allowed to continue – but Ben could see no obvious way out. He kept his foot down hard and sawed at the wheel, deepening the crazy slalom of his course until the wheels were slithering for grip on the road and threatening to break into a skid. He yelled, 'Valentina, are you all right back there?' She responded with a muffled squeal, 'I'm scared!'

'Hold on, Sweet Pea,' Yuri called to her, holding on tight against the rocking, gyrating motion of the van and twisting in his seat to make eye contact with his daughter; but she was tucked low out of sight in the nook below the rear seats. Ben could only pray that the bulkhead behind her was as solid as it felt.

Yet another strafing, rattling burst of gunfire raked the back of the van, and this time Ben felt the chassis give a lurch and the wheelbase kick out sideways as a tyre blew. The left rear wheel started banging and thumping noisily, the shredded rubber flailing against the inside of the wheel arch. He sawed at the wheel, trying to contain the skid, but the forces of physics quickly took over and suddenly the view out of the windscreen became a blurred kaleidoscope of colour and light as the van went into a spin. A jarring crash slammed him painfully against the driver's window as they careened sideways into a row of parked cars, shunting them violently aside and mounting the kerb with a thump that sounded like the whole underbody of the van being torn off. The facade of a building flashed towards them and Ben, wrestling with the steering, only narrowly managed to avoid crashing straight into its doorway.

The van lurched to a momentary halt, rocking on its suspension, listing slightly on its blown-out tyre. It took Ben a second to regain his bearings and realise that they'd turned a complete three-sixty and were still facing in the same direction. The headlights of the pursuing cars seared his retinas in the mirror. He gunned the accelerator and took off again, flattening a parked motorcycle and bumping a damaged Lada out of their path as he hammered back down off the kerb and onto the road.

The street ahead was narrow and the van's steering had suddenly become much less responsive. Ben carved a lurching path between the rows of parked cars, scraping to the left, now to the right, somehow maintaining a more or less forward trajectory with his boot hard down to the floor and his fists clamped on the wheel. Daring to glance back, he saw the twin black Mercedes picking a path around the wreckage of battered cars they'd left in their wake.

Yuri let out some expletive in Russian as he glimpsed what lay ahead. They were speeding towards a T-junction where the little street joined a busy artery of night-time city traffic. The lights were against them. An unbroken stream of cars and trucks and motorcycles was shooting across their path with scant regard for speed limits. It would have been sheer suicide to plunge out into the fast-flowing river. But they were being funnelled straight towards it, and with Calthorpe's men coming fast up behind, to stop for the lights would be even more fatal.

That was when Ben spied the sidestreet to his right, flashing up so fast that he was barely able to slow down enough to take the turning without overshooting the apex and slamming them headlong into the corner of the buildings. By the time he had registered the pedestrians-only sign, he was already committed. The van went screeching into the mouth of the sidestreet.

And moments later, Ben realised his mistake. After only a few dozen yards the way ahead suddenly dropped off the face of the earth, as though the street engineers had simply abandoned their work and left the road hanging off the edge of a sheer precipice. Yuri gave a squawk of terror as the van's front wheels hit empty space and the vehicle's nose dropped over what seemed to be a vertiginous brink. Suddenly the way ahead was visible again. But it wasn't a reassuring sight. There was a reason for the pedestrian-only sign. A long flight of stone steps led down a steep hill flanked by tightly arrayed crumbly old red-brick houses.

Ben scarcely had time to say, 'Hold onto your hats, guys,' before the van was hurtling down the steps, banging and lurching and shaking and veering uncontrollably to the left and right. Using the brakes was not an option. All Ben could do was hang on tight, keep the van pointing downwards and pray they didn't flip nose-over and go tumbling and rolling to their deaths.

Surely no one would be insane enough to follow them down here. But a glimpse in the rearview mirror informed him someone was. First one Mercedes and then the other came roaring over the top of the steps, flew into space and touched down with a crash, front wheels disappearing into their arches as the suspension hit the stops, showering sparks where their undercarriages bottomed out.

Then the chase was back on as both cars came slithering and careening after them. A man's head and shoulders poked from the front passenger window of the car in front; then an arm, clutching a small machine pistol. He managed to let off a burst of fire, but he was soon about to come off much worse than his target. The slewing car jolted too close to one of the houses. Before the shooter could whip his upper body back through the window, he was squashed against the brickwork. Ben heard the short, sharp scream even over the cacophony of noise inside the van. In his mirror he saw the car swerve away from the wall and its passenger door swing open as someone inside booted out the mangled body of the injured man and he tumbled from the open door like a sack of garbage. The second car rolled right over the top of him.

The van had about a fifteen-metre lead over the cars. At last it reached the bottom of the steps, where a narrow pavement separated them from an adjacent street. A romantic couple ambling past arm in arm managed to scramble out of the way just in time to avoid being run down as the van burst by them and hit level ground with a crunch and a shower of sparks. The front bumper, now smashed away entirely, went clattering over their roof. Ben could go left or right; he picked left and hit the gas again. The van responded with a clattery rasp and reluctantly accelerated up the street.

Another mistake.

Yuri yelled, 'It's a one-way system!'

'How was I to know that?' Ben replied, swerving this way

and that as oncoming cars honked their horns and flashed their lights in anger. 'Valentina, are you still okay back there?'

'Make it stop, Ben!' came the muffled cry from behind the seats.

'I'm working on it,' he replied through gritted teeth. He took the first corner he saw, screeching hard right with two wheels off the road. The van careened onwards, thumping and banging and scraping, piling half blindly into the night. The wind whistled cold and shrill through the smashed windows. Every ounce of Ben's concentration was focused on escaping from their pursuers. He had no time to look at the sat nav and no idea where he was, still less where he was heading. Imposing last-century buildings and street signs flashed by as they sped along a boulevard where the night-time traffic was heavy in both directions. The two Mercedes were still in pursuit, but had dropped back some distance. Calthorpe's men seemed to be unable to catch up with them as easily as before. Ben wondered whether the lower-riding Mercedes saloons might have sustained more damage from the steps than their own vehicle.

'We're losing them,' Yuri gasped. 'We might still have a chance.'

But things that appeared too good to be true generally were.

Chapter 57

Just as it seemed they might indeed have half a chance of getting away, a beaten-up yellow taxicab suddenly emerged from a junction right in their path and lurched straight out in front of them, before the driver saw the van coming and panic-braked to a slithering halt.

Ben was going too fast to stop. He swerved hard to avoid a collision, but the van's sloppy steering and burst back tyre caused him to lose control. He barely heard Yuri yelling as the van went into a violent skid. The GAZ Sobol glanced like a ricocheting bullet off the flank of an oncoming car, spun across the road, ploughed down a sign on a post and narrowly missed a head-on smash with an oncoming bus as they spun into the chaotic midst of a busy multi-way intersection. Lights dazzled Ben from all directions. Choruses of horns blared. He somehow brought the van back under control without getting them pulverised, and they were sucked into the fast-moving current like a boatman falling into white water rapids.

A stretch of dual carriageway was now leading them towards the mouth of a brightly lit underpass. Their pursuers had made up the distance between themselves and their quarry, aggressively forcing their way through the traffic with their horns jammed on. They were close behind now, like predators nipping at their heels, looming large in Ben's rearview mirrors. Surging up to the bullet-chewed rear end of the van as if about to try to ram it from behind. Probing for opportunities to overtake. Other motorists, sensing danger, braked or swerved to give them a wide berth. It was just a question of time before some concerned citizen called the *politsiya*, and then the chase would take on a whole new dimension.

Ben was spurring the van on much too fast for a vehicle with a shredded tyre. The flailing tread sounded as though it was beating the rear wheel arch to pieces and might rip its way inside the passenger compartment at any moment. The steering wheel was vibrating so badly in his hands that they were getting numb and it was becoming harder to contain the vehicle's erratic handling. It felt as though they were dragging a parachute in their wake. Then the last shreds of torn rubber let go of the wheel rim; the thumping ceased instantly and Ben saw black strips fly off in the mirror and slap off the windscreen of one of the cars behind them, before tumbling away down the road. The van was still virtually impossible to maintain in a straight line, but with the remains of the tyre shed the drag was noticeably less and the throttle felt more responsive. Ben felt a fierce glow inside him as the speedometer needle began to climb once more.

Just then, he saw a movement in his side mirror and realised that the lead Mercedes was trying to flank them on the left. Before he could react, its nose had pushed on by them and it was drawing up alongside. A rear window was rolled down. Ben glimpsed hard, grim faces staring up at him and the black O of a gun barrel pointing his way, ready to strafe the van broadside. The flimsy door skin would stop bullets about as well as wet cardboard.

He twisted the wheel and side-slammed the car with all the force he could bring to bear. Both vehicles went into a weave. Ben feared he was going to lose control again, but contained it. The Mercedes dropped back and he swerved to block it from a second attempt.

Now their speeding convoy was dropping down into the mouth of the underpass. Two fast lanes in each direction, separated by barriers and squat concrete pillars. The two cars were so close behind the van, Ben could almost have locked eyes with the men in the front of the lead vehicle. Something had to give. There was no way he could hope to outrun these men. It was time to try something else. Reaching behind him, his fist closed on the cool steel of the pump-action shotgun. He thrust the short-barrelled weapon into Yuri's lap. 'Use this.'

'I've no idea how!' Yuri protested.

'It's easier than breaking codes, Yuri. Work that pump, point it and pull the damn trigger.'

Yuri grasped the gun, as bewildered as if he'd been asked to defuse a ticking bomb. He unclipped his safety belt, twisted painfully around in his seat and looked through the shattered rear window at the searingly bright headlights in their wake. He wedged himself into the gap between his seat and Ben's, awkwardly racked the action of the shotgun and was about to fire when he seemed to think better of it. 'I'm scared of hitting Valentina,' he yelled above the engine racket. 'I can't shoot over her head.'

'Then hang out of the bloody window,' Ben yelled back.

The passenger window had already taken a couple of glancing bullet hits and was badly cracked. Yuri smashed the remnants of glass away with the stubby muzzle of the gun, leaned out into the wind with his long hair streaming in black ropes, brought the shotgun to bear, squeezed his eyes shut and jerked the trigger. The booming report of the gun was all but lost in the wind and engine roar. The recoil almost pulled the weapon from his grip.

A clumsy shot, but a pretty effective one. The lead vehicle braked sharply in retreat, a pattern of silver-edged buckshot holes now punched into its bonnet and the lower edge of its windscreen covered in a web of fissures. It wobbled left, then right; then its front wheels lost their grip on the road and the car was suddenly turning broadside, spinning out of control before it flipped and rolled and hit one of the central pillar supports in a spectacular eruption of flying wreckage and debris. Then it exploded in midair. A rolling fireball expanded in all directions and seemed to fill the entire underpass in the van's wake with liquid orange and yellow flames. Ben felt the heat on the back of his neck.

Still hanging half out of the window, Yuri let out a garbled cry of something between triumph and horror. His eyes met Ben's with a fleeting expression that said, 'Did I do that?'

Ben had no time to muster a reply. Out of the wall of fire that scorched the back of the van, the wreckage of the Mercedes came tumbling and hurtling towards them as though flung by a giant hand. A direct hit could have crushed them flatter than roadkill. Two tons of airborne scrap metal smashed into their rear with a glancing blow that lifted the van off its rear wheels and almost sent them flying headlong into another of the support barriers. The impact very nearly jerked Yuri right out of the open window, if Ben hadn't shot an arm across the cab and seized hold of the Russian's belt. The van's rear came crashing back to earth and the vehicle swerved and weaved all over the road, its three tyres screeching and scrabbling for grip.

Then, somehow, they were bursting out of the opposite

end of the underpass and back out into the night. Yuri fell gasping into his seat. 'Ben – I lost the gun.'

'No use in crying over it.' Ben wasn't sure if they'd need the gun any longer, anyway. All he could see of the underpass in his mirror was roiling fire and billowing black smoke. Other motorists had been well out of the way of the conflagration, but the second Mercedes had been inches behind its leader. Close enough to have been caught up in the smash. Was it over?

Even before he'd finished asking himself that question, the second Mercedes came bursting from the fiery mouth of the underpass, scorched and battered but still very much in the game.

Yuri yelled, 'Shit!'

Traffic was streaming the opposite way, but the road behind was virtually empty apart from their solitary remaining pursuer. A pursuer Ben could now only hope to lose by luck or ruse.

The road climbed. High-rises and apartment blocks, new housing developments and redevelopments streaked past, the gaps between them offering snatched glimpses of Moscow's light-spangled panorama stretching far off into the distance. They were in the outer suburbs now, though in which section of the city Ben had no idea, any more than he could guess how much longer the stricken van could keep going on this, for certain its final journey. The handling was all gone to pot – but worse, he could smell an acrid burning smell coming from somewhere. The temperature gauge needle was edging deep into the red. Dashboard warning symbols were flashing like angry little beacons, daring him to ignore them.

Keep going, he told the van. *Just keep going while I still need you.* But the van was losing power. Something was horribly wrong. A bullet must have done some sinister damage deep inside its mechanical innards, and now the Mercedes was inexorably gaining on them again. And the men inside still meant business, with plenty of firepower left to spare. A few shots cracked out, then paused. The men were going to save their ammo until they got closer.

'They'll soon be right on us again,' Yuri said, glancing back in alarm. 'What do we do now?'

'Get ready for a standoff,' Ben replied. 'Whatever happens. We tried, Yuri. All anyone can do is try.'

Yuri boggled at him for an instant, eyes liquid and bulging, his whole face tremulous with emotion. Without a word, he started tearing off the bulletproof vest that had saved his skin earlier, then clambered out of his seat and over the row behind to throw the vest over Valentina like a protective blanket. Ben could hear the child sobbing as her father spoke reassuring words to her in Dutch.

Beyond the edge of the housing developments was an industrial zone where old factories and warehouses were being torn down to make way for the expanding city outskirts. Towering cranes and derrick towers stood silhouetted against the night sky. Far away behind them, Ben saw bright white lights hovering and blinking high over the city. He thought he could hear the distant thud of helicopters. The police were joining the show at last. How ironic, he thought, that the very people he was least anxious to see might be the only ones able to step in and stop him, Yuri and Valentina from getting shot to pieces.

But it was unlikely that the cops would get here in time to prevent the final showdown. Ben and his companions were on their own.

Chapter 58

The remaining car was now right behind them again. Its back windows rolled down and two of Calthorpe's crew poked their head and shoulders through, hanging out over the road at each side like outriggers, faces contorted and eyes narrowed, the wind ripping at their hair and clothes as they brought to bear the automatic weapons they were grasping.

Then the chattering, rattling gunfire started up all over again, shredding what was left of the van's rear bodywork. Yuri was pressed down out of sight between the rows of seats as bullets spat and thunked into the backrests above his head and he covered his daughter's body with his own. Ben felt a bullet graze his shoulder, though he hardly registered the pain. Another perforated the head restraint by his right ear. Another tore through the steering wheel an inch from his left thumb and shattered the windscreen. Forward visibility suddenly dissolved into a mass of cracks. He ripped Bezukhov's pistol from his belt, lunged forward and used the gun to punch the glass out so he could see to drive. A hurricane of cold night air blew into the cab, snatching the breath from his lips and making his eyes stream with tears.

The van had absorbed virtually all the punishment it could withstand. Ben knew it was soon going to die, even before the smoke started pouring from under the bonnet and the engine began to pack up. As it lost power and speed, the Mercedes surged up alongside. A burst of machine gun fire shattered what was left of Ben's driver window and forced him to duck low behind the wheel. He thrust the pistol out over the door sill and squeezed off four, five, six shots, firing without aiming as fast as he could work the trigger. The car's brakes gave a squeal and it dropped back a few metres. Ben wasn't sure if he'd hit anything, but at least he'd given them something to think about.

In the handful of seconds Ben had been driving blind, as he now realised, the van was hurtling towards a narrow bridge that spanned a barren area of wasteland. An old iron monster of a thing, probably built back in the old days to ferry materials and work crews to and from the now derelict factories and warehouses. Its rust-red girders and arches stood supported on enormous, weathered concrete blocks that jutted from a steeply sloping grassy embankment littered with junk, rotted-out drums and remnants of Communist-era vehicles. A low iron mesh parapet each side was all that stood between the asphalt surface of the bridge and a forty-foot drop to the wasteland below.

The van passed under the first iron archway, weaving crazily from side to side to stop the Mercedes from flanking them again. But it was hopeless. The dying GAZ Sobol was losing speed with every turn of its wheels. Its engine was pumping smoke as though it could burst into flames or seize solid any second. The temperature gauge was all the way into the red.

And still the Mercedes hung on in their wake, its battered front end almost visibly grinning a victory grin as the pursuit finally neared its inevitable conclusion.

Or maybe not so inevitable. If Ben had learned anything

in his life, it was that no matter how desperate things got, even at the last ditch, there was always one last trick you could play.

'Hold on tight, folks,' he called out over his shoulder. Then to the van he murmured, 'Come on, baby. Show me what you can do. One last time.' He shoved his foot down all the way to the floor. The expiring engine gave a cough, seemed about to stall, then suddenly rallied round and came up with the goods. One last heroic spurt of speed, enough to make the speedometer flicker and the gap between them and the Mercedes widen by a car's length.

That was all Ben needed. With a silent 'thank you', he took his foot off the accelerator and booted the brake with sudden force. He felt himself being thrown forwards, a dart of pain searing through his shoulder where the seat belt bit into his bullet-creased flesh. The frantic pumping of the anti-lock braking system hammered against the sole of his boot. The van's three remaining tyres hissed and screeched on the surface of the bridge.

Ben steeled himself for the impact.

Then the Mercedes, unable to stop in time, pummelled headlong straight into the back of them. The car's nose impacted against the van's ruined rear end with a crunch of splintering and rumpling metal and plastic. Bits of bodywork from both vehicles went spinning. The car was much heavier than the van, and far more solidly built. It tore away the Sobol's other back wheel, the one that had still had a tyre on, together with most of its rear suspension and chassis cross-members. The impact sent the car cannoning sideways. Its grippy low-profile tyres bit the road and arrested its lateral slide, but all that weight and momentum had to go somewhere. As if in slow motion, the big Mercedes went up on two wheels. Once Newton's laws of dynamics took hold, nothing could stop the car from rolling and flipping. It hit the bridge parapet and tore through the rusted iron mesh like a cannonball fired into football goal netting, upended and somersaulted into space to go tumbling end over end down the embankment.

Then, in the immediate aftermath of so much noise and violent chaos, all was eerily silent.

Ben opened his eyes and blinked a few times, and realised that he was lying pressed against the driver's door, now strangely underneath him. There was blood running down his cheek where he must have banged his temple against the window in the impact of the collision. The van had been overturned and was lying on its side. The dead engine had fallen silent. There was only the murmur of the night-time wind singing against the iron gridwork of the bridge. Then, from behind him, Ben heard a cough and a splutter. He levered himself up on one elbow and tried to speak, but at first all that came out was a dry croak.

'Valentina? Yuri?'

'We're okay,' came a weak reply. 'We're alive. I think.'

'Can we go home now?' said Valentina's voice, and Ben almost laughed out loud with relief at the sound of it. 'Yes,' he answered. 'Yes, we can. But I think we might need another vehicle.'

He struggled free of his seat belt and crawled back through the overturned cab to join them. It took all of his and Yuri's strength to scrape and drag open the Sobol's buckled sliding side door, now a roof hatchway for them to clamber out of. Ben pulled himself out first, then reached down and grasped Valentina's upstretched hand to haul her up. Yuri came last, looking stunned and dazed as though waking from a nightmare.

If it had all been just a bad dream, it was over now. Or, almost over.

Ben looked down over the edge of the parapet and saw the wrecked Mercedes at the bottom of the embankment. It had hit the ground nose-first and come down on its roof. One door hung open. Nothing was moving down there.

'Where are you going?' Yuri said as Ben clambered over the parapet. Ben made no reply. He scrambled down the slope, boots slithering on fresh dirt where the tumbling car had churned deep furrows in the grass and weeds. It took him over a minute to make his way down to the darkness of the rock-strewn, garbage-littered wasteland at the foot of the embankment, using Arkangelskaya's phone as a flashlight. He had his pistol in his belt, but something told him he wouldn't be needing it.

One wheel of the capsized Mercedes was still lazily spinning. The roof pillars were crushed and buckled and the front wings and grille were a crumpled mess from where the car had rear-ended the van and then ploughed through the bridge's parapet. The driver was dead, his bloodied body protruding half out of the shattered windscreen. Another man had been thrown clear of the vehicle when the door had come open. He'd crushed his skull against a rock and would soon be joining the driver in heaven or hell, whichever way they were headed.

Ben walked around the car, bending to shine his light and peer in through its cracked windows and outflung door. He could smell leaking gasoline from a perforated tank or ruptured fuel line.

Three other men were still inside the wreck. The only one still living was Aubyn Calthorpe.

Chapter 59

Ben crouched by the car's remains and wrenched open the buckled rear door next to where Calthorpe lay twisted and bleeding on the upturned ceiling.

'You're not looking quite so hale and hearty, Colonel,' Ben said, casting the light up and down over him.

'My legs,' Calthorpe moaned. 'They're broken.'

'Then again, you're not going anywhere,' Ben replied. 'You won't be needing them.'

Calthorpe reached out a quivering hand. 'Help me,' he croaked.

'You mean, no hard feelings, let bygones be bygones, water under the bridge and all that?'

The smell of spilled fuel was intensifying, along with the sharp ozone stink of burning plastic wire insulation. Something was arcing and sparking and liable to set the leaking wreck off like a firebomb before too long. A fact of which the trapped survivor was all too acutely aware.

'Get me out,' Calthorpe said. 'Please. I'm asking you to do the right thing.'

'The right thing?'

'One ex-soldier to another,' Calthorpe begged, trembling fingers outstretched. He blinked as the bright light shone in his eyes and brought out all the wrinkles and crevices of his face. 'Doesn't that count for something?'

'It didn't before,' Ben said.

Calthorpe let out a wheeze of pain and his features screwed up until he could speak again. 'For God's sake, man, I was just doing what I was told. I'm only a go-between.'

'Fair enough,' Ben said. 'But I didn't come down here to help you. I came to tell you my reply to your offer, in case you were still wondering.'

'I'd rather assumed the answer was a flat no,' Calthorpe replied with a weak grin that turned into another agonised grimace.

'Life's all about compromises,' Ben said. 'I have a counter-proposition to make you. But for that, I can't speak to a go-between. I need to speak to the Chairman.'

Calthorpe managed to shake his head. 'Nobody speaks to the Chairman.'

Ben made to get up. 'Okay. Bye.'

'Wait!'

'Second thoughts?'

'What do you want?' Calthorpe hissed desperately. Smoke was beginning to trickle out from under the buckled seams of the car bonnet and into the upside-down passenger cabin.

'Give me your phone,' Ben said. 'The one you use to talk to your boss. Bring up his number for me.'

'And then?'

'Then I'll do the right thing by you. Quid pro quo. You have my word on that. One soldier to another.'

Calthorpe managed to twist one arm to fish a mobile from his pocket. He activated it with his thumb and squinted at the little screen as he urgently scrolled down a menu of numbers. Finding what he needed, he thrust the phone towards Ben. 'Take it! Now get me out of this bloody thing. Hurry!'

'All in good time, Colonel,' Ben said, taking the phone and putting away Arkangelskaya's. He stood up, brushing dirt from his trousers.

Left alone in the darkness of the wrecked car, Calthorpe began to panic. His voice was edged with terror as he cried out, 'Where the hell are you going?'

'To make a call,' Ben replied calmly. The smoke was pouring thickly from the car, stinging his eyes, and he moved away a few steps towards the slope of the embankment. He could see the spangled lights of the city from here. Somewhere far away was the wail of sirens as fire crews descended on the scene of the underpass and police hunted for the perpetrators. The helicopter lights were still moving across the night sky, a long way off. He glanced back at the car. Calthorpe was thumping on the upturned floor pan and braying, 'Hope! Get me out! Come on!' He had only a couple of minutes, at most, before the wreck began to burn. What Ben had to say to the Chairman wouldn't take that long.

A very British voice answered the phone. Statesmanlike and grave, befitting an elder politician of great stature. Which, Ben could well imagine, the man probably was. A trusted establishment figure. Bastion of the realm.

'Am I speaking to the Chairman?' Ben said.

'Who is this?' the voice said. Not a man easily fazed, by his tone.

'The name's Ben Hope. You know who I am, and I know who you are, so let's save ourselves the intros because I intend to make this quick.'

'Go on,' the voice said.

'I also know where Object 428 is, not to mention a good deal about a certain illicit operation that goes by the codename

"Ploughshares". And someone with my mouth could cause a lot of trouble for you people. With me so far?'

'You have my attention.'

'So here's the deal,' Ben told him. 'The terms are simple. One, Yuri Petrov and his daughter are to be let free and never touched. Two, don't ever come looking for me. If I get even the slightest hint of you people sniffing around my door or theirs, I'll make burning you down my new hobby. You personally, and your entire operation and everyone even remotely connected with it.'

'I see,' the Chairman said. 'In other words, we leave you alone and you'll leave us alone.'

'The way you'd treat a hornets' nest. Or else, get ready for a war.'

The tiniest of smiles could be heard in the Chairman's voice as he replied, 'And what makes you seriously think you can go up against us? You're only one man.'

'And I'm only just getting started,' Ben said. 'That is, unless you're willing to let it go.'

The Chairman was silent for so long that Ben thought the line had gone dead. Finally he replied, in the same calm, unflappable tone, 'You're a very direct man, Major. So am I. I like that in people.'

'Then give me a direct answer. A simple yes or no. Then it ends here.'

Another thoughtful silence. 'Thanks to Colonel Calthorpe, this escapade has already cost us dearly in terms of manpower and resources. I might be willing to consider ways of cutting our losses.'

'You're a wise man,' Ben said. 'Then do we have an understanding?'

'I'm unclear as to how Colonel Calthorpe fits into the equation.'

'One of the losses,' Ben replied. 'Or soon to be.'

'Is that an additional term of your proposition?'

'Call it the cost of doing business.'

Over the line there sounded the unmistakable clink of ice on fine crystal as the Chairman sipped his nightcap. It was late there, well past bedtime for normal folks while the secret rulers of the world worked late.

'He can be replaced,' the Chairman said with a grave finality that was as cold as the ice in his glass.

Ben gave a dry smile. 'Who can't?' He paused. The Chairman said nothing. Ben said, 'Then are we agreed?'

There was another silence. Then the Chairman said, 'Very well. We're agreed. Goodbye, Major Hope. It was a pleasure doing business with you. I shall not expect to hear from you again.'

The line went dead before Ben could end the call. He walked back towards the wrecked Mercedes and tossed Calthorpe's phone in through the open door. Taking out Arkangelskaya's, he shone its flashlight beam inside the car. Calthorpe's pain-streaked face was pale in the light, his pupils shrinking to little black pinpricks of fear. 'I thought you'd buggered off and left me. Quickly, get me out of here before this bloody thing goes up in flames!' He stretched his hand out, yearning. 'Hurry!'

Ben didn't take the hand. He drew out Bezukhov's Smith & Wesson and clicked off the safety. The glint of nickel in the light caught Calthorpe's eye and he seemed to shrivel in terror. 'W-what are you doing?'

'The right thing,' Ben said.

'You can't . . . You promised!'

'And I always honour my promises.'

'Come on, old man,' Calthorpe quavered. 'Be a sport.'

Ben weighed the pistol in his hand as he crouched by the

open car door. 'There's another kind of brain implant you never mentioned, Calthorpe. It's not very high-tech and it costs just a few pennies but it does the job every time. Made of lead, wrapped up in a shiny copper jacket. It's implanted at high speed, using a special tool. And guess what, I happen to have one of those right here.'

He aimed the gun at Calthorpe's head.

Said, 'This is for Katya.'

Calthorpe's last yell of defiant fury was drowned out in the short, sharp crack of the report.

Ben got to his feet, tossed the pistol into the car and walked away. He could feel the heavy weight of sadness descending on him like a fog. *Post-operation melancholia* was the best way he'd found to describe it. He loathed killing, and he hated death. Yet he seemed to do so much of one and see so much of the other.

Moments later, there was a fizz and a spark from the wreckage, followed by a deep, guttural WHOOMPH as the leaking petrol ignited. The carcass of the Mercedes erupted into a mass of flames.

Halfway up the embankment, Ben paused and watched for a short while as the all-consuming blaze devoured the car and everything inside it. The smoke rose up into a black tower that slowly drifted towards the night lights of Moscow.

Then he turned and continued up the slope, towards where Yuri and Valentina were waiting.

Chapter 60

Adrien Leroy and Noël Marchand were waiting anxiously by the Kaprisky Corp's Gulfstream's hangar at Vnukovo Airport, the jet standing by and ready to leave at a moment's notice as instructed. The long minutes had kept ticking by since they'd landed back in Moscow, and there was no sign of their pickups. No contact since the brief and mysterious call their employer had received from Ben Hope hours earlier, to say only, 'Send the plane. We're coming home.' The Kaprisky household had been thrown into a turmoil of speculation, nobody quite sure what 'we' signified and terrified to jump to any hopeful conclusions. The old man was going apeshit and chewing carpets back home.

The longer the pilots waited, the more their spirits sank until they became convinced that they would be returning empty-handed once again. Leroy was pacing the floodlit tarmac in agitation with his shoulders hunched and hands in pockets, while Marchand had retreated to a corner behind the hangar to steal a cigarette in defiance of all the No Smoking signs that plastered the private jet terminal. Let someone come to give him grief over it. He was in just the mood for a good punch-up.

'What d'you reckon?' Leroy called over to his colleague, for about the fortieth time.

'Reckon they're not coming, is what I reckon,' Marchand called back sullenly.

Leroy suddenly straightened up from his slouch and cocked his head. 'Wait, I hear something.'

Marchand was about to brush him off with some disparaging comment when he heard it too, and flicked away his cigarette. The co-pilot was something of a bike enthusiast in his spare time, and there was no mistaking the flat-twin thud of an approaching motorcycle. Fancy limousines and SUVs were a common enough sight at the private jet terminal, but . . . ?

The pair exchanged baffled looks, then followed the sound – and both men's eyes opened wide in astonishment at the sight of the strangest-looking contraption rumbling towards them across the tarmac.

Marchand would have been able to tell Leroy that it was a Russian Ural, the nearest thing still being made to the old Wehrmacht BMW military sidecar outfits of World War II, if he'd been capable of speech at this moment. Even more jaw-dropping than the vehicle was the state of its three occupants. They recognised its rider as Ben Hope, but as they'd never seen him before, bruised and bloodied as though he'd turned up fresh from a battlefield somewhere. Yuri Petrov was perched on the pillion, wild-eyed and hairy like a bedraggled refugee from a labour camp. Sitting in the crude open sidecar, her pink gilet and jeans torn and filthy and her hair all awry, but beaming a smile ten times brighter than the airport floodlights, was little Valentina. Marchand and Leroy's hearts leaped both at once, and they went running to meet and embrace her with tears of joy. Even Leroy's promise to smash Yuri's teeth in was forgotten.

'Sorry we're late,' Ben said. 'We got a little waylaid en route.'

'What . . . where . . . how . . . ?' Leroy was so full of questions for him that he was logjammed and couldn't blurt a single one out.

'Don't ask,' Ben said, and pointed at the waiting aircraft that stood gleaming under the lights. 'Now, I suggest we get out of here pronto, before the Russian authorities start to cotton on to what we've been up to in their lovely city.'

They were ready for takeoff within minutes. Ben parked the sidecar outfit next to the hangar, and on a scrap of paper scribbled an apology note for its owner who would be waking up tomorrow morning to find his pride and joy stolen. If Ben hadn't been in such a rush to get his charges to the airport he might have been able to procure them something with a roof and proper seats, but the Ural had served its purpose just fine. Now he and his weary passengers made the extreme transition to the comfort of an ultra-luxurious private jet. As long as MiG fighters didn't shoot down the Gulfstream before it left Russian airspace, there would be no more stops between here and France.

And three perfectly uneventful hours later, they were landing at Le Mans-Arnage. There to be welcomed by a motorcade that would have made the French President feel inadequate. Auguste Kaprisky and his niece clambered from their limo as the plane taxied to a halt, Eloise bursting with anticipation and the old man so jittery he looked as though he was afflicted by St Vitus's dance. What followed was the most joyful homecoming in the history of the Kaprisky dynasty. Floods of tears were spilled all over the runway as Valentina was reunited with her mother and granduncle. Yuri somewhat self-consciously kept himself at a distance, and went to sit alone on a wheel of the stationary aircraft.

Ben had taken a long, hot shower on the plane, patched up his shoulder as best he could with the on-board first-aid kit, and knocked back quite a number of whiskies. All he wanted now was a soft, warm bed. But that wasn't about to happen just yet. No sooner was he released from the smothering of kisses he received from Eloise than the old man was all over him with clasping handshakes and tears of gratitude and a thousand questions he couldn't begin to answer. 'You are a hero,' Kaprisky kept saying. 'A saviour. A knight.' Ben felt like none of those things, but to protest would have been pointless. Meanwhile Valentina hovered around Ben like a little butterfly, talking incessantly, bubbling with laughter, cheeks flushed, eyes sparkling every time she looked at him. Spotting the solitary figure of her father sitting under the aeroplane, she ran over with a cry to grab his hand and tug him across to meet the others.

Yuri wasn't the only one reluctant to be reunited with his former family. The old man's face hardened like steel at the sight of him, while Eloise turned to stare at her ex-husband and the smile fell from her lips. 'What is *he* doing here?' Kaprisky said icily.

'You've got Yuri wrong, Auguste,' Ben said, putting a hand on his arm. 'Both of you have. It's a long story, but trust me when I say that no man ever loved his little girl more than he does. He'd die to protect her. And I mean that literally.'

Ben's words must have counted for something. He watched as Eloise went over to Yuri and the two of them tentatively embraced. Valentina clasped her parents' hands and looked at Ben with a glow on her face that would have melted the most implacable heart to sugary goo.

At last, the motorcade sped back to the Kaprisky estate, which was lit up like Versailles to greet the homecomers. Valentina rode up front with her mother and granduncle, while Yuri travelled in the second car with Ben. 'Well, we did it,' Ben said. Yuri mournfully shook his head. 'No, my friend. You did it.'

On arrival at the chateau, Valentina was whisked off by her mother and Yuri wandered off to be alone with his thoughts, his sadness for his dead friend Grisha and his concerns about the uncertain future he now faced. Kaprisky homed in on Ben like a goshawk and ushered him to a private drawing room the size of Winchester Cathedral, where they sat in vast leather armchairs and toasted the success of the mission with Louis XIII cognac from a Baccarat crystal decanter. Ben spent the next hour debriefing the old man in as much detail as he felt able to give him.

'And so we will never know what this mysterious cipher contained,' Kaprisky marvelled when Ben had finished giving his account.

'No. Not even Yuri. The thing turned out to be uncrackable. Except his former boss was convinced he was trying to run out on him. Like I say, that's what this whole thing was about. Yuri's actions were solely to protect his little girl. If you want to pin a hero badge on anyone, it should be him.'

Kaprisky was silent and pensive as he swirled his brandy around in the glass. 'What you tell me is truly amazing. Were it from another man, I must confess I would find it hard to believe. Yet everything now makes perfect sense to me. Little wonder that Yuri went to such lengths to conceal from us the truth about his past career. And if I have erred in my judgement of my former nephew-in-law, I will be the first to admit it, and to atone for my mistake.'

'The question is what happens to Yuri now,' Ben said. 'He can never return to his own country. He's sick and hurt. His friend is dead. He has no home, no career, no money, nothing left to live for. Except Valentina.'

Kaprisky waved that aside. 'Yuri need not worry. He can

be provided with all he will ever need. A new home, a new life, even a new identity if required. Anything is possible. He will be able to see Valentina as often as he wishes. As for his state of health, I happen to own a modest medical clinic nearby. It will be a top priority to ensure he makes a full recovery. And you too, my friend,' he added.

'I'm fine. A couple of scratches, that's all.'

'Oh, no,' Kaprisky said. 'You are in pain and exhausted, Benedict. And you will oblige me by accepting the care that the hero of the hour merits.'

Kaprisky's modest clinic turned out to be one of the finest private hospitals and health spas in northern France. Despite his stubborn reluctance as well as the unearthly time of the night, the hero of the hour was coddled and fussed over like a prince and seemed to have been allocated an entire staff of doctors and nurses all to himself.

Ben spent the next two days under informal house arrest at the hospital, supposedly convalescing. Which mainly meant wandering about its extensive and prettily landscaped grounds, sneaking packs of cigarettes from a friendly porter and smoking them when nobody was watching. It was on one of his long exploratory walks through the gardens that he last saw Yuri Petrov. The two of them sat on an ornamental bench in the sunshine, overlooking a sweep of green lawns and country park. Yuri wore a fluffy hospital gown and a pair of crutches leaned against the side of the bench.

'I could get used to this,' Yuri said.

'Makes a change, all right. This clinic's a bit nicer than the one in Moscow.'

'Maybe the old man isn't so bad after all.'

'Deep down, he's just a sentimental fuddy-duddy,' Ben said. 'Whatever people might say about him.'

'You know, Eloise has been to see me. Twice. Things are
. . . well, things are a little better between us now. I should
have been more honest with her. No more secrets.'

'I'm happy things are working out,' Ben said. 'You deserve
it, all three of you.'

'I'm forever in your debt, Ben,' Yuri said earnestly. 'A
debt I can never begin to repay.'

'There's nothing to repay,' Ben said.

'You're family now. To me, to Eloise and to Valentina.'
Yuri smiled. 'Uncle Ben.'

'Like the rice,' Ben said.

Yuri chuckled. 'Actually I think it goes deeper than that. I
get the impression that my daughter wants to marry you.
Which, if she were ten years older, would be just fine by me.'

'Twenty-five would narrow the age gap a little more,' Ben
said. 'I'm flattered. But it'll soon pass.'

'She asked me to give you this.' Yuri reached into the flaps
of his fluffy robe and pulled out a small pink envelope. 'It's
a letter, I think. She's too shy to give it to you herself.'

'May I open it?'

'Go ahead.'

Ben gently broke the seal on the envelope, unfolded the
single sheet of pink notepaper that was inside, and read.
The letter was in French, written in the neat cursive hand
of a well-schooled child, and said:

Dear Ben,

  *Thank you for what you did for me, and my Papa. I
will never forget you. I hope that you'll come and visit
us very very often.*

  Love from your best friend in all the world,
Valentina
XXXX

Ben folded the letter away, feeling deeply touched. 'Please tell her I'll always hold on to it,' he said.

Yuri smiled. 'I'll do that.'

For a while, the two of them just sat and enjoyed the warmth of the sun and the view of the gardens. Breaking the silence, Ben said, 'One thing I meant to ask you.'

'Hmm? What's that?'

'For the record, just where exactly is Object 428? It seemed to vanish quite suddenly.'

'I fed it to Alyosha,' Yuri said. 'The microfilm and the flash drive, too.'

'Grisha's dog?'

'After we left the trailer, when we stopped on the way to that broken-down farm. I didn't know then that we were going to be separated. It was the only safe place I could think to put the stuff, so when nobody was watching I rolled it all up together with a bit of old tripe I'd found in my pocket.'

'You generally walk around with pocketfuls of old tripe?' Ben asked.

'Grisha and I were always bribing the brute with chunks of it, to make him shut up, though it never worked. Anyway, he swallowed the whole lot. He'll eat anything, that dog. Ate a can opener once. I suppose I was hoping to recover the brain chip and the plans later, although I probably wasn't thinking very clearly at the time.'

'Well,' Ben said. 'That's one way to dispose of the evidence.'

'The fact is, Bezukhov was going to kill me whether I gave it to him or not.'

Ben couldn't disagree with that. 'Not such a pleasant bloke.'

Both men might have thought about it then, but neither chose to mention how, and specifically by whose hand, the intelligence chief had met his end. Some secrets should remain unspoken even between those who shared them.

Yuri shook his head sadly. 'Poor Alyosha, though. He was a nuisance sometimes, but I hate to think of him suffering. I wonder what'll become of him, running free like a wild animal.'

'A dog like him will survive fine,' Ben said. 'You said yourself, he'll eat anything. Maybe he'll find a new home for himself, earning his keep by keeping down rats on some farm or other. Wherever he ends up, the brain chip won't stay inside him long. If it's even still there now.'

Yuri cracked a sudden wicked grin. 'No, if the bastards want it they'll have to poke around inside every dog turd for a thousand square miles of wilderness.'

Ben checked out of the clinic that afternoon, itchy to get back to Le Val. He stopped off at Kaprisky's estate to pay his regards and pick up his Alpina. The old man spent a long time expressing his heartfelt thanks all over again. If Ben couldn't be prevailed upon to take payment for his services, then at least he'd accept a ride home by helicopter? The car could easily be delivered to Le Val by a chauffeur.

'No, thanks, a nice long drive is what I need,' Ben replied. And he was looking forward to it, with Miles Davis on the CD player and a fresh pack of Gauloises to attack on the road.

'And you're quite sure that—? I mean, it doesn't seem right that I don't—'

'I don't want any money, Auguste,' Ben repeated. 'But if it makes you feel better, you could always make a donation to the Le Val expansion fund.'

'Rest assured it will be done,' Kaprisky said, much relieved.

'Goodbye, then,' Ben said, and headed for the door.

'Until the next time.' There was an insinuating note in the old man's tone, and a twinkle in his eye, that hinted at a deeper meaning. Ben halted at the doorway.

'There won't be a next time,' he said vehemently. 'I'm done now. No more adventures. From now on, I'm Mr Stay-at-home. Carpet slippers in front of the fire and a pipe, just like Jeff said. And I mean it.'

In all the time Ben had known him, he had not once seen Auguste Kaprisky so much as chuckle. Now the poker-faced old billionaire, the man who never laughed, broke into peals of thigh-slapping giggles and he wept until the tears of mirth were spilling down his parched, wrinkly face.

'Did I miss something?'

Kaprisky wiped the tears from his eyes. 'How you delude yourself. For you, my young friend, there will always be another adventure. You will never stop doing what you do. Not until the last shred of injustice has been purged from this world and there are no more wrongs to right. It is the life you were born to lead.'

And as Ben sped back towards Le Val with the music blaring and the wind blowing through his open windows, he wondered how on earth the old geezer could have got such a daft and ridiculous notion into his head.

WILL BEN HOPE UNCOVER THE TRUTH?

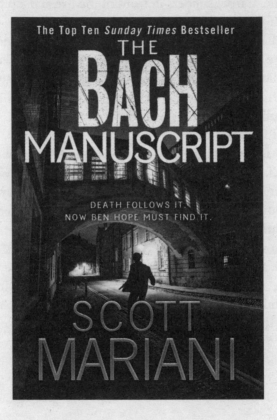

The master bestseller is back.

THE HUNT IS ON . . .

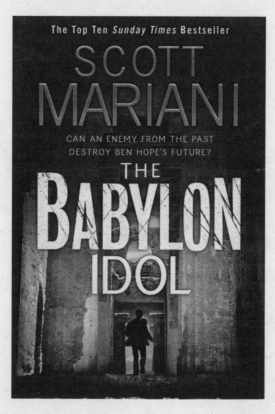

Don't miss the action-packed bestseller.

WHERE BEN HOPE GOES,
TROUBLE ALWAYS FOLLOWS . . .

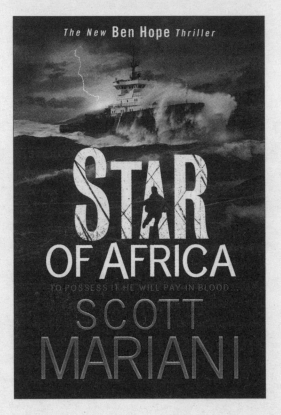

The first in an explosive two-book sequence.

HAS BEN HOPE FINALLY MET HIS MATCH?

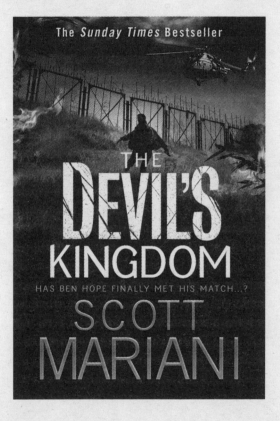

The thrilling sequel to *Star of Africa*.

Read on for an exclusive extract
of the new Ben Hope thriller
by Scott Mariani

The Rebel's Revenge
Coming November 2018

PROLOGUE

Louisiana, May 1864

Built in the Greek Revival style, encircled by twenty-four noble Doric columns and standing proud amid a vast acreage of plantation estate, the mansion was one of the most stately and aristocratic homes in all of the South. Its dozens of reception rooms, not to mention the splendid ballroom, had hosted some of Clovis Parish's most celebrated social events of the forty years since its construction, positioning Athenian Oaks, as the property was named, at the very centre of the region's high society.

On this day, however, the grand house was silent and virtually empty. Deep within its labyrinthine corridors, a very secret and important meeting was taking place. A meeting that its attendees knew very well could help to swing in their favour the outcome of the civil war that had been tearing the states of both North and South apart for three long, bloody years.

Of the four men seated around the table in the richly-appointed dining room, only one was not wearing military uniform: for the good reason that he wasn't an officer of the Confederate States Army but, rather, the civilian owner of Athenian Oaks. His name was Leonidas Wilbanks Garrett.

A Texan by birth, he had risen up to become one of the wealthiest landowners in Louisiana by the time he was forty. Now, fifteen years on, the size of his fortune and spread of his cotton plantation were second to none. As was the workforce of slaves he owned, who occupied an entire village of filthy and squalid huts far out of sight of the mansion's windows.

But it was by virtue of L.W. Garrett's renown as a physician and scientist, rather than his acumen for commerce, that the three high-ranking Confederate officers had made the journey to Clovis Parish to consult him. For this special occasion they were majestically decked out in full dress uniform, gleaming with gold braid. The most senior man present wore the insignia of a general of the C.S.A. He had lost an eye at Second Bull Run and wore a patch over his scarred socket. He had also lost all three of his sons during the course of the conflict, and feared that he would have lost them for nothing if the Yankees prevailed.

A bitter outcome which, at this point in time, it seemed nothing could prevent. Since the crushing defeat at Chattanooga late the previous year and the subsequent appointment of Ulysses S. Grant as General-in-Chief of the Union forces, the turning point seemed to have come. Rout after rout; the tattered and depleted army of the South was in danger of being completely overrun.

'Gentlemen, we stand to lose this damn war,' the general said in between puffs of his cigar. 'And we will lose it soon, unless saved by a miracle.'

'Desperate times call for desperate measures,' said the second officer, who was knocking back the wine as fast as it could be served. He was a younger man, a senior colonel known his fiery temperament both on and off the battlefield. The last cavalry charge he had personally led had resulted in him having his right arm blown off by a cannonball. It had been found two hundred yards away, his dead hand still clutching his sabre. He now wore the empty sleeve of his grey tunic pinned across his chest, after the fashion of Lord Nelson.

'Indeed they do,' the general agreed. 'And if that yellow-belly Jeff Davis and his lapdog Lee don't have the guts to do what's necessary to win this war, then by God someone else must step in and do it for them.'

This provoked a certain ripple of consternation around the table, as it was somewhat shocking to refer to the President of the Confederate States of America, not to mention the revered General Robert E. Lee, hero of the South, in such harsh language. But nobody protested. The facts of the matter were plain. The dreadful prospect of a Union victory was looming large on the horizon. Leonidas Garrett, whose business empire stood to be devastated if a victorious Abraham Lincoln acted on his promise to liberate all slaves in North America, dreaded it as much as anyone.

After another toke on his cigar and a quaff of wine, the general leaned towards Garrett and fixed him with his one steely eye. 'Mr Garrett, how certain are you that this bold scheme of yours can work?'

'If it can be pulled off, which I believe it can, then my certainty is absolute,' Garrett replied coolly.

The third senior officer was the only conspirator present at the top-secret gathering who was yet to be fully convinced of Garrett's plan. 'Gentlemen, I must confess to having great misgivings about the enormity of what we are contemplating. Satan himself could scarcely have devised such wickedness.'

The general shot him a ferocious glare. 'At a time like

this, if it took Beelzebub himself to lead the South to victory, I would gladly give him the job.'

The objector made no reply. The general stared at him a while longer, then asked, 'Are you with us or not?'

'You know I am.' No *sir*, no display of deference to a man of far superior rank. Because rank was not an issue at a meeting so clandestine, so illicit, that any and all of them could have been court-martialled and executed by their own side for taking part. What they were envisaging was in flagrant contravention to the rules of war and gentlemanly conduct.

Silence around the table for a few moments. The dissenter said, 'Still, a damned ugly piece of work.'

'I'm more interested in knowing if we can *make* it work,' said the one-armed colonel.

'It isn't a new idea, by any measure,' Garrett said. 'Such tactics, though brutal, have been used in warfare throughout history. Trust me, gentlemen. We have the means to make it work, and if successful its effect on the enemy will be catastrophic. It will bring the North to its knees, cripple their infrastructure and force those Yankee scumbellies to surrender within a month. But I must reiterate,' he added, casting a solemn warning look around the table, 'that not a single word of this discussion can ever be repeated to anyone outside of this room. Not *anyone*, is that perfectly clear?'

Throughout the meeting, a young female negro servant dressed in a maid's outfit had been silently hovering in the background, watching the levels in their wine glasses and meekly stepping up to the table now and then to top them up from a Venetian crystal decanter. Nobody acknowledged her presence in the room, least of all her legal owner, Garrett. As far as he was concerned she might simply have been a well-trained dog, rather than a human being. A dog, more-over, that could be whipped, chained up to starve, or used as target practice without compunction or accountability at any time, just for the hell of it.

Like Garrett, none of the three southern-born officers gave an instant's thought to the possibility that this young slave girl could be absorbing every single word of their discussion. And that she could remember it perfectly, so perfectly that it could later be repeated verbatim. Nor did any man present have any notion as to who the negro servant woman really was. Her role in the downfall of their plan was a part yet to be played. Just how devastating a part, none of them could yet know either.

'So, gentlemen, we're agreed,' the general said after they'd spent some more time discussing the particulars of Garrett's radical scheme. 'Let's set this thing in motion and reclaim the South's fortunes in this war.' He raised his glass. 'To victory!'

'To victory!' The toast echoed around the table. They clinked glasses and drank.

Her duty done, the slave humbly asked for permission to excuse herself and was dismissed with a cursory wave, where-upon she slipped from the room to attend to the rest of her daily chores. Though if any of them had paid her the least bit of heed, they might have wondered at the enigmatic little smile that curled her lips as she walked away.

Chapter 1

Ben Hope had often had the feeling that trouble had a knack of following him around. No matter what, where or how, it dogged his steps and stuck to him like a shadow. If trouble were a person, he'd have felt justified in thinking that person was stalking him. If he'd been of a superstitious bent he could have thought he was haunted by it, as by a ghost. Whatever the case, it seemed as if at every juncture of his life, wherever he went and however he tried to steer out of its path, there it was waiting for him.

And it was here, pushing midnight on one sultry and thus-far uneventful September evening in the unlikely setting of a tiny backstreet liquor store in a small town in Clovis Parish, Louisiana, that he was about to make trouble's acquaintance yet one more time.

If the most recent round of airport security regulations hadn't made it more bother than it was worth to carry his old faithful hip flask across the Atlantic among his hand luggage, and if the bar and grill where he'd spent most of that evening had stocked the right kind of whisky to satisfy one of those late-night hankerings for a dram or two of the good stuff that occasionally come over a man, then two things wouldn't have happened that night. First, there would have been nobody else around to prevent an innocent man from getting badly hurt, most probably shot to death.

Which was a good thing. And second, Ben wouldn't have been plunged into a whole new kind of mess, even for him.

Which was less of a good thing. But that's what happens when you have a talent for trouble. He should have been used to it by now.

It was nine minutes to midnight when Ben walked into the liquor store. It was as warm and humid inside as it was outside, with a lazy ceiling fan doing little more than stir the thick air around. An unseen radio was blaring country music, a stomping up-tempo bluegrass instrumental that was alive with fiddles and banjos and loud enough to hear from half a block away.

The sign on the door said they were open till 2 a.m. Ben soon saw he was the only customer in the place, which didn't surprise him given the lateness of the hour and the emptiness of the street. Maybe they got a rush of business just before closing time.

The entire store could have fitted inside Ben's farmhouse kitchen back home in Normandy, but was crammed from floor to ceiling across four aisles with enough booze to float a battleship. A glance up and down the heaving displays revealed a bewildering proliferation of beer and bourbon varieties, lots of rum, a smattering of local Muscadine wines and possibly not much else. He was resigned to not finding what he was looking for, but it had to be worth a shot.

Alone behind the counter sat an old guy in a frayed check shirt and a John Deere cap, with crêpey skin and lank grey hair, who was so absorbed in the pages of the fishing magazine he was reading that he didn't seem to have noticed Ben come in.

'How're they biting?' Ben said with a smile over the blare of the music, pointing at the magazine. The friendly traveller making conversation with the locals.

The old timer suddenly registered his customer's presence and gazed up with watery, pale eyes. 'Say what, sonny?' He didn't appear to possess a single tooth in his mouth.

It had to be thirty years since the last time anyone had called Ben 'sonny'. Abandoning the fishing talk, which wasn't his best conversation topic anyway, he asked the old timer what kinds of proper scotch he had for sale. Whisky with a 'y' and not an 'ey'. Ben had never quite managed to develop a taste for bourbon, though in truth he'd drink pretty much anything if pushed. He had to repeat himself twice, as it was now becoming clear that the storekeeper was stone deaf as well as toothless, which probably accounted for the volume of the music.

Finally the old timer got it and directed him to a section of an aisle on the far end of the store. 'Third aisle right there, walk on down to the bottom. Hope you find what you're lookin' for.' The Cajun accent was more noticeable on him, sounding less Americanised than the younger locals. A sign of the times, no doubt, as the traditional ways and cultures eroded away as gradually and surely as Louisiana's coastal wetlands.

Ben said thanks. The old man frowned and peered at him with the utmost curiosity, as though this blond-haired foreigner were the strangest creature who'd ever stepped inside his store. 'Say, where y'all from, podnuh? Ain't from aroun' here, that's for damn sure.' Ben couldn't remember the last time he'd been called 'partner', either.

'Long way from home,' Ben replied.

The old timer cupped a hand behind his ear and craned his wrinkly neck. 'Whassat?' They could still be having this conversation come closing time. Hearing aids obviously hadn't found their way this far south yet. Or maybe the oldster was afraid they'd cramp his style with the girls. Ben just smiled and walked off in search of the section he wanted. The storekeeper gazed after him for a moment and then shrugged and fell back into squinting at his magazine.

Following the directions, Ben soon found the range of scotches at the bottom of the last aisle, tucked away in what seemed a forgotten, seldom-frequented corner of the store judging by the layers dust on the shelf. He began browsing along the rows of bottles, recognising with pleasure the names of some old friends among them. Knockando, Johnny Walker, Cutty Sark, Glenmorangie and a dozen others – it wasn't a bad selection, all things considered. Then he spotted the solitary bottle of Laphroaig Quarter Cask single malt, one of his personal favourites for its dark, peaty, smokey flavour. It had been sitting there so long that the bottle label was flecked with mildew. He took it down from the shelf, wiped off the dust and weighed his discovery appreciatively in his hand, savouring the prospect of taking it back to his hotel room for a couple of hours' enjoyment before bed. The precious liquid had come a long way from its birthplace on rugged, windswept Islay in Scotland's Inner Hebrides, for him to stumble across here in southern Louisiana of all places. Maybe this was something more profound and mean-ingful than mere serendipity. Enough to make a man of lapsed religious faith start believing again, or almost.

Ben was carrying the bottle back up the aisle as though it were holy water when, over the blare of the music, he heard raised voices coming from the direction of the counter. As he reached the top of the aisle he saw a pair of guys who had just walked in. One was big and ox-like in a studded motorcycle jacket with a patch on the back showing a gothic-helmeted grinning skull and the legend IRON SPARTANS MC, LOUISIANA. He was slow-moving and wore a calm smile. The other was a foot shorter, wiry and wasted in a denim vest cut-off that bared long, skinny arms with faded blue ink. He was agitated and angry, eyes darting as if he'd snorted a tugrope-sized line of cocaine.

The pair might have been regular customers, but Ben guessed not. Because he was fairly sure that, even in the Deep South, regular customers didn't generally come storming into a place toting sawn-off pump shotguns and magnum revolvers.

Great.

The armed robbers were too intent on threatening the storekeeper to have noticed that the three of them weren't alone. Ben retreated quickly out of sight behind the corner of the aisle and peeked through a gap between stacks of Dixie beer cans. The hefty ox-like guy had the old timer by the throat with one large hand and the muzzle of the sawn-off jammed against his chest in the other. The store-keeper was pale and terrified and looked about to drop dead from heart failure. Meanwhile the small ratty guy tucked his loaded and cocked .357 Smith & Wesson down the front of his jeans, perhaps not the wisest gunhandling move Ben had ever seen, and vaulted over the counter to start rifling through the cash register. He was yelling furiously, 'Is this all ya got, y'old fuckin' coot? Where's the rest of it?' The old man's eyes boggled and he seemed unable to speak. The big, disconcertingly calm guy with the shotgun looked as if he couldn't wait to blow his victim's internal organs all over the shop wall. It was hard to tell who was more dangerous, the little angry psycho or the big laid-back one.

Ben puffed his cheeks, thought *fuck it*, counted to three. Then sprang into action.

Six minutes to midnight, but the evening was only just getting started.

Chapter 2

Fourteen hours earlier

It had been Ben's first visit to Chicago. Now he was sitting in the departure lounge at O'Hare International, counting down the minutes to his flight while gazing through the window at the planes coming and going, and sipping coffee from a paper cup. As machine coffee went, not bad. It almost quelled his urge to light up a cigarette from the pack of Gauloises in his leather jacket pocket.

It was a rare thing for Ben to leave his base in rural northern France for anything other than work-related travel, whether to do with running the Le Val Tactical Training Centre that he co-owned with his business partner Jeff Dekker or for other, more risky business. But when the chance had come to snatch a few free days out of Le Val's hectic schedule and with no other pressing matters or life-threatening emergencies to attend to, Ben had seized the opportunity to jump on a plane and cross the Atlantic. His mission: to pay a visit to his son, plus one more objective he was yet to meet.

They hadn't seen each other in a few months, since Jude's somewhat rootless and meandering life path had led him to relocate from England to the US to be with his new girlfriend,

Rae Lee. Ben knew all about rootless and meandering from past personal experience, and while he accepted that it was fairly normal for a young guy in his early twenties to take a few years before finding his feet in life, he worried that Jude had too much of his father's restless ways about him. It was Ben's greatest wish that Jude could instead have taken more after the saintly, patient and selflessly loving man who raised him as his own son all those years when the kid's real dad was off merrily raising hell in some or other war-ravaged corner of the globe.

Every time Ben reflected on that complicated history, he felt the same pangs of heartache. Years after the event, the deaths of Jude's mother and stepfather, Michaela and Simeon Arundel, were a wound that would always remain raw. The subject was never discussed between them, but Ben knew the young man felt the pain just as keenly as he did.

Rae was a couple of years older than Jude, the only daughter of a wealthy Taiwanese-American family, and occupied a nice apartment in Chicago's Far North Side overlooking Sheridan Park, where Ben had stayed with them for only one day before feeling it was time to move on. The brevity of his visit might have seemed unusual to more family-orientated folks, but Ben's and Jude's was not a normal father-son relationship and Ben was anxious not to overstay his welcome.

Ben got on cordially with Rae and liked her well enough, but wasn't completely sure that she was right for Jude. Jeff Dekker, never one to mince words, regarded her as a busybody and a do-gooder – and there was some truth in that. She was a freelance investigative journalist with multiple axes to grind over anything she considered worth protesting about, and seemed to be pulling Jude deeper into her world of political activism despite the fact that he'd never hitherto expressed the slightest interest in politics or causes of any kind. They'd met during one of her trips to Africa to expose the human rights abuses of the coltan mining industry. A trip that had achieved nothing except very nearly lead her to a gruesome end, and Jude with her.

Having had to come to the rescue on that memorable occasion, Ben worried that the next idealistic crusade might turn out to be one from which nobody, not even a crew of ex-Special Forces and regular army veterans ready to do whatever it took, could save them.

Still, if Jude was happy, which he seemed to be, Ben could wish for no more; and even if Jude weren't happy it was none of Ben's business to interfere in his grown-up son's personal affairs. He had said his goodbyes and left with mixed emotions, sorry that he wouldn't see Jude again for a while, yet quietly relieved to get away. Now here he sat, waiting for another plane – but he wasn't planning on heading home to France just yet.

At last, Ben's flight was called, and a couple of hours later they were touching down at Louis Armstrong International Airport in New Orleans. Which struck Ben as tying in very well with his other reason for being in the States.

As a dedicated jazz enthusiast, albeit one who was incapable of producing a single note on any instrument yet invented, Ben had for many years been a fan of the venerable tenor saxophonist Woody McCoy. Now pushing 87, McCoy was one of the last of the greats. He'd never achieved the stardom he deserved in his own right, but had played with some of the most iconic names in the business: Bird, Monk, 'Trane, Miles, and Art Blakey's Jazz Messengers, to list but a few.

Now at long last, after a career spanning six decades, the man, the legend, was hanging up his spurs. But doing it in fine style, taking his Woody McCoy Quintet on a farewell tour all up and down the country. A few weeks earlier, Ben had seen the announcement that Woody was due to perform his last ever gig in his home town of Villeneuve, deep in the rural heart of South Louisiana, in mid-September.

When the opportunity had arisen to free up the date in his work schedule, and with Jeff's insistent 'Go on, mate, you know you want to' in his ear, Ben had decided that this last-ever chance to hear Woody McCoy play live was not to be missed. He rarely allowed himself such indulgences. But he'd allow himself this one, as a special treat. Now that he'd cut his stay in Chicago a little shorter than planned, it meant he had a couple of days to explore Woody McCoy's birth-place, sample the local culture, relax and take it easy.

Ben stepped off the plane in New Orleans and found himself in a different world. Welcome to Planet Louisiana. Though over the years he'd visited more places than he could easily count, his past travels around the US had been limited. He'd been to New York City, toured the coastline of Martha's Vineyard, spent some time in the rugged hills of Montana, and had a brief sojourn in the wide open spaces of Oklahoma. But he'd never ventured this far south, and had only a vague idea of what to expect.

The first thing that hit him was the humidity. It was so thick and cloying that for a moment he thought he must have fallen down a wormhole in the space-time continuum and found himself back in the tropical furnace of Brunei redoing his SAS jungle training. He cleared security, strolled through the hellish heat over to the nearest car rental place with his new green canvas haversack on his shoulder and was happy to find that the near-blanket blacklist that bugged him in many other countries didn't seem to apply here. For some reason, the likes of Europcar, Hertz and Avis objected to his custom on the grounds that their vehicles never came back in one piece, occasionally in several, and other times not at all. But the nice young lady at Enterprise breezed through the paperwork and handed him the keys to a gleaming new Chevy Tahoe SUV with a smile like warm honey and a 'Y'all have a good day, now' that was Ben's first introduction to a real-life Southern accent.

The airport lay eleven miles west of downtown New Orleans, amid one of the flattest and most panoramic landscapes Ben had seen outside of the Sahara. He opened all the windows, lit a long-awaited Gauloise with his trusty Zippo lighter, which the airport security guys had scrutinised as though it were an M67 fragmentation grenade, and headed off with the wind blasting around him and a four-hour drive ahead. He intended to enjoy every minute of his freedom.

Ben Hope was an unusually skilled and capable man who claimed little credit for his many gifts. One he lacked, however, in common with most people, was the gift of prophecy. If by some strange intuition he'd been able to foretell what lay in store for him at the end of the long, dusty road, he would have pulled a U-turn right across the highway and jumped straight onto the next plane bound for France.

Instead, he just kept on going.

But that's what happens when you have a talent for trouble.